THE HANDFASTING

Series

BOLD, TANLGED & TORN

BY

Becca St. John

Enjoy! Becca St John
Pioneak Day Arcadia
21 March 15

~ Destiny brought them together ~

<u>BOLD</u>

Two stubborn people, each fighting for their own way.

After The MacBede battle cry, "For Our Maggie!" and the impossible victory it spurs, Talorc the Bold, the Laird MacKay vows to marry the lass for the power of the clan. Maggie MacBede refuses to risk her heart to the sword. Give her a poet, a bard, any man but a fighting man, and she will find her match.

<u>TANGLED</u>

Two passionate people, tangled in a skirmish of love.

Cornered into a Handfasting, a marriage for a year and a day, Maggie MacBede finds herself plunked into the lap of danger and all because of Talorc the Bold, the Laird MacKay.

<u>TORN</u>

Two powerful people, whose enemies would fight to divide.

An enemy lurks deep in the belly of the clan sabotaging their Laird. By winning his bride's love, Talorc may just lose her life.

~ if only for a year and a day ~

Table of Contents

Contents

The Handfasting Series

BOLD

Part 1

Dedication

For the generosity and insightfulness of Judy
Kehoe, Sue Weeks and Kathy Long who
labored through my first novels.

And to all my family – by birth, by marriage,
by choice – you are the reason I write about
Love.

CHAPTER 1 - THE MEETING
1224 Scottish Highlands

They could all be dead

Their bodies strewn across battlefields, lifeless.

Like her twin, like Ian.

Maggie MacBede pressed fist to eyes, spun away from her friend and the empty view they shared. She would not cry. It was Cailleach Bheare, bitter old crone of a north wind, who stirred up the tears. There was naught to fear. Her brothers would return.

They would.

Then she would kill them herself.

Seven brothers born, six still alive, and all she could feel was the pain of the losing. Not that her surviving brothers cared. Och, no, not by half. Ian barely in his grave and off the great hulking oafs go to battle. Not once, not twice, but three times in the six months since Ian's death, they leave her to fret and worry; would they return by foot or bier?

Caitlin moved up beside her, slid an arm around her shoulders. "Don't fuss now." She crooned.

Not fuss? "We've been here since daylight, it's nearly evening now. They should be here. The messenger said so."

"They will be," Caitlin soothed. "I promise, and the thrill of it will be worth the wait."

Maggie snorted, wrapped her plaid close as she turned back to a bleak view of dark heather and a black ribbon of river threading its way through a valley shadowed by ragged hillsides.

No hint of warriors.

"Maggie," Caitlin sidled up beside her. "Don't you think you'd be knowing if they weren't coming? Just like with young Ian."

Maggie looked to the gloomy valley as she searched for an explanation. "Ian was different. He was my twin. We shared dreams. I never had that with my other brothers."

"Never once with the others?" Caitlin frowned. Her husband Alec, one of the men they watched for, was Maggie's older brother.

"No." Maggie raised her hand, shielding against the last streak of sun as she studied the horizon.

Caitlin followed her gaze. "You knew when Ian wasn't coming back, Maggie. I was there. You crumbled as if that sword had pierced your own belly. I've no doubt you would do the same for Alec or any of your other brothers."

"Enough!" Maggie faced her squarely. "Ian and I were the youngest in a family of strong men. We needed that closeness or the others would have run right over our wants. It's you, Caitlin, who will know when Alec goes. Not me."

"He won't go, though." Caitlin argued.

"Don't be foolish." Maggie snapped. "Alec is a warrior and warriors die." She slapped at her chest, where her heart should be. "And all you feel is the pain of the losing.

That's all Caitlin." She eased away. "Just
sorrow, hovering over a pit of numbness."

"Ah, Maggie."

They both fell silent as the autumn chill
seeped through layers of dress and plaid,
through the soles of boots clear into the heart.
Finally, Caitlin shook Maggie's shoulder.
"We've been here too long for naught," she
said, "Let's go back to the keep."

"Aye. No sense waitin' and freezin'
when the Bold has no care for the kin of his
men." She grumbled, as she brushed at her
plaid.

"Now Maggie, you shouldn't be talking
about the Laird that way." Caitlin started to
sign the cross. Maggie grabbed her hands,
stilled them.

"Stop it. He's not a bloody saint,
Caitlin. He was the one who called Ian to his
death, for a battle that was not even ours to
fight."

"He's a great, grand warrior, he is."
Caitlin countered.

Plaid pulled tight over her head,
Maggie closed out the cold. "If he's so mighty
and great, why does he send messengers to
ask our clan to fight? Why can't he come
himself?"

As there was no answer to that, Maggie
argued on. "Coward outside of battle, that's
what he is, to send others to call men to
death!" Warmth of conviction coursed through
her. "I know his kind, Caitlin." She shook a
finger at Caitlin's back, raised her voice as
the girl headed up the hill. "He'll be a great
scarred and ugly man who feasts on wee
bairnes for breakfast. He'll only have one eye,
the other a grotesque pocket of twisted and
puckered flesh from some ancient spear
wound.

"Life means nothing to a man like that. Not without conflict." Anger spurred her up the steep climb. "I would love to give him conflict, I would."

Surprised by the lack of reprimand, for no one disparaged the Great, Grand Laird MacKay, Maggie looked up to see Caitlin at the crest of the hill, still as a statue. She turned, face aglow with tears. "They're here." She whispered. "They've come from the other way."

"No! Oh goodness, no!" Maggie reached the top, grabbed hold of Caitlin's arm as she took in the scene before them.

Below, a train of men and carts crossed under the archway into the courtyard of the keep. All that commotion and they had been too far to hear it.

"I wanted to greet them, and do so properly." Maggie moaned and set off down the hill, Caitlin running along beside her.

"They're here!" Her throat stung with the cry as she charged for the keep.

Despite twenty years and strapping body, Margaret MacBede sailed like a child over the rough land until she could hear the laughter and voices and shouts of welcome ahead of her.

Caitlin, struggling to keep stride, stopped her at the keep entrance. "Will you look at that?" She asked, breathing heavily. And Maggie did.

So many men, not all MacBedes, and a slew of animals. Boisterous hurrahs could be heard from the courtyard, vying with the bawl and bleat of livestock. Wagons piled with pillaged harvest pushed through the mélange.

Her brothers returned with more goods than had been stolen from the MacBedes in three seasons past. Her kin had championed their clan. Thank the skies. These highlanders would eat this winter.

The reward was to more than their bellies. It had been a long wait since they'd heard the victor's song. Too much stolen from them with no successful recourse. Too many lives sacrificed to no gain.

"Come on!" She shouted to Caitlin.

Skirts held high and out of the way, heedless of others, Maggie hurtled forward, straight into the huddle of her brothers and leapt, without warning, into the arms of her brother, Jamie.

"What have we here?" Jamie held her straight out from him, as though she weighed no more than a straw doll. She dangled in midair, her grasp firm on his arms. No small lass, she towered over other women and quite a few of the men folk, but she thrilled to the knowing she would never outsize her brothers.

Just in time, Maggie tensed, held her body straight and true, arms crossed at her chest, legs twined about her skirts to hold them secure. As she knew he would, Jamie tossed her in the air, parallel to the ground, tested the weight of her, same as he would test the weight of a caber.

"I think I've found the biggest faerie in the land," Jamie mused.

"Biggest faerie?" Nigel shouted. "Here, toss it here. It looks naught but a mass of hair and plaid to me."

Maggie gasped at the outrageous slur, as she sailed through the air to be caught yet again. Her childish cry sounded the delight, for she loved the game, loved to fly as though nothing could pull her to earth.

Nigel caught her neatly, adding a spin as he tossed her high again. Maggie pulled in tighter, lest a flailing limb strike out at her brother.

"Aye, 'tis naught but a mass of rusty red fur and rags."

She rethought the striking out business, but there was no time for action. Airborne and twirling, Maggie shut her eyes against the dizziness of it.

"Umph!" It was Douglas this time. "Can't be our Maggie." He groaned, "Too heavy for our light, little Maggie. Here." Maggie pulled in, prepared for the toss. "You see if she's not too fat!"

She should have hit while she could.

Douglas hurled her with an ease that belied his goading. This twirl she landed face to the skies, eyes wide.

Good Lord! She'd not landed in the hands of another brother, and well she knew it. Nay, these hands were even greater in size. They nearly spanned her waist and it was no small waist. But it was not the size that felt so different. It was . . . oh goodness, she didn't really know what it was other than to know she had never felt it before.

Bounced, a test of weight, like the jostle of a bag of coins to guess their worth. With each landing, shivers quivered through her, his touch an arrow that found its mark, candle to flame. A horrible, strange thing.

She cried out, when the man spun her to face the ground. To face him. A stranger as rugged and beautiful as the mountains surrounding them. He had the high cheekbones so common among their clan, yet they did not look common. Dark eyebrows raised in humor, as the lines of his face fitted easily to his smile.

She recognized him, in the way a moment or a thing can be familiar even

6

though it is not. She knew just how wavy his hair would be if it weren't pulled back and tied by a bit of leather. That it was not really black, as it looked now pulled tight against his head, but more the color of cinnamon when moist. The slash of eyebrows, emphasizing his pleasure, could as easily pull into a frown just as eyes, sparkling with merriment right now, could be as blue and cold as ice in winter.

She knew it, knew it all, though he was a stranger with no right to be holding her at all. No right to laughter when she was a riot of confusion.

No right for him to look as though he knew her as well.

He played with her senses.

She batted at his arm. He stilled, holding her aloft. Eye to eye, she stared, wary and vulnerable, fearing he could see deep into her very soul, before he gave a sharp nod of satisfaction with her none the wiser why.

She glowered at his smug audacity. How dare he take liberties just because he had arrived with her kin. So what if looks like his could make a lesser women swoon. Maggie refused to be taken by looks. There were plenty of handsome men to be found in the highlands. She would take that smirk from his face.

Tossed again, grandly high, Maggie was too confused and angry to thrill in it. Instead, mid-air, she glared at Douglas for being the traitor who passed her to this man.

"Nay, Douglas," the man boomed, hearty voice for a hearty man. Her head snapped back, scowl intact. "Feisty but not fat." He had the gall to squeeze her waist with each landing bounce though his eyes were focused higher than her waist, lower than her shoulders.

Maggie shifted her arms, crossed on her chest, to better hide her bosom. He winked.

"Not fat at all."

She swiped at him again, toppled so he had to side step to catch her. "Nor too lean." His smile broadened, which she'd not thought possible. "To my mind, Douglas," slowly he lowered Maggie, "Aye." He nodded thoughtfully. "'Tis true, to my mind she is just rrrright!" His relished R's tumbled through her in a chaotic dance.

The moment Maggie felt the purchase of land, she shoved away from the man, stepped back on legs that wobbled, straightened her plaid with hands that trembled too much to manage. In defiance of any weakness, she lifted her chin.

He towered over her, a massive brute of a man. It was no surprise he could toss her high. His muscle-corded arms were the size of cabers themselves. His chest, och, he had naught covering it but a width of plaid. Not that anything would fit across that expanse.

He was nothing of the sort that Maggie could appreciate. She liked her men long and lanky, with more brain than brawn. This man was all brawn. She doubted he had a brain, not if he'd be playing with her while her brothers watched. They'd get him for that, just as they dealt with any man who looked at her sideways.

She shot a glance toward each of them, and with every sighting her confidence fell.

Nigel, James and Douglas all beamed at her. Her oldest brother, Feargus the younger, strode up to the man and slapped him on the back. They both laughed at some hidden story. Feargus' friendly pats could send a man reeling. Not this one, which made her brothers even more genial.

All right then, if her brothers would not stand against him, then Maggie would. She would stand strong and firm, just as she did with her brothers. It was the only way to win concessions with their lot.

A toss of her head shifted her hair off her shoulders. She straightened her back, showed her own strength, like mare to stallion. His smile quirked, displayed a mouth full of straight white teeth. He sent a nod to her brothers, Crisdean and Alec, who had just pushed their way into the crowd. Both grinned back. Even her da looked ready to explode with mirth.

The man won them over. Had everyone siding with him, rather than her. The cheek of the brute.

He'd be no easy opposition. Aye, but she'd not been raised with brothers to forget how to taunt them. Hold your place and hold your tongue. It was as good as ignoring them, certain to drive them crazy.

Maggie silently stood her ground, confronted with his cocky grin and the glances he threw at her family. The yard, filled with a watchful hush, hinted that everyone knew what she did not, and they all watched to see what she would do. Aye, she was that mare again. Wild and corralled to be tamed, while spectators stood at the fence. The thought spooked her to step back. A blush of humiliation blazed up her neck.

She had never, ever backed away from confrontation. She couldn't with a family the likes of hers. She would never last a snap if she didn't stand against continual teasing and testing. But she had, just now, with this . . . this . . . great beast of a man. One step back and her fortress crumbled, her fear disarmed her, shattered a confidence she never doubted.

There was no help for it. Her mother was behind her, somewhere, and at this moment, for the first time since leaving childhood, she needed her mother's protection. To add to the mortification, when she bumped into her ma, she grabbed her hand. Hard. The blush deepened to a scorch.

This was the first time, in her entire life, she had given ground. It was this man and his laughing eyes. She'd not forgive him. She'd never forgive him. He made her feel peculiar. She no more liked it than she understood it.

With as much dignity as she could summon, Maggie slipped behind her mother, and felt ease and reason in the united pose. Mother and daughter, standing together to greet guests. Her retreat was no retreat. No one could think differently.

Buoyed by the thought, Maggie dipped her head, a regal bow to her subjects. Still, no one spoke. They waited. For her? Even her parents held silent. So be it.

With as much condescension as she could muster, which was difficult as she felt a bit puny herself, words tumbled out with no sifting of thought. "Who do you think you are, to be touching my body and saying I'm just rrrright!"

Touching my body . . . She could swallow her tongue.

The courtyard exploded with raucous humor, but it was one tremendous roar that rocked her. Him. That man.

Brute.

Eyes narrowed, she squeezed her mother's shoulders as though that could shut-out the sound. Her mother tugged Maggie around to her side.

"Settle yourself, lass," Fiona fussed at the drape of Maggie's plaid, brushed at her tangled curls. "You must show some respect."

Maggie gaped. All was topsy-turvy. Her brothers, who never let a courting man near, tossed her to this . . . this . . . mocker of women. Instead of a bellow of rage, her da choked on his pleasure. And now, her mother tells her to be respectful.

"Child," her ma whispered in her ear, "'Tis Talorc the Bold, the great Laird MacKay. You must greet him proper."

A shudder racked through her. The Laird MacKay. Two eyes full of merriment, neither a grotesque pocket of twisted and puckered flesh. He had scars, to be sure, clear and visible but they enhanced rather than disfigured. He was not an ugly, hairy beast, but a man.

Talorc the Bold. A legend. A man who was whispered about in the deep of the night with stories too grand to be true. A warrior who instilled their part of the Highlands with a sense of comfort and safety . . . unless you proved yourself the enemy, then he'd have you for dinner.

He was near to worshipped.

He could do no wrong.

Well, he was doing wrong now and, as far as Maggie could tell, he wouldn't stop. It was in that arrogant roar of laughter. Her fiery blush turned to a flush of anger.

This self-same man called Ian out to a battle of no return. This man was alive and well. Her twin brother dead. There would be no respect from her. Not that he offered her any, treating her like some toy doll. As if anyone noticed.

Her family saw Ian's death as an honorable outcome to inevitable battles. Maggie was not so generous. The Bold may have them all in his palm, but he'd not get the best of her. Och, no. He'd never get the best of her.

The chaff of fear blew away, her anger honed on the memory of her twin's body draped over a horse. Maggie moved away from her mother and approached The MacKay. She could see she startled him by doing so, that it pleased him. Too full of himself, he was, to think he could scare her off so easily that any return took admirable strength. She was not so puny.

"Bold," she addressed him without title, "Whatever business you have here, I hope it ends quickly, and you can be on your way." That raised an eyebrow. Maggie's smile was not pleasant. "And while you are here, I hope you'll be taking time to visit our Ian's grave, as you were so kind as to send him there."

She spun on a chorus of indrawn breaths; stalked away, grandly, on the wave of shocked murmurs and apologies. She did not get far before the Bold's voice rolled over her.

"Aye, Maggie MacBede, I will visit the grave of a brave warrior just as I will see my task accomplished by morn." Her face half turned, she offered a nod of acknowledgement, anxious to be away.

"Maggie." He stopped her. "Is it true, did you really take a Sassenach out with one rock, when you were no more than a wee babe?"

How dare he?

"Did you run the walls during battle and give sustenance to your clansmen?"

He couldna' know what he was saying, couldna' know what his words were about.

"Don't you dare make fun of me, MacKay."
She challenged, for she knew the depth of
embarrassment, humiliation, his words
provoked.

Brows puckered in surprise, he moved
closer. "I'm not funning with you, Maggie
MacBede." He touched her cheek, feathered a
line to her chin. "I'm wondering if the tales
are true."

She wished him to stop touching her,
distracting her, but his finger lingered, an
absent gesture, that meant nothing. He
continued to query her, his voice soft. "I'm
wondering if it's true. Before a MacBede
warrior sets off on his maiden battle, to face
death for the first time, do you in fact give a
piece of plaid with soil and heather to remind
him of what he fights for?"

Nothing he had said, nothing he had
done could have hurt her more than that
question. She shoved his hand away. His
touch may slay her senses, but she would not
be felled by his words. She had stood the test
of those packets and she would stand them
still.

"Once you give to one, you give to all."
She held on to her pride, because that much
was true.

A fool, she had been, to hand them out,
to think it a grand thing to do. The reality
held meager thanks. Parcels meant to be a
prize, proved no more than a worthless bundle
that embarrassed giver and receiver both. She
didn't know how to stop it, though she knew it
would be up to her to do so.

* * * * * * * * *

Talorc watched the straight line of her
spine as the lass escaped. He would catch-up

to her soon enough but first he would ease the chaos left behind her. The MacBedes were caught between loyalty to one of their own and the realities of life. War came to them, they had to meet it or be run over. Men died, honorable lives lost to keep their clans safe.

He had not killed Ian, but the Gunns had. Though she wouldn't know of it, it was thanks to her that the guilty had paid for their sins.

Her brother, Ceadric, jostled his arm, "I told you she was spirited."

Talorc nodded, "You did that. But you didna' say she blames me for your brother's death."

"Aye, she does that," James answered him, "and she can be a stubborn one, but she's not stupid. She'll be civil, soon enough, or she'll have us to contend with." He gestured to all of the MacBede men.

Talorc didn't doubt that she was as stubborn as she was feisty. His task would be more difficult for it, but a lass easily come by was no great winning. Maggie's appeal was all the more powerful for her reluctance.

The truth of it was, fight it or no, she would soon come to learn that he was the right man for her. He knew it as a certainty when he saw her run through the courtyard, straight for him, her lush body shifting with every stride. Before that moment she had been a heady dream, built on stories others told. Innocent stories about a beautiful lass with courage and honor. No one could know how those stories had turned into erotic dreams, filling him with a passion for a faceless goddess.

He had expected to be disappointed when they met in the flesh; had not expected the site of her to fill his blood enough to

14

explode. Ample bodied Maggie MacBede, bursting with life, saturated every thought, every feeling.

She failed to sense his presence. The lass had been totally unaware that he stood a mere breath away. With nary a glance, she jumped, not into his arms, but straight into her brother's.

One shake of his head cleared the haze of fantasy. He had anticipated this meeting for weeks. She stepped blindly into it. If she had known of it, there's no doubt, she would have been as prepared for battle as he had been for a union.

Time. He could give her that, once he had her at Glen Toric. He would engulf her with his presence, with the fire that burned between them. Until then, there was no time. They had to leave on the morrow.

Together.

He lifted his head, searched out the surrounding people, to catch William's eye. The slight nod told him what he needed to know. If he could not use his Scottish tongue to good advantage, and woo her with words by the end of the night, his plan would be enforced. In the meantime, his men would keep a close watch on his lass.

By morning, through gentle persuasion or abduction, she would be his.

Talorc headed toward the door Maggie had taken. It was time to start his assault.

CHAPTER 2 - THE CHALLENGE

In the quiet sanctuary of the keep, Maggie sank against the hard stone wall and let the tremors have their way. She could barely stand, even braced as she was. Conflicts whipped through her; what she imagined of the Bold versus the reality of him: big and handsome, not battle beaten and ugly. Laugh lines in place of frowns or scowling furrows.

A draw that sucked her in without revulsion.

But she could still hate; hate the hands that held her, the ripple of confusion provoked.

She touched her cheek, the lingering caress of a sworn enemy.

He was not the kind of man she sought, too big, overpowering. No malleability in him, none at all. He had drawn her twin to his death.

She had challenged him.

"Oh God," she moaned. You never challenge a man like the MacKay, who lived for the fight, thrived on it.

Why did he have to come here, himself, after years of sending messengers? Why did he choose now to appear, and churn-up her life, overwhelm her with the chaos of sensation?

The sound of the keep door opening, nudged her away from the wall, to shift around the corner, into the tower square.

"Maggie MacBede?" The call tickled through her like water in a gurgling brook. Her traitorous body recognized the deep rumble of the MacKay's shout, tempted a response.

She closed her eyes, willed herself not to react.

"Where are you lass?" His boom reverberated through the hall.

The shift of feet, the crunch of soles on the rough stone floor moved toward her. Resigned, she opened her eyes to find him in the doorway of the tower, watching her.

"What do you want?" She snapped, wishing he would step away.

He moved closer.

"Maggie, I promised Ian I would come to you."

"Promised Ian?" her heart racketed against her breast. Of all she expected from this man, this was not it.

Nor did she expect the tenderness in his eyes, the softening of his voice as he explained, "It was in my arms that your brother died. I promised him that I would come to you. It's taken me too long, but I am here now."

Tears welled. The Bold cupped her face with one large palm, his thumb soothing the side of her cheek.

"He knew you would take it badly. He told me to tell you he was proud, and he would not desert you."

"Well, he did desert me." She bit her lip against a tremble.

"No, he's here," one finger tapped at her temple, "in your memories. And he's here."

He laid his hand between her breasts, over her heart, "in your love. Like salt to water, he is everywhere."

Silent, they stood there, his eyes meeting hers, one hand holding her shoulder, the other over her heart. She was certain he felt the beat of it, pounding, flooding her world by his mere presence. An innocent touch offered, yet it turned her thoughts from Ian, stole her mind, gave her body rule so it asked questions never questioned, created temptations when she had never been tempted. Again, the image of a mare came to mind. How she would nip and bite, buck at a stallion, yet allow him to mount her. She wanted to let this man, this huge stranger, overpower her senses.

Attraction beyond reason.

"I promised your brother," he stood even closer. Her breath caught in her throat, "to give you this," he leaned in, kissed her, a butterfly's touch to her cheek and she whimpered. Not because it was from Ian. Ian had never sent lightning bolts through her with a mere kiss. No one had.

She fought to tame her reaction, but the bewildering whirl of confusion proved too wild to cage.

The Bold whispered, "and I want to give you this," his lips touched hers, a light, airy, brush along her mouth. She pushed him away.

"Just a kiss, Maggie girl."

Innocent, perhaps, but she was not stupid. His idea of a kiss would never be a mere 'just.'

"When do you leave?"

"In the morning." A simple answer, but his eyes shifted away. So there was more to his leaving than that.

She pressed for clarification. "You will be gone then?" If he was to go, could she allow herself this liberty? One kiss, knowing she would never have to face him again? May never face this enticement again?

"In the morning I will be gone." Still, his eyes did not meet hers, but followed the arc of his finger as it traced the side her cheek. The light touch ricocheted through her body.

She shivered and nodded despite a twinge of uncertainty. Surely there was no room for falsehood in such a straight reply.

"Just a kiss." She pushed.

"Aye, just a kiss." He murmured, as he lowered his head.

She had been right. There was no 'just' about it, no feathery caress of lips but a journey begun with the press of lips, the taste of her mouth. He tickled the seal of her lips before moving on along her jaw to nibble his way to her ear.

A kiss turned to whispered words, sweet and soothing, of a language she did not know. It rippled, danced clear to her toes. Dormant senses blossomed.

The carnal trail shifted down her neck Maggie clutched his shoulders. He pulled her close, surrounded her, captured her.

A mere kiss.

To him perhaps.

Reason reared, for one valiant fight. She fought herself, fought him, pushed against that broad chest. Only half a battle as half still clung to the kiss. He lifted his head, eased his hold.

Her father and brothers had warned about men, her mother issued cautions against unwedded desire. Everyone spoke of young

Alicia, who disappeared one day, drawn by
desire to an evil stranger she spoke of but no
one ever saw.

The Bold would leave in the morning.

She would not be so foolish as to leave
with him.

What harm to steal this moment, this
one time, to allow desire free reign in a
stairwell where it could not go further, with a
man she would never have to see again?

"Meet me in this." The whisper brushed
her lips.

Always impetuous, she charged
heedless in to frays more dangerous than this.

"You will not best me at this, Bold."
She pulled his head down to hers.

The Bold seized her opening, lifted her
against him. She refused to hang, toes
dangling above the floor. Hands gripping his
hair, her mouth as hungry as his, she lifted
her legs, wrapped them tight around his waist,
reveled in his shocked stillness.

He pulled away long enough to chuckle,
or was it a groan? She didn't know, didn't
care, too focused on his mouth as it suckled a
line from the tender skin behind her ear, down
her neck. Thrilled, as he pressed her against
the wall, against the core of her. Shocked
tremors ricocheted through her.

It was not enough.

Wild, untamed, raised among a people
who spoke of earthy pleasures, instinct led
her game. No demure lass but a woman with a
new found appetite for the battle of desire, to
be desired. To take.

He stilled, pushed her legs down, set
her to the ground, eased away. She grabbed
his arms, to pull his attention back.

"Shhh."

Laughter, orders, whispers sounded in the hall. The clan moved back to the duties of life. Everyone but Maggie. She drew in a deep breath, tried to settle aroused uncertainties.

He pulled her deeper into the shadows under the winding tower stairs and leaned his head against hers. "Maggie mine," a hoarse croak, "with the heat in you, it's a wonder you don't have a dozen children by now."

"You miserable swine." She batted at his hold. Voices in the hall reminded, she lowered her voice, "You shouldn't be teaching me such things."

"Did I teach you, Maggie? I wonder if you're not teaching me."

Stunned, Maggie stammered for words to fling, only to find she had lost him to something over his shoulder.

She peeked around the side of him.

Her brothers stood in the doorway, arms akimbo. Grand, great men. A wall of them. Her protectors. Pride swelled at the sight of them. She had met him in the battle of senses and now her brothers would kill him for taking her to that battleground.

The Bold turned to face them, his arm still wrapped around Maggie, forcing her around as well. "She's mine," was all he said. No request, no rights to others, just pure possession.

"Aye," Douglas nodded, "I'd say she better be."

Rage soared. "You say nothing, Douglas!" she fought for breath, "He took advantage, as you've warned a man might. He pushed beyond manners!"

Her brothers did not rise to her anger but smiled. James answered for them. "We think you've met your match, Maggie MacBede. Time a man took charge of you."

The Bold squeezed her closer, she
shoved away, furious with him, with her kin,
with herself. "I am no one's! Do you hear?"
she stalked past her brothers, but not without
ordering, "You are to protect my honor." She
reminded them. "So you best take care of him.
He's nothing but a boastful braggart of a
scoundrel!"

They all laughed. Laughed! She
refused to listen. Refused to think of what her
body had tried to tell her. She was a woman
of intelligence. She would not let her flesh
dictate what she would do, who she would do
it with. All it took was keeping that man away
from her.

CHAPTER 3 – BAWDY WOMEN

Aulay Gunn looked to where the man pointed.

"See that?" Old Ros wailed. "See those holes?" His hands trembled with distress. "They've been punched in there." Tears threatened. "How am I to go out and get fish? How are we to feed ourselves?"

This was not the first fisherman to have lost boats to sabotage.

"Aye, you'll not be using that boat this day. You tend to it, see if it can't be made seaworthy again. I'll get young Taran to help you."

"And you'll go after the MacKays, now?" Ros's voice firmed, fueled by retribution.

"Oh, aye," Aulay promised. "Don't you worry. We'll get the lousy MacKays if they're the ones who are doing this."

"Of course they're the ones who are doing this, mon. Who else would do such a thing?"

"I don't know, Ros, I just don't know." Aulay shook his head, fretting over just that. The MacKays might be mortal enemies, stealing livestock and raiding goods, but that was no different than the Gunns were want to do.

Malicious destruction for its own sake was not something The MacKays would condone. The man had his sense of honor. This was not honorable.

Much as Aulay hated to admit it, he and the MacKay were not that different. On separate sides of the fence, but with the same responsibilities. The MacKays had no reason to start a war with the Gunns. Everyone in their part of the world knew the man had just filled his stores. Why do something that would drain those resources? It made no sense.

"If it's the MacKays, we will get them for this. But I want to find out just who the vermin is before we strike."

"Bloody MacKays, that's who it is, mon, who else would go against us like this?"

And that, Aulay knew, was the crux of his problem.

* * * * * * * * * *

Maggie slipped through the keep headed for the kitchens, relaxed, as always , amid scents that embraced, succulent and heady as only a kitchen can be. This was her home, her place, amid the bustle of clan's women, within this room rich with roasting meats, spicy steam and yeast. As a child she had helped tend whole haunches skewered on spits set before the huge fire with ovens placed in the wall around that fire. It was here the clanswomen baked cakes and bread while the warmth aided the brewing of strong, dark beer in heavy casks set deep in the shadows.

Simon, her young cousin, stole a bannock cake straight off the rack where it

24

cooled. Maggie chuckled, but did not try to stop him,

"Did you see The MacKay?" Sibeal, wife of Maggie's oldest brother, asked any who would listen.

Simon headed to the spit handle he had abandoned. Maggie shooed him away and grabbed the handle herself, near enough to hear the chatter, far enough removed that, she hoped, no one would notice her. It was no more than gossip, the women were about, but Maggie found she was drawn to their foolish natter.

"Oh, aye," her cousin Muireall sighed. "What a man that one is." Maggie snorted. Everyone knew Muireall thought the same of all men.

"He's even larger than The MacBede." Another cousin brayed. Too true, Maggie glowered.

"Did you see his eyes?" Muireall trilled, "I've never seen anything so blue in my life. They're as clear as the summer sky." Summer sky? Nay, not so simple. They were more like a gem and its playful light, fire and ice all in one place. Just as likely to burn as to make you shiver.

And shiver she did, remembering his eyes when he looked at her. Thoughts of him were like a fierce undertow. A body could drown in it while scrambling for a shore that was safe and secure. Maggie released the spit's handle, startled by her own thoughts. She had to get out of the room, away from the talk, talk, talk.

"Are you fancying him then, Muireall?" Alec's wife, Caitlin, lured Maggie back with her question. "For you must know when a man is that large, he's that large allllll over." Maggie blushed, remembering what she felt, pressed against him in that tower. T'was more than bunched cloth, which meant Caitlin's words were truth.

"You're not telling me anything I don't know." Muireall bragged, "My own Malcolm, God rest his soul, was no little tyke."

"No," the others laughed together, "no he was no small man, and a shame it was he had to go so soon. He's missed."

"The missing wouldn't be so bad," Muireall confided with a laugh, "if it could be shared with someone like the MacKay, now. And as he's been widowed these three years, well . . ."

"Och, Muireall," Nigel's wife, Leitis, humphed, "he's not looking for a widow such as yourself."

"And why not?"

Maggie snorted. There was no need to turn around to see the glances passed from one woman to another. They'd all be looking about, wondering who would do the telling. It was Leitis who finally admitted, "He's not going to look for a lady willing to share the warmth in *any* bed. A man such as the MacKay will show more discretion."

You tell her, Leitis, Maggie thought sourly, only to feel guilty moments later when Muireall countered, "Say what you like, but you can't ken the loneliness of an evenin' alone. You don't know what it's like to have your man taken in his prime, not even married a full year and no bairn to wake me in the night with cries. The loneliness, och, it's a terrible thing."

"Oh, aye, Muireall," Leitis admitted, "it is a sad thing, I'm sure, but you know it's a worrying thing as well. You have to watch yourself. Too many see, too many tell. And what that means is there's just too many."

The women burst into laughter, all but Muireall, who looked about, her brow furrowed. "Too many what?" She asked.

Laughter descended to snorts, as Leitis quipped. "Too many men in your bed."

Both Sibeal and Caitlin offered, "That's not being fair to cousin Muireall, now. She didn't take on Puny Piers."

"He had Maggie's eye, then, didn't he?" Leitis chided.

"Well," Muireall defended, "I've never warmed myself with Babbling Birk the bard."

"For the same reason."

"And now there's Maggie's Hamish the tailor," Agnes tossed in, "Muireall hasn't gone near him!"

Once again the room erupted with laughter as women called out, "Who else would notice those scrawny buggers but our Maggie?"

"They're not fit for anyone."

"'Tis Maggie and her love for the runts of the litter."

"Stop it!" Maggie swirled about, anger as wild as her wind-tossed hair, "you know nothing about it. They are good men, each and every one of them. Just because they aren't as big as a mountain and as thick in the head doesn't mean there isn't some goodness to them."

"Oh, aye, Maggie, I'm certain you have the right of it." Caitlin eased.

"Besides," Maggie swallowed pride to loyally defend her men, "it was I who was not good enough for them."

"Don't be daft." Sibeal snipped.

"Aye, it's fact," back straight, chin up against the humiliation of reality Maggie admitted. "Not one of those men would have me now, would they?" The silence of the room told her what she already knew. It was the truth.

"Ach, lassie," Muireall sighed, "you should be praising God that you weren't landed with those boys." Maggie kicked the fire's coals.

"Come on now, Maggie girl," Neili and Roz beckoned her, "Don't be listening to them. We've need of your light hand with the pastry here."

Fine ones to talk, those two. The same age as Maggie and they'd been married for years and before that they'd been courted by a number of good, decent men. Warring men. They could have them.

"Flattery now?" Maggie mumbled, but she went to help them as two men sidle in through the back doorway. Maggie snorted. If they wanted to be invisible, let them try, but with their size, their sex, and the fact that they were MacKay Clansmen, and therefore unfamiliar, they weren't likely to be overlooked in a roomful of women.

"Are you so lazy you want me to help you?" She asked the two pastry workers.

Neili and Roz took no notice of Maggie or her taunt. No one did. The only response to her words was the spit of the fat dripping into the fire. Unlike Maggie the others couldn't carry on once two strange men had walked into their spheres. Huge grins gleamed white against tanned faces, the only features discernible in the shadow where they stood.

Predictable as ever, Muireall preened. Maggie grunted and chuckled to herself with a quick glance to see what the men made of her cousin. Only they didn't look at Muireall, didn't seem to notice her at all. They had their sights fixed firmly on Maggie. She swallowed her chuckle, grabbed a dollop of dough. The feel of it a familiar distraction, she bent her head to the task, worked the lump of dough smooth, turning it round and round in her hand. The men may as well stand right behind her, breathing down her neck, for the way it prickled.

Fortunately, Muireall was not one to be ignored. She went into action, grabbed two mugs from the counter, splashed ale into them from the pitcher on the table. "Is there anything you'd be wanting?" she asked them, her voice husky with innuendo, as she moved about. "Drop of ale?" She lifted up the mugs. "Bannock cake, perhaps?" She swiped some off the cooling rack, and stood in front of the men, mugs filled, a plate of steaming cakes on offer, before they could answer.

Maggie tried to watch from the side, her eyes cast down. Muireall stayed with the men, one hand at her waist, the other holding the pitcher of ale braced on her hip, her head tilted flirtatiously. She was a site, for certain. Men rarely ignored Muireall, but though the three talked in low murmurs, the men never dropped their sights from Maggie. She was trapped in a web that made no sense. They were the Bold's men. They were there in his interest.

Enemies, to her at least.

Muireall left them against the far wall and sashayed back to the table. The women resumed their work. The men whispered to themselves, bannock cakes gone in a bite, ales sipped slowly. Stilted silence hung over the room, testament to their presence.

Sibeal, who would not, could not, let a conversation drop, broke the moment to lean over and pat Maggie's shoulder. Maggie jerked back in horror even though Sibeal managed to keep her voice lowered.

"Maggie," Sibeal whispered, "it wasn't that those boys were better than you. They just knew what we already know."

With a hard shake of her head, Maggie tried to stop the conversation. "Leave it Sibeal, you don't understand."

Propelled by the humiliation, Maggie worked the pastry flatter and flatter between her palms. People teased her, as if her choices were a joke, a bit of fun. No one understood the shame of it, of knowing what you want, who you want and knowing that they didn't want you in return.

"Maggie, don't you see?" Sibeal continued. "You're just too much for them."

"Stop it." Maggie shot a quick glance to see if the strangers had heard.

"She's right," Neili countered. "There's nothing to those men, not in body, not in mind. You're just too much woman for them."

"Oh, aye," the others chorused in comforting whispers.

"Too much spirit." Caitlin chimed in a bit louder. Maggie shot her a silencing frown.

Muireall, who loved to have an audience, ignored Maggie's distress. "Maggie lass," she boomed, "Take a look at yourself! Don't you know, you're just too much," she hefted her own bosom, "body."

30

The word exploded in the room, followed by a barrage of earthy squeals.

Maggie glared. Her curves were no more than God's way of balancing her height, keeping her in proper proportion. There was naught she could do about that.

"Oh aye." Leitis trilled, discretion forgotten. "Can you not hear the gossip 'Puny Hamish the tailor dies with a smile on his face. Drowns in the full- bodied womaness of Maggie MacBede.'"

Hoots filled the air. Even the MacKay men, who tried so foolishly to blend with the wall, boomed their amusement. People would hear it across the loch. You'd think the kitchen was full of rough and rowdy men rather than a passel of women. And what did any of them know?

"They were a disgrace measured next to you." Leitis offered, as she fought to catch her breath.

Maggie pressed dough in her hands, thinner and thinner, her head bent to her task, anger building with each round of pastry.

These women knew nothing. Look at Muireall, who angled for a brute of a warrior having already lost one husband to the fight. Didn't they see what they were asking for? Did they all wish to feel the loneliness that Muireall suffered?

"You weren't made to be the wife of a runt."

Harder and harder she turned the dough until it was a circle so fine you could see through it. She placed her latest effort on the pile of finished tart shells and tried to break the flow of humor. "You know," she tilted her head, the shrill crack of her voice the only sign of irritation, "I think it

31

was not exaggerating you were up to, Neili!
I'm thinking you spoke the truth! I do have
a fine hand with the dough."

"Oh, do you?" Roz elbowed Neili.

"Aye, I'm thinking that my pastry
shells are the best."

"Well then, whatever you say,
Mistress Margaret." Neili winked at Roz.
"And as you are the best," Roz sidled away,
"you should do them all!"

"You wouldn't." Maggie hurled the
pastry at the giggling girls.

Like a spirit, appearing from nowhere,
Fiona caught the dough in mid-air. The room
stilled. Out of the corner of her eye, Maggie
noted that the men stood straighter, their
smiles wiped clean.

Fiona sighed at Maggie. "Enough of
chattering and playing, daughter. You need
to be getting yourself ready."

"Ready for what?" Nosy Muireall
asked.

"For The MacKay, of course." Fiona
answered. "He is to be our guest."

"What does that have to do with me?"
Maggie snapped, not that she wanted to
know. Not that she wanted any one to know.
But she had opened her mouth and the worst
came out. Quiet settled on the room. Maggie
sighed.

One of the MacKays, so silent up until
now, spoke. "Lady MacBede, you speak as if
you know what the Bold is here for?"

Fiona shook her head. "Nay."

The man accepted that as answer
enough. This time Maggie's sigh was full of
relief.

Fiona turned to Simon, "Have some
lads send more hot water up to my chamber.
I'm going to see to the men's baths." She

faced Maggie again, "And you, young lass,"
she took Maggie's shoulders, looked her up
and down with a shake of her head. "Look at
the state of you. Your hair is naught but a
tangled mass. You need to be seeing to
yourself."

"But Ma."

"No buts, daughter. I'm not knowing
the why of it, but the MacKay is here to see
you." She turned to the men, "Is that much
not so?"

Their stupid grins were back in place.
"Aye, mistress, 'tis a fact."

"Well then, child," Fiona flipped a
strand of Maggie's hair from her shoulder,
"you'd best make yourself worth seeing!"

Nothing, absolutely nothing, moved
within the room except Fiona. Oblivious to
the reaction she'd created, she swept past
the other women.

The frozen state lasted for as long as
one woman could hold her breath, then all
manner of chaos erupted.

"The MacKay?"

"Oh, aye, isn't that a ripe one."

"Our Maggie?"

"You don't say? Well, it's about
time."

"And here she had us all thinking she
was sweet on Hamish the tailor."

"Och, wouldn't the MacKay be just
the one for our Maggie?" Letice looked to
the MacKay men, who nodded their
agreement. Slyly she added, "He'd not die
in her womanness."

"He'd thrill to it."

"Rise to it is more the way of things."
One of the men blurted out.

"Ohhhhh!" The stunned laughter
swallowed Maggie, as all the women

gathered around, pushing her hair from her face, pinching her cheeks, taking as close a look as they did when she was a wee babe, barely born.

No one had looked at her that closely in as long.

It was better that way.

She was none too happy with the attention now.

CHAPTER 4 - A STORY PROMISED

Talorc moaned with pleasure, as he eased into one of two bathing tubs set before the fire. "Ah man, 'tis weeks since I've bathed in anything other than a frigid stream or a frozen loch."

From the other tub, his host, Feargus MacBede, chuckled. "Keeps a man strong."

"Aye, it does." Heat curled around Talorc, as he settled deep, knees bent until they poked out from the surface. Better cold knees than a cold neck.

He glanced around at the soft sound of a door opening, but couldn't see beyond the bathing screen.

"It's my wife." Feargus explained. "She's a great hand when it comes to washing hair and backs, don't you wife?" Fiona moved within the light of the fire. "Can near put you to sleep, she can."

"Och, flattery, that's what you're doin'," she teased, as she ran her fingers through her husband's thick head of white hair.

Talorc watched, curious. His own father had always said, look to the mother to see what the daughter would become. Fiona was tall and regal, her movements smooth as a gliding falcon. There was a hint of mischief in her smile.

Without warning, she dunked her husband until his entire head was drenched.

More than a hint of mischief!

Feargus came up sputtering. "I hope you don't treat our guest like that!" But his grumble was lost in a sparkling glance. The man had known it was coming.

It was good to still be playing games when you had eight grown children . . . correction, there were only seven now. He knew that well.

Talorc closed his eyes, his head against the rim of the tub. The couple's companionable banter lulled as gently as the warm water within his bath.

"MacKay?" Feargus butted into his thoughts. "The Gunns grow more vicious of late. Foul as they are, they are not the sort to come at us like they've been."

"Aye," Talorc nodded. "There's no understanding to it. They get angry with no ill treatment from us, burn our crofters' homes, steal in a way that leaves a clan starving. Hunger we know how to live with." He gripped the sides of the tub, "But now someone's been thieving young lasses out from under their parents' care."

Feargus grunted. "Aye. One of our crofter's daughters has gone missing. Young Alicia. No sign of her for months now, and we searched."

"The same tale can be heard from the Raeys and the Bainses."

The older man bent his head. "Many a loss, these years past. Young females, good fighting men."

"The glory of the fight does not take away the sorrow of loss. It was a sad day when Ian fell to the sword." Talorc reached for his soap, as he searched for words not easily found. "These battle losses are mine to bear." He admitted. "I call the men to fight. They trust me. But there have been too many problems, too many things gone wrong."

He looked to the older man. "Feargus, you fought with my father, you've raised strong men who don't shy from the fight. Our families have been united for generations. There's no other man in the highlands I would trust more than you."

"The MacBedes have always done their part."

"Aye, more than their part. You've offered good counsel. So I am telling what I've told no other. I think we have a traitor in the clan."

"Impossible!" Feargus barked. "It's the Gunns, that black hearted Angus Gunn! You know, I know, it's him."

"Oh, aye, the Gunns play a part." A traitor was unthinkable but not impossible. Clan loyalty was taught from the cradle, instilled in every highlander. Still, it was possible.

He tried to explain. "There are those thrown out of the clans, the outlaws." Feargus nodded slowly, as Talorc continued. "Some still have family inside our care. Loyalties can be divided."

It cleared his mind to finally speak of this. "For the life of me, I can't think of who would turn against us. There's only one MacKay who has family with the outlaws and there was no love lost when he was banned."

Soap in hand he lathered his chest, his arms, drawn to the smell of it, pine and bay with a touch of spice. A fine odor for a man to wear.

"Laird," Feargus argued, "you have it wrong. We are not a people for turning on our own. And the Gunns have been there to fight when we go out. They'd not fight the renegade's battles."

The room quieted but for the crackle of the fire, the soft splash of water, as Fiona scrubbed her husband's back.

Feargus broke into the silence. "Your wife was a Gunn, rest her soul. I've heard they think you murdered her. Anger festers and grows. Do you think that's what causing these problems?"

"Aye, they claimed I murdered her," Talorc agreed, "but that was grief speaking and too long ago to still be fighting over."

"She died in childbirth." Fiona remembered. "That's no uncommon thing."

The weary rustle of his breath shuddered through the room. "She was a wee thing, my Anabel." A petite lass, who tended towards floral soap for man and woman alike. With her gone, the soap of his keep smelled of lye and fat. A man needed a wife for such things.

"If I failed to get her with child, the union would have been for naught. If I did get her with child, well then, what happened could happen. I lost Anabel to the birthing. It was that desperate, we were, that we didn't want to lose the babe, as well, so I cut her open."

"That's not so strange. We've done the same." Fiona encouraged.

"The Gunns claimed I tried to take it from the mother while she was fit and fine and waiting for the pains. But I don't believe that's the thorn that's causing our problems. I think we have a canker of another sort. I just can't fathom what it is."

Both men sat, frowning as they held their own counsel. Fiona moved over to

Talorc, eased him forward to wash his back, "Your late wife, Anabel, did you love her?" She asked, as she'd lulled him to peace.

"Loved her?" Talorc scowled.

Feargus sputtered and barked. "Don't be ridiculous woman, everyone knows The MacKay married for his clan, not for foolish notions of love."

"No," Talorc argued, "women wish to know these things, although in truth, I don't know." He admitted, adding, "Holding my wife was like embracing a delicate flower. Your heart swells with the beauty, but you fear you'll bruise it. No," he shook his head against the memory. "It would take a stronger lass to win my heart, I'm thinking, one who could meet me on my terms." He looked over his shoulder at Fiona. "Your Maggie is a strapping lass."

With one hefty push, Fiona shoved him under.

"I didna' say anything," Talorc sputtered as he surfaced, "that you dinna' know."

"Oh, aye." Fiona admitted sweetly.

"Did you dunk me for speaking of your daughter?"

"Why would I do that?" Fiona hedged, adding, "but I was wondering if it's true, are you here because of our Maggie?"

"Aye." Talorc admitted.

The fire crackled, water splashed, as he reached for a sheet on a stool by the side of the tub. Standing, he wrapped the long sheet around his waist, used another for drying.

Husband and wife looked to each other. "You don't know much of our Maggie if you've come for her." Fiona warned.

"Do you mean that she likes her men puny?" Talorc vigorously rubbed his hair.

"Aye," They both frowned.

"She's not meant for a puny lad, you know." He tossed the extra sheet over his shoulder. "And I've a mind to help her understand such things."

The MacBede stood from his own bath, scowling. "How do you mean to do that?"

Talorc pulled a shirt over his head, his words caught in the folds of fabric. "Well, MacBede," his head popped out of the opening, "with your permission, I'll marry her. She'll come to understand in time."

Fiona shoved a warmed sheet at her husband. "You'll not get her to understand after the wedding. Laird or no, you force Maggie to marry and she'll make your life a misery. You'll never win her that way."

"I mean to have her agree to the wedding." Talorc defended.

Fiona laughed.

Talorc argued. "You could help persuade her."

Feargus slumped on a stool. "It's more than that, Laird MacKay. You're a fine man, I couldna' hope for such a grand husband for my lovely Maggie, but she's more stubborn than the lot of us. She doesn't want a warrior."

"You're her father. You could make her."

"Oh, aye, I could force it on her, but my Fiona is right. We won't send her to the altar in tears, and if she goes against her will, there will be tears aplenty."

"From a lass such as Maggie?" Talorc was appalled.

MacBede chuckled, "Aye, strapping lass that she is, she's still a female."

Fiona ignored the understanding that passed between the men and nodded at her own thoughts. "You know," she said, "you might make it work, if you could spend some time with her, win her over and then stay away when she says nay to a marriage. She'll pine for you, then come around."

"There's no time for that. I want to take her with me tomorrow."

"Tomorrow?" Feargus stormed. "Never, lad. I'll see her settled in her feelings first."

"Timing, MacBede. You know, I know, timing is everything. It has to be now."

"Why?"

"You'll understand tonight, when I tell my tale."

"You'll be telling me now."

"No." Fiona's soft words broke through. "No, he is right, husband. Maggie doesn't need time to come up with excuses and reasons not to marry him."

"You can't be serious, wife?"

"Aye, I am, and as her mother, with your approval, I will give my blessing if he can convince her to marry him on the morrow."

"He'll never do it."

"Perhaps not. But I'm thinking, if he fails, it will be our Maggie who will lose in the end."

"I'll not fail." Talorc claimed.

Fiona nodded at his confidence. "Fail or no, I'll not grant my blessing until you promise me two things."

"Aye."

"You'll not force yourself on her. She has to give of herself willingly; otherwise, we'll not accept the marriage."

Talorc agreed. "Neither would she, and I know that, but I also know she'll come around. The bond is there already, she just doesn't recognize it."

"Aye, well and good." Feargus nodded. "But you know, if she doesn't come around, if she keeps her distance, we expect her back in the same pure state she'll have left us. I'll not see her returning with a kerchief on her head for the whole world to know she's not a maiden anymore."

"Aye." Talorc agreed. "I'd want no different for my own daughter, if I'm ever blessed to have one."

"You will also vow," Fiona continued, "never to hurt my daughter, to strike her or beat her or punish her in any physical manner."

"I vow to you she shall never be harmed by me or mine, in any manner. If I fail in that, I will return her to you."

"So be it. If you can convince her to say yea, you may have my daughter."

"Oh, for a certainty, she will say yea. She'll have no other choice or she's not the woman I think her to be."

CHAPTER 5 - BETRAYAL

It was a clear night with a full moon, eerie shadows and the shimmer of silver light that teased of spirits lurking. It was the season for Lughnassadh, the time for the summer sun to loosen her hold to Tannist, the stingy winter's day. It was a season of the festivals of old.

Talorc the Bold, The Laird MacKay, would be leaving soon for the Samhain. At least he should be, for no Laird of any worth would be away from home when the spirits of the ancients walked freely upon the earth; when the clan would celebrate those newly deceased, as well as those to be born.

Maggie hurried past the gardens, grateful that the souls were not yet free to roam in the fey light of a full moon. The only ghosts here were the shadowed furrows of the vegetable beds, empty of all but the withered rubble of a harvest now past. Today's bitter northern wind brought frost, prelude to a carpet of snow.

Snow. Maggie looked toward her destination, the small area surrounded by a low stone fence, peppered with Celtic crosses. It was home to her ancestors, home to all the family who had passed beyond this life. Home to her brother, Young Ian. Her twin.

This Samhain they would celebrate Ian's glorious death in battle. He would be

honored, praised for going as he had gone. It
was selfish of Maggie to wish it any other
way, but wish it she did. She wanted to
unwrap her plaid, lay it upon his frozen bed,
to warm him until the snow could play the
part of blanket. But to do so would ignore the
chance of his soul rising free of the earth's
embrace. She could not risk the insult.

It didn't take her long to reach his
grave, to see the covering of heather she had
planted, gray in the moon's light, sparkling
with the frost. A part of her had died with
him. Praise God that it wouldn't resurrect,
that her ability to love so deeply would never
claim her again.

She thought of the MacKay, and his
peculiar hold on her. "I'll not leave you, Ian."
She promised. "Whatever The MacKay wants,
it can't take me away from here." She fell to
her knees, leaned to the side and supported
her weight on one arm. "This is my home."
She picked at the heather. "This is where I
belong. These are my people, our people."

There were no tears this time.
Normally, when she visited Ian's grave,
emotions brimmed and spilled. Perhaps she
was getting used to his absence.

"Do you know what it is he thinks? Can
you watch, from wherever you are? Can you
see what's happening?" Maggie looked up at
the sky, before studying the sway of trees that
surrounded the graveyard. She'd often
wondered if Ian watched.

When he was alive, she would have
known what he was thinking without saying a
word. The loss, an emptiness that could not be
filled.

"You would laugh, you know." Could
he hear her even if she couldn't hear him?
"Our warriors told tales and the Bold was daft

enough to listen. They turned-around all I ever did to grieve them, until you would think I was the bravest and wisest of women. Really, they did!

"Do you remember the time I threw the rock and hit that Englishman dead on? Och, the look on Nigel's face. He slung me over his shoulder, as if I had caused the battle, carried me past every warrior on the battlements, through all the soldiers in the yard and into the crowd of the Great Hall. He dumped me. Like no more than a sack of oats, he tossed me at our mother's feet.

"Aye, you were there. You laughed till your sides split, but it wasn't funny."

Humiliation still stung, remembering Nigel's order, *"keep her out of our way."*

She was no warrior.

God willing, the Bold would never know the depth of embarrassment flung at her when he asked about the packets.

A silly impulse and a sleepless night produced them. No more than ten years old, she had imagined being lauded for those little pouches. One for each warrior before he left for battle. They were to serve as a symbol of all they fought for.

They brought no more than absent pats on the head and embarrassed chuckles. Every ounce of her pride had been gobbled up from that day to this, for she didn't know how to stop it. What she did for one, she had to do for the others, or it would be a sign of favoritism. A Highlander would take great insult on such a slight.

"What would The MacKay think if he knew the truth of it?" She asked, as though her brother could answer.

The wind kicked up. Maggie's sigh rode on it.

"If you were here, Ian, you'd protect me, you'd sit by my side and keep the MacKay at a distance. Och, and the way he makes a body feel!" Maggie fought for words to explain and fisted her belly, as though to press away the flutters within. "Ian, be grateful that you'll never have to feel the way he made me feel. You can't lose it."

A swift look over her shoulder, toward the keep, was reminder enough that she needed to head back.

"Do you think I could be missing the meal?" She sighed against the hope, her eyes focused on the gray slabs of stone that made up her home.

A movement, near the last tree of the orchard, caught her eye. Two soldiers stood there, watching her with steady interest. In the meager light she could not tell for certain, but she thought they were MacKays.

Ian's resting place pulled her once more. "What am I to do?" She rose and dusted the dirt from her plaid. "Who can I get to sit with me if not you?" She studied his grave. "It's not like I have any great suitors to . . ." she paused, her head high, as if to catch a sound. "Ian, I have it. Hamish. Hamish will sit with me, and then The MacKay will know that my affections are taken and . . ."

She glanced over her shoulder to see the two men still watching her.

"They'll be leaving soon." She comforted her brother, for he'd fret for her otherwise. "And Hamish will be there for me, even if for naught but friendship. We have been friends for such a long time."

Her head snapped back to Ian's grave. For the first time since she'd lost him, there was an inkling of thought traitorous enough not to be her own.

46

"Don't you dare, brother!" She wagged her finger at the heather upon the grave as it swayed with a fresh breeze. She could almost see her brother brushing his hand over it, as he argued with her. "Don't you dare start putting opinions in my head now. If I want to take Hamish to dinner with me, then I will." The niggle continued to tug at her decision. "You'd have me sit with him? With The MacKay? You're no better than the others." She snipped, as she spun away from her brother's memory.

"I'll not listen," she hissed into the wind.

Defiant, she stomped away, head high as she passed the two warriors. MacKays, of course they were. The MacBedes would have left her to her mourning without notice.

Her step quickened, as she heard them turn to follow. Nosey brutes. This was her home, with people milling about everywhere you turned. She'd not come to harm.

"You've no need to follow me," she shouted over her shoulder.

"We'll see you safely home."

"This is home." She informed them, and picked up her pace.

They lengthened their stride to match her near run.

She had to lose them, for it would do no good to have them see her beg Hamish to sup with her tonight.

"Go away."

"We're to see to your welfare, Mistress Margaret."

She pivoted, faced them.

"And what makes you so happy?" She bit out.

"You're a bonny lass."

Humph. She started off again, through
the inner yard, into the outer yard, down the
path until she came to the tailor's two story
workshop and home.

She banged on the door.

"One of her puny choices?" One warrior
asked the other.

She'd not turn around.

The door opened a crack to show Colin,
the tailor's apprentice. He tried to shut the
door on her.

"I'm needing to see Hamish," she
blurted and shoved until the poor lad could do
no more than let her in. She slammed the door
on the two MacKay clansmen. A loud
rhythmic creaking filled the room. Maggie
looked to the ceiling.

"Hhhhhe's nnot hhhhere." Colin
stuttered, trying to get beyond Maggie to open
the door again.

Maggie ignored him and moved to the
ladder that led to the second story. "Whatever
is that noise?" She asked Colin before
shouting, "Hamish! It's Maggie MacBede.
I'm needing to speak with you."

Abruptly, the creaking halted, replaced
by smothered voices and the rustling of
clothes.

Frantic, Colin tried to stop her,
"Mimimistress Mamargaret, I think . . ."

Someone pounded at the door.

"Ignore that, Colin." She told the lad,
as Hamish's long narrow foot and spindly
ankle came into view, followed by a hastily
wrapped plaid.

"Ah, Hamish," Maggie waited,
impatient for his descent. The minute his foot
touched the ground she rushed up to him,
gripped the front of his plaid where it crossed

48

his sunken chest. "I'm needing your help! Och, and it's dire you aid me!"

"Aye, Maggie."

She cocked her head at his tone, cringed as he patted her hands. She hated to be treated like a child, with pat to her head or her hands.

The pounding started up again.

"Go away!" Maggie shouted before turning back to Hamish. "I need you to come sit with me at dinner." She told him.

Bewildered, Hamish looked from Maggie to the door. "Colin, who's out there?"

"Nothing, no one," Maggie lied. "Just a couple of The MacKay's men. Don't think of them."

"Warriors?" He gulped.

"Hamish, forget them, just promise me you'll come to the hall to eat. I'm needing you to sit with me."

Even in the dark of the tailor's shop, Maggie could see his face turn ashen. She gritted her teeth, determined to convince him, but was stopped as a woman's head, hair all tousled and loose, popped through the opening at the top of the ladder. "What are you about Hamish?" Nora Bayne demanded.

"Nora?" Maggie frowned. "What are you doing here? And what are you doing up there?"

"Now, Maggie," Hamish pulled on her arm, "You're not to be thinking . .."

"What am I not to be thinking?" She tried to glare at him, to look angry, but her heart sank too deep to fuel her anger, her outrage. Hamish was just another man who didn't want her. "What is Nora to you Hamish?"

"Maggie, now," Hamish soothed, shooting wary looks at Nora, "you and I have been friends for a long time."

"And what's wrong with friendship, Hamish?"

"Well, it's just, you know, I'm not, I mean, well, the truth of it is, Maggie, I'm planning to marry Nora."

Nora's cooed, "Oh, Hamish," was swallowed by Maggie's keening, "Nooooo!"

In all fairness, Hamish only reached out to comfort Maggie, and no more, when the door flew open. He didn't have time to pull away or surely he would have before that sword was stuck to his throat. Granted, it pricked only deep enough to bring a spot of blood, but for Hamish, that was enough.

He fainted.

Colin wet himself.

Nora squealed.

And Maggie glared, as she swatted at the arm holding the offending sword. "Put that stupid thing away, man!" She barked.

Nora, wrapped in no more than a blanket, scurried down the ladder to pull Hamish's head onto her lap.

Colin raised a trembling finger to point at the men. "Mmmmaggie," he stammered, "ththththey're warrrriors, you shouldldldna' be talking to them so."

"Of course they're warriors, Colin." Maggie said with no bit of respect, "But that doesn't give them permission to come barging in here when no one's done anything wrong."

"You screamed," One of the MacKays defended.

"Och." She ignored him, turned to look down on Hamish, whose head was nestled in the soft pillow of Nora. "So you'll not sit with me at dinner?" It was more statement than question, quiet enough to admit to the shame of asking in front of these men.

Hamish was beyond speech.

"He's mine," Nora snipped. "And you'd best stay away from him, Maggie MacBede."

"Oh, aye," Maggie pulled her plaid in tight around her. "I'll stay clear of him, and be happy of it." With chin lifted, she wrapped her embarrassment as tightly as she wrapped her plaid, strode past the warriors, stepped over the threshold and out the door. The MacKay men fell in step.

"Stop following me."

"We have to see to your safety." They told her respectfully, though they did drop back. Unfortunately, it was not far enough to silence their banter.

"Aye, she has spirit."

"Feisty."

"She'll not tame easily."

"I'll not tame at all." She snapped, her eyes on her destination. Someone would answer for this.

As heads turned to watch the progress of the threesome, Maggie realized that she would have to be the one to take matters in hand. So she would. Determined, she spun around to confront them.

"Do you know, this is MacBede land?" She kept to her most ladylike voice. "And that I am a MacBede?"

"Aye, we are knowing that." They grinned stupid grins.

"Well, then, I don't know how it is at the MacKay keep, but here a woman is safe to walk on her own."

"You'll be safe on MacKay land." One of them offered.

She stumbled on that, bewildered. There was naught she could say, but still she hesitated. Even when she turned to walk off again, she did so with a great deal of wariness. They were fools if they thought she would ever be in MacKay territory. She'd never left MacBede land and had no intention of doing so.

She should set them straight. Walking backwards, she told them. "If I ever visit the MacKays, which I doubt would be soon, I'll be remembering that. But for now, kindly leave me be."

She stood still, waited.

They stood still, focused on her.

"I'm only going up to the keep," she informed them, as if they were simple in the head.

They nodded.

She turned, took a step and looked back. They hadn't followed her, but their grins were as wide as doorways. She hoped their faces ached from them.

She walked a few paces before she checked on them again.

"You'll do us proud, Maggie MacBede," they told her.

Harumph. She strode up to the keep, without another turn.

She was not a pleasant person, right now. In truth, she was feeling a mite shrewish, and it was all the MacKay's fault.

● * * * * * * * * * * *

The swarm of people within the great hall helped break the chill of the changing season. The MacBedes and their guests milled about the central fire pit, as smoke rose, curled about their heads before drifting higher and out the window slits.

The main doors flew open. Fire flared, as smoke swirled wildly into a dancing specter. Maggie stood upon the portal, fists planted on her hips, head high. Her glorious mane billowed about her.

Anticipation speared Talorc. She was proud and magnificent and soon she would be his.

"Shut that door, Maggie," her father called across the cavernous room, "and come speak to The MacKay."

Talorc watched her advance. Two of his men, William and Bruce, filled the entrance, shut the door and followed in Maggie's wake.

Aye, she was magnificent, and raring for a fight. Talorc waited, knowing he was in her sights, knowing that she'd stop no more than a foot's distance. Far enough that she'd not get a crick looking up at him, close enough for confrontation.

There'd not been a day in Talorc's memory when a woman, other than his ma or even his grandma, had railed at him. Aye, for that, he could not remember a time when a woman had been a challenge.

He wanted to laugh, felt it rise inside of him. Not in jest, never in jest. His Maggie was no laughing matter. This was pure exhilaration. He had to fight it, for she wouldn't understand the smile on his face, and she was riled enough already.

He pictured her taunting him, goading him with her luscious body, using a mattress for the battlefield. His body tensed, nostrils flared. Now was not the time for this.

For distraction he focused on William and Bruce. They followed her path, close enough to grab her if need be, far enough to give Maggie her own head.

"Where's Diedre?" He called to them. He brought Diedre as a companion for Maggie when they left for Glen Toric.

"Visiting with the women in the village." Not the answer he wanted.

Talorc's scowl matched Maggie's when he looked down to where she now stood. As predicted, no less than one foot away.

Unfortunately, as his scowl fled a smile spread. She'd not care for that.

"You're looking fine, lass," he told her, sure that the compliment would ease the tension.

"Am I now?" She trilled, all wide- eyed and false friendliness.

"It's as I said," Talorc offered cautiously, more comfortable with her straight forward anger than this show of girlish cunning.

"Ah, so fine, perhaps, that you're thinking someone might want to snatch me up and run away with me?"

They couldn't have told her. Talorc glared at his men, but knew they'd said nothing. They would never betray their plan. Still, her scenario was uncannily accurate.

"Or maybe," she told him sweetly, conversationally, "you think there is evil lurking in the streets."

She was determined to play the young innocent, the coquette. Talorc decided it did not suit her.

"I'm thinkin'" she continued, with mock solemnity, "that you don't consider the MacBedes able to care for their own."

"William?" Talorc ordered.

"It's not what you're thinking, Laird." William offered.

"No, 'tis no wrong doing of ours." Bruce added, bringing Maggie's fury around on himself.

"No wrong doing on your part?" Maggie snapped, finger aimed at Bruce, but the two warriors were on the far side of the fire pit. Talorc, being so much closer, drew Maggie's ire. She spun back and shoved at his chest, as if she could push him away.

"Hoi, Maggie." He grabbed her hand. "Tell me what's troubling you."

But she didn't. She didn't say a word, nor did she move. The touch, her hand to his chest, his hand to hers, froze any action. Her eyes widened as she stared, stunned.

This time, there was no hope but to smile. For she stood before him, her chest rising and falling, so you'd think the air had grown too thin and she needed more, yet couldn't get enough. To be true, the slight contact sizzled.

He shook his head, knowing all this was new to her. Unsettling.

He raised his free hand to quiet the murmured bluster that surrounded them. God help him, he'd rather have been holding her with both hands.

"Maggie," his voice a hoarse whisper, not by design, but it suited the moment, made it more intimate.

She tried to pull her hand free, to tug it loose, causing him to press it more fiercely against his chest. The room settled, or so it seemed. Perhaps he just didn't hear it any more, as his focus, every bit of him, was centered on Maggie. When he lowered his free hand to reach for hers, the movement was instinctive. Never did his eyes leave hers. He understood the wariness, the caution in her eyes.

Did she see the promises, the questions in his? Perhaps, for she lowered her gaze, which drew his glance to her lips. Full and red as a summer's berry, dipped and curved as neatly as his bow. The luscious fruit parted,

as the tip of her tongue snuck out to slowly
wet what he so hungered to taste. Talorc
swore time slowed, each movement measured
by an eternity of sensation. He couldn't
breathe, couldn't think, felt the whole of his
body tense with tortuously exquisite
reactions.

"They . . ." Her words a whispered
breath. "They followed me, wouldn't let me
be."

He leaned closer, not understanding her
complaint. "You mean William and Bruce?"

"Aye," she broke the moment with a
swift look over her shoulder. The sight of his
men brought a return of her fury. When she
tugged at her hands, he let them slip from his
grasp, not surprised when she tucked them
behind her.

He didn't consider her step away from
him to be cowardly. They needed distance, if
any rational discussion was to take place.
Straightening, clasping his own hands behind
him, Talorc waited for her to continue.

"You know, Laird MacKay," He
watched, as she took a deep breath and
smoothed her plaid down her sides, "I was
born here." When he nodded, she
acknowledged it with one of her own as she
turned to pace. "And I was raised right here in
this keep." She pointed to the rush-covered
floor that she crossed, back and forth, before
him. "To be sure, by marriage and blood I'm
kin to everyone within the walls of this
place." She halted, her brow knotted
thoughtfully, before she looked up at him.
"Do you get my ken?"

Again, Talorc nodded for her to
continue, for he didn't have the slightest idea
where she was going with all this.

"Well, now, I'm not saying things are different for the MacKays . . ."

Talorc stopped her, wanting to make sure she understood they were not so different. "The MacBedes are descendants of the MacKays, and well you know that. We are kin, Maggie, distant mayhap, but . . ."

"Och," she stilled him, "What I'm saying is that on MacBede land, within the walls of this keep, I am safe from harm. No one would hurt me. Now, mayhap, a MacKay woman is not so safe . . ."

"You go too far, woman!" Talorc roared, the MacBede men joining in against their own.

Maggie ignored them all, as she leaned in to face Talorc, head on with the fury of her own anger. "Then tell me," she snapped, "why these brutes find the need to follow me? Here in my own home. On the land where I've run free as the wind. In the keep that comforts my heart? Why would they be thinking I need protection? They insult us, Laird MacKay."

Talorc said nothing, just looked to his men who no longer smiled.

"We didna' intrude until she screamed." Bruce vowed.

"Screamed?" Talorc, Feargus, all of Maggie's brothers rounded on her, their hands on the hilts of their swords. For the second time that evening, third time that day, Maggie backed away. She did not like the feel of retreat.

"Why did you scream?" Talorc asked, his voice far too calm, far too quiet.

"It's not what you're thinking." She backed up further.

"Maggie," her father barked, "where were you when you screamed?"

Ah, anger, that she could face. She turned to her da. "It was naught but a yelp of surprise."

"Laird MacKay," William started, "I think it was . . ." But Maggie spun on him before he could go further.

"'Tis not your story to tell," she bit out, "and it's no one else's business but my own. There was no harm meant or done, so go away and stop following me." Maggie ordered.

She gave them her back, stormed to the kitchens rather than wait for an outcome. She could not miss the sound of Talorc's voice as he asked where she had been. They would answer him, there was no doubt to that, and then everyone would know of her humiliation. Her life would be a misery.

"Maggie," Fiona caught up with her, turned her daughter around for a good look. "Ah, Maggie, mine, you've grown into a fine lass, love." And gave her a hug, tight as could be.

"Don't say that so loud, ma. The others will think you've gone daft."

"Nay, but I'm going to ask you to be a bit kinder to our guests." She shoved Maggie back, fussed with her hair, "You're a Highlander lass and a MacBede. You'd not shame us now, would you?"

"Is that what you think? That I'd shame you?"

"You don't treat him as you treat our other guests, Maggie, and you know it's true."

She wanted to remind her mother that their other guests did not call her brothers to battle, but she knew her mother would object. "Our other guests don't treat me the way he does."

"He's not unkind."

"Nay."

"He's not rude?"

Maggie might have argued that, as well, but to no better results. "Nay"

"Then how does he treat you different that you act so queer around him?"

Maggie shrugged, digging at the floor with the toe of her slipper. "I don't know what it is Ma, he just . . ." She looked away, avoided her mother's eyes. "He just frightens me so."

Fiona frowned, "He leaves in the morn. Can you hold your temper that long?"

"In the morn?"

"Aye."

Maggie studied the man who had caused her to misbehave. "For tonight?"

"Aye."

"That I can do, Ma, for tonight. But it would be best if we keep apart."Maggie." Fiona touched her daughter's face. "You say he frightens you. I've never known you to be frightened. Ever. And it can't be the size of him, for you know enough of grand men."

"He's a great beast of a man, Ma."

"He's not so much grander than your da or Jamie."

"But he's so..." Maggie fought to explain what she'd yet to understand. "He makes me feel peculiar, Ma. He makes my insides tumble about something fierce. I think he's got the power of spirits so they jump and dance inside of me when he's close. I dinna' like it. I want him to leave us."

Mother looked to daughter, as though for the first time in a long while, and was startled by what she saw. With a shake of her head came laughter, light and loving as a joyful embrace. At the same time, tears filled her eyes. It made no sense to Maggie. No sense at all.

"Ah, daughter mine," once more, she gave a quick, hearty hug. "A day will come when you'll be wishing for just that sort of feeling."

"Never."

"Oh, aye," her mother laughed again, as she pushed Maggie toward the kitchens to oversee the last of the preparations. "And I've a mind to sit him right beside you, so you can find out what it is I'm speaking of."

"You wouldn't, Ma! You wouldn't do that to me, would you now?"

"Oh, aye, I would." Fiona chuckled. "Just as soon as I speak to your da." She shoved Maggie off as she turned back to the great room.

CHAPTER 6 - THE PLEA

To be disregarded, fresh on the heels of Hamish's defection, was no aide to Maggie's temper. Yet there she sat, her brother Nigel on her left, reaching around her, grabbing the notice of the man to her right, as though Maggie were no more than the chair she sat in.

Recently returned from battle, in high demand or not, the Bold could try to speak with her. Unless the taint of Hamish's rejection had put him off.

The problem was, as much as she wanted to have nothing to do with the Bold, she wanted to have everything to do with him. He had awakened something inside of her, something deep and dark and secret. Her senses buzzed with his nearness.

He even smelled good.

Damn the man, anyway. Coming here, catching her, saying she was just rrrrright and making her ma believe he was there for Maggie, herself, when it most certainly was not true. Or, if it was, then he had changed his mind. Men were, after all, a fickle lot.

"You're scowling again, Maggie MacBede."

She dropped her knife, choked on a bite of meat. Talorc slapped her on the back.

"Am I?" Too flustered to be coy, she challenged him. "And how would you be knowing when I do or do not scowl?"

Before Talorc could respond, Nigel reached past Maggie, to grab his arm.

"Hey man, look at that, will ya'?" He gestured to a lower table where a MacBede and a MacKay clenched fists, elbows set squarely on the table.

Maggie shoved at her brother's beefy arm.

"What are ya' doin' Maggie?" Nigel scowled. "I'm wanting to show the Bold how Conegell is bettering Domnall at the arm!"

"And I'll be getting the better of your arm if you don't stop shoving it in my face."

Talorc's bark of laughter reminded her that she was not acting the lady. It didn't help when Nigel snorted. "You know, Laird MacKay, if you take her, she'll be a thorn in your side."

"He'll not be taking me though, will he Nigel. You'll be stuck with me to plague you forever more." Nigel slunk back on his bench.

Talorc touched her chin, guided her around to face him. Heat rushed up, passed the place where his fingers lay, and scorched clear to the roots of her hair. She jerked away, angered that he could ignore her than take such a right as to touch her.

"You've a becoming blush, lass."

"I don't blush." She lied, wishing it were true. "It's the heat."

"Ah."

He leaned back in his chair. Unlike the small bench she sat on, his chair was a grand piece of furniture with sides that blocked all but his fingers, steepled at his chin. He raised an eyebrow when she leaned around to confront him.

"It's your fault you know? You make it hot in here. Like anger, you make the heat rise in me. Why do you do that?"

His half smile coursed through her as his knuckle traced her jaw. Again, she jerked away. "Don't."

"I can't help it. My skin wants to feel yours."

How could words touch her more surely than his fingers had moments ago? Whatever magic he used, she would fight it. "You're not helpless, you can stop yourself."

"No," he shook his head, "no, I don't think I can."

She snorted. Fought the flutter of flattery. Warriors were notorious with the ladies, not that she could blame them. Too many lasses were foolish enough to want one. She might not be immune to this man, but she refused to be thrilled by pretty words.

"Why are you here," she blurted, "when you've never come before?" Riding the tide of surprise, so evident in the focus she had just gained, she continued. "You've sent others to ask the MacBedes to fight your fights, to risk their lives. So tell me Bold, what's so important now?"

He didn't respond straight away, though. For the first time that evening, he ignored the jests and calls that had been demanding his attention throughout the meal. Even her da tried to gain his attention, but Talorc didn't acknowledge anyone but Maggie. A heady feeling.

"You've a good question, Maggie." He bent close. "But I want you to know that I'm not here for trouble, at least not to my mind."

"I'd not be knowing how your mind works, Bold. But you've made people think you're here for me, while I know better."

A young lad moved between them, a tray of roasted meat held out in offering, reminding them both they were here for a feast.

"Maggie," Talorc explained, as he served both of them from the tray, "When someone is sent with a call to arms, I'm already deep in the fray. There's no time for me to leave a fight. Others, who are swift of foot, but not so handy with the sword, are sent to call for help. We all have our roles to play, don't you see."

"Aye." The word did not come easily, she didn't want to understand, but honesty demanded she do so. Not that he had cleared himself of wrong doing, or that she would let him get off so easily.

"Earlier I told you that Ian's last words were of you, that his death would not sit well with you." He touched her cheek. This time she allowed it, welcomed the warmth, needing the heat to balance the cold of her loss. How quickly that cold could come upon her, when she least expected it.

"I want you to know your brother lost his life in an honorable battle, Maggie. He fought bravely, he saved others. The need to fight that fight will be proven when you still have food for your belly on winter's edge of spring."

"And that's why you came. You believe you can convince me Ian needed to be there, with you, when the Gunns don't come on to our land."

He tsked, like a teacher to a student. "Don't fool yourself, Maggie, you know they've been in your fields, taken what's yours."

She looked away, bit at her lower lip, hesitant for the first time. There was truth in

his words. She was not so angry she would deny that. But her Ian's death was still a raw wound.

"Aye, but we never lost as we've been losing these few years past."

Rather than insult, her words gave him pause. He nodded, admitting. "We were losing like the saints were against us. Aye, that is true. One ride out, the food didn't go with us. Another, what we ate was tainted. Small raiders, neither Gunn nor clan, attacked when we least expected."

"You're to expect everything."

"Aye." He reached for her then, as though it were true, that he had an uncontrollable need to touch her. Fingers spread, he cupped her cheek, stroked it with his thumb. She didn't stop him.

"Maggie," Talorc took her hands in his, "Do you know how you avenged Ian? Do you know the role you played in turning the tide, bringing abundance?"

She pulled away, insulted. "Don't use your words with me. That's all they are, just words. I have done nothing. Nothing," she snapped.

"Aye, you have and the MacKays want to thank you. Come to Glen Toric with me."

She sat up, turning fully to confront him. "You ignore me all evening, then suddenly, quick as you please, you're asking me to leave this place? This is my home, these are my people. I've no reason to leave."

"Ah, but you do, Maggie girl, you do," he murmured, as he bent to the platter of meat, cut-off a morsel, speared it. "You gave us an idea that we're growing with. You are changing the need to battle for all we have."

Before the tip of his knife could get the meat to her lips, Maggie took it with her fingers. Moist and succulent, the stewed juices ran down her hand. She tried to catch the rivulet with her tongue.

"Oh, no, Maggie. Let me." He caught her hand, pulled it to his lips, and took the liberty of capturing the droplet with his mouth, licked the rivulet with a slow tongue.

For a breath, a long breath held, Maggie didn't move. The hall could have been empty, the noise pure music, before she caught herself and tugged her hand free. Talorc was not ready to let it go.

"Stop." She hissed.

He looked into her eyes and with one bite, took the meat from her hand. "You taste better than the meat."

"Oh, Lord." She pulled free, stumbled, toppled her bench in a rush to be away from him. He reached to help her but she ignored his hand, scrambled to rise on her own.

Nigel laughed. "You drunk already? It's still early, lass."

"Laugh all you wish, brother, for I'll return the favor soon."

Quick as that, his amusement ended. "Have a care, Laird MacKay, for when she sets out for revenge, she could teach the lot of us a thing or two."

Maggie brushed at her skirts. "He'll not have need to worry, brother, for why would I be wanting revenge on the likes of the Laird?"

"Why indeed?" Talorc asked, as he reminded her, "I'll be leavin' on the morrow."

"Aye," she acknowledged, trying to catch Nigel's eye as she reseated herself. Nigel refused to look her way.

"I want you to leave with me."

She laughed. "Leave with you?" Patted his arm. The man had barely talked to her all evening. "I'll think of it," she lied, "and when next we see each other, I'll consider your request."

"Not later, Maggie," he caught her hand upon his arm, held it tightly in place, "tonight, this night. When I tell my story, if you truthfully find you cannot go with me, then I will accept your decision."

"Tonight? You want to tell me a story tonight and then expect me to leave in the morn?"

"Aye. Tonight."

She laughed. "Does my father know of this?"

"Aye, as does your mother." He moved so they could both look to her parents, who watched with uncommon wariness.

Their wariness made no more sense than anything had this day. Her parents knew that nothing could induce Maggie to leave her home, not tonight, not ever. And, as far as she was concerned, not with a warrior; especially not with a warrior. Her parents knew that.

Talorc blocked them from Maggie's sight. "But they don't know the story, have yet to hear it. When they do, when you do, they've agreed to go along with your wishes."

"Even if I choose to go away with you?"

"Aye."

Maggie relaxed. "You can save your breath. This is my home, my friends and family. If I left, I'd be leaving young Ian behind. I can't be doing . . ." He stopped her with a finger to her lips.

"Bold!" a man yelled from the far end of a table. "Tell us of the final victory! We want to hear the tale of the fight!"

A chorus of agreement rang out. Maggie tried to get away, to leave him to his tales of battle, but he wouldn't let her go. "This is the story I'm going to tell, Maggie," he said for her alone. "Hear my story, then tell me what you will or won't do."

"I'll not go."

"Hear me out first."

She wanted to respond, but there was no chance. The meal had wound down, musicians were playing. Soon the bard would entertain with his own tales of war and love and the strength of the clans.

Talorc freed her hand as he stood. She thought he meant to excuse the two of them, so he could address her in private, away from the prying ears of the family, the clan and his warriors.

Like a wave, solemn silence moved over the room. If Talorc had sought attention, his timing was immaculate. He acted as if that was just what he wanted.

This would be no private telling.

The realization hit with the impact of a horse. Alarmed, Maggie tugged at his arm. Immediately, he lent down, focused on her.

"You know, I've no ken for large men?" She whispered, "I've vowed never to promise myself to a warrior."

"A solemn oath?" An oath was a sacred thing to a highlander.

She swallowed. "Everyone's heard me say so."

He repeated his question. "Did you pledge this as an oath?"

She shook her head. "Why should I? My mind is made up."

"If you didn't pledge yourself, there's nothing to fret over, lass. It's no more than dreaming of the future. Not for us to foretell." He turned back to the tables lined with watchful clansmen, both MacKay and MacBede.

"Oh Lord!" Maggie sent the plea heavenward. "Oh, Lord, please help me here." But she knew it was her own fault for wanting him to flirt with her. As usual, she had brought this on herself, overestimated her ability to deal with a situation.

All eyes were focused on the Bold. He tugged on Maggie until she stood beside him, within the curve of his arm. Her legs trembled until she thought they couldn't possibly hold her upright. Talorc gave her waist a squeeze, as if that would reassure her. He was a fool if he believed that.

As though they were alone, as though the whole world were not watching, he bent over her and whispered. "Will you listen to my plea now?"

* *

Not all the MacBedes made it to the dinner. Far from the keep, beneath the full moon, Roddie MacBede whimpered, "I beg of you anything, anything you want," he pleaded from beneath the foot of the man in green. Six other harsh, ragged men raised spears, anticipating any attempt to flee.

"Anything?'

"Aye," he sniffled, hiccupped a sob of fear.

"You've been cast from your clan."

"No, no," he stuttered, as the man in green pressed his dirk further into his chest, between two ribs, above the heart.

"Why not?"

"No one knows, but they all hate me," he slobbered, "I've not any chances left with the clan."

The pressure of the dirk eased.

69

"No one knows what you do," the man looked over at a bundle of fabric barely disguising the limp form beneath it. "Not what you do," he shook his head, "but what you did, and to a child? Other children?"

"I've never killed one," Roddie cried. "I shouldna' of done it, I know, I shouldna' done it, didn't mean to, just wanted a little fun. She's my sister's child, she was going to tell." Once again, the dirk pressed hard.

"Why not? Why not do it? "

The question startled Roddie, the lilt of it skewed from reality. Wrong. Just as his joy in destroying the small body was out of step. Not real, except she would not wake.

"Tell me? Why not kill the lass?" Whimsy turned hard, cold. "You enjoyed it. Admit it."

Roddie nodded, sure, now, the blade would pierce his black heart.

"The bairn would have destroyed you if ya' had not destroyed her."

Roddie nodded.

"We can find you more lassies who will fight you and lose. Would ya' like that?"

Roddie shivered against a flicker of excitement. He looked up into eyes dark with the same lust he fought and knew he'd met the devil. He hadna' meant to do it. He was a better man than that, he knew he was.

"Well?"

"Aye, I would like that." Whimsical thoughts, that's all they ever were. Urges not to be fed. Only he had fed them, and this one time, when he silenced his victim, he was caught for the deed.

The blade left his breast, a hand offered. "Rise, join us. Let us make merry."

CHAPTER 7 - A STORY TOLD

Talorc's hand rested upon Maggie's shoulders. Reassuring it was not, coming from a man too wild to anticipate, and far too confident. All evening he overlooked her and then, just like that, expected to convince her to go away with him, as though she had no mind of her own.

"To all you men who joined me in the battle against the Gunns," Maggie jumped as Talorc's voice blasted out across the hall. "Have we not failed to honor the one who pulled us through?"

A roar rose to the rafters, matched by the thunder of stomping feet and fists that pounded table tops. Dishes clattered and shook, some fell to the floor.

Maggie looked about, to see who they were honoring, but all the warriors faced forward, sights set on the Bold, who shouted above the noise.

"I'll do my telling," He bellowed, "for everyone to hear the glory of our Maggie MacBede!"

Maggie MacBede? The thought of it nearly suffocated, as the cheers crescendoed. Her whole body trembled, as warrior after warrior moved forward, crossed right hand to left shoulder and bowed low to Maggie. Her legs wobbly, Talorc had to help her stand.

She nodded to each man who offered obeisance to her, stunned by the clamor of the hall.

"Maggie, Maggie, Maggie . . ." They chanted.

She could take no more, held her hand out for them to stop. "Please," she asked, and immediately they silenced. "I would like to hear what this is about."

She stood firm lest they feel they'd frightened her, though frighten they did. And it was the Bold's fault. She was certain of that, because never before, no matter how many battles the MacBedes had fought, had personal honor come to her. It was a heavy weight she never asked for.

The men took to their seats again, stilled as the Bold had not been able to still them. Once again, Talorc sat her, a hand to her shoulder, before nodding to her parents, and again facing the tables of warriors before them.

"It is no secret that these past years have brought great sadness to the Highlands. Sassenachs have been trying to send their fancy Lords and knights to rule our land, our people. Men from the North, the powerful mighty Norsemen, have not ebbed in their pursuit of what is ours. Are the Gunns not more Norsemen than Scot?"

Belches and curses fouled the air, just as the idea fouled their thoughts.

"Brave and glorious the Clan MacKay and all our septs, including the MacBedes, have faced great losses and grand great warriors. Our babes have cried with hunger 'til our souls were torn apart.

We've faced the mockery of the Sassenach, who see glory only in the silver they eat with and the fancy cloth they wear. They laugh at the way we live, as comfortable upon a bed of snow as a mattress filled with down.

"These English are men with no hearts, men who have no care for what we are, who we are and the land we breathe for. And yet they threaten to rule us.

"And so, with these sorrows and woes upon our hearts, we battled the Gunns over disputes that were not of our making. We did this in search of food for our bairnes, to keep them safe and fed through the winter months.

"And we did this to avenge the deaths of the likes of the MacBedes' Ian."

Maggie shifted with the unpleasant reminder that she had loudly resented Talorc's call to arms.

"The MacKays, the MacBedes, the MacVies, the Baynes and the Reays, we all stood strong, charging into battle, our cries heralding the boast of victory.

"But victory did not come."

Shoulders rounded against the burden of losses.

"Again," Talorc continued, as mournful as the drone of a bagpipe, "grand men were lost, taken from us, dying honorable deaths but dying the same."

The hall had grown so quiet Maggie heard the rustling of a mouse within the reeds, the spark of a fire-pit none too close. She looked to the men, their faces grim and sorrowful. Aye, it was a fact, the deaths of those they lost meant greater burden on those who survived.

She looked up at the MacKay, to see where his tale would go, only to find him studying her, a wistful smile upon his lips so contrary to the sorrowful faces of his men. She was glad to see he had the sense to wipe it from his mouth before facing the crowd.

"As was my way, after the second day of fighting, the second day of terrible loss, I walked through the shadows of the camp, looked to the men, fought for words to carry them past the grief.

"The MacBede men drew me. They were no different than the others, sitting before their fires. As brave as they are, worrying sorrow comes with a battle lost, that mayhap we would lose again. There had been too many defeats in too many years to bolster our spirits.

"That was when I learned of Maggie MacBede."

The use of her name didn't touch her at first. She was listening to a story that had naught to do with her. But then, as he stood in silence, his words ran back through her mind to suck the breath right out of her. He nodded, as though he knew, had waited, for just that reaction, before he continued.

"As I watched, as I fought for a way, any way, to encourage each and every man, as I felt the despair of my task pull me under, Conegell MacBede asked any who would listen. 'Do ye remember the time young Maggie gave us our talismans?'

"Talismans, I thought, thinking of old hags and their mysterious witchcraft. But the man did not speak of an old hag, or of sorcery. Nay, straight on the heels of his asking, another chuckled. Oh, aye, he remembered the lass, no more than eight years, and there she was giving the men more strength in her little parcels than any drop of draught could do.

"I'm telling you now," Talorc placed his hands flat on the table, as he leaned out in his telling, "the curiosity alone drove away my wretched worries. I stood and listened as others were beginning to do, for the MacBede fire pit held the only voices to sound the sound of vigor. They chuckled, they spoke of strength being given. It was a night when all were hungry for such sounds.

"So, as the other men left their fires to stand around the MacBedes, the tales continued. I learned that an eight-year-old lass strode out to the courtyard, as the MacBede warriors prepared to leave. She ignored wives and mothers and sisters who stood near their men, and approached each and every warrior to hand him a small parcel.

"It was a square of plaid, no more than a scrap, and inside that plaid she'd placed a piece of heather amid soil from the land. Then she told them, in her earnest child's way, to carry that parcel with them, for it would remind them of what they fought for; the land, the name and the wild glory of both."

The cheers of earlier were no match for these which shook the very walls of the keep. And, as Maggie looked out at the wild shouts she saw, to her amazement, that every MacBede man held his little packet of plaid and soil and heather in the grip of his hand. Some so old, soil spilled from the worn fabric. Others, bright and new.

They had kept them? They had not tossed them in a stream as they left the land? They had not laughed at her, or thought her so foolish that they could not answer her?

"As you can guess, the men were stunned beyond words for fear tears might fall. That a child, a mere little child, bonny as she was, could speak what each needed to hear . . . ah, she was a one to be remembered."

Maggie slumped upon her bench, startled by what she was hearing, seeing.

"But it did not stop there, Maggie girl," Talorc said, directly to her, though his voice filled the entire hall.

"Nay, it did not stop there. For tales abound of the young girl, Maggie MacBede, of her throwing a rock and downing a Sassenach, of topping an enemy who tried to climb over the wall.

"There's talk of a little bairn, six years at the most, making a nuisance of herself on the battlements, carrying water and lugging pebbles, whatever she thought the warriors would need.

"My heart swelled with the hope that one day I would have such a daughter, when the stories turned, and this wee lass was not so wee anymore. No, she had grown, in the space of the telling, into a strapping lass whose honor was much sought after. It took all seven of her brothers to keep suitors at bay."

"There were not so many!" Maggie snapped, slapping her hand over her mouth in embarrassment.

The Bold laughed, an audacious bellow.

"You think not, lass?" He calmed enough to ask, "And why do you think you're left with nothing but puny men to look to?" Maggie could do naught but shake her head. She wanted to say that puny men were all she wanted, but she could not, so Talorc continued. "The rest, my sweet, the men more worthy of you, have been warned away. Which pleases me no end." Talorc confided to the whole of his audience. "For I mean to make her my own."

"No!" She screamed, pushed beyond control by his bluntness.

No one took any notice. No one cared that her hands shook at the way he was openly courting her, putting her in a place she didn't want to be. A place she might not be able to extract herself from.

The Bold continued his tale. "I am The MacKay, the Laird of our clans, and yet this woman, your fine, gentle and true Maggie MacBede, rounded the men with spirit and fire.

"The following day was dark with the omen of death, but it was not a fearful day for us, nor was it our deaths the day spoke of. Hearts full of tales of Maggie MacBede, we stood tall and bold, strong in the face of battle, and shouted our warrior's cry,

"For the land . . .

"for the name . . .

"for the Wild Glory of each!"

The men started to stomp, in unison, a pounding of feet like a drum roll. Talorc's voice rose above it, clear to the rafters . . .

"And for Our Maggie MacBede!" His cry echoed through the keep, rained emotion strong enough to wring tears and shouts of triumph from all who listened.

Maggie could see the testament upon her mother's cheeks and she wanted to weep herself. Not for the glory, but for the foolishness of it all. She was no saint to be worshiped. She was no grand person to be bowed to. She was just Maggie, daughter of Feargus and Fiona. Daughter of this home, this piece of land. As passions grew within the room, Maggie felt her own wither and die.

Talorc continued, though to Maggie his voice came from very far away. "With ease, we won that battle, and each one that followed. We went on to greater victory on the creaghs, bringing food enough to feed our people for more than a winter. And we did all, fueled by the strength and loyalty of one wee woman. Maggie MacBede."

She sat, waiting, knowing deep in her bones that she did not want what was to follow. Her strength, her loyalty, were for the MacBedes and her home. She did not want to leave this place, her clan, to go off with a stranger no matter how peculiar he made her feel.

As though he sensed her need for thoughts, Talorc waited, watching her, before he spoke again.

"And so I ask you, Maggie MacBede, come with me to my home."

Her heart sank.

"Be my bride."

Fear spiraled.

"Birth me daughters."

Her stomach plummeted.

He continued, "Wee lasses, as loyal and stout of heart as their mother, and valiant, brave sons to fight by my side.

"I need you, Maggie MacBede. The Clan MacKay needs you, and all of her septs. Come with me as my bride and together we will save the whole of the Highlands from the Norsemen and the Sassenachs."

How could she deny him?

"Be my bride."

He stood, his hand held out to her. She had no choice but to take it, to allow that tug that had her standing by his side, though her limbs quaked, her hands trembled.

"I'm not what you would think." She whispered, for pride kept her from speaking to all those who listened eagerly.

"Aye, you are, Maggie." He told her softly, "you are everything I think. It is you who knows not what you are."

Looking directly into his eyes, all too aware of his bold assurance, she allowed him to see her fear. With a gracious force she had never thought to conjure, she replied. "I will think on what you have said, Laird MacKay. By spring, you will have your answer."

He began to shake his head, before she had even finished her telling.

"Maggie, I knew you were the one by the first victory. It was then that I vowed to wed you for the clans. But today, when I saw you running through the courtyard, your plaid flapping like a flag, your auburn mane flying behind you. It was then that I knew I would be wedding you for myself."

One tug and she was close enough for him to rest his hands upon her shoulders.

"What I hadna' expected was the feel of you, Maggie MacBede, when your brother tossed you into my hands. 'Twas a brilliant jolt. A shock of lightning coursin' through me. I knew right then, I would marry you for the grand power of our mating and the bonny bright bairnes that would bring.

"Marry me tonight, Maggie MacBede. Be my bride, for the strength of our clans and the future of our kinship. Do it for the land, for the name and for the wild glory of both!"

CHAPTER 8 - TRAPPED

She couldn't say 'no' any more than she could dispel the wild thump of her heart. The wait for her response hung heavy as rain upon the room.

With perverse irony, the pounding of her chest carried her to childhood, and a memory. She had been no more than a wee thing when she found a frantic little sparrow trapped within the stillroom, a dank dark place. How the bird managed to find its way inside the room, heavy with the scent of malt and burning peat, Maggie would never know.

The thick oak door, framed in the opening of what was no more than a cave within the mountain, had been shut tight. The only light from a small window covered with a thin oiled sheet, its ledge as deep as a child's arm was long.

Maggie's plan was to hide inside and hear how the whiskey was made. She'd come ahead of the others, using all of her weight to get that monstrous door open a crack so she could slip inside. It was then she'd sensed the creature, feared it was a bat.

But it wasn't. It was a poor, helpless sparrow, startled by the light that the door offered. It dodged and darted, as frightened of Maggie as it was of its plight.

She'd caught it then, held it gently within the palms of her hands, as she tried to soothe its trembling. The wild beat of its heart could be felt in her fingertips, bringing prayers to Maggie's lips. Over and over she begged God to be merciful, to allow the creature to live long enough for the men to arrive, for she daren't let go of the sparrow in order to open the blasted door.

She'd received a telling measure of censor, for being within that cavern, for being in a place that she never should have entered. But it dinna' matter to her, the bird was free, flying off without a care, without so much as a circling thank you. It was free and that was gratitude enough.

There was no one now, to hold her, comfort her and wait for an open door.

She was trapped with no savior in sight.

Her brothers, ever so quick to stall suitors, were obviously part of this plan. Her parents? Maggie knew, without even looking, the pride that would be shinning in their eyes and the eager hope that Maggie would succumb to this odd manner of courtship.

And it wasn't just them, her parents and her brothers, who had been caught in this man's tales. The wretched beast had the whole of the clan in his hand. Maggie could see, with one furious glance, the rapt anticipation, the delight that one of theirs would become the Great Laird MacKay's wife.

Talorc the Bold was just the sort they would all want for her, a man who was larger than life itself. Larger even than the tales they told about Maggie. They all knew her, knew the truth behind each of the stories, and yet they chose to believe his words, believe the testament of cheers that had rung through the hall but moments ago.

They were fools. They were all fools.

Warriors did this before a battle. They would stoke the fire of aggression with the fuel of former battles that grew far beyond reality. With each telling the stories became grander and bolder and more daring. A warrior who knew his way around words could convince his men of anything in those moments, even that to die in battle was a glorious thing.

Pah! As if risking a life were not foolish in the extreme.

Oh aye, and the Bold knew what he was about. Hadn't he taught her that? His timing was impeccable, waiting until the whiskey had filled the men to just the right point, until they were puffed-up with a false bravado, a sense of largesse, yet not so far gone as to be sloppy, or to forget the Bold's words.

Aye, the men were seeing their world as a bigger and brighter and bolder place, including one wee lass.

Even knowing this, Maggie could not say no.

But neither would she say yes.

"You've given me little time, MacKay."

"Aye."

"Some would say you're trying to trap me." She could feel the tension in the room ease with the anticipation of a spat. They were highlanders; a fight no less than entertainment, especially when they were certain of the outcome. They'd not have respected Maggie if she let him have his way without a battle.

He had wound them all in with his stories, but Maggie knew, just as well, how to ease that coil, if not unwind it all together. Or so she hoped.

"Aye, perhaps." He admitted, answering her accusation of entrapment, "just as I once cornered a horse crazed with fear. We were in a burning wood. Had I let him go, at the least he would have burned to his own death.

"So you see, Maggie, I trapped him to save him."

He was a more agile opponent than she had expected.

"And you think to be saving me by trapping me?"

He didn't respond, nor were there the telling little quips coming from their audience to boost her side of the quarrel. It was time to change tactics.

"How," she asked practically, "do you plan on wedding me when there isn't a Priest within the Highlands? It is nearly the Feast of Fleadh nan Mairbh, and no decent man of the cloth would be found near folks who celebrate such things."

"Does it matter, Maggie?" He asked her gently, "Do we need a church man to make vows? Are you not a Highlander? Is your word not strong enough without witness?"

Those were fighting words, they were. Maggie narrowed her eyes.

"I would like the blessing of a power greater than either of us, Laird. Surely you can understand that . . . wait for that."

"There is no time, Maggie. We, the MacKay, and all her septs, need our wedding," he ran his finger along her cheek, caught her jaw in his palm when she tried to pull away. "Just as they need the presence of our son."

"There's no guarantee of that, Laird." She defended.

He laughed, threw his head back and laughed. Maggie kicked him.

"Oh, Maggie," he grumbled good naturedly, rubbed his shins to the raucous laughter of the crowd. "Life never offers guarantees, but it can make promises. You're a healthy lass, a surprise blessing to a ma and da that had already born seven sons. And should you bear me a daughter you'd not see more delight, for there's ne'er been a daughter in my line for three generations. Give me a son, or a daughter, and fail that-- we'll raise those of our clansmen, and teach them our ways."

He was more of an opponent than she'd ever faced before. She was fighting for all she knew, all she wanted in life, and yet he could come in and take it all from her with one fell swoop of words.

She admired him for it.

She hated him for it.

She willed the tears away, closed her eyes against them, as she fought for the only argument he had yet to slaughter. "And you cannot wait, one season, for a priest, a man of cloth, to bind us?"

Talorc looked to the ground, muttered to himself, then looked up straight into Maggie's eyes. He was well aware that he pressured her, she could see it, and she knew that he knew, with time she could break this thing.

If he'd give her time.

"Maggie," he sighed, and she knew a concession was coming, "in the tradition of old, in the ways of the Highlanders, we will clasp hands, vow to each other. If you canna' make vows for life, then promise yourself for a year and a day. Handfast me, Maggie."

Och, Dear Lord, God in Heaven, Help me. She cried within, though no answering cry returned. Ian, if you're there, help me, for no one else will.

Talorc reached out, took her hands in his, "Handfast me."

Ian's voice failed to ring in her heart.

"I couldna'" she tried to pull away, "it wouldna' be right."

"Why wouldn't it be right? We are Highlanders Maggie, this is our way. Are you so different from the rest of us?"

The flutter of panic in that poor bird's wings so long ago, was no match against the flutter of Maggie's heart. She was trapped. She could feel it and the panic overwhelmed her.

She shoved the Bold straight aside, looked over at her parents, so she could confront them, but her Da would not look at her. He looked to his plate in deep contemplation. Her Ma, oh . . . Maggie's shoulders slumped with what she saw there. Her Ma's heart was breaking. She had wanted Maggie to agree to the wedding but if not, then even her Ma was willing to push her into a Handfast.

A union where, in a year and a day, the Bold could walk out just as easily as Maggie herself could.

". . . should you still not be certain of the match," he continued, "you can walk away. No holds, no binds, you're as free as that horse was, once I steered him away from the fire."

"We know nothing of each other but tales told by others."

"Maggie, the Handfasting is for you, to give you the chance to walk away. 'Tis not for me. I've made that clear. But, I will also make it clear, should you give yourself to me, between the end of the Handfasting and now, should you find that there is no better for either of us, then the priest will bless the union, whatever season he finds us."

"Aye, Aye", the men cheered, the women sighed and wept, caught in the thrill of a courtship unfolding.

"Ma?" Maggie tried once more, but her mother only shook her head. It was Maggie's decision to make, and no other. In truth, she dinna' have a choice.

"I will think on it." She hedged.

Talorc shook his head. "No, Maggie, my people, our clan, they are waiting. They want me to bring you back with me, to settle you in amongst us before the Feast."

"It is not possible," she countered "I have to be here for Fleadh nan Mairbh. I promised Ian."

She'd startled them all, judging by the mumbles and grumbles of the people.

"Maggie," Talorc watched her closely, "you do not invite the dead to come near."

"He was my twin."

"You have a right to your life. His time had come, do not invite your's away." Talorc spoke with care, for everyone knew that the Feast of the Dead was a time of caution. It was a time to hide from the folly of those passed beyond. No one would court such danger.

"It would be more to your purpose to create new life to fill that void. To give your child the name of Ian, in his honor."

"No." She backed away from his words, as the snare of them tightened.

"The two of us, together, this very night."

"But. . ."

"Marry him, Maggie, Marry him . . ." The cheers rang through the hall, the stomping, the clapping, the voices raised in unison, to billow and settle around her.

"Not tonight." She cried.

"Then in the morn, Maggie, for we leave when the sun shows herself."

The chorus had died down, all eyes intent on Maggie and Talorc.

Maggie turned to face them all. "It is what you want?" She cried out, one last plea to the people.

"Oh, aye, lass," Old Padruig played the spokesman, "there's no better for you or for him!"

"Do you all agree?" She shouted, bringing on another resounding cheer. "Then I shall do it." She promised, with a nod of her head. "And the consequences be upon your heads."

Pivoting, she faced Talorc, "In the morn. There is too much to do tonight, if I'm to leave at daybreak."

He raised their hands high as everyone joined in cries of delight. As soon as she could, Maggie spun away, headed toward the stairs that would take her up to her room. Chairs and benches scraped back, as her mother and kinswomen hurried to join her.

They reached her first, though Talorc was not far behind, despite the delay of those who wished to toast his victory.

"Maggie?" He stopped her.

"Aye."

"I'd thought," he leaned in, whispered for her ears alone, "that you would prefer to have our first night together here, with your mother close by to attend you, settle you."

She stared at him, at his lapse in conviction.

"Are you saying I'm to be so terribly alone when away from here?" When, not if. She'd given her word.

"No," he shook his head, frowned, "That's not what I was saying, have no fears on that count. It's just that a mother is a mother . . ."

"And you choose to take me from mine. So be it, if there's any guilt in that, then feel free to feel it." She snipped.

His frown deepened, though he failed to respond. With a tilt of her chin, she swirled away, her entourage of relations a wake of women behind her.

"Tomorrow." Talorc shouted, when she was halfway up the stairs.

Maggie stopped, looked down at the man she would Handfast in the morning. "Tomorrow," she promised with a grim determination, so at odds with the enthusiasm he obviously felt.

Tomorrow she would be promised to a man bold in his battles, both on the battlefield and off. Life would never be easy. If she thought getting her own way was difficult with her brothers and a bear of a father, winning concessions with this man would be all the harder. Hadn't tonight proved that?

* * * * * * * * * *

Maggie scrambled to hide as the earth quaked and shook about her.

"Maggie . . . Maggie, wake darling, 'tis time."

Groggy with sleep, she stirred, opened her eyes. A circle of candles surrounded her bed, lighting the dark of the night. Kinswomen, her mother included. Why?

"Oh Maggie," Muireall swooned upon the bed. "Are you not thrilled? Are you not the luckiest lass in the whole of the Highlands?"

Still muddled, Maggie rubbed her eyes.

"Oh, aye," Leitis smiled, "if Nigel had courted me like that, I don't know what would have happened."

"I do!" Sibeal brought on a chorus of laughter that the older women tried to hush in deference to Maggie's innocence. Quick as the flicker of a candle, Maggie understood why her kinswomen were here, why they spoke the way they did.

Come daylight, she would be riding away from this place, her home. "What's the time? Is it anywhere near to morning?"

"You've an hour at most." Fiona sat beside her daughter, shooing the other women off.

They had all worked late into the night, deciding what Maggie could take with her, what would need sending, what would be saved for her children. They had teased and sighed and oohed over Maggie's fate. Only Maggie didn't take to the fussing. She remained practical; it was the only way to get through what she needed to get through.

It was bad enough that she would have to marry a warrior who came with the near promise of widowhood. God forbid she be left as hungry for male company as Muireall. And with a warrior, a great huge beast of a man, well . . . she would have to be just as strong in spirit. If not, he'd trounce her in every manner of will-- just as he'd done last night when she was fighting for life as she knew it.

The worst of it was that he didn't know her, and when he did come to see who she really was, when all the grand stories proved to be no more than a blown up grain of truth, would he want her? Or, would he turn to all those other women who swooned at the mere thought of him?

Could she ever hope to hold a man such as Talorc the Bold?

As if to spite Maggie's thoughts, her mother took her hand, "He's a splendid man." Then she brushed the hair from Maggie's forehead. Maggie pulled back. How many times in the past had her mother done just such a thing to ease an illness, a pain, or to soothe the frustrations of the young? But those gestures would be too far away to be of any comfort when Maggie faced the confusion and fear of a new home.

"She'll be the envy of every woman," Caitlin cawed, unaware of the sudden wariness between mother and daughter.

"Oh, aye," Siobhan responded, "he makes me quiver."

"How I wish I could be you on the bedding night." Someone else said and they all sighed and nodded.

The words poured around Maggie, too many to take in, too forceful to ignore. Confused, shaken, she lifted her head to knowing smiles. They jostled each other with elbows, raised eyebrows, their comments, now whispered, growing more suggestive by the moment, and suddenly Maggie found a new emotion, a new fear, to completely overwhelm all the others she'd ever felt since meeting this man.

If they were all so eager, why hadn't they asked to be sacrificed? Why hadn't they saved her, possibly the only woman who didn't want to be in this place?

Fiona must have sensed what was happening, for she wrapped a protective arm around her daughter's shoulders, quieting the others.

"Don't go frightening her, now." Fiona warned, but the protective care had come too late. Maggie yanked free of her mother's hold.

"You knew what he was up to, didna' you?" She snapped, and saw her mother's guilty start. So that was the way of it. "Last night, before we even sat to dine, you knew. You led me into that, without a word of care."

Throwing off the covers, she scrambled out the far side of the bed and yelled. "How could ya' do that? How could you let him put me in that corner, where there was no turning back, no matter how I felt?"

"Oh, Maggie, I didna' think . . ."

"You should think! I'm your only daughter and now I've no home here. Why do I wait to be bathed and dressed? Why don't I just go down there and take his hands and make my promises and leave? For you've sent me away from the only home I've ever wanted to know. To a place where who knows what waits?"

Although she paused, to gather breath, to settle the rising hysteria, the others were too stunned to break her momentum.

"Do ya' think he lived there with no woman in his bed?" She asked. "Do you think I'll have my own around me when they carry his body back, all bloodied and broken after a battle? Do you think I'll be pleased with a man not of my own choosin'?"

"Aye!" Angrily, Fiona broke through the shock of her daughter's attack with a succinct nod, "I do!" She shouted back, rounding on Maggie. "For the first time I'm grateful for your brothers' interference. For 'tis true, no man dared court their sister. But your brothers would not dare to interfere with

the Bold. Nor would I have allowed it, as I
did in the past."

She took her daughter by the shoulders.
"He's perfect for you, Maggie, even if you're
too fool to know it."

They stood, both rigid, linked by
Fiona's hands on Maggie's shoulders, when
suddenly Maggie flung herself into her
mother's arms. "Oh mama, I'm so
frightened!" And finally the tears came, as
mother and daughter clung to each other, each
full of their own sorrows for the parting.

Fiona would lose her daughter, to fret
and worry, with no way of knowing how her
own little lass fared. And Maggie, to face
marriage to a stranger, to confront the
unknown, without her mother's wisdom and
care.

"Oh, lass, you'll be fine, you will."
Fiona cradled her daughter's head upon her
shoulder. "I'd not let this happen if I thought
it would be any different. And you remember
now, if you just can't see it in you, to give
yourself to him, then come home. For this
will be your home, forever, for always.Even if
you are married with a dozen children, you
are always wanted here."

Maggie pulled away, swiped at the
tears, unaware of the quiet bustle about her,
as the others prepared a bath, warmed towels,
sorted out the best of her plaids with discreet
peeks at the two women.

"Mama?" Maggie asked, now needing to
know the whole of it. "What is it you mean by
giving myself? Talorc said the same thing,
that if I give myself then we are truly wed,
but if we Handfast . . . mama? Why do you
look that way? What am I saying that you . .
."

"No," Fiona rushed, "no don't be thinking anything, I was just surprised. A mother doesn't imagine it's possible to raise a daughter, with so many older brothers, in a place as busy as our home . . . well . . . where people are so careless with what they say," Fiona put her arm around Maggie, guided her away from the others, toward a window still inky black with night, "It's just that a mother does not expect her daughter to be quite so innocent of thought."

"You didna' look so much surprised as . . ."

"But I was surprised." Fiona broke in.

"You're also thinking to use your words to your advantage, or is it to his advantage?" Maggie startled herself by realizing. "I'm thinking you've his interest in mind over my own."

"Never." Fiona snapped, "Never." She repeated more calmly. "Though 'tis true, I often wonder if you know what's best for you."

"That doesn't answer my question." Maggie badgered.

"About giving yourself?"

"Aye, you ken that's what I'm wanting to know."

"Well," Fiona lifted her chin, "you've heard the women talk about the wedding night?"

"Aye, I know all about that. That's when he takes me to wife."

"You know what takes place?"

Maggie snorted in disgust, "You are right on that mother. This place is not quiet about such things, nor do the animals care to go into hiding when it comes to mating. But what does that have to do with giving myself? A husband has rights and he takes them. An

animal has instincts and they follow them. So
. . . what of me?"

"You," Fiona said with conviction,
"have a heart to give or to withhold. You do
according to your heart, you give to your
husband, absolutely, or you withhold. Let
your heart decide, not your husband. He
cannot take what you do not give."

"Is that it?" Maggie sagged upon the
window ledge, and welcomed the freshness of
the fall breeze as it brushed over her and
rustled her hair. There was clarity in its
coolness. "A matter of my heart?"

"If you let your heart rule what you do
or do not do." Fiona hedged.

"Then if I do not give my heart, I do
not give myself?"

As Fiona took a deep breath, Sibeal
marched up to them.

"Maggie, there's no more time, lass.
Get over there and into that tub, or you'll be
wearing a drying cloth to your Handfasting."

She straightened, looked to her mother,
"If it's as you say, then you can prepare to
have me back here in a year and a day from
this moment. For I'll not give my heart."

Rather than join the throng of women
caring for her daughter, Fiona stood quietly
and watched, as Maggie crossed to the bath.
The lass had regained her spirits, 'twas in her
step, in the way she let the others tease her.

Quietly, Fiona touched three fingers to
her forehead, her heart, to either shoulder.
When the others cast glances her way, they
thought she made the sign of the cross in
preparation of prayers for her daughter. They
could not be knowing that Fiona was praying
for forgiveness for the half-truth she'd been
telling.

For a half-truth, meant a half- lie.

94

A Handfasting was no more than a betrothal. Oh, aye, the couple would live together, may even share a bed but, despite bawdy innuendos to the contrary, should they mate, should the relationship become more than a promise, married they would be. Priest or no priest.

The whole of the Highlands knew this. That Maggie didn't came as a surprise. God's will, Fiona prayed, for she had used Maggie's naiveté mercilessly. Aye, it was for Maggie's own good but still, it had not been with clear honesty. It was just that the girl didn't understand what was in her best interest. And if Fiona judged things right, what was between Maggie and the Laird MacKay . . . well . . . it was nothing, if not physical.

Heart or no, they would be wed before the night was out, or Fiona didn't know her daughter.

CHAPTER 9 - SACRIFICE

She was a stranger to herself.

From her seat on the broad back of a placid gelding called Tairis, Maggie reached for those who stretched to touch her, waved to those who stood high on their toes, necks craned for a view of her, as though they hadn't just talked yesterday.

Somewhere between the dark of night and the sun's glow, she had become someone else, someone extraordinary, someone she didn't recognize. She had been perfectly happy with the old Maggie MacBede, thank you very much.

How many times had she resented her brothers' stoic farewells? Their restless need to be gone when everyone wanted a fair share of good-byes. Now, she was the one in the saddle, desperate to be away from the fawning praise, off to do what must be done.

If she didn't leave at once, she may not leave at all.

Old Maighread reached for her. Maggie bent low, risked the woman's sensitive fingers. The woman had a fey touch, her fingers seeing what her eyes could not.

Old Maighread nodded. "Don't fear child. The one who sings of crows will receive its message."

"Crows?" Crows meant death.

"Maghread!" Fiona snapped.

"No, mother," Maggie shivered with the old woman's warning, took her gnarled hand in her own. "Who?"

"They will try, child," Maighread's cackle rose above the gathering, "they will try. But keep an ear to Ian. He will keep you safe. And your man there, don't let him have fear. You are stronger than anyone thinks, including yourself."

"Grandmother," Fiona pulled Maighread away, "don't fret the lass."

Was she strong? Maggie wondered. She didn't feel strong right now. She felt hapless, helpless, caught on everyone's whim but her own. Tears threatened. Frantically, Maggie sought out the man to blame for her sorrow.

The man who had vowed his life to hers forever.

She had only given him a year and a day.

He was near enough to grab her reins, as though he half expected her to bolt. Silent though it was, he acknowledged her frantic appeal. With a nod and a wry smile, he raised his fist, let loose a warrior's bellow. As one, with no more warning, The MacKay Clansmen stormed through the bailey, out the gate, with Maggie and Talorc in the center of their charge.

Maggie fought to keep her seat, clung to her mount, her head low upon its neck. In any other time, circumstance, she would have thrilled to the challenge, but not today.

Today an old woman had warned of crows. Too true. Life, as Maggie knew it, was dead. Maggie who used to be, was no more. That her body would follow suit made perfect sense, for everything happened in threes, did it not?

Shouts and calls rose, a raucous banner flying in their wake. They rode hard across the flats, just as her clansmen had done countless times. Men on foot jogged behind, the rear guard to the troupe of them. At the base of the closest hill, they slowed their mounts, traversed the steep rugged hillside, around to the back, until they reached the top, out of sight below a ragged crest.

Her clan, the entire lot of MacBedes, would be gathered below, as Maggie herself had been on so many leave takings before. This was the first time, in the whole of her life, she would not be with them, to shout out blessings and well wishes for safe journey. To wave a final farewell.

Her heart thundered in her chest. She swallowed hard, kept her eyes away from that crest. She would not break. Nor could she face the final goodbye. They had sent her off, against her own will. She would not wave a last time. She would be back.

"Lass?" Talorc rode up beside her.

Anger steadied her. She held it close, acknowledged it by refusing to look at him. The shouts of his men, up on the ridge, could be heard.

"Maggie," Talorc reached over, took her chin, forced her to face him. She jerked away. "You have to show yourself, they're waiting to send you off."

She looked down at the ground, the earth that had cradled her feet from her first footstep to this day. Drew in the scent of heather, of blue skies and loch. This was her home. This was where she belonged, a MacBede, with the MacBedes. She blinked against tears, narrowed her eyes, willed resentment to overplay sorrow.

Damn him for being right. Damn him for pushing her beyond her strength.

She looked right at him then, straight into his eyes and felt a power there. It surged between them. He took her fisted hand, lifted it to his lips. With one gentle kiss warmth spread through her body, melted the rigid barricade to fear. Thawed icy defense.

He believed stories, thought her powerful. Fool that he was.

So be it.

She would not show him her weakness.

With a jerk, Maggie reined Tairis sharply to the left, kicked and he bolted. Too fast. This was a docile animal, or so Talorc had claimed. Maggie never expected it to stretch its legs at such speed. Stunned, she gave him his head.

Wind stung her eyes. She swiped the tears away. The ground a blur, the crest, she knew to be no more than a meager outcropping, came closer and closer. Tailis did not slow, showed no sign of halting.

Maggie pulled, hard, her eyes shut tight against disaster. As sure as he bolted, Tailis stopped, pitched Maggie forward. Her cheek to his cheek, half over his haunches, she wrapped her arms tight about Tailis' neck, and clung. Eyes wide with fear. There was no mistaking the yawning distance below.

This creature, promised as gentle and sure, reared, stepped, as though a dancer, right on to the edge of the precipice. Rocks scattered and tumbled, sound testament to a sheer drop. He turned, in a circle, an acrobat of a horse, a showman, leaving Maggie with nothing below her but air.

It was Talorc who gave her this bloody beast to ride. Had he known the animal would do this?

They will try, child, they will try.
Maighread's words came back to her. Talk of
crows, of death, and then those fateful words.
What was the Bold trying to do, kill her?

She'd not give him the satisfaction.

"Get down, you bloody beast!" Legs
wrapped tightly along its belly, Maggie
commanded the animal back to secure footing.
It faced away from the ledge, toward the
valley beyond, full of restless energy. It took
little to encourage him to head off again, past
the MacKay men, past the Bold. Down the
hillside she galloped, around a small copse of
trees. To a valley below, where a stream cut
through the land.

And privacy.

Maggie reined in her ride and realized,
for the very first time since she'd sat to sup
the night before, she was alone, out of sight
of everyone.

She slid from the horse's back, dropped
to her knees, huddled on the ground. All her
barbed emotions unraveled, the anger, the
fury, the rigid fear. It was his fault, his kiss
of her hand that had disarmed her brittleness,
bared raw pain. Sobs, silent, for no sound was
strong enough to carry the weight of them,
rose from the depths of her, poured out, wave
upon wave. Her body stretched toward the
sky, a plea, to carry away the keen that came
from the darkest corner of her soul.

* * * * * * * * * * * * * *

Trained warrior, a seasoned fighter
who could act without thought, Talorc froze,
unable to move. His heart plummeted to the
bowels of hell.

He'd thought she was going to ride
straight off the rise. He was certain of it, was

too far away to stop it. His men thought it a trick, did not interfere. They had applauded and cheered. And then her mount rose on its haunches danced a dance, made a show.

Had she heard the thundering cries from her clansmen? Had she done it on purpose, as his men thought? If she had, he'd kill her with his own bare hands, after he'd clung to her.

She was more than he could handle.

"You've got yourself one hell of a lassie, boy!" Thomas shouted.

Talorc was too shaken to respond. She'd already charged off madly beyond sight, east when they were headed north. He was capable of no more than pointing toward the proper route. His men followed with alacrity, he set off to find his mate.

She hadn't gone far, straight down into the valley below, no further. The sight of her, a crumpled heap upon the ground, racked with dry sobs, tore a brutal hole in his anger. He dismounted, crossed to her and lifted her into his arms. She fought him, fought to be free.

Ignoring her meager blows, he sat upon a large boulder, Maggie cradled in his lap.

"Don't you dare think to comfort me." She punched his chest. "This is your doing." She pounded him again. "What do you care that I have no one? What do you care?"

With a fell grip, he captured her hands, "I care."

"Hah!"

She strained against his hold, his handfasted, his partner, his helpmate. Did she not feel the invisible bond wrapped around them?

"Look!" He pressed their clasped hands against his chest, "You have me lass! You have me, here, for you." Frustrated anger rode high in his blood.

"You?" She shouted back, "I have you? What good is that? You who create changes so drastic, my own clan don't know me anymore."

"You are changed."

"Never!"

"No?" His smile mocked. "You don't think so?" She stilled, guarded. So she should be. He had waited a lifetime for this woman, hungered for her before he even knew of her existence. Now that he had found her, his loins ached, urged for release, anything, even the simple taste of her lips.

Ravenous, he would wait no more, could not bear to. She was his, to love, honor and take. Past time she knew of it.

"You," he stopped, to settle the race of blood that challenged his lungs. "You," he started again, "changed the moment we touched."

He tugged at her hair, pulled her head back, looked into her eyes. Wary, aye, for she saw the truth in his words.

"From the moment you landed in my hands, you knew, you sensed, you felt what you've never had before."

Unwittingly, she licked her lips, whetting his desire. Still, he didn't kiss her, though he imagined doing so.

Not just yet. She had relaxed. He would use that, eased his hold, lifted a finger to trace her mouth, felt her soft huff of breath. Again, she moistened her lips, only this time she found the tip of his finger. He eased it inside.

"Taste me." He ordered. She hesitated then nipped, nearly undoing him. "Do you know what you're about?" He wondered out loud.

"No," she whimpered, and buried her head in his shoulder. "I don't. You are right, I am not who I was. I am a stranger with strange thoughts, wants . . ."

"You've nothing to fear with me."

"It's not the fear that frets me."

Gentling himself, Talorc stroked her back, fought his need to have her closer. "We're handfasted, no need to feel shame."

Face still pressed to his collar, she shook her head.

He cupped her chin, tilted her face to his, to see the thoughts written there. "Maggie, what do you know of what's between us?" Before the words could be asked, Maggie jerked from his hold, indignant, proud. She looked straight at him and he had his answer.

She would not shy from what she felt, but she'd never felt it before. "Ah, lass," his words a smile, "You have old knowledge, but it's all too new to you. Confuses a body. We need to catch-up your learning to your knowing."

"Old knowledge?" She frowned, the haze lifting from her eyes before Talorc wanted it to.

"Maggie," he distracted her with a caress to her ear. She sucked in a breath, as the soft roundness of her breast lifted.

"Don't." She ordered, but there was no weight to her words.

"Because you don't like it or because you want more?" She turned away, and he knew it was better that than to lie. "You love my touch, Maggie. That's what has changed you."

"But I hate you."

"No you don't, Maggie. You wouldn't crave this if you truly hated me."

Finally, their lips met, though it was not much of a kiss, more a gentle brushing of lips. A tease, soft enough to ease her fears. She allowed it, allowed the gentle pressure that grew from that first touch, accepted the gentle brush of his tongue along the seam of her mouth.

As if she knew what he wanted, her lips parted, provoking him to take more. He eased his tongue between her lips, which, in turn, created more hunger. She returned his desire, participated in the tasting. It was the hunger of a powerful man, met by his equal. No matter the turmoil it caused, she was honest in her response. The thrill coursed through his veins. He devoured her, she demanded of him and fire raged.

He wanted her here, now, in this field, below where his men on foot marched, near enough to the keep that any could come upon them. Rather than tame, the thought incited. To show-off her abundant softness, the wild passion focused on him, had him rolling her to the ground, pinning her beneath him, her hands held tight above their heads.

"You are mine!" he pressed against her, widened his legs to urge hers apart until she cradled him.

"Oh, aye," she allowed, "For a year and a day." She pulled his head to hers.

He allowed it, long enough to know she was saturated with wanting. He risked lifting up to look down on her, at the lush rise of her breast, at lips swollen from his kisses, cheeks flushed from desire. "You don't shy from this, yet still expect to leave me?"

"Imprisoned by Handfast, I will reap whatever rewards I can." Hands bound by his, she arched her back.

He didn't understand her willingness. The hunger, aye, for it was that strong between them. But that she would risk, even incite, mating, he could not comprehend. Not when she wanted her freedom so fiercely. But the Bold was not named so for missed opportunities.

One hand still holding hers, he used the other to tease with a gentle stroking, along the side of her body, barely brushing the side swell of her breast.

"You are so bloody luscious," he gave in, filled his hand with her, molded, squeezed as he lowered his head to suckle. He couldn't resist any more, freed her hands to fill both his with her softness. "You make me hurt, ache with wanting you. Since the first moment I saw you, my blood has risen so high I fear I'll burst. Ease me, Maggie girl, ease my pain."

She made it more insistent, urging the heat in him to rise even higher. She pulled his head to hers, kissing him with a full mouth. Her hips rose to his, circled impatiently, as he thrust against her.

Too much cloth between them, Talorc thought of his knife, to slice it away, to give him access to her breasts as he wadded her skirt in his hand, lifting it higher, higher. He wanted to see her legs, her hips, raised himself to do so, but stopped.

"I'll not have you caught like this," he thought out loud. "We've barely made our pledge, left your home and already I'm ravishing you. Your clansmen will certainly see the change in you then."

Her eyes met his, so fierce, so wanton he was surprised by her words. "This is not how they see me as different, Laird MacKay."

She was battling him with words when he was still battling his body. Trying to calm it.

She continued. "What they think is that I am more than I am."

"Aren't you proving that as we speak?" He asked, fighting for breath, fighting to tame the wildness in his veins. It didn't help that she arched her back, squiggled her hips trying to pull from beneath him. He wasn't ready to let her go. "They know you, Maggie. They've always known you, they just didn't recognize you as I do."

She snorted. "Know me or no, you dinna' get my ken last night."

"You said you would Handfast, you gave your word."

She lashed out. "Oh, aye, I had no choice. You wouldn't listen, would you? You had to keep going." She shoved him aside, freed herself of his hold. "Like a boulder down a mountain, you are. But I told you, over and over. Know me or no, I don't want you."

"You don't know what you want."

"Ach!" Maggie rose, twitched her plaid straight with trembling hand. "I do know what I want!" She railed. "That's how little you know me, because I have always known what I wanted. I want my home, I want my family, I want a simple life without all the complications of a man like you.

"I don't want to fight to be heard, fight to be listened to, fight to be believed or to have my way."

"You want to be in control." Talorc nodded. He understood the desire, not that he was going to let her have her own way.

He stood, towered over her.

"Aye, I want control of my life, no one else's, just mine." She dragged her hair from her face. "Is that so much to ask for?"

Talorc shook his head, caught a stray lock of her hair with his finger and tried to push it behind her ear. She slapped his hand away.

Her sigh was weary and old as the mountains. "Lord knows, you're a fine enough looking man, and you have an uncanny way with a woman's body," she granted, "There are plenty of women who would want you. Why does it have to be me? Why, when you are nothing like what I want?"

Frustrated, and knowing there was no hope for it, Talorc snorted, "I'm not scrawny enough for your tastes? Is that it? You won't be able to rule me as you might a lesser man."

"Hah." She snuffed, rose to his bait. "Of course, you would think that just because a man is of lesser build he would be a lesser man."

"He'd not be able to protect you as I would."

"I have brothers enough for that. And I know how they are, how they try to bombard my wishes for their own. I've known you less than a day and already you ignore my wants, my cares."

Talorc smiled, "Every man will try to have his way, in his own kind. Don't underestimate a male's hunger for control, just because he's closer in height to you."

She looked as sorrowful as a wee lamb tangled in the bracken. He had torn her from her home, her family, but he had a home and family to offer her. With time, she would understand that. "It is a brave thing you do lass, leaving everything that's familiar to you.

107

I mean to make it up to you, to prove that it will be worth the pain you are feeling now."

She turned to him, trails of tears long since dried, lined the length of her face. "The only comfort I have to that pain is knowing I will be home this time next year. My Ma promised me, if I don't give you my heart, then we would not be wed. And that, you can be sure, will be easy."

Startled, he moved, to better see her. She was a lusty lass for one who wanted to walk away from a Handfast. This explained that. "Is this what she told you?"

"Aye," her eyes narrowed, "is that not the truth of it?"

"Oh, aye," he mumbled, certain her heart would rule her body. She just didn't know that. But he was coming to understand her openness to his touches. She didn't fear their passion, because she didn't consider it a threat to her singleness.

Now that he had her attention, Talorc wasn't certain he wanted it. She didn't know that, should she share her body with him, should they mate, they'd be wed. The chance of a child was enough to bind the least likely of couples.

The attraction was strong. The past moments were proof of that. It wouldn't be long before he slid between her thighs, no cloth to bar him, and slid into the core of her, toppling their Handfasting into marriage.

They belonged together. Their passion was his strongest weapon against her denial of their bond. Her mother would know that. She had played his hand for him.

Intriguing.

"Do you not think you could give me your heart?"

Maggie was still fighting to right her plaid, the MacBede cloth. Not so different from his own. Not really, but the colors were off, dyed by plants grown in a different soil and the MacBedes' had a thin orange line that couldn't be found on the MacKay cloth. Talorc frowned, he'd not noticed, others would. It would make her a stranger, a visitor, to them until the day she wore his colors. He wanted that change soon.

"My heart was ripped apart with my brother's death. You know well enough that a scar can cause lasting damage."

"I've patience enough."

She snorted. "Patience? Is that why you said your vows as you did? Is that why you bound yourself to me, this day? 'I take thee, Maggie . . .'" she mimicked. "Not 'I will take thee,' at a future date. No, you say, 'I take thee.' You commit yourself to now. Why would you do that MacKay, why would you pledge yourself for life when you knew I would not match those words? Why would you put that upon me, if you have the patience you speak of?"

"I trust in what the future will bring."

"You think you know me better than I know myself?"

"Aye, I do." He stalled her sputtering denial with a gentle finger to her lips. "I've seen more of the world than you, Maggie. I know what is out there, I've been married before. Between us, there is more than the best of marriages have. You just need to learn of it."

She stood, courageous and straight. It reminded him of their vows, their Handfasting. She had been brave then, yet so vulnerable. She had kept her head high, her sight on whatever wall was before her. She

109

didn't look to the people, would not look at him. If she had, would the joy in all the smiles have softened her heart?

He had watched her then, from where he spoke with her father. Dowry, land and furnishings, handed over with a pledge, simple transactions.

She had not come so willingly.

The ladies had to surround her, one lamb to be shepherded to his side. He had lifted her hand, placed it upon his arm. She barely allowed it to rest there, barely touched him. By the time he had led Maggie to the top of the entrance stairs, every available MacBede had been below, in the courtyard, to witness the joining.

She had not wanted to be there, continued to refuse to look at him, or the people below. He was the one to take her right hand in his right hand, her left in his, their hands bound in an unbreakable pattern of forever. His had been sure and warm, hers trembling and cold.

When he married Anabel, she had trembled as well, though there'd been a shy smile upon her lips. Not so with Maggie. Stoic, brave Maggie. He'd have to bring that smile to her lips and when he did, he doubted it would be shy.

"I suppose 'tis time we were off." Maggie sighed, bringing him back to the present.

"You spoke your vows loud and true, Maggie, I'm thanking you for that."

"I said I'd Handfast with you. I'd not go back on my word."

"The whole of the courtyard heard you."

"'Tis what they were there for."

"They're dreaming of happy endings."

"They're allowed their dreams. It's reality that I must face."

"I'll give you a dream, if you'll let me." He'd caught her wary attention again.

"And what do you mean by that."

"We can have a happy ending."

Her hair shifted, a silken mass upon her shoulders, as she shook her head. "Nay, life is not a happy thing. Don't be making promises you can't keep."

"Trust me, Maggie. Trust me to do what's right for you."

She looked at him then, keenly.

"I would like to, Talorc, I would like to, but you've not given me much ground for trusting you, if you ken my meaning."

"Aye," he nodded, frowning. It was true, he had cornered her into hHhandfasting. He had skirted truths and played games to get her where he wanted her, but in the end, it would all work out. He said as much.

"We'll see," she acknowledged with a touch too much defeat for his Maggie.

That weary wariness troubled Talorc, but there was no time to fret. The men had ridden on. It was time Maggie and Talorc join them. As safe as his lands could be, bordering the MacBedes, there was no telling what the Gunns were willing to risk for retribution. She was his to protect now. He'd not come this far to lose her to his enemy.

CHAPTER 10 - THE WICKED

Chants rumbled on the breeze.
Shadows from the flicker of torch flames,
writhed against monstrous standing stones,
much as he expected the women would
writhe this night.

His blood throbbed in anticipation.
The steady stomp of his men's feet, the
thumping of their wooden staffs, ensured
they felt the same.

Amid the acrid scent of a burning
carcass, leftovers from a feast, women
moved with solemn grace, circled a stone
altar stained with the blood of sacrifice. A
lamb led to slaughter, much like the
youngest of the lasses this night, too naïve
and trusting to understand the trap set for
them.

They desired rituals of old, the
promise of magic. It was not the season of
Beltane, or dances of fertility, but they
wanted celebrations. He was not at fault for
turning their desires to his.

An owl passed over low, a sign: the
wisdom of the ages looked down upon them.
Fanciful superstition over no more than a
predator looking for prey.

He withheld laughter. There would be
time enough for that, once he broke through
the circling, the twined lines of men in
capes green of the forest, women wrapped in

the brown of earth. The shades of their cloaks were faded, the hems ragged, for they were outlaws, with no warm home and hearth full of spinning and weaving. All they had was wickedness and the power it gave them.

Through deeds so perverse there was no forgiving, clans banished them. Sent them to live in the wilderness, as if that diminished their threat. As if they would not find each other, these renegades. As if they would not bond in their despicable ways, and grow as any family would grow.

This very night, they would dance a devil's dance and prove the lassies of the highlands no safer from outlaws banished than with them nestled in the bosom of their kin.

Nor were the clans themselves safe, which was his doing. He played mischief with them, pitted one against another, never risked his own hide or that of his people. It was a deliciously devious plan. He had used their own might, their own vengeful selves, to create their demise.

They would destroy each other and he would rise up to have his way with the highlands just as he would have his way tonight.

He looked to the woman who stood opposite him, a deceitful, cunning and blasphemous whore. He licked his lips, his body aching for release.

She was the one who promised power from the old ways, taught the women to move as the sun and the moon, east to west, knowledge to intuition. She explained how the men, with their cocky strides, were to travel from earth to strength, north to south.

She was a willing partner in these dances, eagerly enticed young lasses to join their troupe, for she knew his taste. The rebellious, the lonely, the insecure were sweet succor to his band.

The moment was ripe. It was time. As the Green Man, he stepped inside the circle, horns upon his head, a wooden staff in hand. She stood opposite, a large vessel cradled at her hip.

It was a familiar game. *Catch me if you can*, she teased. He was willing to be diverted. He knew how the night would end.

The human chain stopped in place, swayed and chanted, captured by the story unfolding before them. They expected the portrayal of his death and rebirth, unaware it was the ruin of innocence they would witness.

He used his staff as a shepherd's hook, he worked to corral the woman, head her toward the altar. They sidled one way, then another, adversaries. He smiled again. He rather liked this sport, becoming The Green Man. It was a shame the season was wrong and he couldn't create a mask of leaves and branches.

He swung out with his rod. Nimbly she jumped, twisted and taunted, beckoned as she did so, managing to hold her distance. He allowed it, drawing out the reckoning.

The wind toyed with their cloaks. The moon, as though in tune, played its game of light and dark. With a dip of his head, he showed off his antlers, a stag's crowned achievement, and held his ground.

The wench stood at the mouth of the south, vessel on hip, offered a saucy smile. The south was his place, the man's place.

Melodic tinkling foreshadowed the emergence of her arm covered in silver bracelets. The other women raised their adorned limbs, shook them, for a musical backdrop to the sensuous dance.

His woman wove hers through the air, a cobra's salute to the piper's tune. Mesmerized, he startled when she jammed that sensuous limb deep within the vessel.

The women of his troupe rang tiny bells of encouragement soon matched by the young lasses who watched and learned; the men stomped their feet, their curdled cries riding on the night wind.

Perhaps there was something to these rituals after all.

Oblivious to the blood draped altar behind her, his night's mate laughed as she lifted her hand high, fingers coated in thick, viscous, honey. Riveted, he watched, as slowly, ever so slowly, heavy rivulets trailed down her hand, along her arm. Head angled, she watched him as she caught syrupy globules with her lips, followed their path with her tongue, darted flickers for taste, wide swaths for hunger. She traced the honey up, up, up to the tip of her fist.

Fight though she did, the fist did not fit in her mouth, it was too big. So she suckled each finger in turn, drew hard, her cheeks no more than shadowed hollows.

He groaned. All the men groaned as the women chimed their bells. Enough was enough.

"You will be as the earth!" He bellowed. "My seed will feed your womb upon the blood of our victim."

Startled, her sensuous sucking stopped. She settled her hand light on her breasts.

"It's a cold night for such things." Sticky fingers slipped inside the opening of her cape. He knew what ripeness was hidden within that cloak, imagined suckling their honeyed sweetness. He loved honey.

"I will make you burn." He advanced.

"You will make me burn," She trilled as lightly as the jingle of her bracelets. Despite her twirls and sways, he was pleased to see she moved closer before she stopped just outside the reach of his staff.

One moment a soft female, the next a forceful presence, up she went, high on her toes, vessel raised to the skies. He swung his staff left then right. Nimbly she jumped each swipe.

Without warning, she hurled the honey pot straight at him. One mighty swing and he shattered her vessel with the knotted head of his staff.

"I will flame your fire."

Bracelets jangled as she clapped. "May the power of my essence incite your passion as I bear your strength."

He knew the younger lasses, the newcomers, were uneasy with the turn of play. They shifted, eyed each other, looked to the older women, but they could not run. His men clamped hands upon their shoulders, for it was their fight, not his, to keep the lasses from running. Foolish girls to trust strangers, to believe they could ever go home again to be comforted by mother or father, sibling or cousin.

One act of disobedience and they chose their destiny. It was their own folly that led them to the service of his band. To become outlaws. That is, if they survived this night.

Their restless movements, the terror in their faces, provoked a lust that had already burgeoned. He pawed at the earth, tilted his head, a stag in rut, and charged. Shoulder to belly, he swooped, lifted, carried.

The men's chants thickened, heightened by the game, over riding cries of terror.

Not to be undone, his woman arched her back, rode him like a ship's mast, opened her cape, offered her nectared breasts. "I give succor to your strength. Taste of my sweetness."

Greedily he accepted, licked and suckled as he carried her through their arena. His laughter rode the night, echoed by the tiny tinkle of bells, as he dropped her upon the altar, hips on the edge, legs dangling.

"You must pay a price!" She commanded.

He chuckled. She was in no position to be making commands, but he would humor her.

"Vixen," he turned to his audience, "Is she worth a price?"

The men stomped and bellowed. "Plunder, plunder, plunder!"

"Honor her, honor her, honor her." Bells jangled, as the women countered the men, some frantic in their pleas.

He was the Green Man, he would make the choice.

Slowing his pace, drawing out the tension, he ran his hands along the sweet curve of her thighs. They were full and round, would embrace his hips with softness. Just the thought, enflamed by the narrowing of her eyes, a sure sign she was ready to challenge him, made him hungry for more.

Without warning, he gripped her legs, splayed them, revealing the shadowed opening to her womb.

Despite her tries to wiggle free, to negotiate the cost of this privilege, he held her firm. Let her know who had the power.

"What price?"

"The MacKay," She inched back, away from the edge of the altar. "I've helped you weaken the MacKay," voice sultry as a promise she lifted, leaned back on her hands, breasts tantalizing mounds in the moonlight. "You've set the Gunns toward failure. But all could be lost."

"I will not lose."

She scrambled onto her knees. "There is one who has turned the tide away from us." Her finger trailed a path from his lips to his chest. "You must kill her," she leaned closer, "kill her," she licked his lips, "kill her!" swung her legs around, encircling his waist.

He was swollen and greedy, more than ready to finish this. "Who is this woman?" He grunted, as he ground against her softness, bringing a moan for his efforts.

Still, she did not leave her plea. "Maggie MacBede." Another moan. "We cannot risk a child born to her."

"You want her blood?" He spread her cloak, lowered it, so all could see as his touch roamed mounds and valleys, squeezed and soothed in turn. Her buttocks were cradled in his arms, her legs wrapped about his waist, her breasts a breath away from his lips, as he strode the perimeters of the circle. A boastful male.

"She wants me to destroy the MacBede girl, daughter of a Chief." He shouted.

Brushing her chest against his mouth, she pleaded. "Promise me The MacKay will have no heir."

Ah, so that was it.

"I want to kill him." He grabbed her bottom, raised her up, to slide her down along his rigid need before placing her, once again, on the altar. "Torture him."

"Her, kill her." She scrambled on the blood slick stone to kneel before him.

He shoved her down, onto her back, her hair tangled in blood, and leaned over her, master of what he beheld. She gripped his arms, as though she knew he would soon leave this subject. "He must live to be humiliated, to see his own destruction. She is in the way. She can die. Must die."

"Devil's harlot." His chuckle was lost as he teased her nipple. "Perfect."

"You promise."

"Oh, my lusty earth bride. I promise, with pleasure. Here, on this altar, we will slice her slowly, little by little. Her screams will make my blood rise. I will want to take you for days afterward. But now, tonight, all bargaining is done. We will think of nothing else, but my plundering you."

Arching his neck he shouted, "Take your wenches men! Seed their bellies!"

He was too late. Two lines had become one thick writhing cord as bodies sank to the ground, chants turned to moans of pleasure, mingled with screams and cries. Cloaks opened, flesh meshed, male to female, a time old chain of fertility.

CHAPTER 11 - A MEANS OF ESCAPE

Days filled with the land opening up to
forever. They skirted the mountain, rode at
the base of foothills, across open stretches
that dipped and fell. Rugged terrain at a
rugged pace, on horseback, when Maggie had
never ridden as much as a morning before.

Many of their group walked. Talorc
refused to let Maggie join them. She wouldn't
forgive him for the pain of it, riding, when
she was not accustomed to such things.

Strong boned and buxom, Diedre rode
up and reached over, giving Maggie's arm a
comforting pat. "Don't fret now lass, the time
will fly."

Diedre, a MacKay companion for
Maggie. A woman who convinced the Bold
that Maggie would need one for the ride.
Female companionship in the likes of the
MacBede's Muireall, the widow. Proof the
women at Glen Toric would not be so
different to back home. Thoughtful of the
Bold. Generous of Diedre, for they were in a
troop of men. She rather suspected that was
Diedre's reason for joining the adventure.

As for Maggie? She was more than used
to the company of men, especially warriors.
Probably more comfortable with them than
women.

Still, she appreciated the gesture, especially as the woman did not hover but left Maggie to herself often enough.

Open and friendly one minute, too close another, before Deidre would go off, flirting with the men as widows were wont to do, sneaking off with one or another. Plenty of men on this ride and only two women. Muireall would have liked those odds herself.

"The Bold may be a great man, but he's also a man. Can't be around one without some ill feeling festering," Diedre claimed, an old mother hen even though they were of an age. "Best to get bad thoughts out of a body or they sour the soul."

Off with someone the night before, Maggie didn't have to wonder about the smile the woman wore.

"Sore?" Diedre asked.

Maggie mumbled, not as comfortable with complaining aloud as Diedre. "Aye. Don't know why he won't let me walk."

"He's the Laird. He's used to telling others what to do."

"And they all listen."

Diedre nodded. "Of course. Like lambs and a shepherd."

"Lambs are slaughtered." Maggie countered and they both laughed. Only it wasn't funny. She was being led as though she had no will of her own.

What had happened to her dignity, to her self-respect? Who was he to tell her she couldn't walk, when riding for days was not natural. She may not be able to walk, if she didn't get down off this beast soon.

Still, she kept the litany to herself, decided to deal with the issue her own way. She halted her horse on the downward slope, lifted her leg gingerly over its neck, and slowly eased off.

"Are you needen' to freshen up?" Diedre frowned. They had only just remounted from a short break. "It would be better if we wait until we reach the bottom of the hill. There's a wee stream down there. See?" And she pointed.

Maggie had seen it, a thin thread winding through the valley floor. "Aye." It took a few moments to straighten her legs against aches in places she didn't know a body could ache.

William rode up. "Is there a problem?"

"No." Maggie handed him her reins before he could refuse them. "I'd rather walk, if you don't mind."

"The Bold says you're to ride."

"He can do as he pleases. I will do as I please."

She didn't want to argue, she didn't want to be persuaded, or treated like a recalcitrant child. She just wanted to walk, so she turned away and strode down the hillside, taking a path with large boulders, difficult for a horse to follow.

"Wait!" Diedre called, but Maggie kept moving as sounds of the other woman closed in on her.

"You needn't run from me." Diedre huffed, out of breath. "If you ask me, he's too high handed by half with you."

"He is that." Maggie snapped.

"The man just up and took you from your home."

"He did that." Maggie lifted her chin. "Just pulled me from my home, my people, what I wanted and then makes me ride that bloody . . ."

Diedre put a hand on her arm. "He has his reasons, I'm sure. And he's a handsome man, no?"

"I'm not blind."

"And you feel something for him?"

Maggie pulled away, looked at the mountains, honest enough to keep silent rather than admit the truth. Aye, she felt something for him, but it was such a muddled mess there was no explaining it.

"You're set on leaving him, are you?"

Was that an insult to his people? She didn't mean it as such. "I didn't want to leave my own."

"No." Diedre sat on a boulder. Maggie turned to see her motioning someone away. Another glance confirmed it was the Bold.

Diedre continued. "You didna' want to leave your home, but you can go back. Just keep that in mind. You can have yourself a fine adventure and then go back. We're not so bad, you see. You'll like the folks of Glen Toric."

"My brothers say the keep is built on caves."

Diedre smiled and nodded. "Aye, scary if you ask me. But they're down there, underneath us, dark and full of the echoes of whatever creatures are hiding in there."

Maggie shivered, pulled her plaid closer around her. "I've never been in a cave, but I don't much care for the dark."

"Hmn," the other woman considered that. "The men are waiting for us."

"Then let's move on down, so they can move as well."

"I think the Bold is going to join us."

Maggie looked, and sure enough, the man was finding his way between the rocks. Agile for such a big man. She would give him

that much. He was just too good at
everything. He was a fool if he thought they
were a match. Foolish and impetuous was
what she was, a far cry from good at
everything.

Her biggest fear was that she would be
foolish and impetuous with him.

"He's a fine warrior, Maggie. I know
you're afraid he will be killed, but he's lived
to now."

"Aye, until now."

"My husband, bless his soul, was a
warrior."

Talorc gained on them. Hoping for a
few more moments on foot, Maggie grabbed
Diedre's arm and aimed them both further
down the hillside.

They were of an age, yet Diedre had
already been married, birthed a child and been
abandoned as a widow. That was the problem
with warriors, they did things like that.
Maggie kept silent. The woman didn't need
reminding of what was.

"You may have the right of things. I
don't think I would marry another warrior.
It's too much of a worry. Waiting for days,
weeks when they go out for the fight. It eats
at a body."

"Aye." Maggie nodded, glad she had
Diedre, that the Bold had thought to bring
her.

Diedre stopped, pulled Maggie around
so they spoke face to face, eye to eye. "Just
don't let him near. Stick with the women folk
and don't let him near. Then you can have a
high time with us, and return home to anyone
you want."

Wise words, only she didn't know if she
wanted to hear them. Contrary, that's what
she was. One minute enjoying the man's

company, the next, angry that he took all her choices away from her.

"You would help me?"

"Aye." Diedre nodded, but didn't have a chance to say more, for the Bold had reached them.

Maggie fought to hold to Diedre's idea through days of travel; despite the aches of the forced ride, she was drawn to the Bold. Though she kept her tongue sharp, whenever he was near, she hungered for those moments. Feared he would acknowledge her hardness and leave her be.

"Are you enjoying Diedre's company, lass?' A shiver of awareness shot through her, as the Bold pulled alongside of her.

"Aye, I believe we will get on."

"Good." He nodded.

Her people were not ones for aimless chat. She had been relieved to see that neither were Talorc or his men.

After a time, he took her arm, signaled to stop and be quiet.

They had just breached a small rise that looked over a narrow valley. Below, a herd of deer grazed along a stream that cut through one side of the flat land.

"See them." The warmth of his hand intoxicated. She pulled free only to have him lean in, one hand braced behind her on the horse's rump, the other pointing. Diverted by the strength of his hand, the sinewy strength in his arm, she failed to see what he was showing her.

"See him?" He jolted her to look where he pointed. "That's Bruce, moving in."

She sucked in her breath, surprised. Below them, blending in with the heather and the rock, a hunter crouched, edging ever closer to the herd, so much a part of the land that it was hard to place him.

She held her breath, as though even that small sound could be heard, and watched, waited, wondering how the Bold could tell, from this distance, who was who.

"He's down wind, so the deer can't smell him." His explanation brushed her ear.

She focused, hard, on the man, Bruce, down on his belly creeping closer still. One of the creatures lifted its head, ears twitching, nose to the wind. The hunter stilled.

"He's close enough now."

Aye, Bruce was close to the deer, but so was the Bold to her. The heat of his body, the brush of his breath drew her away from the action below. She looked at him, her Handfasted.

He didn't acknowledge her gaze, kept his on the action below, so she took her time, considered just what it was that pulled at her senses. Why was he so different from the other men she knew?

The compulsion to trace the scar that ran along his cheek, to touch the crinkles that radiated from his eyes, had her hand poised between the two of them, as though some magic controlled her better judgment. The dark tan of his skin, common enough among any who spent their days out of doors, fascinated.

"You're going to miss it if you keep looking at me." He said, without once shifting his gaze away from Bruce.

Maggie snapped back just in time to see Bruce's fluid adjustment from crouching to standing, aiming and shooting. He downed the animal in one shot, as all the other game fled.

"No need for more. That will keep us for the journey." Talorc told her and heeled his mount forward.

She urged her ride to catch up, confused by her compulsion yet not ready to fight it. "How did you know who that was down there?"

"I can recognize my men, how each moves." He looked to her. "As I do with you."

She snorted, "A stiff and bowlegged lass. Enchanting."

"Oh girl, what I see you can be verrrry proud of." He teased.

With her best glare she changed the subject. "You knew the deer were there, but didn't go to hunt."

"Couldn't have shown you if I had been down there."

His thoughtfulness defeated her. "You knew I would want to see it."

"Aye."

"I've never hunted."

"And you've always wanted to, no doubt. I'll be teaching you then." Finally he stopped, turned, and looked at her. She refused to look away, put her chin up defiant against her own reluctance.

"I would like that."

He was studying her as closely as she had studied him. She fought the urge to squirm.

"No doubt, you'll be good at it." He stated.

He couldn't know that, but in her defense she admitted, "I can tickle fish better than my brothers."

His chuckle echoed through her, rattling the foundation of her resistance. Over and over she tried to remember Diedre's words.

Just don't let him near. Stick with the women folk and don't let him near. Then you can have a high time with us, and return home to anyone you want

By the next day, her resistance was firmly back in place.

CHAPTER 12 - LOVE LOST

Talorc looked to the sky. Clear and bright and cold enough to freeze the ground. A relief after the wet, muddy journey of neither snow nor rain, but a muddled mix of both that slapped their faces and melted on the ground.

Soon, the sun would set. By mid-day tomorrow they would reach Glen Toric. He planned it that way, so the sun would be high in the sky, shining down on his home in its most magnificent glory just as they rode up to it.

Despite the chill, they took time this afternoon to bathe in the loch below, wash away the long muddy ride before trekking up to this camp, an outcropping of stone off the edge of the woods.

From the higher vantage point, aided by a bright moon, the tall square keep of Glen Toric could be seen, the substantial wings flaring out and back from its sides. The long narrow climb up to it proof of the safety it offered. Not fancy but strong, and sturdy, and easily defended. Large enough to hold all she needed. Much like him.

He nodded to Liam, the last of the guards he met on his round of the watch, and headed back toward the camp. Positioned in the woods, his best men would watch for trouble while the others slept free from

attack. This close to home there was little fear
of that.

Diedre passed him as he wove through
the woods. She had a parcel. Food for Liam,
her latest love. Fair enough, the man had to
eat. He also had to keep his wits about him.

"You're not to distract him." Talorc
warned.

"Perhaps you're the one who needs
distracting." She offered. "You've got to be
frustrated as a mad bull with her within reach
but out of touch."

Oh, aye, he was frustrated as hell. Had
expected to be wed three nights ago, the night
of the Handfasting, but a warrior's camp was
no place to woo a wife. And he needed time.
Time to decide if he should warn her of what
their coupling would mean. That she would be
his wife at the end of it. It was a fine line of
trust he walked.

But Deiedre knew he'd not take the
bait. Never had with her, never would. In the
past, discretion stopped him. Diedre didna'
understand the concept, proved as much
tonight when she offered her game with
Maggie right there in the camp. Empty gesture
or no, it showed a poor sense of decency.

"You get my ken? Give him the food
but get back to the others."

"Aye, I get your ken."

He nodded, left her, trusting she would
follow his orders.

He stopped just outside the light from
the fire, the first one lit on this journey. He
risked it as they were tight within MacKay
land.

As he looked over the men, as was his
way, he assessed the mood, warm from the
fire, spirits high as they were so close to
home. He made certain he accounted for

everyone, everything before he let his sights rest on Maggie.

She stood speaking with some of the men, oblivious to her own power as a woman. Every man seen as a brother or cousin of sorts, she was comfortable with them, all of them, except him.

He made her nervous, he knew that, understood what it meant. She didn't. Soon, he would teach her.

So he gave her ground, distance, thought that would ease the way for him, but he thought wrong. Rather than earn her trust, she grew more wary by the day. He wasn't quite sure how to breach that divide.

Aye, Diedre was right, he was frustrated as a mad bull. He'd nearly broken when she bathed this very afternoon, with him not ten feet away, back turned. No easy thing to do. Sounds enticed, the rustle of clothes as she undressed, the catch of her breath from the frigid water. All it took was one splash and his mind reeled with images; rivulets caressing where his hands had, and hadn't been. Droplets taking a lazy journey between high firm breasts with nipples puckered from the cold. He knew the curve of that breast, the weight of it.

But the water would go further than he had advanced. It would trail down across her body to pool in her navel, just waiting for him to dip his head, lave and sip. Sparkling beads would be caught in curls at the apex of her thighs. His fingers would weave past them to dip into the heat of Maggie's own moistness.

Soon, they would dance that dance. When he had her to himself. Alone, so his hand could roam as free as the water. His lips would travel the same path and his heat would find the source of hers.

But not tonight. Not until they reached Glen Toric. Not until they had a place to bed without fifty men surrounding them. And not until she had learned that the love of her body was the love of her heart.

He had an idea, was waiting for just the right moment, needed her trust to move into action. That was why he stood back, as fifty men blustered and blushed with the sound of her voice.

It could not have been easy for her brothers to keep suitors away. To do so proved a disservice. Maggie saw all men as extensions of her family, like brothers. So much so, he was amazed she had not tied him with that same rope. Then again, he knew how singular their attraction was.

Thomas leaned over her, his smile as wide as his face could stretch, and said something. She chuckled, a tease of sound that rode the breeze and trailed across Talorc's shoulders like a lover's caress.

She swatted at Thomas and shooed him away, then swung her head, so her hair waved back and forth before the heat. There was no provocative intent in what she did. She was too busy prattling on about nonsense, totally unaware that as her neck arced, so did her back, and with her back bowed the roundness of her figure stood out in stark relief. A rich, lush, virginal offering.

Blood rushed through his body. She was a heady temptation, blocking out the rest of the world, in the midst of a warrior's camp.

They were not alone. He must not forget, they were not alone.

His gaze snapped to his men. Wide-eyed and slack- jawed they stared, as unable to move as he had been. He cursed.

132

"Maggie." As expected, she shot straight with the sound of his voice, her eyes wary, for she was coming to be cautious of him and of what they shared. As abruptly as she sat up, his men moved away, released from the spell she cast.

That was as alone as they would be tonight.

When he neither moved nor spoke, Maggie shrugged her shoulders, reached back to braid thick strands of auburn tresses. "How much further to Glen Toric?" She asked.

He stayed where he was, didn't move closer, though he couldn't have said why. "Another day, a short one. We should be there before dark."

Four days they'd been riding when the entire journey only took two. He slowed the pace for Maggie.

"You've had bad dreams?"

Every bit of her went still. "Why would you say that?"

Unable to sleep, he had watched her of a night, close to the fire. Only Maggie had not slept, not properly, she tossed and turned and called out.

"Ian. You asked for Ian."

"Did I?" She studied the ground beneath her feet.

"My guess is he responds, for you settle."

A blush crept up as she shook her head. "I don't remember." She looked about, as though to bring the dreams back, then looked at him. "Did I really?"

"You settled." And was pleased to see her smile.

"Come," he was close now. "There are fish in the stream, just beyond the trees, over there," he pointed. "waiting for a tickle."

133

"Are there?" Her smile turned playful. "You want me to show you how it's done?"

She was teasing him. This was good. It proved her barrier was not a solid one.

"We'll see. Why not a wager lass? I win, I get a kiss. You win and," he reached out, hoping she would take his hand. "What, Maggie girl, what do you get?"

"To walk!"

"You ask the world, Maggie, and all I want is a simple kiss." But he was happy now for she had taken his hand, was letting him lead her to the stream.

He saw Bruce aiming for them and shook his head. This was the closest he had been to Maggie in days, he did not want to upset that.

Bruce ignored his scowl, sidled up beside him. "Bold."

"I'm busy now, Bruce."

"Not too busy for this."

He squeezed her hand, looked to her, not willing to let her go when she pulled free. A reluctant withdrawal.

"You go, Bold." Her wistful smile worried him, for it spoke of a chance lost forever when there should be so many more in their future.

Damn his responsibilities.

"It's important, Laird, or I'd not break in."

"Wait for me?" He asked Maggie but she didn't answer, just waved a small wave as she backed away. The distance loomed far wider than feet.

"Bold," Bruce pressed. "You'll be wantin' to hear this now, not later."

"What?" He snapped.

"There's sign of riders coming toward us. They veered east just short of Dunegan's Woods."

That caught his attention. "Riders? Have you told the watch?"

"Aye. But that's not the worst of it."

Talorc watched Maggie head toward the bush for a bit of privacy and frowned. Diedre should be back by now, should go with her into the woods.

Unease burgeoned as he looked back at Bruce. "What is the worst of it?"

"Someone's playing with the old ways. They've built an altar, for sacrifice."

"In Donegan's wood?"

"Aye."

"Are you certain that's what it's for?"

Bruce shifted on his feet. "The markings are there, and it's been used. It's covered with blood stains. From the looks of the bones by the fire, more than animals have been on that stone."

"How old are the tracks?" Some of the dis-ease settled, as Maggie stepped back into the clearing.

"Within a day, but Bold," Bruce looked away, as if he couldn't face his leader, "it looks like they were preparing for another sacrifice. There's fresh wood laid out, and . . ."

"This is our land," Talorc bellowed. "This is happening inside our borders!"

"I know, and I've doubled the guard."

"Did you not destroy that altar?"

Bruce stared at the Bold. "No, the men wouldna' touch it."

Talorc dampened his fury, it would only cloud his thoughts. The first thing was to protect Maggie, guard her at all times. He turned, to find her backing away from the trees, shaking her head, tears on her cheeks.

"Ian?" She stumbled toward the outcropping, then she turned to him, eyes wide, full of tears. "Ian's there, can you see him? Blocking my way . . ."

There was no time to finish, for Deidre staggered from the woods, her clothes stained with blood. She shook, raised her hand, a bloody hand, knife still clasped in it.

"We were attacked." The boisterous woman whimpered. "Liam's dead!" With her wail the woods purged, a flood of wild men, painted, armed, ready for battle.

Warriors' battle calls filled the night. Undulating cries rose from the woods, the heavy pounding of shields. They were cornered on that outcropping, nowhere to go but back and then down, a fifty foot drop.

Maggie. They must protect Maggie. "Surround her!" Talorc ordered, as he raced forward, no question that the men would form a protective body guard around her.

But she was only safe if the battle was won.

It was turning dark, the worst time for attack, to distinguish friend from foe. His claymore in hand, Talorc charged for the trees, toward the heat of the fray.

Arrows rained down upon them. Men wearing naught but painted symbols poured from the woods, heaved rocks, waved claymores and dirks. MacKays outnumbered the band, but the attackers had targes to shield them from blows and the advantage of surprise. The MacKays barely had time to gather their wits, let alone weapons and shields.

He wielded his blade, slashed and stabbed, swung from side to side, front to back to confront foe after foe. A fierce battle, a focused fight, pushing them further back toward the edge of the rocks.

Spurred with worry, he lunged in attack, swerved to see the circle of his men with Maggie in the middle. They had her safe, despite the onslaught of arrows and rocks still coming from the cowards in the woods. Damned if she wasn't struggling to break free.

Mikey broke from the circle, charged a giant of a man who drew too near. Talorc leaped toward the open hole, as his men tried to close it, but Maggie pushed past them. A stone flew through the air where her head had been. She reached down, oblivious to the near miss, and grabbed it. With the strength of fury she heaved it at the nearest target. He went down.

Diedre grabbed her arm, pulled her toward the edge of the outcropping, a sliver of space where no one fought. Maggie pulled hard, brought Diedre around, revealing a wild man behind her. Maggie grabbed the knife still clutched in Diedre's hand, aimed it so the two of them stabbed. As he fell, Deidre twisted free, revealing the swing of the man's club, already high to bring down on Deidre's head. It crashed down on Maggie's instead, as he fell on top of her.

Talorc charged toward them, too far to catch her, close enough to hear the crack, as her head hit the rocky ground. Talorc tore the man off her as if he was no more than a blanket. Dead, he was dead. The Bold spun around, blood pumped with violence, looking to lash out, finding only stillness.

One moment there were too many attackers, then, suddenly, none. Noise, commotion ended as quickly as it started. The battle an illusion except the sight and smell of

wounds, of death, of Maggie, a crumpled heap
upon the ground, blood pouring down her
face, the dead man's club beside her head.

She had killed the man, avenged
herself, when Talorc should have kept her
safe. Vowed to keep her safe.

Talorc fell to his knees, oblivious to the
stunned silence surrounding them, the sudden
halting of those returned from the chase. He
lifted her lifeless form, curled her body into
his heaving chest. He shut his eyes against the
fear her body would stay that way forever.

Diedre approached. The only one with
the courage to do so.

"Let me look." She eased Talorc toward
a boulder, to sit, as she gently pulled Maggie
back from his shoulder. Blood streamed from
the wound to her forehead, a wound that
would soon grow large and dark with bruise.

"You should leave her here, Bold. Let
the carrion get her, let those sods come back
for her"

Talorc's head snapped up. "Are you
mad?" He hissed.

Diedre stood firm. "At best, she'll die
from that wound. Worse, she'll be a half-wit.
She'd not thank you for saving her for that.
Leave her here, tell her kin she ran away,
straight into this band of men. Tell them you
tried to retrieve her, to save her."

Douglas approached. "Laird," his eyes
focused on the wound. "You've seen it before,
wounds to the head. This is a bad one and if
anyone knows the consequences, it's Diedre."

"No." Talorc stood, shaken from shock.
"I'll not tell the MacKays I left her dead on
the road."

Diedre leaned in, forced him to focus
on her. "You wed her for life, Bold. You did
not give her half a vow but the whole of it.

138

She refused that. She refused you, has done her best to be free of you. Let her death be measured by that."

"Aye," Douglas argued, "you've not joined. You're free to leave her."

The woman nodded. "There's another you could marry, Bold. You know it, we all know it. Give this one up before you return and the breach between the two of you can be crossed."

Give this one up? When he'd just found her. For what? To appease gossip of the past? Gossip that held no truth? There was no other but Maggie. Never would be.

Tired of the old pressure, Talorc ignored it. "I'll not leave her here for those heathens to dishonor." He brushed at Maggie's hair, locks coated in blood. Too much blood.

"And if she's a half-wit?" Diedre challenged.

"Then she will be my half-wit." He vowed for life. He would honor that vow.

Diedre tried to speak, Douglas stopped her with a shake of his head. Talorc understood their exchange. Maggie suffered a double crack to the head, worse than the blow that widowed Diedre. "My half-wit." Talorc echoed and strode off with Maggie in his arms.

The Handfasting Series

TANGLED

Part 2

Dedication

To my husband for sweeping me off my feet
and leading me into a land of mists, castles
and history rich enough to inspire dreams.
Love you boyfriend.

CHAPTER 1 – GLEN TORIC

Maggie's head spun, her inners heaved and surged. Bile, bitter and hot, stung her throat. She fought against it.

What wretched thing roused her, when all she wanted was to go back, deep, into darkness. She must be on a boat with its pitch and sway, seasick and in a pain so sharp it hurt too bad to think.

She licked lips, dry as ash. Thirst. She was thirsty, and incapable of doing anything but moan. Surely her mother was near.

"Maggie?" A deep voice vibrated against her throbbing head.

Not her Ma.

Someone shifted her. She groaned, flinched as sunlight pierced the veil of her cocoon.

The boat stopped. Voices floated like jetsam in a harbor.

"Is she awake?"

"Ah, the lass is goin' to be alright!"

"Eh?"

"Shhhh," that deep voice hushed all others. Comforted by the protection, she snuggled back toward the warmth of the body that held her.

"Maggie girl," his voice gentled. "We're almost there." The rocking started

again. She hated boats, and this one smelled
of horses. Sounded of them to, the clump of
hooves, the snort of breath, close, too close.
The boat lurched, the stench. . .

"Oh," she tried to push free, "I'm going
to be sick."

Guided over the flank of a horse, she
heaved, eyes shut as shattering pain racked
her head. It lasted too long, and then it was
done. She clutched at a wet cloth put to her
mouth, pressed it there to hold back agony,
and opened her eyes.

A foot, dripping with sick, hung below
her head. She snapped her eyes shut,
disoriented, as she was swung back up, into
the arms of the man with the voice.

A drinking bladder pressed against her
lips but, thirsty as she was, all her fuzzy mind
could register was the horse. She was on a
horse, not a boat.

"Drink up lass. It will make you feel
better."

"Aye, Talorc." She froze. Her mouth
acknowledging what her fuzzy mind refused.
Talorc the Bold, the man her clan pushed her
to Handfast, to marry for a year and a day.

A man the whole of the highlands
idolized and she just christened his foot but
good. Shame mingled with her moan, and then
she remembered. This man took her from her
home, the place she loved, the people she
knew, where she was safe.

Humiliation be damned.

She struggled to speak. "What
happened?" but the words slurred, the effort
to try again so beyond possible she gave up
thinking altogether.

"You caught a rock between the eyes.
You've a nasty lump and you've slept for the
time it took to reach Glen Toric."

The horse started forward again, jarred her stomach, jolted her head. She sounded the ache, clear from the depths of her.

"I'm sorry, Maggie mine, but we are in sight of the castle, and I dare not stop. You need to be tended to."

She would not answer to Maggie mine. It would hurt too much to try.

"I'm going as slow as possible."

"I don't want to be sick again."

"Nobody would blame you if you were."

The vibration of his voice rumbled through her. If he just put her on the still ground, left her to die, she would be happy. He wouldn't though. He would push her again, force her to wait to die, or at the least make her wait for unconsciousness.

He said they reached Glen Toric, his home, her home for the next year. These people would be her people. She refused to disgrace herself by meeting them in a dead faint. She would stand on her own two feet.

Only, just now, it was an improbable goal.

Curse the man for bringing her here, and the dizzy hum from a voice so deep she felt it as much as heard it. "Do you ken the slant of our climb? Glen Toric sits atop a steep mound. Bruce rode ahead to tell them you are with us. They are all coming out the gates to greet you, Maggie."

"With sick all over me."

"You were injured in battle, lass. There's honor in that."

"Who?" Snippets of memory rolled through her awareness, as much dream as reality.

His hold tightened. "They wore no plaid, and we took no prisoners. The dead offered no recognition, but we think they were renegade Gunns."

"MacKays safe?"

"We lost some good men."

The horse stumbled, Maggie whimpered and remembered. "I killed."

Talorc snorted. "At least one and good on you."

"Wish more."

His bark of laughter shocked a cry from her.

"Sorry, Maggie, I'll try to stay quiet." Quite right, he should sound contrite.

She tried to peek at his face, but only saw plaid. The slope of the ride forced her to sink against him, a solid cradle that rocked with the lure of sleep.

"Maggie," a voice nudged at her consciousness. "Are you awake, lass?"

Leave me be. All she could do was groan.

The hem of her skirt tugged. "She's a strapping lass."

"Hey now, give her room. She's injured, y' know."

"The poor thing."

"Take care."

In the hush, whispers crept through the milling crowd.

"Is this what the dream meant?"

"Och, couldna' be, she's alive."

"But a crow, on a bride's shoulder."

"She's not a bride, she's a Handfast."

"Who dreamt it?"

"Hilde heard it from Seonaid. The lassclaims someone dreamt it."

"Aye, I heard the same."

"She'll live," Talorc snapped, silencing the whispers.

Bully, Maggie thought. Death would be a sweet welcome, would stop the spinning, the churning of her stomach and the anvil's pain of her head.

"Seonaid didna' say what bride."
Another hissed, and the murmurs resumed.

Maggie could only catch bits of the exchanges, could make little sense of the import.

"Did she really save your life, Bold?"

"Bruce said she took a sword and used it."

"Every stone she threw hit its mark."

"Aye, a fine lass, boy. Fine woman to have by your side."

Talorc's lips brushed her ear, "You've impressed them, lass."

"Easily fooled." She breathed.

"Oh, they're wise ones, they are," he told her, as the buzz of curiosity grew.

Their movement ceased. "We're at the steps, Maggie. It'll jar you a might, getting down, but I'll be as easy as I can."

"I'll stand," she goaded herself with the declaration.

"No, you'll not stand." Talorc slipped her from his lap to the horse's back so he could dismount, then eased her into his arms.

The man robbed her of her pride.

"Let go, Talorc." He held her closer. "I'm needing to be sick."

Close to the truth, the fib worked. Talorc set her down, eased her around. Braced between his back and arm, he kept her from collapsing on wobbly legs.

Maggie blinked. A swarm of features moved before her, as vague as a reflection in a murky pond.

"Give her room." He barked, and the blur shifted.

He eased a lock of hair away from her eyes. A collective gasp thundered at Maggie. She fought to keep upright, as the sound pummeled her.

"Would you look at that?" It asked with reverent horror.

She pushed into Talorc's hold.

Another nearby reached out. Instinctively, Maggie jerked her head back as Talorc clasped the woman's wrist just shy of Maggie's face.

"Steady now, leave her be."

"She'll be needing some cold against that, Laird. And belladonna for the ache of it."

"Aye, Laird, she'll need tending."

"They clipped her good."

"Filthy heathens."

Another rumble of sound, as shapes moved, leaned toward her. She reached to explore a prickle on her head. A piece of hair? Drop of moisture? Perhaps a spider had fallen down on her. She tried to touch it, brush it away but found, instead, a fist sized lump, stuck right in the middle of her forehead. Split and wet. She held her fingers before her eyes, saw a dozen fingers instead of five and blood.

Blood?

Too stunned to feel at first, sensation returned with a blast. One moment Maggie stared at her hand, the next pain ricocheted, violent, aggressive, against her skull. Blessed darkness answered. Like a rag doll she crumbled.

"At least she didn't see it, Bold." Thomas offered, as he looked at the hideously purple protrusion.

An old lady tsked. "Or know that she has two great black eyes to go with it."

"Aye," Old Micheil sported. "She's a fine lass, boy, a fine lass indeed."

* * * * * * * *

Talorc's shadow shifted across the shale floor, as he turned from the fire to look back at the bed behind him. Ealasaid, drenched sponge in hand, bent over Maggie, dripping water into her mouth.

"Go on down to the celebrations, Laird. It's the eve of Samhain. You've reason to be thankful, the larders are full, you won a difficult battle. Your clan wants to celebrate the feast with their Laird. They can't do that if you stay here, and look only at what might be lost."

She walked over to him, placed her hands on his arms, as she looked into his eyes. "You've been here for as long as she, and naught has changed. Go on down, see to your people. I'll send for you. . . " Ealasaid hesitated.

"When she wakes." Talorc finished.

"Whatever happens," the old woman answered honestly. "You have to accept, Bold. Since she's been with us, the lass has done no more than breathe. She might not be wakin' at all."

"She's not to die."

"Bold," the old woman snapped, then gentled, patted his chest, where his heart beat. "It's life's way. We live and we die without any say of our own."

He thought of whispers of dreams, of crows, the messenger of death, of Seonaid. "What do you think Seonaid's playing at?"

Ealasaid snorted and left Talorc for her patient. "You know as well as I, Bold. You grew up together, you were close. Seonaid was never one to share."

"I was never hers, she was never mine, and I know her well enough to be certain she does not have the sight."

"She talks of dreams often enough, though she never claims them as her own."

Bold studied the woman who had raised him when his own mother died. "You don't believe her dreams any more than I do."

"No," she sighed, "no, but the others do. This crow could just as easily be the brother of your Handfasted. His death is still new, and there's a bond with twins."

He shoved off the bench, crossed to the window and opened the shutters. Shouts and laughter swept into the room. Bonfires, to celebrate the eve of Samhain, backlit odd grotesque shapes of people covered in animal skins, some with horns perched upon their heads. Others dressed in their plaids, their faces and bodies painted to disguise against spirits who had free reign to roam the land this night.

Honor the dead, but don't let them take you back with them. That was the way of Samhain, when the spirit of those gone, those to come, walked among the people.

Ealasaid spoke as though she heard his thoughts. "Even without Seonaid's dream, the eve of Samhain is a dangerous time to be hanging on to life. It's too easy to go and frolic with the dead. To leave this world."

"She's not to die. I feel it in my bones. She is mine, my chosen, mate of the soul."

"There is no finer means of death than battle. She would be honored."

He looked at Maggie's still form and remembered the night he proposed the Handfast. *I have to be here for Fleadh nan*

Mairbh. I promised Ian. As though Ian couldn't find her here. Talorc rather thought Ian might.

He had never fought a ghost before.

"Seonaid doesn't worry me. But Maggie's twin does."

"There's naught you can do." Ealasaid smoothed Maggie's hair, like mother to child.

Talorc understood action, it was this waiting that broke him. He would not wait.

"Ealasaid," He stalked toward the door, "talk to her, even if you think she does not hear." Why had he not thought of this sooner? "I want her mind full of the sounds of Glen Toric. We will take her down to the celebrations."

"You're mad!"

"Aye, well, so be it. You get her ready, talk to her as you do, of everyday things, of life among the MacKays. We need to make her want to wake to us. I will see that a pallet is brought. We'll move her on that.

"You could kill her in the move."

"No." Talorc shook his head. "If a move would do that, she'd be dead now."

"She'll not be freer of her brother in the hall."

For the first time in days, Talorc smiled, the same grin he wore in anticipation of a battle well- planned. "You could be right, Ealasaid, but down there the MacKays' call will be louder than any damn ghost."

CHAPTER 2 – CLAN MACKAY

She could hear the flute, and the sound of voices in harmony. Laughter, mugs clinking and someone full of tittle-tattle whispering in her ear. Pain overshadowed her dreams, great standing stones hard and menacing, like the ones in the field. Gray things, she tried to skirt around, hide from, as she searched for the merriment.

Every time she moved, those stones shattered, shot piercing pieces straight to the center of her head. Desperate, she tried to twist away from the explosions, but something held her still, kept her from moving and the pain, unerringly, found its target.

So powerful was that hurt, it turned to sound, billowed from her depths, to be purged. Somehow it worked. The sound turned her from the stones to face a wide stream. Water, cool comfort, enticing her far, far away.

"Maggie . . ." The whisper floated on the wind.

"Ian." She looked, searched the opposite shore.

"Maggie . . ." his voice touched her shoulder. She snapped her head to the side, to see, but the result was a shatter of sensation that blinded her.

"Shhhh, quiet Maggie." It was another voice, a deep rumble.

Water washed across the source of suffering. More dripped onto her lips, into her mouth. Greedily, she licked at them, which earned her another refreshing taste.

Comfort of the stream drew her, the pleasure of submerging in its depth for relief. "Ian?" He had drawn her to it, could help her find it again. "Ian?" She willed him to return, brushed at the merry making. The noise of feasting too insistent, loud, it interfered, stopped her from hearing the whispers.

A gossip poured urgent words into her ear. Maggie pulled away, cringed against the squelch of noise. "Ian, come back."

He did.

He stood on the far bank. He stood there and smiled, but he was not the man she last remembered. Instead, he stood as a small child, different but like her twin of years before.

"Mamamaggie." He reached out with chubby arms, for her to come and lift him. His smile wide, but changed from what she remembered of her brother. And his hair had gone dark, the redness not so strong. Ian's hair a brighter red than Maggie's own.

"The water." She said. She tried to walk to the stream on weighted legs. She wanted to go where the hurt could be washed away, cleanse her to join the child Ian. But the child was no longer alone, with him was Ian the man.

She did not understand.

"Stop." She begged the boisterous party makers. She wanted the calm of the river, the man, the child.

Her brother picked-up the boy, held him in his arms.

"The bairn will stay with me until you're ready." He told her.

She tried to crawl to the water, but a fierce hold on her shoulders kept her close to the pain, too close to the pain.

"My namesake, Maggie. You'll give him my name."

"Ian, help me . . ." again, she wanted the relief of the stream but someone slapped her cheek hard. She cried out, not from the pain, but from a different hurt. Loss. The world of Ian vanished, naught but a huge hole in her heart.

"Maggie, wake-up, girl. Come on now, open your eyes."

"Ian?"

****

Talorc closed his eyes in relief. She may have called to her brother, but this time she was awake, eyes wide and bewildered mayhap, but open.

"Ian?" Like thistle down, she touched Talorc's jaw, as though she were afraid he would dissolve.

Damn straight. That's exactly what should happen to a spirit. "Ian's dead, Maggie. You are here, at Glen Toric, with me, with the clan MacKay."

She tried to jerk free of him only to wince with the pain. "You sent him away."

He tightened his hold on her. "You've no place with him, Maggie. He's dead and gone."

"Talorc," she squirmed and whimpered with the movement, "You're hurting my arms."

Stunned, he looked, "Och, Maggie," he eased his bruising hold. "I'm sorry." And let go, though he could not pull away. Instead, he slid one arm around her shoulders, to hold her upright and awake. "I was afraid you'd hurt yourself." *I was afraid,* he didn't tell her, *that you would leave me for your brother, go to a land of no return.*

Ealasaid reached behind Maggie, to fluff and arrange the pillows.

"Lay her back, Laird." The older woman commanded, as she filled a mug with water.

He was loath to release her, wanted her to feel him near, to sense his presence and let go of dangerous dreams.

"Go on now, lad," Ealasaid chided, "those pillows are softer than your arm."

As he eased her back, she whispered. "Ian was here. I saw him."

"Ian is dead, Maggie. You are not."

"He was here." Her hands flew to her head.

"No Maggie."

"Dead or no, I saw him, Talorc, talked to him and the boy, the wee one."

"The wee one?" Talorc's sight jerked to her eyes. Eyes dulled by a sorrow that ran too deep.

"Ian wants me to take the babe . . ." her lashes feathered down.

"No, no, no, Maggie," fear clutched at his inners. She'd already slept too long, "wake-up, think about what you said."

"Talorc, stop . . ." she groaned, "let me sleep, let me go back to the boy."

"Oh no, Maggie," harsh and loud, he insisted, "listen," her eyes opened, "listen to me. A wee one. It's Samhain, time for those who have passed on, and time of those to be born." He shook her shoulders, jostled her to wake. "To be born, Maggie! It was our babe.

Who else would pass that child on to you, but Ian?" He could barely get his breath, as he moved in close, so only she would hear as he begged her to listen. "The wee one, it has to be ours, girl. Our babe."

The brush of her lashes against his cheeks alerted him. She had heard. He pulled back to study her. Her dream told it all, she would live, have his child.

"He didna' say it was yours, Talorc."

He laughed, he couldn't help it. Weak and aching, she could still tussle with him. "Are ya' sure now, lass? Are you absolutely certain, he didna' say the boy was mine?"

Her brow wrinkled and she shook her head. "Oh! Talorc." Gingerly, she touched the bruise. "I do ache."

Contrite, he leaned back, made room for Ealasaid to move closer.

"You just lie there, lass, leave the pain to me." As the older woman turned to rinse the cloth, to cool it again, another, smaller woman, offered a steaming bowl.

"Beathag?" Talorc tried to frown away his late wife's nursemaid.

Full of worried innocence, the small woman looked at him, offered the bowl. "I've a broth for her." Talorc tipped back, horrified that she might try to pour the stuff down his throat. Not bloody likely. Not from her.

Even his late wife had been leery of Beathag's concoctions, and she was the one to bring the rodent of a woman to Glen Toric. She was a small thing who slipped nervously along the edges of a room. Slight, aye, timid, true, but as determined as a mouse to cheese. Talorc was never certain how to deal with her.

Thankfully, Ealasaid took over. "Beathag, what have you made here?"

Ealasaid's brusque, robust way managed to soothe with practicality.

"It's a broth."

"So I see. And what have you put in it, Beathag?" Ealasaid leaned in to sniff at it, "For you see, I've already been giving the lass a drop of tincture. We wouldn't want to confuse her poor, hurt head, by mixing up the wrong mixes, now, would we?"

Beathag gave a sharp shake. "Oh no, Ealasaid. We wouldn't want to do that." And she slipped back into the crowd, a mouse to a crack in the wall.

Ealasaid shrugged her shoulders and rolled her eyes.

"Who was she?" Maggie was getting more alert. Talorc took her hands in his.

"Beathag, an old nurse maid," Her hands were too cold. He rubbed warmth into them.

"Talorc?"

"Aye?"

"The rest?" She lifted her chin toward the foot of her pallet. "And where am I?"

He had forgotten that the others were there, that her bed was here, a pallet upon a table in the great room, before the fire. His clan, her clan now, formed a circle around them.

"It's the Clan MacKay, Maggie. But I wouldn't be thinking you'd be ready to hear all the names."

Her eyes closed as she shook her head gently. "No, not all, but some, I should know some . . . the one with the cool cloths."

"Ealasaid, Maggie. She is as close to a ma as I have."

Ealasaid flustered with the notice. "You'll be needing another." Overly enthusiastic, she replaced the warmed cloth with a fresh one.

"Aye, thank you, Ealasaid." Maggie adjusted the rag that hung drunkenly over her forehead. "And who whispered stories?"

Talorc had erred before, he may have done so again with Una. She had the breath for a tale, but it was gossip, aimed for drama, not reality. Talorc never thought Maggie would remember what was said, only be urged by the voices. He realized he should have listened, should have censored what the woman said.

Una scrambled up around to the fire side of Maggie's pallet. "It was me. I could tell you heard every word. No one else believed that you would, but you did, did ya not? Oh, you were sooo . . ."

Una had been a mistake. Talorc nodded toward Conegell, Una's husband.

"Come on woman." Conegell tugged at her arm. "Canna' you see, she's suffering from a sore noggin?" When his wife resisted, the calm man warned, "you'll make it worse if you don't stop that chatterin.'"

"I'm the one who woke her."

"No you're not," Deidre snorted, "It was her dreams of the boy. The Laird's son. She knew she had to come back from that."

Maggie had gone back to sleep. Talorc lifted one of her eyelids.

"Just resting, Bold," she whispered, "just resting."

Una ignored her husband. "Do you want me to keep talking to her?" Talorc shook his head. "No, Una, that's enough."

"Una?" Maggie whispered, "You remind me of a cousin."

"I do? I remind her of her cousin." She preened to the crowd.

156

Leaning down beside Maggie, Talorc murmured in her ear, "saucy wench. I've met your cousins and I know exactly which you were speaking of. 'Twas no compliment you just paid Una."

"Who's to know?" She whispered back.

"Aye. You warmed her, you made her feel proud," he tucked the covers around her, as she fell back to sleep. He shot a look at Ealasaid, in question.

"Don't you fret now, laird, she's fine to sleep. It's just the pain."

"She'll wake again?"

"Oh, aye, she'll wake again, now." The older woman promised, as she shooed the others away.

The mighty Bold held onto his Handfasted's hands, bowed his head to rest it next to hers.

"You gave me a scare girl. You gave me a good scare." A shudder racked him with the surge of fears he had kept at bay.

Maggie returned to her dreams. Talorc was not so fortunate. He could do no more than sit by her side and watch for the tussle of attraction. To see if she would struggle to return to her brother.

In the end, after she had been moved back to his bed chamber, after a night and a full day of Maggie rising and falling, between slumber and wakefulness, without a word of Ian, Talorc gave way to sleep.

* * * * * * * * * *

The MacKay woman stood at the top of the hill, her arms wide, hair caught on the wind. He thought of her naked and willing on the slab of stone and grunted as the cold whipped about him. She had been furious. So had he.

"Yes, Cailleach Bheare," She sang to the wind. "Fill me with your breath of life." She turned toward the setting sun, "I vow we will give you blood. May the day set on the MacKay. May he fall below the horizon, give rise to a new day, and an old way."

He watched her, his new plaid pulled tight, and smiled. They may not have succeeded capturing the MacBede woman, lost good men in the effort, men they couldn't afford to lose. But they had a reward, the woman's trunks. New clothes for his men, fancy embroidered dresses for the lasses.

He couldn't wait to wear the MacBede plaid in an attack against the Gunns. Their retaliation would be a stunning blow that would go far to balance out their failure.

He looked behind him. This time it was a small deer upon an altar, body dissected, entrails removed. Someone read fortunes in the splay of its guts. It should have been the MacBede lass's inners they were studying.

She had power. She had broken the chain of loss he fought so hard to ensure.

The MacKay woman had finished her supplications, to whatever she called God. He felt her reach him, the warmth of her body, the scent of her.

"You failed." She sniped.

He grunted, refused to respond.

"Despite my invocations, she has survived. You know that?"

"One loss," he reminded her. "One loss."

"Yes, the only plan I was not a part of."

He turned on her then. "Careful." He warned.

"I was the one who saw to it their food was spoiled. I was the one who ensured their supplies would not travel with them. I have been the one to undermine the MacKay."

"Using my ideas. You know what is to come. We will not fail in this."

The woman nodded, wrapped her arm around his. She had been right. The MacKay's success was due to the MacBede lass. One, unanticipated woman.

"I need to return. I need to be there, to see that she questions her place at Glen Toric, his loyalty to her . . ."

He shared her frustration. They had been so close. Patiently, with deliberate steps, they had undermined the MacKay's confidence. Just one more sneaky little victory against the MacKay, and his glory would have turned to rust. Insecurity would have destroyed his clan.

The MacKays would have crumbled, blamed the Gunns, faulted their enemy. Pursued nasty little revenges. The Gunns, pompous in victories not of their making, would destroy themselves in arrogance.

All the clan confidence they had worked so hard to destroy had flooded back because of Maggie MacBede.

But they had one small victory, another fissure in the foundation of their security. The Mackay warriors had found the altar in Dunegan's Woods. It scared them. They didn't have the courage to destroy it. Fear was a grand weapon that weakened. The weak made mistakes, left room for a new order.

Blood lay in a pool below the altar. Soon, it would be her blood to bless them. For now, the deer would do.

One day.

Soon.

This little band of outcasts would have their way.

CHAPTER 3 – INTRIGUE

Ealasaid pulled at a sleeve too short for Maggie's arm, gave up, and brushed lint tangled in the intricate weave of the finest embroidery. "It fits well enough for now. We'll see that you have something finer by tomorrow."

Finer could not be possible. A better fit would be good though. One where she could breathe, without fearing a split seam. Looser, as women wore in this day and age. Surely, this had been from his mother, which meant these people were extravagant enough not to reuse the material. Wasteful.

"All my trunks were lost?" Her only link with home, her life, all gone. No matter how many times she asked, the answer never changed.

"Aye," Ealasaid fussed about the room, tidying all the other garments Maggie had tried. "Such a shame. No doubt you've a better hand with a needle, but there it is, nowhere to be found."

"Oh, aye." Maggie lied, as she looked down at delicate threads of gold and silver. Threads her own people could ill afford. She didna' have to leave the room to know Glen Toric was filled with riches beyond the reach of her people. A fancy carved bed, tapestries with enough detail to record an entire battle,

not just a simple hunt or some singular
meeting.

She did not belong here.

"You stay put, young lady," Ealasaid
pointed a finger at a chair, "I'll go find the
Laird."

"I can manage the stairs without him."
Maggie argued, half-heartedly. In truth, she
was happy to have Ealasaid leave, to give her
time to herself.

With a swipe of her hand, the older
woman brushed Maggie's argument aside and
headed out to the hall.

Alone, Maggie stepped to the window,
set deep with a seat beneath it. Opened
earlier, the shutters allowed a cool breeze and
bright sunlight, so often absent this time of
year.

It was not the sun she sought.

Ian had come to her in a dream. All
these months she had been waiting and now he
chooses to appear, each time as a warning or
promise.

This was no promise.

What was she to do? How could she
convince anyone to help her with no way of
knowing if the dreamscape was real or if the
girl she had seen, frightened and running, was
truly lost?

She scanned the land beyond the castle
wall, the vista no match to the image in her
mind. A vision too easily inspired by too
many highland lasses gone missing.

Only a dream, that's all it was, a simple
if not tragic, dream.

But if it was more? If Ian truly came to
warn her, prompt her?

Och! There was no hope but to sneak
out of the castle, find the stables and steal a
horse long enough to look. Another horse

journey, after she vowed never to get on a horse again.

She looked to the courtyard below, the steady stream of people heading toward the keep. One more example of the wealth of the Bold's home. His rooms weren't even in the tall, square fortress but in a separate wing altogether.

She leaned out further and saw the stable along the wall, closer to the gates. Talorc emerged with a tall lithe lad, deep in discussion, crossing the courtyard quickly. He held the lad's arm as they walked, bent in to listen. Ealasaid's voice rang cross the distance. The two looked toward the castle.

There wouldn't be much time.

Having spotted the stables, but not the rise and fall of land she sought, Maggie crossed the vast room. Another set of window enclosures framed the bed. This chamber must be on a corner with an outlook in two directions.

Even as she approached the outlook, she realized the sound and scent, with its promise of views beyond anything she had ever seen, had been there all along, in the background. An undefined constant, just another new noise, new thing to be absorbed. She reached the window to witness a wild crash of waves, as a powerful surf slammed against huge boulders, pulled back only to arch and rise again, an angry spray of foamy white.

Further out, the false calm of the water smoothed and sparkled blue, reaching to forever.

The ocean.

Her brothers told stories of this salty water that guarded one side of Glen Toric. Tugged to the view as fiercely as the draw of tide she'd heard tales about, this was not the

rise and sharp drop of heather and gorse she
so desperately sought. With a shake of her
head, she looked away from the fascinating
beauty.

What direction could it be? Nothing
looked like her dream, not the courtyard, nor
the hillsides beyond. Certainly not the ocean.

Hopeless, Maggie stifled urgency with
practicality. She would need a cape,
something warm. She turned back into the
room and gasped.

A small, bent woman with grizzled hair
stood inside the doorway.

"She left you alone, did she?" So very
tiny, with a meager smile stunted by timidity,
disquiet etched the old woman's face.

Maggie crossed to the chair before the
hearth, held on to the back of it. "Ealasaid
went to get the Laird."

The small head popped up with interest.
"She will be awhile then." With surprising
purpose, she came into the room, closed the
door behind her.

"My name's Beathag. I'll watch over
you. Mustn't leave you alone. We don't want
him to lose another wife. Not so soon
anyway."

Maggie stepped back.

"I've frightened you?"

"No." Keeping a distance did not mean
fright. A chance to get her bearings was all.

The woman scurried over, took
Maggie's arms and led her to the chair by the
fire, pushed at her until she sat.

"Do you want a drink? A blanket?"
Without waiting for a response, the mouse of
a woman bustled about, pouring water,
grabbing a lap blanket, handing the one over
as she plunked the other onto Maggie's lap.

Too stunned to argue, or stop her, Maggie sat still, allowed the ministrations. She did not drink the water.

"I'm very good at taking care of the Laird's wife," Beathag peeked up, as she pushed edges of the blanket around Maggie's legs. "I was his first wife's maid, you see. I came here with her, was with her when he cut her open." Tears pooled in the beady, obsidian eyes, "so sad, so very sad that he had to do her in like that."

"He was married before?" But of course he had been. She knew that.

A vague recollection of the women at the MacBede keep, and talk of Talorc being a widower, came to her. Back then, the information had not prompted thoughts of a wife. An actual woman, who he would have cared for, lived with. Maggie's gaze shifted, to look at the huge bed she had been sleeping in.

"Aye," Beathag's voice matched her movements, quick, furtive and done before anyone noticed. "That was their bed. The bed my Anabal died in." She paused, head tilted, watching Maggie. "Some say it was murder, but our Laird wouldn't do that, would he?"

Would Talorc do that? A man like her father, her brother, determined to protect and avenge, not to murder a woman with child, his child.

A wife dead from her husband's knife?

Her dream of Ian came to mind. There was no time for this.

The little woman kept speaking. "The Gunns just sent her off, traded her for peace. She was such a sweet little thing. As delicate and . . ."

Maggie didn't doubt he swept the other woman from her home. This man was well

versed in that, but to kill her? She had been a
Gunn, a sworn enemy, but the ramifications to
his soul, let alone the clan, would be foolish.
The Bold was no foolish man.

The door opened with a whoosh and
there he stood, filling the opening with
strength and steadiness. Her heart thumped
wildly. Relief, she promised herself,
distraction from this odd woman and the
thoughts she provoked.

"Beathag? What are you doing here?"

The old woman cringed.

Talorc eased the sharpness of his
question. "The people have gathered below
stairs. You should be with them." Words
directed to Beathag, while his eyes held
Maggie's. Did he sense her distress?

Beathag bobbed and curtsied and
scuttled out of the room. He watched, ensured
she left.

"She's an odd one, Talorc."

He turned to study Maggie, head to toe,
as though searching for injury, beyond the
blow to her head.

"She never hurt me."

"Good." He nodded, as though he did
not believe her but would let it pass.

"You were married before." She stood,
straightening the blanket, laying it over the
back of his chair, feeling the draw of him,
dangerous as any undertow.

He cursed the door Beathag had scuttled
through and rubbed the back of his neck.
Maggie noted his wet hair and clothes, clean
and tidy as though it were a feast day. In no
mood to celebrate, she remembered the cloak
she needed and crossed to the trunk Ealasaid
had filled with clothes from earlier. A
massive thing carved with scenes of a boar

hunt. She lifted the lid, determined to get out of the castle.

"It is no secret that I was married." He crossed to her. "Though, I don't remember Anabal much when I'm with you. Truth told, I was certain you knew, didna' question it." He watched her rifling through the clothes. "What are you looking for?"

Maggie's cheeks burned. "A cloak, or a plaid."

"Are you cold? Perhaps you should be back in bed."

"I'm well enough."

He frowned. "I'll carry you."

She raised her eyebrows. "You can keep your hands to yourself. It was my head that was hurt, not my feet."

He dropped his hands, let them hang by his sides. She knew the look, useless as any man faced with illness. She patted his shoulder. "I'm fine," and thought of a way to escape, "just need fresh air. The outdoors. Do you have a cloak for me?" She hadn't found one in the chest and time was short.

He reached into a wardrobe, brought out a folded length of plaid. The colors a wee bit different than at home. Grand as this place was, their plants did not offer the same depth of color as the ones at home.

"You've none of mine?" He could know things Ealasaid didn't. She frowned and reached for his offering.

"No, your trunks were lost. But we'll find them, we'll keep looking."

"All of my clothing?" She tsked as she wrapped the folded length of plaid around her shoulders. "All the hours I spent embroidering lost?" She hated needlework, resented the time it took, and it showed. All those tedious hours for naught. His chagrin did much to ease her loss, though she took little time to savor it. Urgency nipped.

"The clan's coming together, below stairs," he explained. "If you go down, they'll want to greet you."

"Bold, I'm no' ready for that. Been closed in for days. I've a need for some time alone, some fresh air first."

He narrowed his eyes. "You'd not meet the people who cared for you, tended to you?"

She looked away.

He bent down, met her eye to eye, "There's something you're not telling me."

Her cheeks warmed. The Bold was coming to know her too well, in too short a time. "Why would I lie about such a thing?" She challenged. "It's as I said. I need some time to myself. There's no disrespect in that."

"Aye, there is, which is not like you."

Flustered, she shook her hands, turned away to pace. "You've foisted change on me, Bold. I'm needing to breathe, out where the breeze can hit my face, where I can look at the land and see it's not so different from my own, without being surrounded by strangers."

Stunned by her own argument, she realized it was true.

"You canna' go alone."

"I could if I were home."

He shook his head. "You could at Glen Toric before now, but a lass has gone missing. That's why the clan is below, gathering to search.

"A lass is missing," she blurted, "and you've wasted time? Washed, fresh clothes?"

He snorted. "I've been sleeping in that chair, in the same clothes we traveled in. You and I have had a rough few days. I needed to wash that time away. But this, this is new, we only just heard. They're preparing for a search."

"For the lass hiding out," she waved her hand toward the northeast, "out there."

He cocked his head. "I didna' say she was hiding."

Maggie blushed. "She's in trouble, afraid, but not near as afraid as she should be, and there's meager cover where she is."

Talorc took her shoulders. "How do you know this? What makes you think we should go a certain way?"

She shook her head. There was no hope, she had to say something. "It was a dream. Ian lead me to a lass huddled in gorse and heather, trembling. Och, Bold, she's only a mite of a thing, weak and frightened, and a dark cloud is pressing closer and closer . . ." Maggie shivered. "And you're going to think I'm mad to be listening to dreams."

Talorc looked toward the window, as anxious as she to be on his way. Still, he hesitated before looking back at her.

"Ian, you say?"

"Aye." She never should have said anything. He would think her crazy and, even if he didn't, how could he use her information without sounding crazy himself?

He surprised her by taking her shoulders, facing her straight on. "No, Maggie." Talorc lifted her chin. "Fey mayhap, and I wished it was anyone but your Ian to talk to you, but not mad."

Maggie sat down hard on the trunk, uncaring of tusks or branches digging into her thigh. "Another lass has gone missing."

"Aye, young Ysenda." He nodded. "A wee mite of a thing, just as you said, and if you know where she is, there's not a soul who

cares where the knowing came from, as long
as it takes us to her."

Again, she rode a horse, to make the
going swift. A rare privilege to these
highlanders but the ache to her head from the
jolt of it hurt so bad she could barely see. Not
that the seeing was any good. It all looked the
same, the roll of the land, the harshness of
thorny gorse and heather.

Few rode, even Talorc was afoot, oft'-
times jogging, leading her mare. The others,
throngs of people, swept out in long lines,
sweeping the area. Most walked, some had
donkeys or ponies. Bagpipes played soulful
notes, as a draw for the lass.

Maggie closed her eyes, fought heaving
her last meal and felt grace when her ride
halted.

That's when it came to her, as sharp
and clear as a bolt of lightning.

"Stop!" She whispered, not opening her
eyes, not looking to see if any listened.
"Quiet."

Talorc promised not to tell about her
dream, or that she had a 'feeling' about where
the lass was, so she didn't know why they all
listened to her, how they even heard her quiet
words, but they did. By signal or look, she
didn't know, her eyes were closed, but as
quick as she spoke, the long line of people on
either side of her stopped. The music wheezed
to a close. Nothing but the sound of the
breeze and a slight whimper.

"There" she opened her eyes. "Do ya'
hear that?" But they all just stared at her.

Maggie slipped from her horse, turned
to see the same land as in her dream and she
knew, knew where to look, though half-afraid
the lass would be gone, or not there yet, or

that the terrifying black cloud would be
hanging over the spot. Still, she turned and
pointed.

"What?" Talorc whispered from beside
her.

"Look," she told him, and knew the
moment he saw, down below them, crumpled
on the ground, what looked to be a pile of
plaid that blended so well with the ground you
would miss it if you weren't certain it was
there.

"Oh my lord!" A woman cried. "It's my
Ysenda! My girl!"

As quickly as they had stilled, everyone
shouted and raced for a way down the steep
drop. One man took no notice but leaped to
the ground below, fell, then ran with a hitch
to each stride. Hurt but not halted.

That mound of fabric rose, stood, a
young girl swaying with weariness.

"Mama?" A meek cry, but there. "Is
that you?" And she tried to run to them,
stumbling and pulling herself up. Her cries
threaded through the hoorahs of others.

Maggie slipped down, cross-legged,
onto the ground, her head in her hands.

"You found her, Maggie." Talorc
crouched beside her.

"No, not me." Tears blossomed as she
felt the fear ripple through her. "The poor
child. The poor, poor lass."

"The poor lass might have been lost for
good if not for you. We were concentrating
our search closer to her home. We'd not have
found her." He brushed her hair from her face.
"If not for a fine faerie, do you think?"

She swatted at him. He pulled her onto
his lap. "No, you're too big for a faerie.
Could be a Sidhe," Caught her wrists, held
Maggie close, while he watched the people

fuss over Ysenda. He continued to tease. "No,
not a Sidhe either. It's a Valkyr, you are, like
the northerners speak of."

Laughter brought pain. "You're cruel!"
She complained.

"Not so cruel to let others know what
you were about." He was serious now. "I've
not told them of your dream, of Ian."

"What of when I asked them to be
silent?"

"You heard her cries."

She let loose a breath she hadn't known
she held. "Thank you." She whispered.
"Thank you. I'd not have your people
frightened of me."

He continued to watch the people
below. "Our people." He corrected but did not
push. "I will need to speak to the lass. Will
you come with me?"

"There's nothing I can do." Her life was
changing, too fast. She couldn't take it in,
worried that she would never be the same,
would never be able to return to her own
without being a stranger. "I wouldn't know
what to do, Bold, but yes, I will sit with you,
as long as you don't need me to speak."

He turned on her, with a fierceness that
startled. "You promised a Handfast, a year
and a day as my wife, a Laird's wife. You'd
not be so small as to skirt that?" Voice lower,
softer, he added. "You knew where she was,
you'll know what questions to ask that I
would not think of."

No, she thought. *No, no, no*. She was
not like that, in either sense. She was not one
to skirt what needed doing but this was not
her land, her people. Even more so, she was
not one to go finding lost lasses. "I'm not fey,
have never done such a thing before. There's
no promise it will happen again."

"Once was enough." He rose, Maggie still in his arms. "But questions can wait until tomorrow. We'll leave Ysenda to her parents for now and get you back to the castle. You're still mending, need your rest.

Maggie pushed out of his arms and eyed the horse she'd been riding.

"Here," he lifted her again.

"Stop." She wrestled from his hold.

"Just helping you mount."

"I'll walk."

"No," he caught her by the waist, "you'll ride, one more time." He settled her on the back of the animal. "We don't know what happened with Ysenda, or who attacked us in the woods, but if they decide to come again, escape is easier on a horse." He handed her the reins and looked toward the people coming back up onto the rise.

"What about you?"

"I'd best see to Ysenda and her family. If they want to go home, they'll need a guard around their cottage."

Maggie looked to the people and saw the lad from the courtyard, the one Bold had spoken with. The boy headed their way. Talorc noticed him, too, signaling for the lad to wait where he was.

"Get yourself back to the castle." He nodded to one of his men. "Bryson will see you stay safe."

She watched him walk away, toward the lad, surprised when he took his arm and bent his head so the two could speak closely, privately.

"Who is that lad?" Maggie asked Bryson.

"Lad?" He asked.

"Aye, the one speaking with Bold."

Bryson took the reins from her and started walking away. "That's just Seonaid."

"Seonaid? That's a girl's name."

"Aye."

Maggie looked back over her shoulder at Talorc and the lad. Things were even more different at Glen Toric than at home if they gave girls names to boys.

Bold listened to Seonaid as he watched Ysenda, her parents and half his clan, move up to the high ground.

"She's worn to the bone, Bold, and badly bruised, but she's alive."

"Has she said anything?"

"No, crying is all."

"Not lost." It wasn't a question. This far from home, it wasn't likely. He thought of Maggie's dream.

"She thinks she killed someone. That much did come clear."

"That little thing?" He scowled, relieved she was safe, even as fury raged. She hadn't been safe, had needed to kill, raged.

". . .*a mite of thing, weak and frightened and a dark cloud is pressing closer and closer*" The threat was not gone.

"See to them, Seonaid, Ysenda and her family. Convince them to come back to Glen Toric." He ordered.

"They'll be wanting to go home."

"That they might, but we need to be sure they're safe. Their cottage is beyond everything else. I'll send them with a guard. That will take time to organize."

"Men have gone looking for the bastard."

"Glen, Ian, and Ben."

"You knew there would be someone to blame."

"And you're going to think I'm mad to be listening to dreams."

He'd not betray her. "The highlands are not as safe as they should be." He looked down at Seonaid. "You be careful yourself. I've a feeling your brother has a hand in this."

Seonaid's nostrils flared, as her hand flexed around the dagger at her hip. "I know how to fight, Bold. No one, not even my brother, can hurt me."

"Aye." He smiled and patted her head, as if she were still the wee lass who used to follow him around. She pulled free of his touch. Still he warned her. "You know how to care for yourself, but you also know how to be rash, so watch yourself."

"Birk!" Maggie pushed through the crowd in the great hall, toward the Bard, surprised by her own eagerness. She had every reason to ignore the man, yet here she was running to him, the lone familiar face in this far-away place.

"Maggie MacBede!" The bard bent his tall, gangly body into a bow so low his head nearly scrapped the floor. As he uncurled, Maggie halted.

"Birk?"

Wide and gentle, his smile did not reach his eyes.

She had loved his eyes, so expressive and kind, yet now hinting at a sorrow she couldn't fathom. Cautious, she reached out with both hands. He took them immediately, lifted them to his lips.

"You look well, lass."

A year ago she would have swooned. But that was a year ago, when she thought he

loved her, thought he would marry her,
dreamed of being the wife of a Bard and
traveling from keep to castle. It had been an
idyllic dream he fanned until one evening,
after filling her with beautiful, treasured,
words of adoration, he left. Without a word of
good-bye, she faced an empty morning
searching.

Babbling Birk the Bard.

She would not be taken in with his
warm eyes and gentle smile again. She pulled
her hands free.

"I am honored you would have me here
at Glen Toric to sing for you, to tell your
story, to spread word of your glorious triumph
and . . ."

"Birk." She interrupted for, with all his
attractions, the man could get carried away
with words. "Why are you here?"

Eyes wide he stumbled to explain. "You
sent for me. Me. I am humbled by your
request, came as quick as was possible to be
here for you." He looked around and she
realized they were encircled by the MacKays,
watching. Birk leaned in close to whisper in
her ear, "you did not want the Handfast, you
do not want a warrior. I know you, Maggie."
He stroked her arm.

"No," she shook her head. "I didna'
send for you. But I'm that glad you are here."
Bothered by the brush of his hand along her
arm, she took his hand, placed it on her
forearm, as she nudged him to walk.

People watched them, she felt it, caught
it in sidelong glances. She didn't care. They
could gossip all they wanted. She did not ask
to be here, surrounded by strangers.

"I'm glad to see an old friend." She
squeezed his arm and, as they passed people,

she nodded to any who were the least bit
familiar.

There were the men who had ridden
with the MacKay when he had gone to her
own home, Ealasaid who tended to her, and
Una the gossip. A few recognizable figures in
a room of nameless faces. An intimidating
thing for a lass who had never been beyond
sight of her home, where strangers were a rare
thing to wonder about, whisper about.

Now she was that stranger.

Babbling Birk the Bard may have
abandoned her, but at this moment he was the
closest thing to a friend she had.

He lent down, to whisper in her ear
again. She scrunched her shoulder against the
tickle of it.

"Are you happy here, Maggie? Are you
happy with your hHhandfast?"

Happy? She looked about, at the people
around them. Friendly, for the most part, even
anxious to please. But they were not so simple
as her own kind, dressed in their fancy clothes
of the finest weave, edges lined with fur from
many pelts, and the jewels! Part of her
wanted to reach out and touch the sparkle of a
gem or the soft fabric of a gown. Instead, she
clung to Birk's side.

"They're fine people." She
acknowledged.

"Oh, aye. But so are the MacBedes." He
covered her hand with his and gazed down at
her.

Was that longing in his eyes? Maggie
pulled free, unsettled by the hope in that look,
confused that she still had her breath, that her
heart didn't skitter with pleasure. "Aye, we
are a fine people, even if our clothes are not
so . . ."

He put his fingers to her lips. "You are good people, Maggie MacBede, with many a tale of strength and honor."

It was good to be with an old friend. She squeezed his arm. "Will you be singing after the meal?

"That I will." As he tilted his head, she suddenly wondered how his skinny neck held his head upright. He really was a scrawny thing.

"I'm not scrawny enough for your tastes? Is that it? You won't be able to rule me as you might a lesser man."

She stepped back, as Bold's words rippled through her. Words spoken when she challenged him for forcing the Handfasting on her. Worse, the thought of him flowed, with the memory filling her with all the excitement she wanted to feel for Birk.

She looked away, not wanting comparisons, not wanting to feel the foolish reminder of infatuation, horrified to think she may have married this man.

He was a friend. That was all.

"I will see you at dinner then," she promised, and turned back to the flock of women who shadowed her.

"I will sing of you." He crooned.

She welcomed the women as they encircled her, moving her beyond the bard, whispering over each other.

"Who is he?" Nora asked.

Another woman slapped Nora's arm. "That's the Bard, you fool."

Maggie smiled.

"Babbling Birk the Bard," the woman tittered. "One of your puny men, aye?" Her eyes lit up, Maggie lost her smile.

These women were not so different from the ones at home.

"Where is Ealasaid?" She asked, rather than feed their curiosity.

"Fretting over that girl." Diedre complained.

"Ysenda?" But she didn't need to ask. Of course she would be tending to Ysenda. That's what Ealasaid did, she cared for others. Maggie frowned at Diedre's lack of compassion, but didn't say anything.

They had been friends of a sort. Diedre, the only woman to travel with Maggie to Glen Toric. The first of the MacKay women Maggie met. She had been full of stories of the people and place; full of advice on how to enjoy this year and a day without being trapped for the rest of her life.

Maggie had not seen much of Diedre since they returned. Even for the search for Ysenda. Diedre didn't appear until they reached the castle. Once she heard the news, she'd not stopped berating since. "Whatever got into the girl?" She snapped. "To frighten her family, her people, like that."

"Come now, Diedre, you know what it's like, living way out in the hinterlands, no young men about." Young Ete, justified.

"But to go off with a stranger? With so many lasses going missing?" Nora MacKay shook her head, confused by the idea.

"Too easy to trust a charming man." Una fretted, as she'd been doing ever since the girl was found.

"Aye, but now we know what's about. Who the blackguard is." Diedre stated.

"But we don't know," young Ingrid whispered, lifting her head to look at Diedre.

Something passed between the two. Maggie wasn't sure what it was, but the shy girl with her long blonde hair seemed to challenge the boisterous Diedre.

"Give her time." Diedre murmured.

Maggie shook her head against her imaginings, tired from too much of a day. She scanned the room for Talorc.

"Och, look at you," one woman moved forward and brushed hair away from Maggie's forehead. "Two black eyes and a lump the size of a goose egg. Who would have thought you'd be out looking for Ysenda with the rest of us."

Nora swatted at the woman. "Don't be telling her about the eyes."

Una laughed. "She should be right proud of those eyes."

Maggie reached up, to feel, but there was no color in the touch. "Two black eyes?"

"Aye," someone else cooed. "You're a grand lass."

She was not so grand, certainly didn't feel grand. If only they would sit at the table, but where was Talorc. Voices floated past. She didn't listen, just scanned the hall until she saw him, across the room, with the lad from the courtyard.

The one who had spoken to him when Ysenda was found. Senoiad.

Only now, despite the clouding pain, she saw that Seonaid was not a lad with a lasses name. Seonaid was a willowy, windswept woman and so close to Bold, the curve of her breast touched his arm.

Stunned, Maggie wondered how she figured it out, for the woman's kirtle was no kirtle at all but a tunic that ended above the knee. She wore hose, like a man and a sword hung from her hip, a dagger tucked into her belt and a knife was strapped to her ankle.

There was just enough curve of the breast and the angle of her cheek bone to make a difference.

Though easily of an age with Talorc, which gave her ten years on Maggie, there was no covering upon the woman's head, just a thick dark braid that had fallen over one shoulder.

The woman tilted her face to laugh at something Talorc said. His smile, wide with pleasure, spoke of a familiarity rich in years.

Do ya' think he lived there with no woman in his bed?

A dart, thrown to make her mother worry and fret and stop the Handfasting. Nothing real, back then.

Talorc thought her to be a woman who inspired victory. But she was nothing other than flesh and blood, often foolish, always stubborn. An imposter, in another woman's place. A simple lass in an extravagant home.

He wanted her for his clan, her clan, and the power of the two together. He wanted her for breeding stock, to bear sturdy sons with the blood from two lines of warriors.

He wanted her because of overblown tales told around a campfire.

There was no reality to his wanting. He didn't know who she, Maggie, was. But he had known who this woman was, the actuality of her. She was not an illusion. She was not a false image. She was just a woman Talorc knew well.

An imagined fear turned to piercing hurt that cramped the heart. A reality. The second one to hit that day.

Maggie glanced back at the woman, the second person that night to reveal a hint of sorrow as Bold now talked to Bruce. As if she felt Maggie's gaze, this woman, Seonaid, met it. Her eyes violet as the small flower, dark and intense.

"Don't you fret about Seonaid." Una startled Maggie by wrapping an arm around her shoulders. "The Bold never thought to marry the lass."

Lizbeth gave Una a sharp elbow to the side, adding, "It's you he watches, as though you might disappear in a waft of smoke."

She looked back to find him watching her. But he hadn't been earlier. She doubted he even remembered she was there.

Deidre moved over to Maggie, as did half a dozen others.

"It doesn't matter anyway." Deidre stroked her hand. "When the Handfast is over, you will be leaving him behind."

You'll be leaving. . . . He never thought to marry Seonaid, words echoed with a thousand different conclusions.

Odd perhaps, in a lad's clothes, but the woman was beautiful and graceful, with dark black hair, and mysterious eyes.

Maggie looked down at her own self. Too much of her own self, all hip and bosom.

"Did she have reason to think he would? Marry her, that is."

"You needn't worry." Eilinor patted Maggie's shoulder.

"I wasn't." Which was true, she hadn't until now. She needed to know. "Did she have reason to think he would? Marry, her that is."

They all looked to each other.

Ingrid broke the silence with a haughty flip of her own braid. "Seonaid is nothing more than a woman who thinks she's a man."

Again silence, then Una piped in. "Let's play the wedding game!" She encouraged the others. "We'll not let the Bold anywhere near you for the whole of the evening!"

A game meant for a bride, which Maggie was not, but she managed to smile, allowed the women their fun despite an aching head and an unruly heart.

As they played interference, came between her and the Bold, Maggie listed all the reasons she was happy to play. She wanted to go home. She wanted a husband more like Birk than Bold. She did not want to love the Bold.

She would not love the Bold.

She refused to love the Bold.

And all the while her mind fought to control her wishes, she found her heart could not play the game.

CHAPTER 4 – CHANGES

A groaning wind rattled the shutters. The banked fire hissed and spit its meager glow. Shadows thick as tar danced, eerie movements illuminating demons upon the walls.

Maggie jumped with every rattle, shivered with each hiss of fire and cursed the man who brought her here to sleep alone, in a huge, ominous room away from her own clan.

The MacBedes knew of Maggie's night fears. They would not have left her alone, even if there were room for that. A single lass never slept in a room on her own. There were advantages to living in a small keep.

But she was not in a small keep. She was in a strange and cavernous room, with any number of hidden tunnels in and out of it.

Eyes wide, she fought to breathe . . . to steady herself . . .

A great snuffle, a snort, ricocheted down her spine, to freeze with a scratch of claws on stone floor. Never, even in her most frightening experiences, had the night been this bad.

"God preserve me." She whimpered.

Terror kicked up the patter of her heart, pulsed hammer blows to her head. To scream would shatter her bones.

This was the Bold's fault. He forced her to be alone . . . in this strange place . . . with strange noises . . . unexplored shadows . . . and sounds of great, huge, ravenous rats.

Rigid, Maggie strained against the gloom, to see what hid in a place too full of hiding places. Another snort and scrape of talons shot down her spine and a cold wet nose pressed against her face. Terror erupted in a shriek, racketing pain throughout her head.

A monster of a beast scrabbled to get on the bed, two massive paws already there, as another mangy head rose from the foot of it. Sound choked in her throat. She would have sobbed, but could do no more than flap her jaw.

The beast grumbled, "Wha. . . Hu . . . Wa"

She heard nothing other than the prayers she mumbled under her breath, her eyes squeezed tight against the frightful image. Desperately, she pulled the covers up over her head.

A heavy weight landed beside her.

"You bloody, bloody, cruel man to leave me here," she cried to herself. "Talorc, where are you when I need you?"

Something tugged at the covers. With fists and teeth she held tight, her body shuddering in fear.

"Maggie, Maggie," the struggle stopped, "I'm here, Maggie," Talorc's voice penetrated her shelter, settled on her, as the comfort of his hands cupped her shoulders through the thickness of covers. "I'm right here, Maggie mine. You've nothing to fear. I'd not leave you alone when you've been so ill."

She lowered the barrier to her nose. One eye opened, then another.

"You great brute." Through the blanket, she punched his shoulder. "You left me alone in this miserable place, and I don't take kindly to it."

"Never, Maggie, I was here."

"Not quick enough."

"Right there," he turned her to face him, pointed to the foot of the bed, where the devil's head had popped up.

"With a beast?"

"Aye," he reached over to pat the head of an enormous dog. Maggie put her interpretation of the animal down to shock. Talorc continued, as if there were not a problem in the whole of the world. "Brutus was here, as well, to watch over you and make sure no one could harm you."

She eyed the animal, and wondered who would protect her from it. He looked big, and mean enough to eat her. And it wasn't a dog she wanted, but Ian or at the least, another person, someone to explain away the ominous shadows.

A shift of focus and she froze, to stare at the fabric in Talorc's lap. A scrunched up ball of plaid. This, his only concession to modesty, barely covered his privates, trailed over his thigh, a train in his wake.

She couldn't help but stare. This was the body that taunted and teased, that made her feel in ways she had never felt. She touched his thigh with a light finger, found it muscled, hairy.

Her gaze rose, but only as far as his chest. That's where it took a turn, along the path just perused.

Fascination washed away embarrassment and fear. She forgot her anger. She, who had grown-up surrounded by men, could not take her eyes away from the arrow

186

of hair that mirrored the arrow of his body. So broad and muscled at the top, to taper down . . . lower down, into the soft folds of fabric that exposed so much, yet hid . . . all by itself, the cloth shifted as though a live thing were hidden underneath it. Her eyes snapped up. His glistened with laughter.

"You want to peek?"

She clutched covers against her own nakedness, and managed a disdainful snort. "You've nothing I've never seen before." She lied. She was quite certain he had something she had never, ever seen.

"I bet you've never seen it in this state."

She could barely breathe. "As if I would want to." She lied again, thinking of how she had felt it through layers of clothes. The curiosity to see, to touch was strong.

To hide her blush, Maggie harrumphed, and flopped over, mumbled about men with little boy humors, and gave him her back.

The bed shifted, cloth rustled. She would not, absolutely not, look. Not even one quick glimpse over her shoulder. She fought the urge by staring straight ahead. The shutter still banged, buffeted by the storm raging outside. The shadows continued to dance. None of it alarmed her. Not anymore. Not with Talorc there, to make it feel cozy and safe.

"You're all right, Maggie. Nothing will harm you at Glen Toric." He lay beside her She wondered if he could read minds to answer her thoughts.

He pulled her into his arms, held her as her brothers would. Neither spoke, as he stroked her hair. She squirmed.

He did not feel like her brother. His caress did not lull her toward sleep, but made her want to stretch, like a cat, so his hands

would move from stroking her hair to stroking
. . . She squelched another squirm. He kissed
the top of her head.

How many days had it been since he
had kissed her properly? Since he challenged
her body? Too many. He treated her like a
child. She did not feel like a child.

And she did not know how to start the
battle of the senses. He had not yet taught her
that much.

"Are you falling to sleep?"

She shook her head, and asked, "Are
you waiting for me to? So you can sleep?"

He pulled back, brushed her hair from
her face, his eyes heavy lidded. "Would you
blame me if I did?"

She nestled back into his hold, rather
than have him see how she felt.

Every night before this one, whenever
she woke, Talorc had been there, in the chair
beside her bed, ready to speak to her, to ease
her fear, to place a cool cloth upon her head.
Always, he was in the room, to watch over
her, make her feel safe. She was better now
and it was true, he needed sleep.

If she had a bedmate, he could go to
another chamber, and get the rest he needed.
At the same time, she would not have to face
the fear of a strange place all by herself.

"It's time I share this bed."

She pulled back, looked at his hand,
poised for another caress, his expressive
features expressionless. She frowned.

"It's just that," the words jumbled in her
head. "Perhaps things are different here, but
at home maidens share their beds. It leaves
more room for others. Glen Toric can't be so
different. Surely, I've put someone out of
their place."

He held the curve of her shoulder. His hand warm, solid. She did not want him to go just yet. She did not want him to let go.

"You're fine in this bed."

She grabbed at that. "I would be glad to share."

Talorc chuckled. "Would you now?"

"Aye."

"It's my bed you're sleeping in."

She blinked. Of course it was. She knew that. His papers, his books, his clothes were in here. "It's not you I'm thinking of sharing with."

He laughed. "Do you want to let me in?"

Aye, she did, but dared not tell him. Refused to let him see how desperately she wanted his mouth on her mouth, on her body. To feel the way his teeth would tease her nipple and his tongue would soothe the nip all while his hands molded her breasts. She would not demand that he push himself against her secret places, rub and buck and draw her into mindless hunger. She would not beg.

"Where's Ealasaid? I shouldna' be here alone with you."

"You're my Handfasted, you're expected to be alone with me."

Maggie's snort was not much different than Brutus's. "I'd not have need of comfort if not for that. But I am doing better now. I can be moved to another bed."

"There's no need for that." He sighed. "But you needn't worry about me climbing under the covers with you. I'm more than comfortable on the floor. It's smoother than the rocky ground outside. And goodness knows I've spent enough nights on that."

"I've never slept alone, MacKay."

"You'll not be alone, Maggie. I will be
right there for you."

"I've never slept alone in a bed. And
I've never shared a bed with someone who
was not my kin."

"I am your kin now, Maggie. Don't
mistake that."

"Blood kin."

Silence, so peaceful moments before,
stirred into something quite different.

"Maggie," Talorc broke the stand-off,
"if you want someone in the bed with you, I'll
join you."

"Never." She thought of the other
woman, Seonaid and wondered if she had
shared this bed with him.

"I'll not pursue you more than you
want." His white teeth gleamed with his
smile.

That she could challenge. "I don't see
you pursuing at all."

He cupped her head, pulled her to his
kiss before she could react, all hard and tense
hunger. He rolled onto her with his body,
thrust against her with his loins. She felt the
long, thick length of him and knew that she
had won. He was pursuing, he was
challenging her.

She had to check him, or he would think
to dominate her with her one weakness. She
had to check herself as well, or she would be
buried so deep in her want for him she would
never leave.

"I'm not wanting." She told him, and
realized it was her third lie of the evening.

"Then I'll not pursue."

This was what she hated about him. The
push-pull, to want him and not want him. The
pit of her fluttered, a hundred frenzied

190

butterflies. Her mind screamed to push him off, tell him to go to the floor.

"You'll have to sleep in a different layer of covers." She was naked. She'd not risk her skin to touch his, certain it would ignite a horrible sensation she could never control. "And stay on your side."

"Aye, Maggie," he didn't pull his plaid free until he was under a blanket. "I'll do that." Settled, he reached out again, pulled her close. "You'll be safe, right here, with me."

"You're not on your side." She grumbled, even as she wriggled against him.

"Aye, I am. On my side of the center. And you are on your side of the center." He tightened his hold.

Tell him to let go, her mind argued, but Maggie stayed mum, until Talorc asked, "Remember your dream, Maggie? When you woke from your wound?"

Impossible to forget. "You mean when Ian came for me."

"Ian didn't come for you, Maggie," Talorc leaned up, and over her. With a reverence that stunned her, Talorc rested his hand over her belly, "He brought you a bairn, my child, Maggie. Yours and mine."

"He didn't say it was yours."

Talorc laughed. "He brought the lad to you here at Glen Toric, to my home, my bed. He'd not do that with another man's child."

His words tugged at her. She did not want the sense of it any more than she wanted to hunger for his nearness.

Talorc lifted a strand of her hair, traced her cheek with it. She brushed him off.

"Maggie?"

She would fight the warmth of him. The security. He was a warrior. A spear-heading, dive into the fray, warrior. He had already played against the odds of survival. He was not a man that a woman could count on to grow old beside her. He was not a man to be content unless he had his way.

He was not the man she wanted to dream of.

"I'm tired, MacKay." She willed thoughts that would turn her against him. "What with all the sleep I've had, I'm still tired." She rolled away, settled deep in the covers.

"Fine," he whispered, "Just remember, I'm here for you."

He was there for too many. That was the problem. Chin over her shoulder she asked, "Were you there for her, too? Did you make such promises to Seonaid?"

His eyes lost the heavy lidded look. "She's nothing to you, Maggie. We grew up together. Her father was my da's right hand. I promised to watch over her. There is nothing more to it than that."

"She's fairly cozy with you."

"Maggie, I'll not treat you false."

She heard the way he held on to his patience. "You've already done that."

"Maggie," his exasperation escaped, "why would you think I could want a woman like that when I have you?" Possessively, he cupped her breast, she moaned. "You, who are so responsive?" He worked his hand under her blanket, trailing it across her belly and lower. She wanted to stop him, but he had started to kiss her again, his words no more than a wisp of air against her cheek, in her ear. The whoosh of it spiraled straight down her inners, parallel to the path of his hand. "You are so brave." Horrified, she felt his fingers thread through the small cluster of curls at the juncture of her thighs. "You don't run from your desire," his fingers were turning to magic. Maggie twisted in his hold, buried her face in his shoulder, "You meet my challenge, come to me like the warrior lass you are." He was stroking that part of her that ached with desire, between the folds of her womanhood. One finger drew a tiny swirling design on the tenderest of places. Her hips lifted off the bed, she whimpered, felt weak and foolish.

She would meet him. She would take his challenge. Quickly, before she could stop herself, she reached below his cover and found that solid hard ridge that commanded her desire. With determination, she wrapped her hand around him, stunned by the size and texture of him. Hard as a sword's handle but soft as a babe's flesh, it drew her with wonderment. She slid her fingers from base to tip, felt its involuntary jerk, felt the drop of moisture that topped it.

"Oh, Maggie." He covered her hand with his, forced her hold to tighten. "How I wish you weren't still mending." He groaned, his forehead to hers, his other hand still working glory between her thighs.

She licked her lips, wanting something, anything, to free her hunger. "I want more. You never seem to give me enough."

"Maggie," Talorc lifted her chin, forced her to meet his eyes. "When I give you enough, it will be with the length and breadth of me."

Oh, good Lord. "You would never fit." She shook her head. "Never, ever, in my lifetime."

He had the cheek to laugh. It was time to back off before he tried to do what he spoke of. For if he tried, she was not certain she would stop him.

"I will fit, Maggie, trust me. But you will not be the same from that moment."

"Then that moment best not happen."

He surprised her with a gentle kiss on her mouth, a slight lick of her lips. "That moment will happen. I promise that. But you must know, when it does, you will be mine. No skirting past that. I will be your husband in body and word."

"Never."

"Aye, bodies chained will make you my wife."

"You don't claim Seonaid as wife."

He sighed, rolled to his back. "Maggie, Seonaid has never tasted of me nor touched me as you have tonight." He sounded as if he meant that.

Maggie rolled her eyes rather than let him know the exhilaration of his words.

"And you, Maggie?" Talorc leaned up, pushed her over onto her back, "While we are talking of pasts, what of the Bard, that was here tonight. Who is he to you?"

Please bed, swallow me up. Maggie did not want to answer.

"Well?" He was not going to give up.

"Why do you want to be knowing?"

"He sang to you, did he do that before?"

"He's a bard, Bold, he sings for everyone. Back home they call him Babbling Birk the Bard because he sings and talks so much."

"He courted you."

No, she thought, I courted him. "We were friends."

"Close enough that your brothers ran him off."

She tilted her head, to see if he spoke the truth. She had never thought of that. If her brothers had run him off, then Birk hadn't run

194

from her. She smiled. There's a grand difference between running away from protective kin and running away from a woman.

"My brothers ran him off?"

She pictured Birk, as he had been this evening. Sweet, hopeful, eager to please. Like an expectant child, next to Talorc.

Talorc could never be seen as a child.

"He's more mouse than man."

She laughed at his predictable response. He sounded just like her brothers. "Birk has a good heart and can sing better than any other."

"He could never love you better than me."

"You don't love me, Bold." He didn't know her to love her. And once he did know her, there would be no chance of love.

"That's not the kind of love I'm talking of."

She snorted.

He kissed her, a slow insistent taste.

"Don't, MacKay." She fought the molten heat that trickled through her with his words, the touch of his lips. He will love my body, but he will never love me. She held the thought like a chant.

"Just one more," he whispered, his mouth pressing against hers, his lips urging hers to open.

"Sleep well, lass." His voice wrapped around her as surely as arms.

It was neither Seonaid nor Birk she pictured as she drifted to sleep, but Talorc. The one man she did not want to dream of.

CHAPTER 5 – MEANS OF ESCAPE

Sun filtered through the shutters in a time of year when the sun was a late riser. Maggie overslept. So had the Bold, sprawled out on the bed as though sleeping with her were a normal thing. He needed to catch up on his rest after nights of watching over her. She, on the other hand, had slept enough since reaching Glen Toric. It was time she started to do something.

Anything.

Only it was cold, she was naked. The cold she could face, had been doing so her whole life. It was the man in her bed that had her hesitating, and an imp of desire that wondered what would happen if he caught her slipping free of the bed in no more than she was born with.

She closed her eyes to the temptation and listened to his steady snores. It would be better if they were louder, deeper, more arrogant. The noises he was making could be mere play. He was on his stomach, his head turned away.

There would be no better chance. Maggie slipped off the bed, onto all fours. Should he wake, he would have to roll over and move to the edge of the bed and peer down to see her. She would hear that, and have enough time to scuttle behind the bed drapes.

Secure in that plan, she crawled to the trunk at the foot of the bed, full of clothes left for her by some of the clans' women. Her chemise hung behind a screen in the corner, but she dared not go that far and risk being seen. Instead, she grabbed the first kirtle she found, pulled it over her head, only to find it too small when her arms got stuck. The reverse process proved harder than getting it on.

The bed sheets rustled. She stilled, then frantically tried to pull the garment off. A great rending rip later she was free enough to use the garment as a screen. Naked, except for the fabric held at her chest, she peaked over the side of the feather mattress.

The Bold snored gently as he resettled into a new position. She risked leveling up high enough to have a good look at the pile of clothes, found a garment in heather green and, with less effort, pulled it on, adding a yellow side-less surcoat to cover. She eyed the MacKay plaid. It would add warmth if she went outside.

She peeked at the Bold once more, grabbed the plaid and headed to the hallway. Once out of the room she stopped, her hand to her head, stunned, for it no longer ached. For the first time since arriving at Glen Toric, she felt like her old self. Cheerful with health, she followed the hallway to the corner that turned to a stairway down to the great room.

It was empty. Which was odd. At home there were always people about. Glen Toric was much larger, with far more people, yet no one was in the great hall.

A door swung open at the far end, leading toward what Maggie suspected were the kitchens. Little Eba, Diedre's daughter, peaked around the edge, then ran out to the center of the room where she skidded to a halt staring up at Maggie. With a giggle she turned, racing into the gallery that led to another set of stairs ending at the entrance of the castle.

Even Maggie, unfamiliar with the castle, knew this was not a good place for a child. Not that the wee one could get out. The door was massive, no doubt heavy. But it was no place for a young lass to run amok. The stairs outside, like the ones Maggie had just descended, were designed for defense; narrow and twisted, with no railing on the outside edge, just a very steep drop.

Maggie hiked her skirts and set out after the child, picking up speed when the groan of the heavy door hinges reached her. The little sprite had managed to get outside.

Images of a broken child flew through her mind, as she raced to stave off the danger. The great door was swinging closed when she reached it. Weighted to be kept closed, it took the strength of worry to push it open and slip through to the top step. Exhausted, she took deep breaths and watched little Eba run safely back around the castle toward the kitchens. Standing at the top, seeing the long drop, she wondered who Eba had followed out. The mite was lucky to be alive. Even standing there, close to the wall, took Maggie's breath.

She chuckled at her foolishness, lifted her skirts so she wouldn't trip on them and turned. Halfway into the pivot something hit her shoulder hard, sending her off-balance against the steep open steps. It happened so quickly she spun with the momentum, reeled, landing without grace, on all fours, as though climbing the stairs, far too close to the edge.

The corner of a plaid caught her eye, nearly caught in the closing door.

Had the door taken so long to shut or did someone hold it open?

Bruce shouted from below.

"Are you all right, Lass?" He raced up to help. "You needs be careful on these."

With the hesitation, the push to follow halted, she sat, not at all certain her legs would hold her. "Yes, rattled but fine." She hesitated. "Did you see?"

Bruce reached her side. "See what?"

"Did you see anyone behind me?"

He frowned. "No, lass. Saw you down, not the tumble. You aren't thinking someone at Glen Toric would topple you on these stairs?"

"No," She rose, using the wall for support, refusing to start her first day throwing accusations around. "Of course not. I was looking for Eba. She ran out here."

"Eba? Diedre's child?"

"I followed her, that's what brought me to these wicked stairs." She chuckled on a sob, determined not to show just how upset she was. "Nearly swallowed my heart when I heard the door open."

"You're telling me she ran for the door?"

Of course it sounded ridiculous, but it was the truth. Maggie knew it was the truth. She forgot all about the fear she'd just faced and took the stairs to the castle entrance.

Bruce reached it first, risking the long drop to step past her, to open it for her. She stepped inside. He followed, and the massive door swung closed.

Maggie watched, aware that the movement meant something, but still too unsettled to realize just what.

It was a solid thing, sturdy oak, thick as the length of her fingers. Far too heavy for a child the size of Eba.

Bruce scowled. "You are saying Eba ran to this door, opened it without a struggle, and ran down the steps." He stood in front of the closed door. "When you followed you were pushed?" He didn't look at her, kept studying the door. There was doubt in that.

"Of course not." It didn't make sense. "I think she followed someone out."

He stepped back. "Open it."

She reached for the massive iron ring and, with both hands, barely managed to turn it. The turning pushed the lever up out of its slot. With an umph, she pushed the door outward. Unwieldy for an adult, but possible. Not so for a wee lass.

"Could it have been left ajar?"

Bruce shook his head, guided her away. Immediately, the door swung shut on its own. "It's designed to fall closed. That's a defense, as well as protection."

"The child could have been crushed."

"Did you see anyone else?"

"No." She hadn't been looking, too focused on saving the child. Maggie didn't blame Bruce for doubting her.

"Please, don't say anything to the Bold."

"He's the laird, you're his lady. He needs to be told."

"I could be wrong, confused. The stumble frightened me." She explained, not believing a word of it. She could take care of her own safety. There was no need to make a fuss.

"You believe you were pushed."

"No." She lied, for she was pushed, she was certain of it. Whoever pushed her had opened the door for Eba. They couldn't have known Maggie would follow. It couldn't have been planned.

She had to find Eba to learn who had let her out that door.

"No." She told Bruce. "It was just the surprise of it. No one wants to think they're clumsy." She lied again.

"Are you sure, lass? Because if you are not, this is no light thing you speak of."

"I'm certain as I can be." And she was, certain she had been pushed.

"Then I will give you a chance to tell the Laird yourself. If you don't tell him in good time, then I will. That's my duty."

"Fair's fair." Maggie nodded. She just had to find Eba and the whole matter would be settled.

****

With the quiet at this time of day, he had no trouble moving through the castle ground. Head bent, the kerchief hiding the sides of his face, he shortened his stride rather than get entangled by the volume of fabric. How did women manage? Not that he cared. After today, he wouldn't risk getting caught on the castle grounds. He just wanted to get close enough to see this Maggie MacBede for himself.

He smiled when he pictured her stumbling on the stairs. It hadn't been planned, just being in the right place at the right time and a little shove.

He found the tower of baskets right where the lass said they would be. Good. It was tall enough to hide his face when he moved past the guard to the store rooms. He thought about killing the guard, but that would alert them to his presence, to the chance that he could breach their defenses. He didn't want them to be that wary.

For now, he knew how to get through the caves to the castle. He knew the weaknesses in their defenses. Soon he would come in, with all his men, and take over.

But not now, not yet. He wanted to see the Bold crushed, first. Then Glen Toric would be his.

CHAPTER 6 – ENEMY WITHIN

Bold couldn't find Maggie. Naill and Sim had been spotted riding hard for Glen Toric and he wanted here there, by his side, to greet them. He wanted her with him when he heard their report.

It was his own fault. When Deidre suggested they do their best to ensure his Handfasted enjoyed the MacKays, he never thought they would keep her from him. They played that game last night.

They could not play the game in his chamber. Temptation and caution tangled in the middle of the night. He felt he'd won that round, if sharing a bed was the prize. He still played the price of caution, furthered by watching her slip, naked, from the bed.

Temptation.

Soon, he would make her his wife, but first he had to find out who was working against the clan.

William caught up with him at the bottom of the castle steps. "Is it Naill and Sim, do you think?"

"Aye, and none too soon." He had been waiting for them too long already.

"This is the first you've heard of them since they set off?"

Talorc nodded. Sim, their best tracker, along with Naill, who was a wily fighter, pursued the men who attacked Maggie on the road to Glen Toric.

"I thought we might have lost them." Talorc admitted with a deep sigh. "I was about to send you and Bruce out to look for them."

Bruce strode into the courtyard, as the two weary riders came into sight. Their horses lathered and steaming, the men looked no better. They greeted with familiar grunts, nods, and slaps to the back. The only words spoken were swift and short. "Ayes" in response to Talorc's, "You're faring well?" and then Niall's, "Your Handfasted still stands?"

"She's a harder noggin than that." He gave a curt nod. "But let's get inside. You men have words to give us."

"That we do, laird," Sim shook his head, "and not good ones either."

The riders handed their horses off to a lad, as the five men headed for the keep. By the time they reached the fire, a pitcher of ale and a plate of cheese had been set out on a table. The bustle of the great hall quieted, everyone aware of the riders' importance, though none left. People milled about in small groups, whispering and waiting to hear what was found.

Sim did not so much sit as collapse at the table, his head bowed low. Niall stood to the fire, hands out.

"They know our lands, Laird." Curt and to the point, he didn't look up with the telling. "They led us straight into our own lands, quick as you please. You would have thought they knew the way better than we did."

"They ne'er tried to hide their tracks. Bold as you please, they were. They took us through MacKay land, then turned, like they were going to go to Gunn territory. So we followed."

"Could you name them?"

Niall turned around, used his knife to cut a hunk of cheese. "They're not Gunns, Laird, for they went into Gunn land and played some mischief. We don't know what for sure, but, well . . ."

"They disappeared." Sim finished. "I lost the track because I was distracted, see, by the Gunns, or true Gunns, if you will." He shook his head slowly. "It doesn't make a wee bit of sense, does it? These men played a trick on the Gunns, and then the Gunns retaliated against us."

Talorc held up his hand. "It makes sense, alright. It's the first thing to make sense in these past few years, why the Gunns have been picking fights." He caught the eye of each of his men, as he admitted. "We've not been dealing with the Gunns. They're not the ones who have been playing us false. It's renegades set on causing trouble."

Such a simple thought.

Naill and Sim looked to each other. "But there are so many of them, all together."

"They've no honor," Bruce spit at the ground, "despicable is what they are, too depraved to live with another. How could they band?" Bruce argued.

"Aye," Talorc explained, "their crimes may be inconceivable to us, so despicable we cast them out. But I wonder if they don't boast among each other. Hearts of thieves."

Naill shook his head, "They had naught to lose, but they've always been too busy fighting amongst themselves to be any sizeable threat."

That they banded together to cause mischief was a fearsome thought. Bold thought of the altars, of the way they tried to get Maggie, and scanned the room to see that she was there, that she was safe.

The danger made too much sense. If the renegades had come together, they did so with a strong leader. A man Talorc should have killed himself, rather than ban.

So what had they done, what contemptible act on Gunn land, brought retribution on the MacKays?

"You said retaliation, did you not? What do you mean? What retaliation are you talking about?"

"The one that sent us back here, before tracking those men again."

"So you said, but vengeance for what?"

Both men halted, looked to each other, then at their laird. It was Naill who finally said, "Old Micheil has been taken."

Talorc froze.

"Taken?" Bruce bellowed. "What do you mean, taken?"

"Our whiskey man's been taken and all his supplies, or what they could carry. What they couldn't take," Naill's eyes filled with tears. "They smashed to pieces, Laird. Nothing left of all you planned. Nothing." And he hung his head, as Talorc looked from one man to the other.

"Everything?"

"Aye." Naill acknowledged. "Sim tracked the kidnap, that's why we didna' finish tracking those others. Sim knows where Old Micheil is."

Cold ran down Talorc's spine. Old Micheil kidnapped along with his whiskey making equipment. Not an easy task. The master distiller, and their new scheme, was the most closely guarded secret of the clan.

Stunned, he looked up and there she was, Maggie, at the threshold of the great room, with Deidre's daughter, Eba. He hadn't told her what they were about because he wanted to show her, to take her around the MacKay's land and show her. There had been no time.

Now, their plans had been destroyed. Someone outside of the clan had known where the whiskey man lived and what he was about.

The MacKays were a taciturn lot, stingy with words that needed saying, let alone those forbidden to be said. It was against their nature to share a secret. Kill, thieve, be a scoundrel, yes, but a traitor, never. It was contrary to who they were. Loyalty was taught from birth. A clan was family, their bond meant sustenance for more than food. It was a tightly woven support system. Who would betray that or even want to?

"What about the guards?"

"There was a skirmish, it drew men away." William cursed, but Naill stopped him. "Patrick stayed behind but was overtaken, a rock to his head, much as your Handfasted. He's up and about now and with the others. They're bringing Old Micheil's family to the keep."

Of all his worries, he could never have anticipated this. "For them to learn of Old Micheil, it had to be one of our own."

He searched the room again and found her, his Maggie, standing in the shadows, near enough to have heard what they had said, without knowing the significance of it.

Windblown, she carried fresh air and sunshine. New beginnings, that was what she meant. It was time now, to tell her.

"You wouldn't be knowing." He had to look away, to gather himself for the importance of what he had to say. When he looked back, he wondered if it had been right to wait, to not have told her sooner what she meant to the clan. Just why he pushed so hard to have her with him now, rather than later. "We've been preparing things for trading. It's a new idea, because of you."

"Me?"

"Aye, you." He smiled, for he knew how she would feel about this. "Your brother, your Ian, shared a story about you, for a laugh." He crossed to her, ready to tell her the clan's secret.

"Laughing at me?" She shook her head. "That sounds like any one of my brothers."

"I've come to see that, but they don't laugh at you Maggie, they laugh with the joy of who you are."

She pulled in on herself then, crossing her arms before her. "And what was it they said?"

"Well now, before you hear what it was, you need to know that it was not so funny, as it made good practical sense."

Maggie stood firm. "Go on then, what was he laughing about?"

"Whiskey."

"No surprise there, they are fond of their whiskey."

"And you're full of telling them so."

She snorted. "Waste of time, that."

"And you told them, if they drank less, they could trade what was left and wouldn't have to be raiding and fighting to keep their families alive."

He didn't touch her, just stood close and watched, as countless emotions shifted her features, like clouds across the sky. Her awed, "You're preparing whiskey for trade?" made him feel proud, fueled him with the same excitement the original idea had inspired.

"Aye." He knew his smile was grand, for the idea of it, the pure simple idea of it. "We've been trading whiskey in a small way for the whole of our lives, but the demand has not been so great until now, with Old Micheil. He's the finest whiskey maker in these lands." He rubbed his hands together. "He's the best in the world, and why we haven't thought to pursue trading I canna' tell."

"You're going into business." She couldn't seem to get past the thought. "Why have you not told me of this?"

"It's still early days, Maggie. We don't know if it will work. But we do know it all started with a wee thought from you."

She braced herself against a table. "You've buckled my knees, that you're . . . I mean . . . you wouldn't need to be fighting."

He steadied her, sighed. "Maggie, we aren't there yet. And fighting is something I will have to be about." He was going to tell her that he would be about it soon, this very day, but she didn't give him the chance to finish.

"Because the whiskey maker has been taken and all the supplies you've been setting up?"

"Aye." Talorc took her by the shoulders. "He's been taken, and everything we've been trying to put together has been broken or stolen, but we know where to find him."

"How many know of your plans?"

And that was the worst of it. "Only the closest to me in the clan, Maggie. Only those on the inside."

* * * * * * * * * * * *
* * * *

The Bold turned to his men, as Maggie stepped back into the shadows. Diedre and Ingrid were busy filling the table with more food and pitchers of ale. Maggie should be doing that herself, it was time she got involved, made a place for herself here, but she couldn't move.

He had taken her idea and turned it into reality. Or, at least, he was trying to. He had taken her seriously.

She couldn't stop staring at him. Like a moonstruck lass, she found the line of his cheek, the lay of his hair, the way words formed on his lips, utterly fascinating. Even the bend of his body, as he reached across the table for a hunk of bread, teased her senses.

He believed in her. The idea of it blew away any resistance she concocted. She had lost the fight to be free of him. Had fallen hard for a great big bear of a beast. A beast who could be tender and caring.

That changed nothing, though. He was a fighting man. There would always be call for that. She had to face it, challenge it, or accept it. Like her family, she was prone to fight rather than accept. It didn't bode for a peaceful marriage.

His men talked on top of one another, but not Talorc. He stood still, silent, a warrior steeled and ready for battle. He would have all his senses opened. Aye and he did too, for he turned as though he knew she watched him.

She was selfish enough that she did not want him to go, even as she knew he had no choice, not this time. With his going was the chance he would not return.

She spun away, accepting that which she had promised herself she would never accept. She had given her heart to a fighting man. The fear of it rose to her throat.

Hand shaking, she reached into the pouch at her side and found the packet; a bit of plaid that held soil and heather, a gift from the MacBedes upon her leaving. Her most cherished possession.

"Maggie." He spoke to her. She brushed away tears, not wanting him to see the ridiculous reaction that swallowed her whole. Even when she turned to him, she couldn't respond, couldn't get words past her throat.

Of course he was going. He had to go. That's who he was, what he was, why she loved him. And she did love him. How could she ever have thought she didn't. She was no cuckoo in the nest. She needed a man like those in her family. She knew that now, perhaps had known it all along. He wouldn't have been such a threat otherwise.

Seonaid picked that moment to enter the hall. Sun peaked through the only openings to the outside, slim slits high on the wall. Meager rays caught on the haze caused by fire and torch light. They highlighted her, tall and aloof, as she scanned the room. She drew Talorc's gaze. He called her over, took her arm and led her to a quiet place, away from the others.

Did he trust the woman that much? Did he confide in her when he couldn't even tell Maggie of his plans for trade? Whatever he said angered Seonaid. She yanked her arm from his grasp, backed away, her head shaking back and forth in denial. His response was lost in the distance, but it fueled Seonaid to turn her back on him and run to the kitchen.

Had he accused her of something? Was Seonaid connected to the renegades? Is that where she went when she left the keep?

Trouble usually looked for trouble. At least now there was something Maggie could do. She set out after Seonaid.

CHAPTER 7 – TROUBLE FINDS HER

The kitchen was a bustle of women filling sacks, preparing for the men to ride out. Maggie wasn't certain how the word had gotten to them, but it had. Judging by the concise way they worked, they knew exactly how many were going and that they were leaving quickly.

How was it then, from this experienced kitchen, Talorc and his men had ridden out with tainted food and lost supplies, as they had only a few months before? Could that have been an accident?

Maggie fiddled with the talisman in her pocket. Love him or no, she had to return to the MacBedes one more time. First, though, she had work to do.

A shout came from the back of the kitchen, a dark corner. Seonaid held Deidre's arms as they quarreled. Other than the one shout, their voices were low, urgent hushed whispers. Still, there was no mistaking the sharp hand movements, the deep frowns, the bits of strident argument.

Busy as the kitchen was, the women gave the quarrelers a wide berth, though no one shied from glancing their way. Eyes rolled when they took their fight to the outdoors.

Maggie wove through the bustle of preparation, down the stairs and out a far door to a courtyard. It was empty.

At a tug of her skirt, she found Eba pointing toward a small mound. "The guard is following her." The lass whispered. "In the cellars. They go all the way to the center of the earth, where great hungry monsters live."

following her Of course, she meant them or her mother but a child doesn't always know which words to choose.

In the caves? Maggie shuddered. Diedre told her about the caves beneath the castle. "Great monsters?" She asked, as they circled to the mound to find a short flight of stairs down to a small door. She could wait for the guard to return.

If that's who he was following. There'd been no time for the two women to move out of sight in any other direction.

She had to find out. Maggie took a step down. Eba held back. "I don't like it in there."

"No need for you to come, Eba. Go on back into the kitchens." She directed, doubting she would like the place herself. Cellars were dark places and Maggie did not like the dark.

Prepared for the worst, she was surprised to find the space lit. A lantern fitted into the wall beside the door, which meant someone was in there.

She stood for a moment, becoming familiar with the chamber, listening.

Caves they may be, but much the same as the storehouses at home. Built below the surface of the ground, they held a steady temperature, perfect for keeping foods fresh.

Like the ones at home, from the outside no more than small mound. Unlike home, this storage area was cavernous with endless rows of goods on shelves, huge barrels lined a rack as sacks, bulging with grain, hung from the ceiling. More food than her clan could eat in years carried on beyond the meager light of the lamp.

Maggie saw a halo of light at the end of the first row of shelves. It illuminated a second doorway.

"Mother of God," she whispered. "Do I really need to go there?" A wasted prayer, for she knew she had to, knew she had to see who moved beyond this great store room.

Caves, dark places, bats and rodents and deep crevices. Nightmares were tamer than this adventure.

Baskets of root vegetables on her left, the wall to her right, Maggie edged through the room, scanned the shadows and the looming dark deeper in the yawning cavity. This was a foolish venture, for sure. The women were merely on an errand and would return soon. Or the guard would bring them back.

On the verge of convincing herself of this, the light that drew her flickered and shifted, dimming as it moved beyond the dark mouth of the second door. Maggie hurried to catch-up.

One step over the threshold of the second room, smacked her with the scent of smoke. It had been there all along, she realized, only now it enveloped her. Some great ox of a person stood between her and the glow of the lamp.

Heart beating a vicious tattoo in her chest, she reached out and grabbed the shadowy figure. Not an ox nor a man, or even a woman. It was a ham. She had moved into a

smoke house or, at the least, the chamber
where the meats were stored.

"Oh Lord," she prayed to herself.
"What have I gotten myself into?" She was
too far to turn back. What little light
remained was moving swiftly away.

Between either, the light at the entrance
and the one carried further on, a hole of
blackness threatened. Maggie shouted for
Deidre, certain she would help, just as the
torch light in front, went out. Her call echoed
back, shuddering through the silence.

This was no mere storehouse. These
were caves that ran forever beneath the keep.

"Seonaid?" Maggie called for help
once more, but even to her own ears it was a
weak attempt. There was nothing for it but to
head back, use the same grounding touch she
had used to get this far. Except she had left
the wall when she raced after the dimming
light. With relief, she saw the way back was
still illuminated.

As quickly as the thought flickered
through her mind, hairs rose on the back of
her neck.

The door to the smoke room slammed
shut.

She didn't like the dark.

An icy stream of fear ran down her
back. Rigid, she searched the black before
her. There were no shadows to run from, no
sounds to alarm, but still, she conjured a
million ways to die a horrible death in this
place.

These caves were the pride of Glen
Toric, a perfect defense against thieves. Ideal
for storing foods but dangerous for the
uninitiated. Deep crevasses, soft ground,
endless tunnels to get lost in, threats enough
when one had light.

"Don't be foolish." She admonished herself. "There's naught to fear." That door would have been weighted to swing shut just as the great door had been. Focused on the only thing she had to do, which was get back to the first chamber, she used the cured meat as a guide.

Despite the self-chastisement, her hand shook, as she reached for the first haunch of meat, calmed as she realized the wall was next to it. She followed that, sliding a foot in front to ensure solid ground would meet her step.

Progress was far slower on the return, but at least it was progress and she did reach the doorway. It was long and narrow. It was also lodged firmly into place. Hard as she tried, the latch refused to lift.

Holding panic at bay, despite a dark heavy as pitch, she felt around the rough opening to see which side the hinges were on, whether the door needed a push or pull to open. They were on the other side. It was easier to push at a door than to pull on a lever that was no more than a simple wooden doll.

That great ham, she had once thought an ox, was too close to give her any room to maneuver. Still, she tried to push, tried to force the door by slamming her weight against it. If only the ham hadn't been in the way. She jiggled and cajoled the latch, but it didn't give. Exhausted, she slid down the wall of wood, used her feet to push at the offending meat.

The ham swung right back, knocking her head against the oak planes of the door, nearly breaking her nose with the mass of it. She could swear she heard Ian's laughter with the ringing of her head.

"It's not funny!" She snapped.

Aye, it's funny, but not so funny as you not seeing what's in front of you!

Maggie stilled, no longer aware of the darkness, no longer frantic to escape, or too exhausted to do anything about it. This time, when she shoved at the huge hunk of meat, she moved out of its way. Certain enough, she felt the air move as it countered the swing, coming back. The door creaked, the hinges rattled.

With no thought but freedom, Maggie moved down the line of hams, setting them swinging on their hooks, one after another until she reached the last one. This one she pulled back, held it as high as she could, then let it go to ram into the already moving line, forcing them to careen hard against the door.

The first effort echoed a thundering shake of the portal but not enough to break through. Determined, she tried again and again, willing the wood to weaken, to crack, to break the hardware locked in place. To do anything to offer hope.

* * * * * * * * * * * * * *

His men were mounted, the horses restless. At the very least, Talorc thought Maggie would see him off. He had expected that much, especially now that she knew what he was about. But something had her running off to the kitchens and he had a good idea what it was.

Talking to Seonaid had seemed right at the time. Would have been if Maggie knew the full situation, but Maggie didn't. Nobody knew and he couldn't tell them, even though it had so much to do with what was happening.

He needed Maggie to trust him. If she
didn't, then he would have to live with the
consequences. If she didn't want to be there
for his departure, he wouldn't lower himself
to ask where she was.

One more time he would check their
supplies and then, Maggie or not, he would be
gone.

She still hadn't come by the time he
was astride, too much time wasted. Everyone
was ready, waiting on him. He raised his arm
in a final wave, opened his mouth to signal
their departure, when another shout stopped
him.

He reared his horse in the effort to turn
toward the caller who ran toward him, her
clothes askew, her hair a tangle.

"Stop Bold." She shouted. "You just
wait now."

He couldn't have moved if he wanted
to. She was coming to him, all mussed from
some adventure, but she was coming and of
her own free will.

When she reached his horse, she bent
over, hands on her knees, heaving for breath.
Some kind of dust covered her from top to
tail. An aroma of cured meats rose from her.

"What is it, lass?" He dismounted,
alarmed now that he realized she wasn't
disheveled from play.

"Got myself locked in the meat room."
There was a hiccup of fear in her laughter.
Hand shaking, she pulled tangled hair from
her face. "And I wasn't afraid of the dark."
She tried to chuckle despite the edge of tears
he was certain she fought.

"Who let you out?"

She stilled at that, turning as though
searching the crowd gathered. There was no
hint of humor left when she looked back at

him. "I got myself out, but I'm afraid I've broken the door."

William joined them. "You had to break the door? It's stout for a lass."

"I swung the meat. The weight of it pushed the moorings out."

"Wait," Talorc held up his hand. "You were locked in the caves? And just how did that happen?"

"A prank, that's all. But I got out. That's all that matters."

He put a finger to her cheek and brushed off the dirt, meat cure. A prank, she'd said. Locking her in the caves, in the dark which she hated. A prank. Fury rose in his throat, capped by William's hand on his arm and a quiet, "steady now."

That stopped him from reacting too swiftly, except for pulling Maggie into him. She was safe. That was the most important thing. He bent his head to hers, smelled sulfur in her hair. She was safe.

And William was right. If this was not a prank, Maggie was in danger. It would be better to convince the culprit that they had no worries.

Reluctantly, Talorc let her go, holding up a warning finger. "Don't you move anywhere. Do you hear? You stay right there."

He took William's arm as they moved aside, where no one could overhear their lowered voices.

"No, Bold," Maggie argued, and reached out to stop him.

"I'm not leaving you Maggie. Just give us a moment."

"No," she shook her head, a bit frantic. She looked more frightened now than when she'd spoken of the dark. "Here," she thrust something at him. Startled he took it as she said. "You have to go. It's who you are, what you are. But I'm wishing you a safe return.

She adjusted her skewed kirtle. "I just want to make sure you know what you go for."

That's when he looked down and realized what she had placed in his hand. "For the land, for the name, and for the wild glory of both." It was a hoarse whisper. He knew how much this little square of plaid meant to her. He had seen the tears in her eyes when her people gave it to her. He saw how she pulled it out and rubbed it when she fretted over something.

By the time he gathered himself together, to give her thanks, she was running to the keep, away from him.

Would he ever understand this woman?

"Bold," William pulled him aside. "We've no' much time, but no one locks anyone in the caves."

"Where was the guard?"

William shook his head. He didn't know, not yet, but they would.

Maggie had been alone when she had come to him. Where were the friends she had made? Where was Deidre?

William continued. "You need to put a guard on her. Put extra patrols on the comings and goings of the keep."

It was worse than that. Talorc rubbed at his side, the injury that had only just healed. "It's not someone from the outside William. Do you not get that? It has to be someone who's close to us, calls the keep their home. It's a friend, William, it's family."

Bruce joined them. "Bold, there's something you should know. This morning, when she looked for Eba, your handfasted tripped on the stairs from the castle."

"The outer stairs?"

"Aye, only now I believe her, where before I couldn't. It didn't seem possible, but she didn't trip, she was pushed."

CHAPTER 8 – A LAIRD'S WIFE

The dark loomed, the fireplace banked to barely a glow and Brutus, that great beast of a dog, made the most horrid of sounds. Maggie was not frightened. She had her two protectors, Gerta and Caitrina. The whiskey man's wife and daughter who had come to the keep for safety. They had arrived as Talorc and his men were setting out.

She wished he hadn't, but Talorc explained to the mother and daughter that Maggie did not like the night. Not only had they insisted on sleeping with her, they made sure she had the middle. Talorc would owe her for this, having her squashed between an old woman who made noises Brutus could be proud of, and her daughter, who continuously puffed the covers with hot wind.

There would be no cabbage in tomorrow's dinner. Not that it wasn't too late already. The bed would never be the same.

Maggie scowled and rolled to face Gerta, only to be poked by straw coming through the mattress. She shifted, fidgeted, and tried to focus on something other than her sleeping companions.

There certainly was enough on her mind for, thanks to the Bold's belief in her, she had found her calling. She hadn't known, hadn't realized what her mother had always known.

Maggie had been prepared for this moment from the day she had been born.

Maggie knew how to organize, dictate and turn ideas into reality, and she was doing just that with all but one plan. Not that she had time to do any more than had already been set in motion, but her one scheme was essential to the clan's benefit. It was a gift she could give to The Bold.

Unfortunately, he banned anyone from leaving the castle and set a guard on Maggie herself; so, her most important task would have to wait.

In the meantime, she had an army of MacKays to accomplish an almost overwhelming load of work. In that case, Talorc's ban worked in her favor. Just as he forbade anyone to leave the castle, he had ordered crofters to move inside the grounds. There were some who would have preferred the risk of attack rather than face Maggie's demands.

The first project was inspired by huge sacks of fleece confiscated in the last raids.

"Whiskey isn't the only thing you can trade." Maggie told the women, "But you'll need more spun wool than you can produce with hand spindles."

She rounded up the woodworkers and a few young lads to help, and set them to building spinning wheels to be followed by enough looms to fill the long shed behind the castle. "If you do several of each piece, as you go, then you don't have to stop and change tools as often." She explained and left them with the promise that the Bold would be well pleased if they had accomplished their work before his return.

If he returned. The fear haunted, but it was a familiar fear. She knew how to live with the nag of it.

While the men were busy with sawing and sanding, she set the women to work in the weaving sheds. Those best at spinning spent their days there. The dyers worked in another out building, coloring the wool as quickly as those who had an eye for design could come up with patterns, for they didn't care to have others wear the MacKay plaid.

She'd set a batch of women to string what looms were available. Everyone took turns between everyday chores and working in the weaving, spinning and dying sheds, while the older children kept an eye on the younger babes.

The castle bustled with happy excitement and purpose. But it was not enough.

Talorc warned her the household had been without personal care for too long. He had spoken true. One snap of a tapestry corner produced a cloud that had her coughing for the rest of the day.

Fair enough, the women were busy so she went to the men, surprising their wives and mothers in her ability to get men to clear the floor of thrushes, gather more, remove the tapestries from the walls. "Far too high for a lass," one man explained. And used their might to swat the dirt from them "Sturdy lasses as we have in the MacKay's, they've no arm for this."

They didn't scrub the floors, but once Maggie was down on her knees, bucket and scrub brush in hand, women came to join her.

With the help of dozens of children, on a lone, hard fought for, adventure beyond the walls of the castle, Maggie managed to gather of fresh flooring.

She took account of the furniture, noted what needed fixing and made a list of new pieces to be made. Once the woodworkers were done with the spinning wheels and looms, they would get to that.

It seemed as though the men were gone forever, as there was even time to brush out the fireplaces and free the chimneys of soot. Outbuilding roofs were checked for leaks and a passel of boys were hard at work mending what they could. It was too late in the season to thatch, but they would be prepared for spring.

But what, of the numerous tasks, should she attack next? Clearing out the kitchen storage? She was determined to return to those caves, except Talorc had them closed off. No one could enter without a guarded escort. Not that the area was quiet. She had seen soldiers going in with torches. Searching, she figured, looking to see if an attack could come from there.

He prepared for a full attack, brought the crofters inside the walls, his men busy searching for weak points.. So far, other than the attack in the woods, the enemy had used stealth, setting one clan against each other. The Bold would be wise to meet with the Gunns, to put aside their differences.

The Gunns were not at fault. If Anabal hadn't died, all the losses, all the battles, could have been averted because the two clans would have communicated.

Anabal. Talorc's late wife, God rest her soul. Not a woman Maggie cared to think about, hadn't thought about her in days. Just the idea of her conjured images. Fragile and fair, that's what she had been. Maggie knew

226

this because she had asked. Beathag thrilled to talk about 'her' Anabal, the perfect lady, who never dirtied herself with chores.

Not like Maggie did.

Anabal had been beautiful, winsome, and petite. Gerta snorted that she was no more than another useless Gunn, but then Gerta was proving to be fiercely loyal to Maggie. The question rising was whether Talorc had adored the woman, loved her? Their relations had been fruitful, produced a bairn. Bless his soul and all.

Anabal.

Talorc would have kissed her, wrapped her in his arms, pressed their bodies together.

Maggie froze. Couldn't breathe.

He would have mated with the other woman. . . . in . . . . this . . . . bed!

Maggie muffled a scream, kicked her way from under the covers, and scurried out and down the mattress.

"What . . . huh?" Both Gerta and Caitrina looked at Maggie, who had leapt off the end of the bed, to land right next to Brutus' head. The dog jumped and barked, the hair on the back of his neck bristling at the unknown danger. The door flew open and a sleepy eyed guard ran into the room, his dagger out and ready to defend.

A guard at all times was a nuisance. Especially now. She blinked. Thankful she wore a shift to bed.

She cleared her throat. Everyone stared at her. "I . . . I just couldna' sleep."

"Me either," Gerta hefted a hearty sigh, "It's worrying about our men folk."

It was Maggie's turn to stare. Gray hair disheveled, lines from the pillow creased Gerta's cheek, her eyes heavy with sleep.

"It's near enough to dawn." Caitrina
offered. "We might as well get up now."

"Aye," Maggie lied, "that's all I was
doing. Rising for the day." The guard nodded,
yawned broadly and backed out of the room,
as Maggie added, "I have a task for us to work
on today."

Caitrina sighed, "As you always do."

"Of course," Maggie frowned, "There's
much to do to run a keep."

"Then I'll stick to my crofter's cottage,
thank you very much." Gerta snorted. "What
is it this time?"

"The beds." She rushed out. "We need
to freshen up the beds before winter." The
kitchen could wait.

The women looked at each other.

Maggie moved up and ripped the covers
from the mattress. "Empty the mattresses, toss
the old filling, and scrub the ticking. The beds
will smell sweet with new fill. We can wash
the blankets as well. If it's as sunny today as
it was yesterday, they'll dry in no time."

"There are plenty of beds and pallets in
this keep."

"Aye, and my guess is they haven't been
cleaned and aired since Talorc's mother was
alive."

Gerta humphed. "You would probably
be right in that. They've probably just put
more straw and heather in, without changing
what was there."

"Ooohhhh!" Caitrina scooted away from
the bed. "There must be a thousand bugs in
that thing!" she started to scratch, as if the
mention of the critters caused the bite.

"Aye," Gerta agreed.

"We'll start with this one." Maggie
didn't wait for their help before she stripped
the mattress from the frame.

CHAPTER 9 – DECISIONS MADE

The Bold was back.

Unnerved by his presence in the chamber, Maggie pulled a cover about her and rose to open the shutters and look at the courtyard below. A feathery carpet covered the ground that would soon turn to slush, melt in the warmth of an autumn day. Harmless in itself, it signaled heavier snows to come.

Her chance of leaving was slipping away and she so desperately needed to go, to see her family, to follow a plan she was determined to see through.

Talorc returned last night with a swooping kiss for Maggie, a dizzying spin in his arms, and a tale that had kept the whole of the clan mesmerized. There had been a battle, the sorrow of a man lost, but they had freed the whiskey maker and the tools of his trade, at least those that hadn't been destroyed.

And he'd returned with two of her brothers.

James and Douglas, the two who had no wives or families to leave behind, had come to see how Maggie fared. They said their mother fretted for news of her. But, of course, the fight had to come first.

They were riding straight for Glen Toric when they found The Bold riding out to fetch Old Micheil. They rode with him rather

than go to the MacKay keep to see their baby
sister.

She braced herself on the window sill,
filled her lungs with the cool air.

They cared little for Maggie's request to
go home. Quiet requests, private, gained when
she cornered each, as they left the hall as men
will do when they've been drinking pots of
ale.

"Och, Maggie, give a man some peace."
Douglas had groused.

"But I can't speak freely in there."

That caught his attention.

"Why not, Maggie? From what I see,
you're treated better here than at home. And
you've got the run of the place. Look what
you've done." He'd looked amazed. "The
Bold sees the changes you've made with more
pride than he sees his own success. You're a
true Laird's wife, what you were raised to be."

"I'm not his wife."

He laughed, like all men do over shared
secrets no woman would understand. "Not yet,
you're not. But it won't be long now." And he
walked away, as if any plea she would make
was worthless.

Everyone believed Talorc would have
his way, and he would. Not even she could
deny that. But she had to make him wait, until
she was settled in herself. Then she would
become his wife. After she went home.

There was only one option left. She
would get a note to her mother. Her ma had
been fretting. If Maggie could make her fret
enough, her ma would send for her.

She had to.

Before there were any more kisses or
touches.

She closed her eyes, willed herself to
forget them. Even as she tried, memories

seeped through her body, her mind's eye picturing his great broad hand roaming over her flesh. She believed him when he said that, should they mate, she would never be the same.

She had to go. Frantic, she looked about, as if to find escape within the chamber, then stilled. Time. That's all she wanted. Time to say good-bye to her people. Time for the Bold to realize he wanted her as she was, or he didn't want her at all.

Travel was still possible. The snow from the night was so light it didn't even hide the charred remains of the bonfire that had been lit for Samhain. Samhain. The night she missed. A night she had waited for from the moment she knew of young Ian's death. There would have been costumes, laughter and a wee bit of fear. The night would have been full of ghosts. She had counted on that, waited and waited for it. She had promised Ian.

Ian . . . Ian and a child. She blinked, as if to switch her mind to another time. She had seen them, or dreamt of them. Ian had spoken to her of a child, a young Ian, who was similar and yet, different, than the brother Maggie remembered.

". . . time for those who have passed on, and time for those to be born . . ." Ian had promised to take care of the babe.

"It was our babe. Who else would pass that child on to you, Maggie, but Ian?"

She twisted around, to see where Talorc lay, deep in sleep. Once she was with child, there would be no travel, no going home to see her own people. Between carrying a child, nursing a child and conceiving another, it could be years before she ever left Glen Toric.

She needed to go home, now.

Again, she looked to the huge man, fast asleep upon the floor. The hound's great, square head was up, eyes focused on Maggie. Lazily, Brutus shifted, rose from the hearth, brushed up against her leg and stopped, to lean against her his head high enough that she could run a hand over it without bending. She scratched behind his ears, smiled as his back foot thumped in time with the caress. He leaned so hard she had to brace herself. Somehow it managed to make her feel better, enough that she scrunched down beside him, to hold that massive noggin against her, stroke his long silky ears.

"You're a great beast, just like your owner."

"I'm not such a beast." Talorc argued. Both Maggie and the dog spun about to see him still lying there, eyes closed.

"You are to me." She stood, let the dog abandon her for the man. It was just as well.

Talorc stretched and sputtered against the dog's eager licks. When he'd brushed Brutus aside, he opened his eyes to see Maggie, wrapped in an old blanket, the sunrise to her back. She was tall and disheveled and utterly delectable.

"How old are you now, Maggie?"

"Oh Bold," she gave a mock sigh, "What kind of man are you, to take on a lass before you even know her age?"

"Twenty."

"I was."

"Twenty-one then?"

"What's the day?"

"You've been with me for near on a month."

"November's nearly gone?"

"Aye."

232

"Then I'm twenty-one."

He thought about what she was saying. Just twenty-one. Twenty when they met. He'd been so busy getting her to join him, taking her away from her home, that he'd never thought of her age, or when it would change.

"You're a woman, fully grown." He couldn't think of much else to say. He certainly wasn't about to make apologies. There was no stopping with those. "Time you're married, with a family, Maggie."

She looked down, then away and he realized he'd hit a tender spot. She'd have been miserable with the tailor, or the bard. Talorc knew it, deep in his bones. The good Lord hadn't saved her for him by mere accident. Any other lass, as special as his Maggie, would have been married by the time she was nineteen. But not this one. She was meant to be a MacKay, the Laird's wife. She was meant to be his.

"What makes you so sad, girl."

She leaned out, over the window sill, her face to the freshness of the outdoors.

"Do you think the child was yours, Talorc?"

He stilled. Wondered which child she meant, and could only think of one. Someone had told her about Seonaid's lad. Silence was not easily won within his keep.

"Child?" he would let her clarify.

She frowned, as though he had disappointed her by not knowing what she meant.

"The one Ian held."

He rose, wrapped his plaid around his waist slowly while the punch of her words settled. Even the thought of the bairn and his body stirred for the making.

A child.

Their child.

"Aye." He told her and crossed to where she stood within the room, with him, yet so terribly alone. "Give us a chance, Maggie. You will see." He placed his hands on her shoulders, his lips to her hair. She smelled of the outdoors and woman. A combination that completed the rearing of his manhood and near buckled his knees.

"Don't, Talorc." She tried to pull away, and, though he lightened his hold, he did not release her. "You do not like my touch?" He rubbed his hands along her arms, to soothe, but she stiffened. This was not like his Maggie. He tried again, one last effort. "My lips against you?" He bent to her neck, where he nuzzled her with warm breath, and butterfly kisses. She whimpered, he heard it even as she tried to stifle the sound. She trembled. His head came up, to see what was in her eyes.

Tears. He released her.

"Is my touch that bad that it brings you to tears?" Instead of answering she reached up, wound her arms around his neck and, with a wobbly voice, ordered, "Kiss me, Talorc. Just this once."

He clasped her head, looked straight into eyes green as spring leaves, and just as damp. He could barely breathe. "Are you sure, Maggie?"

She sniffled, nodded. "Just this once. I need you . . ."

He didn't understand the stricture, on last time, but there was no waiting for her to explain. He wanted to go slow, to ease and woo, but her confession slayed his intentions. He crushed her, his lips hungry and urgent on hers.

She wanted him. She didna' want to, but she wanted him. Needed him. The proof was in the way she matched his hunger, met the fever of his kisses. She did this every time they came together, from inexperienced maiden, she flamed to temptress. Without taking his lips from hers, he reached down and caught her behind the knees, to lift her to his chest. She angled her body toward him, her breast crushed to his.

As he crossed to the bed, he released her lips, nudging the blanket from her breast to greedily suckle her. She cried out, startled, stunned as he laid her on the bed, careful not to put his full weight on her. She pulled at him anyway, as though she welcomed it, as if she could not get enough of him. Her back arched, her breast raised for better access.

Oh, Lord, her impulses played havoc with his intentions. If she was hungry for his suckle, he would give it to her. In age old rhythm, her hips moved against him, he added his own measure, lifted enough to look at her eyes glazed with passion, her body a ripe offering. He groaned.

"Why, Talorc?" she breathed, more than spoke. "Why do ya' make me feel like this?"

"Because you're mine, and your body knows it, even if you don't."

"No, I'm not yours. Not yet, anyhow." Her eyes cleared. Desperate to distract, he urged his hardness against that soft apex he craved and watched as her head bowed back. A soft moan left her lips. "Oh Talorc, you make me . . ."

"I make you mine."

He should have kept his mouth shut. Even before the words were uttered, she was fighting the haze of sensuality.

"Not now," she argued, "I'm not ready to be yours."

"You can't fight it Maggie." She tried anyway, tried to push him off of her, but he held her still, just long enough to say, "It's good for the clans. It's what your body wants, I want. Accept it Maggie. We are meant to be."

"No," she rolled away, off the bed, to tug at the blanket, pinned beneath him.

He let it go, watched as she wrapped it securely about herself. Her breasts now flattened and hidden. He tried not to moan as he got off the bed.

Timing was everything.

"Maggie, you are fighting a losing battle. You want me as desperately. . "

She didn't let him finish, didn't let him calm the way, before she turned on him, shoved at his chest.

"All fine and dandy for you!" She ranted, her passion turned to anger. "You're preparing for a war. What happens when you don't come home from the fight? What happens when the likes of Seonaid make promises of sweetness to you, when you have a wife as tart as sour apples? Will you be true to me, then? In your heart?"

"Don't bring Seonaid into this. She's naught to do with us!" He would have to tell her about Seonaid, claims that her child was his, but not now, not yet. Maggie was too upset to give him the chance.

"Seonaid, battles, whatever. You have all manner of mistresses! What happens if one of those becomes spiteful? What happens if the battle turns against you? Sends you to the otherworld?"

She stopped, glared at him, as though her fears were already truth. "You'll be fine

236

and dandy in your celestial home, but what of me? Left all alone with no chance to meet another that compares with you. Left to raise a small tyke who will grow up to be just like his father? Another warrior to desert me." She took a breath, her hands at her blanket. "And don't go telling me that he won't grow up to be just like you, because he will, just as my brothers grew up to be like my da. Just like you grew up to be like the great warrior whose seed you carry. He'll grow up to go out and fight and leave his mother broken with pain."

When she shoved past him, he was too stunned to stop her. She stormed through the room, tossed down the blanket and whipped a kirtle over her head, settled it to all the curves he craved to caress. He watched as she wrapped a plaid about herself, a MacBede plaid, no thanks to her brothers. That was all he needed now. A fine reminder that she was not his. Not yet.

She tossed one last glare his way before she stormed out the door. Where ever she thought to go, he hadna' clue, but he'd leave her to it.

Aye, she'd lost one brother. One brother out of seven. Her da was still alive, just as the father of their children would stay alive. Talorc would see to it.

But she needed to do her fuming. He understood that, too. She needed to run around and around in her mind, until she was worn weary of the thoughts. Then she would settle in with him, accept the inevitable.

He hoped it would happen quickly. He didn't know if he could stand the wait. He looked at the puddle of blankets on the floor. They'd come so close to being man and wife.

If only he'd kept his mouth closed.

* * * * * * * * * *

Mother, Maggie wrote, then stopped.
She had to be very careful with the way she
phrased her life at Glen Toric. If she told her
mother that she was well, that Talorc treated
her with respect and honor, she would be
there for the rest of her life.

If she told her mother that the people of
Glen Toric looked up to her, saw her as a
great and wise woman, her mother would
never believe it.

But she would want to.

Mother . . . Maggie began again, the
point of the quill on the parchment. She
pressed, as though that would bring words to
her mind. No cohesive thought came. She
lifted the pen tip. A large drop of black ink
marked her lack of inspiration.

Maggie dabbed the pen against the
blotter, as she thought. She hated to waste a
whole piece of parchment for one slight
mistake. Unable to look at it, she turned
aside, her eyes narrowed with thought.
Nothing. All she could think about was the
black mark and the pitcher of water beside the
basin at the end of the table that was straight
in her line of sight.

She shot a glance at the small wet dab
of ink on her paper.

With an air of innocence, though who
she tried to fool she couldna' tell, for no one
else was in the room, she crossed to the
pitcher of water, stuck her finger in and came
out with a wetted tip. Carefully, she held her
finger upright, with the drop of water on it, as
she walked back to the parchment.

Paper held at an angle, one flick and
her stain became a spilled tear.

Hah! She blew, sanded, then waved the paper until it was good and dry and wouldn't run anymore. She set to her task with fresh enthusiasm.

> *Mother,*
> *May this find you strong and well. My brothers will tell you that I am up and about, no thanks to the rock to my head. It happened on the way to Glen Toric, after I mortally wounded one of the attacking Gunns. It was my first time in battle. While my soul does shudder from the memory, the Laird MacKay is quite proud. I think he means for me to join him in all future battles. To his mind, I am a strong and able soldier.*
> *Strong warrior lass or no, I was felled, down for three days and four nights. The clan MacKay thought the Gunns had killed me. But my head can take a stronger bruising than that.*
> *The worst of it was, young Ian came to me in my dreams, but the MacKay would not let me go to him, so I have no message for you from that quarter.*

She would not tell her ma about the wee boy. There was no guarantee that it was Talorc's. She would not encourage her mother to have such thoughts.

Maggie bent back to her writing.

> *My head is mending, the headaches are less severe. The women help to ease my work, especially a woman called Seonaid, so I don't suffer too terribly... They all say she had no*

*reason to believe the Bold would marry
her. The two are quite close, you see,
but he is determined to sacrifice himself
for his people, just as he did with his
first marriage. It saddens my heart to
know that I keep the two of them apart.
She is ever so full of emotion when she
sees me.*

*There is talk that he murdered his
late wife.*

*But I am fine. Give my love to our
Laird, my father, and to all the others.
It was good to see the brothers. As you
have taught me, I do not let on that my
heart is broken with missing my own.
Nor do I allow the brothers to witness
the odd way the MacKays treat me. (Do
you think it is because of this Seonaid
woman?) I will keep my silence, so our
men will not fret. They do not have the
strength in such things that we women
have.*

*Please, if there is ever any
problem at home, write. I will come to
you as swift as a sparrow. If not, I fear
Glen Toric is my judgment.*

*With all my heart,
Your Loving daughter
Maggie MacBede*

It was a fair bending of the truth, but
she was that desperate.

With quick movements she sanded,
blotted and folded the letter, top to bottom
and side to middle, then sealed it with the
mark of her broach. The MacBede marking.

With a deep breath, she stood, stuffed
the letter in the cross of her plaid, and headed
to the front of the keep where her brothers
prepared to leave. With this missive, she

would wish them God Speed and hope they returned quickly, before the snow.

She got to the top of the stairs and stopped. If she was writing letters, it meant her brothers were truly leaving. She would miss them, terribly. But they would be back soon. Jamie had, after all, taken a fancy to Lizbeth.

They would be back.

She hated goodbyes. Hated leave takings with all that standing about, watching, trying to find just the right parting words when none would do.

She dawdled, as if that would keep them there longer, or give her the strength she needed not to cry with their departure. She went to the kitchen to ask Eilinor for something special to send with them.

Then she stopped in the great hall, to have a chat with Eba.

When she finally reached the great doors, she saw Mary move toward Douglas with yearning eyes. Too shy, she turned away, hurried up the steps, her head bowed. She had a piece of MacKay Plaid made into a small packet. She nearly ran into Maggie.

"Oh." She whispered.

Maggie nodded toward her hand.

"For your brothers. I thought they might want a parcel with MacKay soil and heather. They can keep the two together, MacKay and MacBede, for added strength."

Gently, Maggie took the packet, rubbed the weave of it. "They're very fine, so soft. Did you weave it yourself?" Mary was one of the girls assigned to the weaving room.

"Aye, spun the wool as well."

"It must be the wool from a kid. It's too soft for anything else."

Mary looked uncertain. "Is that not what you do?"

Maggie laughed, "I'm no dab hand at spinning and weaving. Mine were just scraps of cloth, not so fine as this. They will be honored, Mary. They will gladly carry this with them." She had to fight to get the words past her throat. She would have to have a word with Douglas. Tell him to look at the obvious. He could do worse than Mary, and probably no better.

When she finally made it down the keep steps, the MacBede men were already mounted. Her delay was meant to make them stay longer, perhaps another day. Instead, she realized they would have left without any good- bye at all.

"Where've you been, Maggie girl?" Jamie called out.

"Do you care? You are ready to ride out without so much as a farewell."

"Thought it was you, not wanting to say your good-byes, you took so long."

She tilted her head up, held her tears back. "That's what you know of things. I've been so long because I went to get sweet cakes for the journey."

"Aye, so did Lizbeth." Jamie smiled down at the woman who stood by his horse. "You women will get us fat."

"You're certain you won't stay for the winter?" Talorc offered, as he'd done the night before.

Maggie frowned. If they stayed, she could not return to The MacBede Keep before spring. That would be too late. They had to go, and quickly.

"My mother will fret if they don't return soon."

"Getting rid of us, sister?" Douglas shouted out.

"Aye, I have my pride to carry. Don't want you to spoil that with foolish tales of when I was young."

They both barked with laughter. "They've heard the stories, Maggie. We didn't cut our visit that short."

"Come, little sister, give your old brother a fond farewell." Jamie called out.

They were really, truly leaving, and if her missive didn't send them straight back, she may not see them again for . . . it could be years.

Push-pull. She wanted them to leave. She did not want them to leave.

"Jamie," she came up close, clasped his hand. "I've a letter for ma, could you see that she gets it."

"Aye, lass. She'd be wanting one and all."

"And," she rushed over to Douglas, afraid that tears would start to run down her face. "Mary made these for the both of you." She handed out the packets, which the men clutched tight, before stuffing them inside the cross of their plaid.

"Mary?" Douglas called out.

"Here," she waved from the top of the stairs.

"You're a fine woman. We'll be proud to carry your reminder of the MacKays! Keep our sister dear."

That was it. Those were their last words. They, each in turn, eased their horses over to Maggie, bent for a brief, close hug. They kissed the top of her head, ruffled her hair with raised brows toward the MacKay, as if to say it was about time their sister wore a kerchief.

Off they shot then, through the bailey, and into the MacKay wilderness.

They were gone so quick, that it was beyond reality for Maggie. She stared at the path they took, wondering what kind of fool she had been to take so long to offer her parting. She should have rushed out, first thing, begged them to take her with them.

She put her fingers to her mouth, sniffled, but refused to cry.

Eight days, fortnight at most, and they would be back.

Talorc put his arm around her, squeezed, but she pulled away.

"I should have left with them, you know."

She took a step toward the keep, but he stopped her, his hand to her chin, forcing her around to face him. "No, I don't know."

"They are my family."

"And so are we."

She shook her head. "No, Bold, you are my friend. They are my family."

"Maggie," but he didn't continue. Instead he took her arm. His hold firm, determined. She had no choice but to follow his lead, beyond the others, across the courtyard, to the nearest barn. "Give us space, Domnall." He said to the lad cleaning the stalls. Domnall asked no questions, just put down his pitch fork and scurried out.

Maggie still at his side, Talorc stood silent, as the barn door closed behind the young man, then he pulled Maggie around and straight into his arms.

CHAPTER 10 – VOWS

The rich sweet scent of hay and oiled leather softened the heavy smell of sweat and horse droppings. Maggie jerked free of Talorc, not realizing how much she needed the support. Unsteady, she leaned against the wall, refusing to look at him. Instead, she studied beams of light that filtered between sod roof and stone wall, watched the dance of chaff floating in that sparse light, and fought against tears.

"You're expected to miss them, you know. No one would think unkindly of that."

She shoved off the stone wall, her arms crossed against a belly so full of emotion she was afraid of exploding.

"They're fine men, Maggie. The MacBedes are a fine line. I'll be proud to mix our bloods."

She snorted.

"And what was that for?" He reached, but she pulled away.

"Is this because of what came between us? Are you afraid of my touch?"

She refused to answer, she couldn't. It would only open the door to a flood of rash words flung to hurt. The tumble would reveal Maggie's own weakness, perhaps even confess a missive just sent.

"Maggie," one word, heavy with weariness. "Do you really think the tailor would have suited you? Or any of the others? Do you really think, if the Good Lord had wanted you to go that route, you wouldn't already be there? Did it ever occur to you, that He was saving you for me?"

"No." She whispered, horrified his thoughts could so easily mirror hers from yesterday morning. Then there had been snow on the ground. By mid-day it was gone and the air mild. Proof she should, could leave.

She turned to face the stone wall, pushed her head against it, as if to grind away the confusion that had set so deep inside.

"You've seen how little prepared we are for guests. You've seen that my people are good, hard workers, but none of them know how to run a keep as grand as this. But you're doing it, lass. The changes you've made in a wee bit of time . . ." She heard him shift, move closer. "I try to do my best, but I need help. You've been trained to be a Laird's wife. Do you not feel right with it? To have a purpose? To be in control of your own home."

Och, he was right and she hated that. For the truth of his words had the power to keep her from her home, her people, her family.

"Would your tailor have given you as much?"

Even when he'd been out, finding old Micheil, she'd felt at home, at peace within Glen Toric. She had more reason, more direction, in this past week than she had ever experienced. She was no longer a joke, but a woman who had a place.

But at what cost?

"Maggie, we can make this work." Talorc put his hands on her shoulders.

She dared not move, not one fraction.
She yearned too wildly for his touch, was
afraid of her own reaction to it. "Your hands
are no comfort." It was the truth. It was no
comfort knowing she had to wait, to hold off
from allowing what she desired.

He nudged her to turn, but she resisted.
"Let me hold you, lass. No more, just hold
you close so you don't feel so alone."

"No." He could keep a hug simple, but
Maggie doubted her strength on that score.
"No," she shoved from the wall, moved away,
toward the door. "I would take it kindly if you
would just leave me be, Bold." She refused to
turn and look at him. "You've brought enough
down on me. Don't make me face more than is
already on my platter."

She slipped through the opening, closed
it behind her, and leaned against it much as
she'd leaned against the wall, in need of
something to keep her upright, when what she
truly wanted was to curl into a ball and mourn
her brothers' departure.

She couldn't do that here. Silent, eyes
closed, she willed herself to move, widen the
distance between them, remove herself from
the awful need to have him closer. He had
nestled into her heart, provoked desire. She
refused to succumb, had to keep away, get
away.

Eight days, fortnight at most, and her
brothers would be back. She would leave.

If she could.

She would.

Maggie opened her eyes to a courtyard
full of MacKays. Hushed, serious, they stared.
Her newfound conviction wobbled as she
searched faces, from one to another. A slight
brush of a breeze pulled a lock of hair, tugged

at an apron string, the only movement among them all.

At the top of the stairs, alone, impressive, stood Seonaid.

Seonaid, gone with Talorc's departure, despite his order against escape. Back upon Talorc's return. Seonaid, who everyone whispered about, but none would talk of openly. At least, not to Maggie.

Seonaid, who spent last evening close to Maggie's own brothers, therefore close to Talorc.

Och, but she goaded a woman.

Maggie swung the door open again, and stepped inside the shade of the barn. The Bold stood in the aisle that ran the length of the stalls, his back to her, head bowed. She must have made a noise, for he looked over his shoulder, frowned and pivoted half-way.

"She's out there, Bold." Maggie snapped. "Seonaid, gone for the length of your departure, returns with you. She is there every time I look to your side."

"Your brothers were with me, Maggie. I'd be a fool to have another, with your brothers right there."

"What is she? Witch or confidant, to know your comings and goings better than anyone else?"

Talorc's frown deepened, but Maggie gave him no time to think.

"Did you send word to her, of your return?"

Agitated, he ran his hands through his hair. "Maggie, she's nothing to me but an old friend. Or she was. She's not such a friend now that we're grown. More a nuisance, sticky as tar that won't be shed."

"She'd like to see us fail."

"Will you give her that?"

The letter was sent. Maggie would be back with the MacBedes for the winter. Would the Bold come for her?

"You push too fast, Bold. You don't give a lass time to think."

"You only get yourself in trouble when you think."

Tangled outrage tumbled into gibberish against his slur. He laughed, cheeky fool, aware he stirred her ire. A deep breath steadied her thoughts.

"What are you playing at man?" She slammed the great door behind her and stepped fully into the barn. "You know I'm on a fence here, half in your hold, half-way back to my ma and da. Yet you make fun of me. As if that will . . . "

She backed up, as he moved closer. "Oh, no. Don't you dare come near me."

"Why, Maggie?"

"Because I don't want you to touch me."

"Afraid?" he challenged. "Afraid that you'll want me to touch you all the more? Afraid that you'll find there's no better man? Afraid it will topple you over into my hold?"

True, she was afraid, but she was not fool enough to admit it. She quit her retreat, stood firm, surprised to see him halt, mid-step.

"Will you meet my challenge, Maggie MacBede? Will you stand the test of my touch?"

He reached out, close enough that she could take his hand, to be tugged into his hold. Temptation urged, but she still had questions to be answered.

"Do you love me?"

He pulled his hand back. "What do you mean, do I love you?"

"Just what I said, it's that simple."

"I've traveled over half of Scotland to find you, promised my life to you, and you ask if I love you."

"You're doing that for your clan, for the safety of the Highlands."

"Och, lassie," disgusted, he turned away, his fingers running through his hair. When he finally turned back, there was a wary defeat in his eyes. "I want you lass, with every ounce of my body, of my soul. You're full of trouble, but I still want you. Is that not enough?"

Was it? "I don't know, Bold. I've no ken of what I feel for you either. Don't you see? There's a fire raging between us, but I've seen a fair number of lasses and laddies get together because they couldn't keep their hands anywhere else, and now, well, there's not much there between them but a babe and the heat of anger."

"There's more between us, I know there is."

She took a deep breath. "You may be right, I won't be denying that. I just don't want to jump straight in, without any thought."

"By all that's Holy, lass, that's the way you do everything else."

She spun in a circle, his words a physical thing sending her reeling. She didn't know whether to counter him or stalk away. But she was not one to run from conflict.

"Naught's fair with that!" She marched straight-up to him and shoved. "You aren't such a temporary thing, now, are you?"

He grabbed her hands before she could pull them away, lowered his voice, as he lowered his mouth. "No, lass, there's nothing temporary about me at all, that's what I've been trying to tell you."

250

He kissed her again, the cheeky man.
Every time he did that, she forgot all else, and
let him wrap his arms around her, and pull her
into him, and kiss her until . . . she . . . . just
. . . couldna' . . . think . . .of anything but the
touch of his tongue to hers. His lips nibbling
her lips. His breath, a feather's touch along
her neck, in her ear, sending shivers coursing
through her, signaling her lowers to heat and
pool.

She wondered hazily if the two of them
were possible, with this to bind them. Would
it be so bad?

"No lass, not bad. Good, so good."

Had she spoken aloud? Oh, grief. It was
his kisses, if she had just one more, then she
would ask him to stop, but first, she'd let him
kiss her neck . . .

"More than your neck, lass, please, just
a wee bit more?"

She felt him ease her plaid away, free
the tie at the neck of her dress. He had to
stop, because she couldn't stand properly on
legs gone wobbly.

Without a word, he hefted her up,
touched her lips, a tickle of attention, her
eyes, the side of her neck. Then, there they
were, pillowed in sweet hay, the glorious
weight of him pressing her into it. She didn't
know how he got them there, but she was glad
of it, glad she could arch her breasts, tease
him with their presence. A sense of glory
blossomed.

She was a woman. The birth of that,
deep within her, was heady and powerful. She
caught Talorc's attention by touching her own
breasts.

"Let me." He ordered, as he held her
bosom, lowered his mouth to suckle her
through the cloth of her dress.

"Oh, Bold."

"Say my name, lass, say my name, I want to hear it from your own lips."

"Talorc." She gave to him. "Hold me, hold me tight, and close."

He did so, pressed their bodies together.

It wasn't enough.

"I want more, I don't . . . yes, please . . . Och, the way you touch me . . . you stroke like a cat . . . " Eyes closed she stretched, just like that feline, despite the agitation, the hunger . . . .

He slid his hands from hip to the pit of her arm, before allowing them to capture her breasts,

. . . . .and more

Through fabric he had one nipple caught between his teeth, the other he teased with his fingers.

. . . .

and more.

"What else?" his words whispered across her skin. Lips brushed, body pressed and his hands, the rough stroke of them, insistent, patient, rough calluses against soft flesh, reminding again of a cat, the texture of its tongue.

Still, it wasn't enough. Why would any two people allow such feelings to build when peace demanded they be quenched?

He lifted his hips away. She grabbed, urged him back to thrust against her. He answered her urgency, but only for a moment before he rose to his knees to straddle her.

Words fought to rise against desire. "If this was all we had, would it be enough?"

"We have this, Maggie," He had his hands full of her breasts, kneading, squeezing. Just the sight of him poised above her, his

eyes hard, intent, made the heat rise within
her. She boiled with want, as she watched his
thumbs slowly draw the loosened neck of her
gown down, lower and lower, until the peaks
of her nipples, tender from his teasing, stood
firm,

"Oh, my Maggie, we have this and so
much more."

It was maddening, so much, so very
much, and yet, not enough.

"What we have is as rich and full as
your body." Slow as a thirsty man who sees
water and fears it might not be real, Talorc
lowered his mouth to those succulent peaks.
"Aye," he groaned, as he eased his weight
onto her, greedy in his hunger. He lavished
her nipples, her breasts with hands and mouth,
as his hips rotated against her in sweet
torment.

Impatiently, he pushed her bodice low,
laved her body with one long stroke from
navel to neck, then suckled his way back.

Maggie arched, met the grinding rhythm
of his hardness, starving for more because no
matter how much he touched, he suckled, no
matter how close they were, it still wasn't
enough.

Not nearly enough.

He moved aside, and she tried to
follow, but he stopped her. With one hand, he
held her hip in place, nudged her skirts with
his knee. His mouth at her breast, trailed
away, up to her neck, her ear, her mouth. All
the while, ever so slowly, his fingers slid
across her belly, down her thigh, back up to .
. .

"Och, no," she moaned, knowing she
would die with want.

"Och, yes," he chuckled, deep and breathless. "I have to have you, Maggie. I'll die of the pain, if you don't let me have you."

She felt him slide his hand between her legs, tried to pull away, but he was too persistent and she could not think. He played magic against her damp flesh. She squirmed, rose for more.

When would the torment ease? She whimpered, pulled back sharply, twisted her body away from the sensation.

"Stop!"

He did, immediately, his breath heavy with the exertion of it. "Please Maggie, don't make me stop. Not now. Please, it's so right, so very, very right."

Her grip on his arm was bruising, she couldn't help herself. "It's too much, Bold, I can't take more of this."

He lowered his forehead to hers. "You've only had a taste, Maggie."

She tried to roll away, to curl into a ball, and moaned when he curled around her, pushed his hardness against the crevice of her bottom, his body her prison.

"No." she cried and tried to explain. "It's like a feast, only the more you eat, the hungrier you get. I can't stand anymore."

"I can make it better, lass." He stroked her hair away from her face, gently ran a hand over her breasts, barely brushing the tips of them, and smiled as her back arched into his touch.

It wasn't fair.

"Maggie, I promise, in the last round, you will feel complete." He was panting, trying to slow it, as he urged her face around. "We will feel complete. Whole. At peace with our bodies, at long last." He kissed her, slow, languorous, his tongue in her mouth. "We can stop the painful throbbing here," He cupped her damp lips, her mound and squeezed. He'd awakened dormant desires that raged to be fed; all of it new, tantalizing and insistent.

"Please." Dazed, she didn't know if she was asking him to continue or stop.

"I can make it all come together, Maggie. That's when we explode with pleasure, fly to heaven and back. That's when you know what it means to be a woman."

"I don't know, Bold." She nipped at his shoulder, unable to stop herself.

"Aye, you do, you just don't want to."

"I've never felt like this."

"No, you saved it for me."

She gulped, her hands gripped fiercely on his arms. She was beginning to think she'd gone too far to turn back.

"If we stop now?" She didn't even know what she was asking, but he seemed to understand.

"No, Maggie, that only makes the wanting worse."

Eyes widened against the dim light of the barn. "It couldna' be worse!"

"Aye. Why do you think you melted so quick? From the morning, you were still ready from the morning. And next time . . ."

"No." she stopped him. "If there's an answer to the torment, answer it, Talorc."

He didn't move.

The man was an oaf! She finally makes her decision and he just holds himself above her, still, watchful. "Now, Bold," she pushed at his shoulders.

He reached down and stroked her, in that spot between her legs that only made it worse. A shiver of blissful agony coursed through her. She couldn't stand any more.

Desperate, she cried, "Do it then, Bold. Make me a woman. Now."

"Now?"

She shook him. "Now!"

"You'll be my wife?"

"I'll give you my body."

He sucked in air. "With my body, I thee cherish," he improvised the Scots marriage vows.

Suddenly, her breath hitched, came far too fast, as she realized she may be asking for more than she meant to. She wasn't ready, had plans before that commitment was made.

"Just for now, Bold. You can have what you want, but just for now." And what she wanted. She was in a panic, hungry, yet uncertain, afraid she would say yea, when she should say nay.

He shucked off his shirt before she could think. Not that she could think, as he eased her skirts higher. Sense told her to be appalled. She ignored that, raised her hips to help him move her skirt up to her waist, revealing the heart of her to his view. It excited and frightened all in one.

He shifted his plaid. She stared at the tall proud length of him, reached out to stoke it.

"You'll never fit." Forlorn, that's what she felt. Loss before she had even had.

Again, she felt his weight pressed against her, his lips, his hands, stealing all sense from her.

She didn't know what she expected when the blunt tip of him pressed at the base of her. Instinct screamed that was exactly what she needed. Her eyes rolled and she moaned.

He slid himself along the portal of her passage.

"Forever, Maggie. This is forever, and you can have it any time you like. But if it's just for now," he pulled away, "then it's not for you."

She angled her hips, urgent to keep the contact. "Bold, don't you dare stop."

"Forever."

She lay with legs spread around his, her skirts bunched at her hips, and her breasts, bare as the day she was born. So close, his body pressed against hers, but he shifted, rose up, bold in the way he looked at her. Hungry and savage. It fueled her desire.

He no longer held all the power. Not by the sight of him, he didn't. His manhood stood, strong and straight and ready to pierce her. She should be quivering with terror, not anticipation. Contrary as ever.

She had to think, licked her lips, fought for reason. "I'm not a sweet thing who will do your bidding."

His smile tilted with amusement. "I like my apples tart."

"You won't be the only Bold one between us."

"Prove it."

She reached down, took him in her hand, and felt it leap with reaction. She pulled away.

"Don't give up so easy, lass." He encouraged her to wrap her fingers and slide them along his length.

"You like that, but what do I get?" she teased.

With a devilish smirk, he pulled from her hold and slid down to nuzzle the back of her knees. His suckling kisses rose higher.

"Oh no." she tried to stop him.

"Oh aye." He challenged, as his mouth covered her bud of pleasure. She felt his

fingers slide inside of her and she screamed
with the incredible pulsing that racked
through her over and over and over. . . his
mouth, all musky and wet, covered her scream
and again, the broad tip of him pushed at her.

She had no power left, just a limp shell
of a body.

"Forever, Maggie."

"You'll leave me." Of course he would,
at the best of times and the worst of times.

"Never, lass, never will I leave you."

"You'll go off to battle and leave me."
She would always be second to the fight.

"I'll always be with you, in your heart,
by your side, in your thoughts."

"You won't be there to give me this."

He chuckled. "You'll be satisfied
aplenty. Too much. You'll be pushing me off
of you."

"Never!" she was truly shocked, to
think she'd say no to this.

His arms closed about her, pulled her
tight. Words whispered through her hair, into
her ear. "Be mine forever, Maggie. Be mine,
say yes, let me fill you."

"You're a big man, Bold."

"You're a grand lass, Maggie, mine. Let
me fill you."

"You won't leave."

"I'll be yours forever."

"I'll slay you if you leave."

"I will never desert you, lass, I promise
to be a part of you, just let me be a part of
you. As one, Maggie, we will be as one."

She opened her eyes fully, looked into
his. He was so earnest, true. He had promised.
She cupped his head, her hands on either side
of his face.

"You stay with me, be a husband at my
side, then you have all of me, God save you."

And she pulled him down to kiss her, a deep, urgent kiss, full of all the hunger that had been building.

Slowly, he eased his length inside of her. Maggie rotated her hips, knowing there was more of him, wanting it but terrified. It didn't hurt, which surprised her, he was so large, filled her so full, stretched her so tight. She wiggled, to urge him further, but he stopped, held poised on the brink of something, but she didn't know what it was.

"Hang on, lassie." His breath came in deep draughts. "Hang on tight." He pulled out, then slammed back into the core of her.

She bucked, once, he rode it, and stilled.

"You hurt me, Bold."

"Aye, just this once, never again."

"I think you lie to me, Bold."

"No, Maggie, mine, I wouldn't lie, but I can't . . ." he pressed into her, even deeper. "Stop," he pulled out only to push again, urgently, "moving," and, he did move, hard, fast, beyond his control, until he shuddered above her, shouting her name.

With a groan, he collapsed on top of her. "Oh, Maggie, I couldna' stop myself. You have that much power over me."

She was still restless, shifted her breasts beneath him, to feel her nipples tugged by the hair of his chest.

"Oh lassie," it was a sigh. He reached between them, to pluck at that sensitive bud he had found earlier.

"Oh, oh, oh . . . " her back arched like a bow, he suckled a nipple, and continued to play. She bucked again, but not in pain, and again. He was still hard inside of her. "Och, Talorc," she screamed.

"That's it, my sweet." He barely had
breath enough to whisper, but she was beyond
hearing. She was soaring into heaven, flying
with the clouds, floating back to earth.

Bliss, contentment, it was everything
and more than Talorc had promised. Even the
pain from the breach of her maidenhead, was
no more than an edge of ecstasy.

She stroked his hair, wet with the effort
they'd shared. He'd not lied. The hunger was
gone. Profoundly gone. He had pushed,
coerced, but he was right. They had joined
and were one, would share forever more.

Talorc shifted to his side, pulled
Maggie along, to lie belly to belly, chest to
chest, legs entwined.

Maggie smiled at the irony of it. "You
know, we have Seonaid to thank for this."

"Seonaid? She has nothing to do with
us."

"She's the reason I came back in the
barn."

Talorc chuckled. "I'll have to be
thanking her, then."

"You'll not be talking to her." Maggie
punched his shoulder.

"She's in the clan, Maggie, I'll be
having to speak to her. But you can stand by
my side when I do, to make certain I'm safe."

"Safe?" she shuddered.

"Maggie," Talorc braced himself on one
arm to better look at her.

"Do you think she's a danger?"

He leaned over her. "Not to us, Maggie.
You're the woman for me."

"No, not that way," she brushed his
words aside. "It's just that . . . when you said
that about safe, it ran down my spine."

"We're not as secure as we were, here at
Glen Toric. But you're not to worry."

"You have a traitor."

"Aye. That's the only explanation for Micheil. No one outside the clan should have known where he was, or what he does."

"Seonaid?"

"No." he shook his head, as if he had already thought of it and discarded the notion. "She may not like your being here, but she'd not turn traitor. She's as much a part of this clan as I am. Her da was a great warrior, my father's closest man. She learned from her father's side."

"Then who?"

"I don't know, Maggie. But now, maybe, I can finally think of something other than your backside!" He gave it a smack.

"You brutish troll!" she rolled him over, braced herself on his shoulders.

The door rattled, a fist pounded on it. "Bold."

Maggie sank down, her head on his shoulder. "Tell them to go away."

"Go away." Talorc shouted, and laughed.

"Bold, you have to come. The Gunns have come out of hiding on our land. Jesse's place is burning."

In the space of a breath, Maggie was on her own, in the hay. Even before he had his clothes to rights Talorc barked, "We'll ride to fight. Call the men to arms!"

"You're leaving?" He had promised, only moments before, crucial moments before, that he would stay by her side.

He looked at her as if she were crazy. "You expect me to stay when the Gunns are riding against our own?"

Of course he was leaving, he would always be going. "You promised." She accused, even as she realized the

impossibility of it. Passion had clouded her
thoughts, made her believe the unbelievable.
Of course he would go, had to go. She would
think less of him if he didn't.

He was a fighting man; therefore, he
would leave.

"I'm not leaving you." He claimed, as
he headed toward the door.

She knew that. But if he wasn't here,
and her brothers came back, who would keep
her from going? She hadn't meant to say it
out loud but she did. "You pushed me too far,
Bold. I wasn't ready and now you'll be gone."

He stopped, looked back at her. "The
Gunns are on our land. If I don't ride, then
who will keep us safe? Who will protect
you?"

"My father stopped following the
battles." It was a foolish argument, but she
was desperate. "You could as well. Send your
men."

"You'd have me do that? Ask others to
do what I would not?"

Only this once, she thought but said.
"You promised."

He moved closer, knelt down to listen,
acknowledge her complaint. "I promised not
to leave you Maggie, but where does that
stop? I can't be by your side every moment,
nor would you want that. I must do what I
must do. Never doubt, I will always be your
husband. I'll not leave you for another, or to
another."

To him, she was his. She was his, and
he was his, which left her with nothing. No
power, no strength, no say. He could come
and go at will, while she was left to follow
his instructions.

Like hell.

"You're leaving, then." It was all she could think to say. It was a fact to be acknowledged.

"Aye, I'm going to do the work of a man. And you can trust I will hunger to be back to you. You are in me," he clasped his fist at his chest, "Here, Maggie, you hold my heart, my future."

"And you hold mine through trickery. That's how you got me here, and that's how you mean to keep me."

He held her still, his hands a heavy weight on her shoulders.

The door rattled, "Bold," it was William, "We need horses and yours is in the barn . . . Oh shite! There goes Seonaid! Can't anybody keep her here when we're off to fight?"

Talorc's hands tightened their hold.

"Go!" she shoved him off, rose herself, straightening her clothes. "And I'll be going to." She stormed past him. He grabbed her arm, spun her back to him.

"You'll be going nowhere."

"Don't push me, Laird." she shot back. "I'll be going to the keep, to prepare the hall, for those who'll want to stay when the Gunns are in their world."

"You'll stay at Glen Toric." It was an order.

"I'll be leaving the barn," she hedged, "Or they won't be able to saddle your mount."

He flushed, or she thought he did, despite the meager light. She left him to it, to his horse, to his battles, to his leaving her.

CHAPTER 11 – LEAVING

It had taken more than a fortnight, but her brothers had come. And it wasn't Jamie or Douglas but her oldest brother, Feargus the younger, and Nigel. Serious business, if her mother had sent those two.

Maggie waited at the top of the keep steps. She didn't run down to jump into their arms, to be tossed about like a caber. It would not be fitting, when they rode so tall and straight and somber. As acting Lady of Glen Toric, she would match their stoicism.

They did not dismount.

Maggie frowned. Men had moved in to take their reins, to hold their mounts and take them off to the stables, but her brothers refused the act of hospitality.

A grave insult.

"Our mother's ailing, Maggie. She's asking for you."

Maggie would have toppled, if Una hadn't been so close beside her, eager for anything new to gossip about.

Was her mother truly ill, or was this in response to her letter?

She must be ailing, for her brothers to be so stern, to refuse the friendly help offered by the MacKays. Still, Maggie could not believe it. "Ill?"

"Aye, and asking for you." Nigel answered.

"You'll come in and warm yourselves, while I prepare . . ."

"You'll come now, Maggie. There's no' much time before the snows come."

She looked up, only to see what she had noted first thing this morning. The day was gray and heavy. Snow for certain and no light sprinkling at that. No matter how fast she moved, they'd still be caught in it.

"I'll get my great plaid. Rest your horses, feed them, while mine is saddled. I'll have food sent out to you." She nodded to Domnall, to take care of these tasks, then turned to flee indoors.

"Maggie!" Feargus stopped her. "Where's the Bold. He should have been out here to greet us."

There was challenge in his tone. If they had come because her mother was truly ill, they would be somber, but not picking for a fight. Right now, they looked to make trouble.

"The Gunns are on MacKay land, to the east and south. They were burning the cottages. He's ridden out to stop them."

"You're not wearing a kerchief?"

Guiltily, her hand went to her head. She dared not look to a single face, embarrassed that someone, anyone, might know what happened in the barn. It was no great secret that they were in there long enough for any manner of mischief.

And mischief did happen.

But she'd not stand alone for all to know. If Talorc had stayed, she would have had him there with the admission. But he hadn't. He left her. She'd not want the world to know what a fool she had been.

265

"I'm free to leave." She lied and wondered if anyone would contradict her. The MacKays who stood near, shifted, turned away from her gaze, but didn't say anything.

Her brothers nodded, and, finally dismounted.

"You have time for a warm toddy, anyway." She told them, and left to prepare herself for traveling, her heart sinking with worry over her ma, with concern at the coldness of her brothers, and the overwhelming ache that she was leaving Talorc.

For the winter, anyway.

The snow that threatened was no meager danger. It would be heavy, deep, she could feel it in her bones. He'd have trouble enough returning from his battles, let alone trying to follow her.

There was the whole of the winter to sort out just how she felt, and assure her people that there was no need for revenge against the Bold. Which there would be, if Feargus and Nigel's hostility was any indication.

It only took a few moments to gather her meager possessions. The pieces that were part of her dowry had yet to be sent to Glen Toric. That would wait until she were truly wed, if she ever were truly wed.

Which she wasn't, or at least, she didn't think she was. There was the year and a day to consider, and Maggie knew of enough women who had bedded without a wedding. Certainly, this was no different than another woman whose passion ran deeper than sense.

It would not be the first time that Maggie had acted the fool. At least it had only been the once. A person couldn't be with child from one mating. If that were the case, there would be far more children about.

"Oh, lass." Ealasaid patted the small bundle that Maggie would take with her, "you've barely settled in, and now I fear you won't make it back until spring."

"The weather could clear," They both knew it was not likely.

"You've been such a dear. The whole clan was hoping . . . " the older woman looked away, toward the bed. Her sheen of tears changed to the dull of grimness. "The Laird will not like this. I can promise you that."

"My mother needs me."

"Aye, your mother needs you." There was no conviction in Ealasaid's words.

"She's never needed me before."

"Your brothers were loath to step on MacKay land."

"It's the snow. They're that worried that we'll be lost in it."

Ealasaid frowned. "You're not telling the whole of it, lass, but I don't think I'm the one who will get you to tell it. The one who could is not here."

"My mother needs me," Maggie argued.

"And so do the Highlands, lass, so do we and all the other clans allied with the Bold."

"I'm only going home."

Ealasaid's eyes narrowed, her head tilted to the side. "Home, lass? Is this not home for you now?"

It was far harder than she expected, for this was a home, of sorts. And she did love the people. That was the problem, she loved them too much.

"I mean the home of my parents, where I was raised."

"Well, there's something I think you should be taking, then."

"What is that?"

Ealasaid offered a head scarf of MacKay. Maggie's hands flew to her uncovered head.

"As I thought." Ealasaid nodded succinctly. "There was talk of a wee spot of blood in the hay. We all waited, thinking you'd want the Bold here, with you, before you faced us all with the fact. But I'm thinking you're not true to your own actions."

"No, it's not like that. He made me a promise and he broke it, straight away, he broke it!"

"What did he promise?"

Maggie shook her head. Talorc would understand, but she wasn't certain anyone else would. Even she knew the impossibility of her request. That was the worst of it. She knew he had to go, he had to fight. She just wasn't prepared to face the consequences.

"I have to go." She wanted to give Ealasaid a hug, unsure if it would be well received.

But she wasn't so chicken as that. Without warning, she hurried over, wrapped her arms around Ealasaid and squeezed. The great woman squeezed her back.

"You let them know you're married, child."

"I'm not. A year's time has not passed."

Ealasaid pushed away. "You let everyone know you're one, and the Laird may not like your going, but he will accept it."

Maggie turned away.

"The kerchief does more than say a lass is married. It says she's a woman now, no longer a maiden. You're not a maiden anymore." She handed out the kerchief.

Maggie looked over her shoulder at it and
pivoted. She did not want to take the cloth.

Ealasaid urged it on her. Maggie had no
choice, but as soon as it was in her hand, she
pushed it between the folds of her packet.

"What if he comes back injured? How
will you be feeling to be gone?"

Maggie's head snapped up. "How would
I feel, to have him return across the back of a
saddle?"

"He'll not be killed. He's the Bold."

"Kings have been killed, slaughtered.
He's no better than that."

"He'll be back."

"Oh, aye, I don't doubt that," Maggie
snapped, "It's how he'll be coming back that's
the worry, and the crux of his promise, and
well he knows that."

Ealasaid frowned. "You take good care
of that mother of yours and hurry back here.
Or know that the Laird will be there to fetch
you."

Deep inside, Maggie already knew that.
But he would have to wait until spring. He
might travel in the snow, but he'd not expect
it of Maggie. He would have to stay with his
clan.

Her brothers were here.

Her mother could truly be ill.

"Ealasaid, will you be the one to tell
Talorc why I had to leave," he could have
been injured. "Will you tell him . . ."

"That he broke a promise?"

Maggie couldn't answer that. She just
couldn't. Her brothers were waiting and her
tears threatened to fall. She choked back a
sob.

"Tell him I'm gone."

The Handfasting Series

TORN

Part 3

Dedication

To my daughters for all their differences,
similarities and joys. You make me smile, you
keep me young, you give me a reason for
being. I love you.

CHAPTER 1 – A TOUCH WISER

Home again.

Maggie expected it to be the same. She expected to step straight back into life as it had been.

She was a fool.

The ride should have forewarned. Rather than teasing affection, her brothers treated her with the wariness of large men in a room full of breakable objects. There was a hint of distrust.

"Ma read your missive and took straight to her bed." Nigel admitted.

"To her bed?" Her mother, Fiona MacBede, never fell ill enough to be off her feet.

"To her bed." Feargus the younger barked. His scowl meant someone would pay. There was no one, except perhaps her father, who would be more protective of Fiona MacBede than her sons.

Maggie shrunk deeper into her great plaid.

"You seem well enough." Feargus continued.

"Aye." But she wasn't, not with the mischief she had played. She felt small. Very small indeed.

She must have sounded so.

"Don't doubt yourself, Maggie. No matter what they may have said, or done, you're a fine lass. The best for the best."

Her brothers blamed Talorc for the offense against their sister, the worry to her mother.

What had Maggie done?

"We thought the Bold was the man. But even we can be wrong."

Maggie's groan was stolen by an eerie moan of wind. An ominous sound, coupled with a dark silver sky and a landscape of brittle heather. The heather was fast turned to white.

Snow had come.

They battled against it the whole of their return to the MacBede Keep. Shoulders hunched, head bowed. Maggie could only see white. It blew against them, blocked sight of their trail, the sun. It froze Maggie's heart from thoughts of Talorc and the MacKays. She didn't know how her brothers knew where they were or where they were going, but they continued on. In the worst of it they traveled through two nights, Maggie tied to the horse so when she dozed, she'd not lose her seat.

"We'll get you home, lass. We'll get you back to the safety of our people. Ma will be that glad to see you."

They reached the MacBede gates before Maggie realized where they were. One moment her head was bowed with weariness, the next she lifted her eyes to see the most beautiful sight she could ever imagine.

Home.

She was home again and this time she would relish it in the way one does when they know they have to leave again. And she would leave. She had come to understand that much.

If the Bold would take her, she would go back to him.

But not yet.

There was the whole of the winter to get her fill of kin, to listen to her mother's advice, to be a MacBede. Come spring, she would be off again, to the Laird MacKay, to be a wife.

If he waited.

If he didn't . . . there was a chance of that, she had to be honest enough to admit. Talorc was a man of action, quick, impulsive action. He wasn't one to take time, assess his situation. Maggie could understand that. She was known to be just as impulsive and she knew the flavor of regret over thoughtless action.

The letter. Thoughtless, thoughtless, thoughtless.

Her clan, her family, pushed her into a Handfast with Talorc the Bold, the Laird MacKay. Marriage for a year and a day, unless they bonded in body, then it was a marriage to be sure. Only she hadn't known that, she hadn't known about the limitations until Talorc told her and now, och, now she'd made a right mess of it all.

If only her clan, and the Bold himself, had given her time to accept the idea, but they hadn't. In one night she went from living among her people to riding off for the MacKay keep. She'd felt the right of it, when she sent that missive off to her mother, implying things were not so good for her in her new home. Only they had been good, and then her brothers had come to take her home. Spoiling for a fight, they were, when all she had wanted was to see her family again.

Impulsive, reckless action.

Talorc was as bad. Hadn't he proposed to her within a few hours of meeting? The truth was, given time, disappointment was known to taint hasty decisions.

He didn't love her.

The curiosity of desire had been fed.

Seonaid, with all her closeness to the man, could press her interest.

He would have the whole of the winter to think that out. And if he chose to leave her with the MacBedes, it would be better to learn of it within the bosom of her own family than held fast to the MacKay keep.

She dampened the recriminations. This, now, was her homecoming. She refused to think of Talorc or the MacKays and spoil the joy of it. There would be time enough to rethink actions in the winter to come.

Bone cold, aching from sitting astride for days, hungry for nothing more than the warmth of her own bed and a hot broth, she was hit with a jolt of energy. Rag doll limp outside the gate, she felt grand with the crossing of it, raised her hand to wave and shout "hallo" to all those around.

Silence stunted her gesture.

Despite the snow, the courtyard was full. All those who would have waved back and called out now stood taciturn and stoic, with the same wary watchfulness that Maggie's brothers held along their journey.

Maggie's newfound energy leached from her as quickly as it had come. She had no heart to prod for fun. No exuberance to challenge their stoicism. That was for them to do for her. But they didn't.

She bowed her head, shameful of the problems she had caused.

"Head-up lass, you've done naught wrong." Feargus growled beside her.

"You don't know, Feargus." His head snapped around, wariness replaced with accusation. Feargus had gone to his sister's rescue. If there was no need for rescue, Feargus would be shamed to the core.

His look burned. Maggie felt significant as ash.

Och, Talorc, what have I done?

But even as she thought it, she realized it was not her fault. They, both Bold and her people, had put her to this. They had pushed her, and pushed her, to accept things before she was ready.

Did they want her to be a MacKay? Fine and dandy for them. She knew those in power married strangers, but at least they were prepared from the cradle. Her own gave her no more than one night, one torturous night to adjust, accept and consider life without those she loved and held dear.

She thought of Ealasaid, and Deidre, Lizbeth, Mary and Eba.

So the MacKays had good people, too.

She thought of Seonaid.

And they had troublesome women, as well.

There were all sorts to a community. Maggie could accept that, if only she had been better prepared, given some warning, time enough to shore up her foundations.

Head held high, she urged her mount a step before her brothers.

Feargus was right, she had naught to be sorry about. But he did. As did her ma and her da and Bold, trickster that he was. She would not feel guilty for wanting to be home with her own.

Except it didn't feel much like home.

Her father reached up, to lift her off the horse. He had not done such a thing since she was a mere child, her head no higher than his stomach. Nor had he ever hugged her with such fierce power.

She didna' know if the tears sprang from the pressure of his hold, or the sudden bout of homesickness that had her hugging him back with the same emotional desperation. Reluctantly, he let her go to her mother's embrace.

"Och, Maggie," finally her mother released her, to lean back and assess, her fingers gripped tight to Maggie's arms. "You've had a birthday since you've been gone." With the words, Fiona's eyes filled to brimming.

Maggie's own salty tears streamed down her cheeks. "Aye, I'm a woman now." The quiet of the courtyard hadn't lasted long. With Maggie's words, it landed once again, like a heavy mallet.

"A woman now?" Fiona's gaze shifted over Maggie.

I can make it all come together, Maggie. That's when we explode with pleasure, fly to heaven and back. That's when you know what it means to be a woman. Talorc's words of passion.

Maggie blushed furiously. That was not what she meant to say, yet it was what they had all heard.

"I'm twenty, now," she defended. "No longer a child."

"Oh." Her mother sighed. "No, not a child any longer." And seemed saddened by the fact. "But let's get you in by the fire, warm you up."

Fiona looked back at her two sons. "You as well, someone can take the mounts. You've done a fine job of returning our

Maggie to us, time to warm yourselves and have a proper meal."

Her brothers were huddled together with her da. Probably speaking of their reception at the MacKays, which was no reception, because they wouldna' leave their mounts. They as good as proclaimed war. Talorc would not be pleased.

She let her mother lead her into Maggie's own chamber, where a tub already stood, filled with steaming water.

"Mother, you don't know how good that looks."

"It was a hard journey?"

"Terrible with the snow and all."

"He won't be able to come this way for a good long time." Fiona kept her back to Maggie, as she moved drying sheets closer to the fire. Maggie couldn't respond. As determined as she had been to go home, she now wished Talorc close at hand.

She eased her damp plaid from her shoulders, from around her waist. "Were you truly sick?"

"Aye," Fiona crossed to Maggie to help with the fastening of her gown. "I'd been fretting ever since you left and when your letter arrived, well, I was beyond fretting."

"My words made you ill?"

"Sick of heart, child, sick of heart." Fiona wrapped her arms around her daughter. "You don't know how hard it is to send a child off. Grown or no, children of their own or no, you never stop worrying about them. And when you've played a hand at sending them out against their own will," a gentle mother's touch traced Maggie's cheek. "Can you forgive me? I truly thought it was for the best."

Tears kept Maggie from answering. Not great gulping sobs but quiet tears of anguish. Never, in her whole lifetime, had she ever hurt her mother, and now she had done so with a vengeance. The worst of it was Fiona had been right. Talorc was a good man in many ways. If he just wouldn't force Maggie's hand so much when she was powerless to stop him.

He was a danger to her. Not in the way her family was thinking, but he was a danger. Maggie would have to put their ideas to right, later, after she was warm, fed and rested.

Fortunately, Fiona didn't seem to need answers. She helped Maggie into the tub as Sibeal, Feargus the younger's wife, came into the room with a tray full of steaming mugs and haggis straight from the stoves. The smell of it, the warmth of the water, the comfort of family enveloped Maggie.

"I'll be staying with you tonight, Maggie. We all know how you don't like the darkness." Sibeal offered.

"Did you tell him about that?" Fiona asked. "Did he know you don't like to be alone in the night?"

"He knew." Maggie reassured her ma. "But I'm too old to be fretting about such things, now."

"Tsk," Fiona disapproved. "He left you alone. These warring men just canna' understand we all have our fears."

"And we need to learn how to face them."

Sibeal pulled a chair near the tub, broke off a bit of haggis and put it to Maggie's mouth, to feed her as if she were a babe. "Was it that bad? That you had to face fears like that?"

278

"No," Maggie pulled away from Sibeal's offer, and reached up to take it herself.

"Well," Fiona shot out, "Your father and brothers would not let you be harmed in battle! And that's the truth of it!"

Reparations could not wait until she had her wits about her. She had deliberately distorted the truth, had exaggerated the distortions, but who would have thought her family would take it as gospel? She was known to be dramatic. There was no choice among a family of boisterous older brothers, and a clan that was no different. She knew to come in loud and grand or be ignored. Of all the times for them to take her on her word, they would have to start now.

There was naught she could do, but defend those she had slandered. "It wasna' the MacKay's fault. I broke through the protection when a man was felled. You know how I can be."

"He should have known."

Maggie forgot how stubborn her people could be, once they took a side.

"We all thought the Gunns had gone, turned tail and fled. They had been gone that long. But you know the Gunns are a sneaky lot. I'm just that grateful that I'm free of them. Talorc thought they were set on capture, and against that he did a fine job."

Fiona fussed over Maggie's forehead. "There's still a lump, lass. He should have taken the blow."

"I'm fairing well, ma."

"You'll fair better, now that you're home."

"Aye, ma, I'll fair better."

* * * * * * * * * *

If only it had been true. That Maggie would do better at home. But she didn't. Her ma may not have been ill, but Maggie surely was. It came on slowly but soon took over her life.

At first, she blamed it on the emotions at battle inside of her. They sucked her dry, like a sawdust doll that leaked its inners. It left her all floppy and listless. But it didn't stop there. No. Terrible little sithichean, fairies by the bucket load, danced and jigged in her belly and soured all she smelled, made her sick, until she could keep naught down.

Her mother hovered, too close.

As all children born in the wee hours of the night, Maggie was expected to be brilliant, as well as wild. Because of that, she had been given a fair amount of freedom. Now, to have her ma, her da, all her brothers and their wives perched so near, was about to drive her crazy. Even when she retched, someone would hold her head, another would hand her a wet cloth, and the lot of them stood witness to the embarrassment of her weakness, for Maggie never ailed.

"How close did you come to be, to the Bold?" Her mother asked, after one such bought.

How close? Maggie moaned, which her mother put down to illness. They had been as close as two people can be. They had also been as far apart as two people could be.

Or had they?

"He was gone, much of the time. And when he was there, he had clan business to see to. He did not follow me about, if that's what you mean."

"Could you be his wife?" Finally, the question had come.

"Mayhap, one day." Maggie hedged.

"I see," Fiona nodded, as if that explained all.

But it didn't. It didn't explain to Maggie why she felt so lonely among the people she loved. It didn't explain the fear she felt, that Bold would never come for her. It didn't explain the hunger for kisses and caresses and soft whispered words.

It didn't explain why she felt those things never felt before.

* * * * * * * * *

Talorc rode into Glen Toric's snow-swirled courtyard well after dark. He doubted the watch knew he was there before he was straight under their noses. Especially as he had traveled alone, leaving his men to their dinner and sleep. They were not as anxious to return to the keep. None were newly married. None had just come to 'know' their wives, nor was the hunger still licking at them to get to know her again.

He told the guards not to announce him. He wanted to surprise Maggie there in the hall, to see her reaction when he stood waiting for her welcome. No doubt, she would be as ravenous for him as he was for her. She proved the truth of it in the barn. It was that good between them.

Together they would go above stairs, ready a bath so she could bathe him. Her fingers would run over his head while she lathered it. Her hands would knead the ache in his shoulders and back, as it warmed the cold that had settled in his marrow. He would teach her how to ease the lower aches as well. To run her fingers from his shoulders, down his chest, across his belly, to his loins.

He stormed up the steps, to the door of the keep.

The memory of Maggie held him fast in hand combat, kept him alive, for he promised he'd not leave her. And he'd not. No more fighting with reckless abandon. Not now. He had enough experience to fight with skill and care. Maggie gave him the reason to do so.

Talorc moved into the doorway of the great room to look over the crowd. Even before he spotted Maggie, he saw Seonaid there with her child. His innards clenched. His head shot around, as he scanned the crowd, suddenly aware of the unusual muted tones. It was Donegal who saw him first.

"Bold."

The quiet turned to calls and shouts, questions about the battle, urgings for him to move close to the fire, have a dram. Someone swiped snow from his shoulders, but it wasn't Maggie.

"Where's my wife?" He hadn't meant to bellow, to frighten her with his need for her. But the escalating fear could not be squelched.

The room stilled, an ominous thing. Una, always proud to be the first to impart news, called out. "She's gone to the MacBedes, but she said naught about being a wife."

Lustful hunger turned to a nest of vipers deep in his gut. "She's my wife. Make no doubt about that. She should be wearing a kerchief."

"Bold," Ealasaid bustled through the crowd, with a grim look shot at Una. "You'd not expect her to face us on her own with such news now, would you? She would need you by her side."

He acknowledged the truth of it with a grunt. "Is it true? Has she left?"

"True."

"How, with who?"

Old Micheil barged forward, pushed his way in front of Ealasaid. "Her brothers came for her. Said her mother was ailing and she should go."

Talorc nodded to Micheil. "Alright then, so she should." He would follow, snow or no, be by her side. Make certain they, Maggie included, all knew he was her mate.

First things first. Talorc crossed to the fire, to warm the cold that ran to the bone. He would warm himself, have a bite to eat and a dram to burn out the cold that ran deeper yet.

Beathag tugged at his arm. "The MacKays refused our hospitality."

"What?" He looked to Micheil, to see the truth of it.

The old man nodded. "Wouldn't even dismount."

"Shite." Talorc grabbed the goblet Seonaid offered and downed the whole of it. The whiskey hit as true as a campfire to his belly. He shook his head, like a dog shaking off water. "The MacBedes are strong allies. Did you not make them feel welcome?"

"She offered it, herself, but they refused to dismount until she insisted."

"Did they give reason?"

"Blamed it on the snow to come."

"Fair enough." Talorc took another swig of life, then sat on the bench before the fire. He pushed for days, to return to her, just to face this reception. He should have waited.

Fatigue hit with the weight of what was said, and what wasn't. It could be far better than it sounded. Or it could be far worse. "Their mother was ill and the weather had taken a nasty turn. Reason enough to be quick about things."

"They asked for you, insulted you weren't there to greet them yourself."

"And did you tell them why I wasn't there?"

"She did, herself."

"Maggie?" In response, the men grunted. Talorc continued to reason it all out rather than succumb to panic. "She offered them hospitality, she explained my absence, she worried over her mother. Is there more to the telling?"

"They'd not speak with us, and wouldn't go to the keep. Just watered and fed their horses, drank their own draft."

It didn't make sense. Maggie may have been angry that Talorc was called away, but her family had no way of knowing. "They were here not six days since. They left with good heart. What do you think happened to turn their minds?"

"Wasn't the same two brothers."

"Ach, crikey! And you wait to tell me this? Which brothers came?"

"Feargus and Nigel." Liam told him.

"Feargus and Nigel? And they were cold?"

"Aye."

"Was there anything untoward that happened? Anything her brothers might report, so the family would send the heavy arms?"

"Laird?" It was a soft voice, buried deep in the throng of clansmen around him.

"Speak up, lass."

Lizbeth moved forward, shy but determined. "Do you think it was something Mistress Maggie put in her letter?"

Mule kicked. Maggie and her ways had that effect on him. "What letter?"

"Before he left, Maggie gave Jamie a piece of parchment for her ma."

"Here lad," Micheil shoved a flask of whiskey into Talorc's face. He swiped it away.

"Did any of you write it for her?" But he already knew the answer. If anyone around her knew how to read or write, Maggie would have hounded to be taught the same. She would have written it herself.

"What do you think it means, Laird?" Ealasaid worried.

"Her mother's not sick, at least not in her body. She's probably soul sick, though, if Maggie had her way."

"But she's your wife. You said so yourself, when you first arrived."

How could he answer that? True, he had had her body, but he didn't have her heart. Not if she would run like she did. Nor had they said the words that would bind them in marriage, and Maggie had yet to learn that with a Handfasting the binding of bodies was as good, if not better, than words.

He halfway wondered at the Gunns' timing. It was just a little too true to their purpose, but how in heaven would they know that? If he had stayed, if he hadn't gone to fight the Gunns, she would have been here at Glen Toric and securely his.

But there was no way the Gunns could know, on the heels of the event, that he had consummated his marriage.

He wanted to believe that nothing would have taken her from Glen Toric, if he'd been there to confirm that she was his wife. But he doubted the honesty of that. He had tricked her into going to Glen Toric. He had used her against herself to keep her, then left at the turn in their relationship.

I will take thee, Talorc MacKay, she had said at the Handfasting. She had yet to say I take thee. One wee word, a teeny wee word and she was still free.

"Laird," Ealasaid said, "She was not so happy to be going, but she truly believed you'd broken a vow."

"I've broken her maidenhead. My seed is in her belly. That's enough that she should be here to discuss her concerns with me."

But she wasn't here, and if his seed had not taken, he didn't know if he could get her back.

CHAPTER 2 - REVELATION

Blade scraped against stone, back, forth, back, forth, rasped against Fiona's nerves. She closed her eyes, took deep breaths, as Feargus continued with his task. Resentment simmered.

Men! Oblivious to a woman's moods, a woman's needs. Fiona opened her eyes to the muted light of late afternoon. She crossed to the fire, to distance herself from the rhythmic rasp, and tried to swallow her ire toward a sound that soothed so many times in the past.

Nothing soothed today.

"Feargus," his head popped, his wary glance proved he knew of her temper. "It's almost time to light the torches, and Maggie's still in bed. She has been since we cleared up from the mid-day meal."

"She's not well. She needs rest." Eyes narrowed, he ran his thumb over the blade of his dirk. Fiona sighed.

Feargus was a warrior. No nuances for a man of his sort. Guilt was cut and dry. He imagined the Bold's neck under that honed edge, and found satisfaction in the thought. A vengeful draw of blood to ease his own conscience. But it would never erase it. Guilt was a gray thing with a wide spread shadow.

Fiona crossed her arms, her foot tapping a swift metrical beat. She didn't want vengeance, she wanted answers. "You're as worried as I am."

"I'll admit she's never been sick before."

"You've seen Glen Toric."

"What has that to do with anything?" His eyes shifted away, culpable. He should have known the Bold well enough, vetted him more strongly. Just because the man was a brilliant tactician and fearless warrior did not mean he was decent husband material.

If Feargus had misgivings, she would force him to face them. "You've been to Glen Toric, you know what it is like, if it's full of disease. Should we be looking to some strange illness Maggie brought home with her?"

Feargus snorted. "It's clean enough."

"Fool me for asking." She rolled her eyes. "As if a man is any judge of such a thing."

Fidgety as Fiona, Feargus rose to pace between the chair and the fire. "I can tell you, there weren't people puking their guts in the streets, woman."

She clicked her teeth, "Impervious probably."

A caustic rumble carried through the high window, voices raised in fight. Feargus frowned, focused on the doorway, as the sound grew with an alarming speed toward the keep. Someone would be there soon, to report the uproar. Fiona shook her head at Feargus, telling him to stay put. They had more important problems to sort out.

She rushed on, as the outer door burst open, intent on gaining information before anyone could get from the door to the Great Hall. "Were there signs that the people were brutal?"

That gained Feargus' attention. She knew it would, had held off asking, rather than plant seeds in a mind fertile with anger. "What are you asking?"

"Are they a brutal people?"

Color raced up his neck, shading his face as he shouted, "Are you finally telling me there were marks on our daughter? If he put a hand on her, I'll bloody kill him, I'll . . ."

"I never laid an ill hand upon her body!"

Fiona spun around, as fast as her husband had, to see Talorc, bold as his name implied, disheveled from a fight, surrounded by a hostile pack of MacBede sons backed by a huge crowd of clansmen. He stood in the entrance to the hall, tall and defiant, as though Feargus the younger and Nigel did not have a grip of his shoulders, captors delivering captive.

The MacBede charged toward them. "What in God's name have you done to our daughter?" He bellowed.

Armed with his own might, Talorc shook away his captors, stepped toward Feargus. The two lairds faced off like raging bulls. Or, at the least, Feargus looked like a raging bull. Fiona tilted her head, studied Talorc.

With seven sons and a warrior of a husband, she was accustomed to fights, knew how to read opponents, how to judge the intensity of the conflict. The Bold would not back off, he stood large, shoulders back, chest forward, confrontational. Feargus' head was forward, prepared for attack. The Bold would hold his own, but he would not be the aggressor.

Good. If Feargus wanted to fight a man half his age, when the other would fight merely to defend himself, so be it. He was on his own.

A sharp sideways nod to Jamie, the only one whose eye she could catch, and word passed round the broad, barbaric circle of men. Anxious to fight, they did not stand still, kicked at the floor as her instruction spread. Grumbles and sideway glances to her ensured they didn't like the message, but they would not jump into the fray. That was as much satisfaction as she could hope for.

The combatants circled, feigned charges, until finally they met with an impact that forced deep grunts from each. They shoved, neither gaining ground. Feargus fought with punches, The MacKay blocked hits, parried each blow with a bark to settle the conflict with reason. A fruitless effort against weeks of building fury.

"Feargus." The Bold shouted above the roar of a hostile crowd. "I'm telling you I never harmed her, would never want to." He thrust The MacBede away.

Broken apart, both men backed off, breathing deeply, to catcalls for violence. Feargus dove in again, struggled. Talorc avoided a direct hit to his mouth, but caught one in the gut.

"You want to fight now, do you," the MacKay bashed into Feargus, caught him in a headlock, "Tell me why you took my Maggie, old man." They twisted and turned, fell to the floor. "She's mine," Talorc hissed.

"Forget that," Feargus heaved.

Talorc pinned him. "She's pledged to me and then you steal her when my back is turned. Give me a good reason for taking her out from under my protection."

290

Feargus snorted. "You call that protection?"

"Steal her away?" The Younger dove onto the Bold, to pull him off his father. "You want to take on someone your own age with that challenge?"

"That would be me." Nigel pushed forward, followed by Alec, who claimed, "Oh no, you don't, I'm more his size."

"Stop!" A good head shorter than her children, Fiona stood, arms akimbo, eyes narrowed, and waited until the entire hall silenced.

"Nora," she called out to the lass rooted by the door that led to the kitchens. "Bring out some chicken and a dram. The man must be freezing from his travels."

"Fiona."

"Ma."

"Mother."

Feargus and the boys complained. She ignored the indignant cries, shooed the other clansmen from the hall. Tone sharp as a pinched ear she ordered, "Let him up, and leave him be. I want to hear what he has to say."

Wary, reluctant, they followed her command. The Bold and Feargus stood, brushed themselves off and refused eye contact. Talorc straightened, his attention on the mistress of the keep. "I heard you had been taken deathly ill, Fiona MacBede, but you're looking fit enough now."

"Cheeky boy," she admonished and wondered if she could shake his irreverence. "I'm not the one who's ailing."

He stood, arrogant and angry, still heaving with the effort of defending himself. He had already proved he had no intention of inflicting harm. He was not out to make

enemies. He was out to fetch his Handfasted.
Fair enough, if he deserved her.

She waited as his anger turned to
impatience.

"I'm sorry others are ill, but I'd like to
see Maggie."

No one moved. Talorc looked at the
somber faces, the antagonism that came with
bereavement. His arrogance froze. He shook
his head, to negate thoughts racing into it. A
flash of emotion shuttered through him.
Emotion Fiona could not read. Concern she
expected, but not with an edge of caution.

"Maggie's not well?"

Only his eyes shifted, his body frozen,
feelings held tight.

Angered that the man wasn't more
frantic with worry, Fiona snipped. "She's still
abed, and it's near dusk."

Crisdean barreled forward. "I've seen
animals go to ground when they've been
poorly treated."

"She's not been poorly treated." Talorc
snapped, but gave little notice to Crisdean,
intent on Fiona instead, as if she held the
answers. "Did she say she'd been ill-treated?"

"There was another woman at the keep
for you."

Talorc cursed. "Not to my mind and she
knew that."

Thank God, Fiona released her breath.
The confrontation between the two Lairds
confirmed Talorc could control his
aggression. It was the worry of another
woman that had nagged.

The Bold did not command his patience
as well as his aggression. "I've come a long
way to fetch her. Where is she?"

Feargus blocked him. "She's no' fit to
travel."

Fiona restrained Feargus, with a hand on his arm. "Settle yourself now, we need to hear what the man has to say."

"We'll hear it from Maggie." Feargus argued.

"If that were true, we'd have heard it by now."

"Has she said nothing?" Talorc asked.

Fiona shook her head and looked to the men who surrounded her. They were all of a size, powerfully built men, who took up space in a hall the size of a practice field. It was more than build, it was their presence. These were men of authority, they carried it with them. Force sizzled in the air around them.

It was not up to a ma or a da or great overbearing brothers to decide whether Maggie left for Glen Toric. It would be up to Maggie and the Bold. Fiona balanced just how to move forward, to protect her daughter without alienating the man.

Gentling the truth, Fiona said, "Feargus is right, we're that worried about Maggie. She has not been well, certainly not fit for travel."

"What sort of illness does she have?"

Fiona had taken his arm, to lead him to the fire, but stopped. "You're not surprised, are you? You've expected her to be ill? You know what it is she's suffering from?" All her worries about sickness at Glen Toric flooded back.

He didn't answer her, but nodded toward the three maids putting food out by the fire. "You offered me a bite to eat,"

Anger billowed. "You expected her to be sick. What are you not telling me? Are others ailing at Glen Toric?"

"I'm wanting to see Maggie."

"And you will." Fiona snapped, "I'll go up and fetch her myself."

"Give me your word you'll not hide her away."

"How dare you." Feargus snarled.

"How dare you steal her?" Talorc shouted right back.

"Stop it, both of you." Fiona glared, "I promise that you will be seeing Maggie within the hour. Though I make no pledge you will see her alone. Now eat." She waved toward the food, as she turned to fetch her daughter . . . who stood upon the stairs.

Stronger for the rest, Maggie watched Talorc with her family, and felt a flood of relief. She had missed him, wanted him to guide her through the change in her place within her own home.

She knew he could, knew he would understand and, when he didn't, she knew he would hold her while she rode the waves. That is, if he were there for her.

He might not be.

She sat on the step, watched through the railings as her da charged into a fight, and her brothers circled and growled, no better than a pack of dogs ready to rip to shreds.

They meant to send him away without seeing her. Without asking her what she wanted. She did not want him to go, almost called out to stop them, until she realized if he did not stand against them, for her, then he did not want her.

She prayed he would make a stand.

Her mother interceded, as she did so often with her brothers, her da. The voice of reason in a volatile family, the hand of calm but firm control. Fiona wielded her power with ease.

Maggie stood, garnering her strength by watching a master.

Talorc's voice rose to the ceiling.
"How dare you steal her?"

That's just fine, Maggie thought, stir up the hostilities. But it didn't. All her da did was grunt. Her brothers followed his lead, their heads up, arms crossed against chests puffed up with a lot of hot air.

Silly posturing.

Her mother turned toward her, saw her and stopped.

At least Maggie was well enough to take a stand to settle things. She called out to her Handfasted. "You've come."

Talorc toppled his bench in his rush to rise.

Good. He was either that glad to see her, or that wary of seeing her. Either way meant he was not glaring at her with accusation.

"Your ma says you've been ill." He called up to her.

"Aye." She started down.

The Bold crossed to meet her.

"Are you better now? Can you travel?"

She didn't know her answer, procrastinated with a touch to his shoulder, "You're wet."

"Aye, it's snowing out there."

"Well, come with me, then." She stepped off the stairs, tugged at his arm, and led him toward the table. "You need the fire and food. I'll not have you thinking the MacBedes don't take care of travelers."

He moved with her, like a docile pet. She bit back a grin, determined to fuss over him as she settled her own feelings. But as they neared his plate, the stench of rotten meat soured Maggie's fragile stomach. She pulled back in horror. "Ma."

"What?" Fiona looked about as if she couldn't find the problem that was right under her nose.

Even her brothers looked innocently surprised by her reaction, but they were good at pulling the innocent when set on pranks. She would put this down to them, although how it got past her mother, was beyond her ken.

"Did you do this?" She grabbed the plate and shoved it at her siblings, mindful to keep one hand across her nose, away from the foul smell of it. "Which of you would insult my Handfasted by bringing out putrid meat?"

"It's fine," Talorc reached over her arm for a drumstick, kept Maggie from pulling it away as he took a bite, all the while, his eyes intent on her.

Horrified, Maggie yanked his arm, to keep the meat from his mouth, and gagged. As the meat juices ran down his hand, bile rose in her throat. She tore away, searched for an exit, made it as far as a bowl left for the dogs and retched, despite a too empty stomach. The foul scent wafted around her, stirred another bout of gagging.

Talorc curled around her back, his arm across her stomach, one hand holding her hair from falling forward. She heaved a deep breath, slumped away from him, against the wall. Talorc took a mug of ale from her mother.

"Are you alright, now lass? Would you like a bite of this bread?" She moaned, shoved his arm away as he tried to give her a piece. The whole of her family hovered.

"She's been sleeping more than you think she needs?" Talorc asked her ma instead of herself. Maggie was sick enough not to care.

"Aye," Fiona admitted, "we told you she was ill." But he didn't pay attention to Fiona's worries. Instead he knelt down next to Maggie and urged her to eat the bread.

"Trust me lass, it will make you feel that much better." She kept trying to move away, as he tried to force it past her lips.

"Leave her be." Feargus stormed, but Fiona waylaid him.

"No Feargus, let him feed her. I think he has the right of it."

Maggie could hear her brothers and her da grouse but, as usual, Fiona had the last say.

Maggie ate the bread, just so he would leave her alone. But he didn't leave her alone. He picked her up and carried her back over by the fire, and that horrible smell. She must have flinched, for he ordered, "Someone take the chicken away."

"There's naught wrong with your chicken." Fiona argued, but she took the plate and passed it to one of the clanswoman who had come out to watch the commotion.

"There's naught wrong with Maggie, either." Talorc had the nerve to smile, an indulgent lift of lips.

"You have no heart," Maggie moaned and pushed out of his arms, surprised that she didn't wobble with sick.

"Feeling a bit better with the bread?" He asked.

"A body always feels better once the sick is out. Besides, that foul meat is gone."

She couldn't read his pleasure, but it was there, in his eyes, in the slant of his mouth. She was sick and he was thrilled. Stupid oaf.

"Maggie," he cajoled, "if you're feeling a mite better, we need to have words."

"You talk to her here." Fiona placed an arm around her daughter.

"Is that how you want it, Maggie?"

Confused over his delight in her illness, Maggie couldn't think, didn't want to. If he was to tell her the Handfasting was over, she did not want to be alone. She nodded.

"Alright, then," He stood, surrounded by the men in her family, confronting Maggie and her ma. "Have you told your family we're no longer Handfasted?"

Her roiling stomach contracted. She should have asked to be alone. Had not truly anticipated his words or the kick they held. But no, she asked her family to stay. A vocal lot, now stunned to silence as he ended their time together.

Pride squashed the urge to turn in to her mother's hold. She broke free, stood tall, and fought for words, as the silence was broken by outraged gasps of her family.

His voice rose above it. "Acknowledge it or no, after what went on in that barn, you're my wife and you know that."

"In a barn?" She didn't know whose bellow it was, or how many were yelling and threatening, but this was her fight.

The blasted man had no discretion. No thought to protect her modesty. Who did he think he was?

She shoved at his chest. "How dare you?" As if to push back his words. "You great big loud troll. You have the mouth of a harpy." He caught her wrists, she kicked him. "I'm so bloody sick of you confronting me with an audience."

"I tried to talk to you in private."

"Well, you could have tried harder."

"Crisdean," Maggie yanked her hands free. "Punch him for me, will you?"

Her da stopped him. Maggie scowled. Her father looked like he wanted to cry and didn't know if he was happy or sad about it.

"Da?" Maggie asked.

Fiona murmured. "She's not sick, then."

"Of course I'm sick. Didn't you just see . . ." her words were dwarfed by Talorc's snort.

Oh Lord, she groaned, batted at Talorc's arms, as he swept her up in his hold.

"She insults me by clinging to a bare head and the MacBede colors." But Talorc didn't look insulted. He looked boastful, the great big loud mouthed brute.

"Oh . . . my . . . Good Lord!" Fiona's hands flew to her cheeks, "Did you hear that Feargus? Did you hear what the Bold is saying?"

"Should you be wearing a kerchief, Maggie?" her da asked.

Maggie blushed, a hot, burning, face reddening blush. "He's sayin' nothin'" Maggie tried to distract them, but no one listened to her.

Maggie was dizzy from looking from one to the other. Her ma, her da, had the strangest looks. Her brothers were not much better. Crisdean blushed, embarrassed, which was impossible to believe, even with seeing. Sibeal, Feargus the Younger's wife had moved up beside him. He had his arm around her shoulder and was smiling at her.

None of it made sense. They talked riddles around her, as if she weren't there. Did her family understand what the Bold was saying? Would he now boast of her begging for him to take her?

"Bold," she warned him. This was private business. And not at all settled, the way he told it.

"Remember when I carried the twins? Remember how I was to the smell of roasting bird?"

Feargus looked like he'd been hit by a bull. "You seduced my daughter," his words ominously soft.

"I'm married to your daughter, you old goat!" Talorc bellowed to the rafters.

"Don't call him an old goat." Maggie stormed. "He's my father, and I never pledged marriage to you."

"Then you better do so, Maggie MacBede."

She pushed out of his hold, settled her skirts with a harsh snap of fabric and a more gentle brush of hands, then looked up, ready to confront him. "Just tell me why, Talorc MacKay." She lifted her chin. "Tell me why I have to do anything of the sort, when I'm safe, here with my family?" Aye, maybe, just maybe, she was his wife but he had a few things to learn before she would be ready to leave with him.

"Maggie." Her mother hissed.

Talorc was gentler. "Maggie, have you not been listening to what we've been saying?"

"Aye, I've been hearing you tell tales that are best left between us." She punctuated her words by shoving at him, glancing away only once at her da's startled bark of . . . well, it wasn't quite laughter but it was far from anger. Which made no sense at all.

Once again, they sided with the Bold against her. It had been the way of things from the first moment of their meeting, as well as his habit of cornering her in front of others. They ganged up without her any the wiser, and ill- prepared for the conflicts that would change her life.

For once, she would like to know what everyone else knew ahead of her.

For once.

But the Bold would never give her that advantage.

Everything was beyond her except for his high- handed tendency to push her into tight places and make her a public spectacle.

She was just as angry with her parents. They always knew what he was up to but they never told Maggie. They let him tell her, humiliate her, take all her own choices away before she knew herself.

Fiona beamed. Maggie scowled.

"Bold," Maggie tugged at his sleeve, "You're right. It's time we had a private chat."

"It's too late for that, Maggie." He took her hand as if it were a precious, fragile thing. She snorted. She was no little blossom. "Maggie, you've been sleeping, you can't keep your food down and my dinner smelled foul to you."

"You've been told, I haven't been well."

"You're well enough, Maggie."

She pulled out of his hold, "Easy for you to say. You tell him ma," but her ma only grinned.

Talorc leaned closer. "Your ma knows you aren't ill, lass. You're with child. Our child. We're going to have a wee bairn."

She blinked. Saw the huge smiles of everyone around her. She stood, like a silent jackdaw, mouth agape. Words wouldn't come. And then she realized, they had all known, her brothers, her parents, the clan members who still stood in the hall. They knew from the twisted words he'd been saying.

He did it again. A huge moment in her life had been laid bare to everyone before she had a clue. As if she was the least affected by

it all. Her scream erupted from the depths of
her, a tormented banshee shriek, loud and
shrill enough to split the drums of the ear.

"You bloody, brutal, warring, skunk!"
She heaved in air, fought to crush wild,
uncontrollable tears.

Married to the Bold, there would be no
romantic, sentimental journeys of memory.
Each one was wiped out by a power play. He
had taken, controlled and conquered. She was
no more than another victory.

In this moment, she hated him.

Her nostrils flared, as she sucked in air,
trembling with the loss of a magical moment.
The Bold's proud pleasure transformed from
joy to a frown, bewilderment to rigid icy
horror. He bent over, a wary look in his eyes
as he met hers.

"We're talking about an innocent bairn
here, Maggie."

Aye, they were talking about her child
as well as his, though you wouldn't know it.
Too angry for words, she spat at the ground.

"Do you hate me so much, you would
hate my child?"

My child, he had said. Fury trembled
through her.

"Your child, is it?" She shoved her
finger against his chest. "Everything is about
you, what you want, the way you want it.
Victory for you, no thought for me." She spun
half way, took a step, turned back. "You're
having a bloody child, but I'm the one
heaving." She shoved him, hard, in the chest,
and ran out of the hall, out of the keep, and as
far from The Laird MacKay as she could get,
to her brother, her twin, Ian.

She collapsed on his grave; lay upon
the snow, oblivious to the burn of ice against

her bare hands, as she heaved air, sobbed dry tears.

"It's too much, Ian. Every time I turn around, there's a change, a massive, never to be the same, kind of change and I'm the last to know of it, the last to be told the truth.

"First you leave me, then the Bold comes into my life. Gone no more than a cycle of the moon, two at most, and I return home to find it's not the same, the people are changed." She rose up, braced herself on her elbows. "At least to me they are. And now . . ." her hand fisted at her belly. "I've a babe, Ian" she told him, in wonder, "I've a babe, right here, in my belly. Maybe it's the boy you showed me."

Tears filled her eyes, different from the ones that had tried to flow when she fled the keep. These were tears of happiness, fulfillment, excitement. She had not wanted the world to know of her and Talorc. She had wanted to have time together, to get to know each other, in that wondrous way they had found in the barn.

And she had wanted to adjust to what leaving her first home meant.

They had more than a few differences to work on. Things had to be settled between them before spring, when, as she had come to understand, they would be united. Husband and wife.

In the spring.

She thought there was time to work at who they were together, before finalizing their commitment.

Then came his announcement. The gall of it, that he should tell the world of their private affairs. Tell them all what they had been about in the barn. Personal enough, but then he tells them she carries a bairn, before she had an inkling.

He lets them know before she knows, when it's her body doing the carrying. The shock of it, especially now, when so fragile, and knowing it was a boy child, like in her dream. Another man to steal her heart and risk it as easily as her da, her brothers.

Alright, so she had been bred to marry a man like Talorc. And he was the man for her. She no longer had a doubt, knew she would never find another, after being with him. But she would not allow him to command her life or push her faster than her emotions could grasp.

"You can stop your tears."

Maggie spun around to face Talorc, his eyes colder than the stone of Ian's grave, voice sharper and harder than the frozen ground. She'd never heard him like this before.

"We've made a baby, Bold." But the magic of it was lost in her words, which faltered over his icy glare.

What was wrong with him?

"Aye, we've made a babe." He wouldn't look at her, not really, he looked at her belly, he looked at the stone before the grave, he even looked at her nose, she was sure of that. But he wouldn't look at her eyes.

"Why are you angry with me?"

His nostrils flared. His fists, held rigid at his side, bunched and flexed. Would he strike her? Never.

"I'm taking you back to Glen Toric, to make sure you don't do any harm to the child. When it's born, you'll be brought back here. Alone."

She couldn't breathe. Why was he doing this? Why had he turned so cruel?

The whole of her body started to shake. "You'll not have my child."

He turned away and spit. "Not your child. My child. You let your family, your whole clan, see well enough how you felt about that."

"What are you saying?"

"You said it yourself. Screamed it, like a banshee."

She remembered now, the look on his face. He did not understand her fury, and took it upon himself to choose assumptions. Well, he could just swallow those thoughts.

She stood. "You tell the world things about me, private personal things, before you even speak with me." She closed her eyes. Even to her, the argument sounded weak, did not warrant the fury she spilled in the hall.

"I thought you were a better woman, Maggie MacBede. I didn't think you would be so greedy for my touch and hate me at the same time. Nor did I ever dream your hatred would carry over to a harmless babe. I never thought you were so . . ."

He looked away.

He believed she didn't want him. He imagined she didn't want the babe. Stunned, she waited to hear just what he thought of her. How wrong he could be.

"Rest assured, you'll be free to go for one of those puny weak men you want, without burden of my child. I'd not have you near it. It's bad enough that you have to carry the wee one for months. I can only hope the MacKays will make-up for that."

He spun around and left her to the frozen ground . . .

to a frozen heart . . .

to a life that appeared as dead as her beloved brother.

CHAPTER 3 – BROKEN

Wind whipped through Seonaid's hair, a banner of dark tendrils in her wake. Sitting straight in the crux of her lap, his face alive with excitement, her son, Deian, rode before her on the grand gelding.

Ingrid was gone. Again. But this time she left Deian on his own. A wee child, barely five years, and she left him alone. For certain, Ingrid held no love for Seonaid, but they had an arrangement. They managed without a man out here on the edges of MacKay land. They helped each other with chores, took turns watching both Deidre's Eba and Seonaid's own young Deian. Without family or protection Seonaid, Deidre and Deidre's sister, Ingrid, needed each other. Power in numbers.

Dear Lord, please don't let Ingrid fall prey to the swine who has been stealing young girls, the same who took Ysenda.

Desperate to get to Glen Toric, Seonaid pushed their mount, goaded by the swell of fear from the moment she walked through the cottage door and felt a heavy, foreboding. It was too quiet, ominously so. Afraid to call, afraid to draw attention, she searched silently, despite the rushes below her feet.

She moved through three small rooms before a small sound, just enough to tell her she wasn't alone came from above, in the loft.

She stood for an eternity at the foot of the
ladder, looking up, waiting for something to
happen, anything, so she wouldn't have to
climb up there, vulnerable.

The thought of Deian forced her to
move, one foot up a rung, then another and
another, all the while knowing whoever was
there would see the top of her head before she
could see anything. Still, she climbed, her
head cocked defensively, stopped, just before
the top. Holding her breath, propelled with
worry for her boy, she pushed straight up. A
set of dark eyes peered at her from beneath
the bed.

"Deian!" She whispered, and hauled
herself up onto the floor to pull him out, hug
him close, rocking, comforting him,
comforting herself.

He wasn't allowed in the loft. That's
where the sisters slept and the drop was too
dangerous for a wee tyke. "What are you
doing up here?"

Squirming, he pushed away. "Can we go
down now?" he asked. "I need to piss." He
wailed, his tunic growing wet even as he
wailed.

"Oh, aye, we can go down." She
promised, not mentioning the mistake, not
pressing for answers. "You just let me start."
She lowered herself onto the ladder and
opened an arm, hunched her body, so he could
climb between her feet and her shoulders.

"I was good." He sniffled. "I tried hard
to wait."

"Aye, you did lad." She comforted.
"How long did you wait."

"A long, long time."

"Och, no," she helped him jump the last
few rungs, "so long, too long I'm thinking."

She wanted him safe, but she also wanted him comfortable.

She looked down at the sorrowful bow of his head.

"She promised me you would be quick." He sniffled.

"Me, now?"

"Aye."

"Ingrid said this? Was she alone?"

He scrunched his shoulders and tried to undo the ties of his braies.

"Here," Seonaid freed his hands, so she could finish the task before he was all in knots. "Did Ingrid put you in the loft?"

"Aye." He wiggled out of his wet breeches. "Told me to wait until you were home. Said you wouldn't be long, but you were long and I'm hungry."

She wasn't long, at least not as long as Ingrid would have expected.

"When did she do this?"

"Before I could finish my porridge." He grumbled through the cloth, as Seonaid pulled the wet Tunic over his head.

In the morning? Ingrid knew Seonaid was seeing to the sheep, that she hadn't expected until near dark.

"Did you hear anyone else?"

He shook his head, as she led him, naked, over to the fireplace. It was cold, but not so cold that it had been put out before the girl left. It had been allowed to burn itself down.

She stared at a glint of hot ash and felt her own anger spark. One spit of the fire would have ignited the rushes on the floor. One snap, and Diean would have been trapped in the loft. She banked her own fury, to focus on getting him out of there and tracking Ingrid.

She'd dressed him in fresh tunic and braies with wool chausses, like a grown man. Clothes Deidre made for him. Clothes that matched the Bold's. She hated putting her boy in them, though he took great delight in feeling so grown-up.

"Do you want to go to Glen Toric with me?" She'd asked, knowing the answer, knowing he always wanted to go up to the castle.

"Will the Bold be there?"

"No, not just now. He's off to find his Handfasted."

The lad loved the Bold, loved the excitement of Glen Toric. As much as he thrilled to the infrequent visits, she hated them. Hated the way everyone looked at him, guessing who is father might be.

Oddly enough, everyone thought it was The Bold. No one realized the lad looked just like the man who seeded her belly. The idea too horrific for them. Still she tried her best to hide him away.

"Will Padraig be there?"

That startled her. "Padraig?"

He nodded.

"Aye, I believe Padraig will be there." She told him, as she wrapped him in his cloak and got them both out of there before anyone could come find them.

* *

Frozen between fury and despair, Maggie's lungs shut down. Her lips immobile, her body rigid. Her eyes the only part of her to shift, narrow, as she watched him walk away.

The great hulking clod. He had his nerve, to tell her where she would be when. To decide whether or not she could have her own babe.

"I'm the one getting sick. I'm the one keeping the child."

He did not turn around.

"Don't you dare walk away from me!" She shouted.

He called over his shoulder. "Be ready to leave on the morrow."

"Who the bloody hell do you think you are? You have no right to take my child. You won't succeed."

Taut fury, barely leashed, Talorc turned. Maggie's blood chilled.

Her entire life had been spent in the world of warriors, but never once had she been the focus of their violence, all the more potent for being leashed. The tremble of his body proved restraint a fragile barrier. Maggie willed him to keep a distance, as her mind raced, a frantic search for a way to deflate his fury. Then she looked to his eyes and realized it was not anger that swirled around her. It was not fury that he kept at bay.

It was despair.

She had broken his heart.

Cautious, against an eruption of emotion, she rose, took a step forward. Talorc didn't move. She took another step, and then another, and another, until she stood close enough that the fog of her breath touched him. But still, other than to turn his head away, he remained immobile. She jammed her finger in his chest.

"You're not a man of your word."

A muscle twitched at the side of his jaw. She had enough brothers to know it for the warning it was. "You don't want the babe."

"You are like all the rest. A foolish, stupid man." She pivoted, to pace, but he grabbed her arm, whirled her back to face him. He wanted to blast her with anger. She cut in first. "You think you are smart enough to tell me how I feel. What I want." Pushed beyond caution, she taunted. "You know nothing. You're as thick as the rest of them. Thick as two short planks." Disgusted, she pulled free, twirled on her heel, went back to Ian's grave.

He caught her by her collar. She turned and bit him. With a yelp he let go.

"That will teach you to stop me when I mean to go."

"Aye, and you left me when my back was turned."

"My mother was ill."

"Ill over a letter you wrote."

She hadn't expected him to know that. Nor had she expected his expressive eyes to be as barren as the winter's trees.

"Do you know what it was like for me? Do you have any idea?"

"Maggie," He raised hands, in appeal, then dropped them, listless, to his sides. "There's no point in going on with this. You didn't want the Handfasting, you don't want to be my wife and you don't want the child. Leave it, leave me be."

He turned away, his shoulders rounded, mirroring the way he pulled into himself.

Let him go she thought, but was beyond holding in the last words. "Ealasaid tried to stop me from going, but it was you who could have. If you'd been there.

"But no, you were off to leave me halfway to marriage and not quite there." She swiped at her eyes, afraid that crying would keep her from talking and she didn't know any other way to stop him. "It's not an easy place for a lass to be."

At least he stopped, though he would only look at her over his shoulder. "You could have told them we were one, Maggie. You could have worn my plaid, a kerchief upon your head."

"Oh aye, wouldn't that have been grand. Announce to the whole world what we'd been about. Nothing to be shy about there, is there? Especially doing so on my own, with the risk you might not be coming back!"

Finally, he turned. "I came back to find my wife had deserted me." Anger. She could use his anger, better than his defeat.

"I came home to see my clan."

"So, to your mind, you're still a MacBede? Is that how you can hate a poor defenseless babe that's not even born?"

"Don't be picturing thoughts in my head that aren't there."

He looked toward the horizon, distorted now by the gloom of dusk. Maggie watched him, the way the wind teased his hair, the strong angles of his face. His throat worked, as though to swallow unwanted tears, and suddenly Maggie knew how deeply she had hurt him.

"I want this child, Bold."

He flashed a glance, but it was gone as quick as it flickered toward her. "Then it's just me you don't want." It was not a question.

"Don't want you?" She raised her hands in argument only to slap them down in anger. He never, ever listened to her. She moved over, to stand in the path of his vision. "You want to know how much I don't want you?"

She was planted in front of him yet he still refused to meet her eyes. "Is it because of Seonaid's lad? It's not mine, you know. I don't care what games she plays, it isn't mine. She never even says it is, just lets people think so."

Maggie brushed that aside. "I never knew she had a child. But I do know, if you tell me Seonaid has nothing to do with us, then she has nothing to do with us. I trust your word over her."

"You do?"

"Aye. You may be a fool in thinking you know what's best for me. But I don't doubt your honesty."

He mulled that over. "So what do you think is best for you?"

Her first victory with the man. "It's best for me to tell you how much I don't want you." His eyes twitched, but he stood firm. She couldn't help but smile.

Life as he knew it was over. Dead and buried and so she let him know. "I wed thee, Talorc the Bold, with no 'wills' about it. Forever more this means." The impact of her own words, hit her. She had not expected that. Tears came to her eyes. "That's how much I don't want you." She sniffed back a sob, horrified.

Talorc stood stricken, his jaw dropped, eyes wide, but she couldn't stop. "Care or not,

Bold, I'm bound to you now, for as long as we both shall live."

"Wait."

"It's too late." She hung her head, realizing that she had pushed him too far this last time. He no longer wanted her, but her impetuous self trapped them both. "What's been said has been said and can't be taken back. You've been storming over my wants long enough, it is my turn to sweep over yours." She lifted her chin. She would not be sorry. She would not be humiliated. "You started this. I have a right to finish it."

He grabbed her by the shoulders, his jaw clenched so tight he hissed. "Just wait." Then he shouted over his shoulder. "William, Bruce, get a MacBede and come, and be quick about it."

"No." Maggie tried to jerk free, but he held fast. "You'll not be sending me away from you. Just try it and you'll find me returning before you can blink."

She half expected him to lift her up and carry her to the keep, he was that impatient. "What changed your mind, Maggie? Just inside you were screaming like the devil was on your heels and now, now you're changing to sweet songs? What changed you?"

A sharp jerk of her shoulders and she pulled free, turned away, rather than face her shame. Breath quick and shallow she asked, "Could you not see, could you not tell how hungry I was for the sight of you?"

His hands gripped her shoulders. "You fled from me." She tried to twist free, but he wouldn't let her go. "Tell me why, Maggie. Why did you run, screaming, as if hell was at your heel?"

Och, but she hated the tears, swiped at them. "Why can't you let me go, let me have a

cry in peace? Why does everything have to be
said in front of a crowd? Why do you tell all
of them, before you even tell me?" He held
her arms, so she couldn't even brush the salty
wet of her cheeks. Turned her, as he pulled
her against him, raised a knuckle and brushed
at her tears. She mumbled against his chest.

"First, it's the wooing, the Handfasting,
then it's what we did in the barn . . ." she
couldn't talk over the embarrassment of that,
it choked her.

"It was beautiful, Maggie."

She hiccupped. "Just like two dogs in
the yard."

"No," he rocked them back and forth,
"No, like a man and woman bonded in the
flesh."

But she wasn't finished with his
injustices. "The babe, Talorc? How could you
tell everyone I was with child before I even
knew?" She pushed far enough away to look
up into his eyes. "You think that's not
wrong?" She pounded at his chest, her face
scrunched up with the crying. "Why do you
always have to see me weak and foolish, when
what you need is a woman who's strong and
inspired?"

He cupped her face in his great
powerful hands and stilled her. "What I need
is you, no one else, just you." He pulled her
close again, held her so tight she could barely
breathe. She told him so. He loosened his
hold, looked down at her, his eyes no longer
bleak with despair, but hard and serious.

She had to ask, to understand, "You
didn't want my words of wedding you. You
told me to stop."

"I told you to wait."

"It's too late for that. The words were
said."

"Why, Maggie? Are you saying you want me or is it for the babe?"

She should give up on him. Should leave him to his misery if he couldn't tell what she was feeling. But she couldn't do that. His hold was too strong. She admitted as much. "I wanted you before I even knew about the child."

"You left."

"To see my family once more, because I knew, after this, my home would be at Glen Toric."

His eyes held her, though he did not say a word.

"Talorc, do you not ken what I am saying?" she asked.

Finally, he spoke, though it only proved how thick he was. "Do I have your heart?"

"Och, you great oaf! You've had my heart forever."

He smiled. She slapped at him, with as little consequence as the brush of a horse's tail. He laughed. "You hid it well."

"Oh, aye," she retorted, "like when we were in the barn. I hid it verrrry well!" Brazen was the only word for it. She ducked her head, to hide her own awkwardness.

"Och, Maggie." This time, when he pulled her close, it was a tender hold. "I thought you didn't want me. I love you so much, and I thought you didn't want me."

"You promised you wouldn't leave, you promised me forever. I'm holding you at your word."

Shouts, the thunder of running feet, came from below.

"Bold!"

"Maggie!"

"Don't you hurt her now!"

Maggie peaked around Talorc's broad chest to see William and Bruce hurrying up the hillside, Maggie's family and clan in tow.

She sniffled, shoved at him. "Let me go."

"I don't think so."

"People are coming and my eyes are all red."

"You look beautiful."

"Talorc, when are you going to learn, I mean what I say?"

His smile was wide, as he shook his head. She butted him, her forehead to his chin. Not as effective as the bridge of his nose, but enough that he released her. She tried to scramble away, he caught her, lifted her up over his shoulder.

"I'll never forgive you for this, Bold. Do you hear me? I'll never forgive . . ."

"What is it, Bold?" William was there first, with her brother, Feargus the younger, both out of breath with the rush. The others weren't far behind.

"Tell them what you said, Maggie, admit it before witnesses."

She closed her eyes, and swallowed. "Can you keep nothing between the two of us?"

"Not this." He let her slide off his shoulder and down his body. When she stood, he took her right hand in his right hand. Her left in his left.

In this, he was right. Witnesses gave it strength. If only he would prepare her for what he meant to accomplish.

"You move too fast for me, Bold."

"You'd outdistance me if I didn't."

"Oh, Maggie," Fiona gasped. Maggie could hear the tremor of her mother's words but it was no time for mothers and daughters. It was the time for a woman with her man.

She looked down at the clasp of her hands to Talorc's. Her nose twitched with an itch, so she lifted their joined fists to rub it. Talorc tugged them down. She looked at him, at the great huge warrior who stood before her, and took a deep breath. "I wed thee, Talorc the Bold, the bane of my life, for as long as we both shall live."

To him alone, the words had been a simple gesture. With all her people around, the significance closed her throat to any more words.

Her life would never be the same, was set on a different course than she would have chosen. A course she was proving to hold to just as stubbornly as the one she had dreamt of.

Talorc squeezed her hands. "And I, Talorc MacKay, wed thee, Maggie MacBede, delight of my life, for as long as we both shall live."

Everyone cheered, as Maggie glared at her husband. He laughed, grabbed her into another bear hug. "I know you wanted it just between the two of us Maggie, but I wanted witnesses. I want the world to know."

"Maggie," Feargus broke in, as quiet as a man could be with a voice more used to bellowing. "Why did you scream like that when you learned of the babe?"

She burrowed closer into Talorc's hold. If he wanted to take charge, she would let him.

"Ah, Feargus, a woman's a delicate thing."

"That yell wasna' delicate." Bruce had the gall to murmur.

"Bruce," Talorc admonished, "Give her a care. One minute her family thinks she's an innocent maiden. Next, they don't know for sure she's married, but they do know she's with child. And they know this before she even has a clue to why she's feeling like she's feeling."

She shoved far enough away to stay in the comfort of his arms, but still able to look at him. "I should know before you."

"You will next time." He leaned down, hooked her behind her knees and lifted her up. "But for now, you've had too much excitement. I'm thinking you need to lie down."

"She's been in bed all day," Jamie complained.

"Aye, well, I'll just have to stay with her, and make certain she's not failing." Talorc announced, to ribald cheers, as he headed for the keep.

"You forgot a vow!" Someone shouted.

She felt him pivot, and then drop her legs, so her body lowered against his.

"Aye, we forgot a vow." He took her hands again, and as soon as everyone was near, he told her, "With my body, I thee worship."

She ducked, to hide the blush that crept up her neck, to her face.

"Maggie, have you nothing to say to me?"

She looked up at him, through her lashes. Stood on her tip toes and put her mouth to his ear. "With my body, I thee worship."

He laughed, a great bellowing thing, and lifted her back in his arms. "Well then, you best come prove it." The crowd roared their approval.

"You have no spine for secrets, Bold."
Bold merely chuckled. "That's how I know, if
Seonaid has a son, it's not yours."

He stopped to look at her. "They were
at Glen Toric when I arrived."

"She's never there, if you're not."

She watched him, but could make no
sense of his frown. When he did speak, it was
as if pulled from deeper thoughts. "The child
is not mine. I never had her, never once."

"But she wants people to think it is."

She felt the jar of his breath, as if he
needed extra air to bolster his words. "I don't
know what she's about. We were close,
friends mind you, no more, everyone thinks it
has to be mine."

"But it isn't."

"No."

"And as Laird, it would be your
responsibility to see that the man comes
forward, to own up to his own kin."

"True."

"And, as you don't, it makes you more
suspect."

He grunted.

"You know who it is." It wasn't a
question.

"Aye, but it's not my place to be
telling."

"He's married." Again, it was not a
question.

He grunted again.

She continued. "Could be trouble if he
had a wife when the bairn was conceived."

"If a man seasoned the broth, he can
drink it, bitter or no. But there's more to it
than that. More that is owed to Seonaid than
to reveal the father."

Now was not the time to speak of
Seonaid. Talorc set off again toward the keep.

"I never didn't want you." Maggie admitted.

"You just didn't want to want me."

She laid her head on his shoulder. "Something like that."

"It could be a lass, you know."

He spoke of the babe, wanted to ease her mind, for it was a certainty that any son of his would be a warrior. But she couldn't forget Ian's words. "It will be a boy. Just like his da."

"I'll teach him to be safe."

"You can't stop fate."

"That's what we are, lass. Fate's fruition."

Maggie sighed. Fate's fruition was her fear. It brought as much sorrow as joy. Would the grief be far behind? She wouldn't think on that, couldn't. Right now, all she wanted were these precious moments of delight. Tomorrow could tell its own tale.

CHAPTER 4 – DREAMS

Heads turned, as she rode into the courtyard. Seonaid kept her head high, held back from pulling Deian's hood further up, to better hide his face. No one knew, no one would suspect, she reminded herself. Bold had promised her as much. Explained away her fears that any would look upon Deian and know who his father was.

Still, she couldn't help but worry and so she challenged every eye turned her way, until none would look directly. It was Padraig who broke the frost, walking out of the stables just as she arrived at them.

"You've returned?"

"I have." She nodded, coldly despite the warmth she always felt in Padraig's presence. A big gruff man with his curly brown hair and blunt features, only his eyes gave away his gentler side. A kindness that led him to go out of his way to check on her at the cottage, or find her in the fields, tending sheep.

He would get down on the floor to play with Deian, sparking a hunger deep inside of her, a virulent desire to have him as her son's father and as her husband.

Impossible. She was spoiled goods, a woman no man would want if they knew the truth of it. Nor could she ever conceive of ever wanting a man in the way she believed Padraig wanted her.

Despite that, she trusted him and Lord knew she trusted few. Few trusted her in return. Hers was a lonely world.

She dismounted, reached up for Deian, but not quick enough. Padraig was already there, lowering her son to the hard- packed yard. Unlike her, the lad didn't need time to adjust to standing, despite being astride for two days, trying to find Diedre and Ingrid in all the places Seonaid hoped to find them. The safest places, anyway.

"The Bold has returned with his Handfasted," Padraig offered, as he encouraged Deian to take one of the horse's reins. "Only she is no longer his Handfasted. She's wearing a kerchief."

Seonaid looked at him. "She was forever pushing him away." As if she was too good for the man.

"She's with child."

Anger flourished, as she followed Padraig and Deian into the barn. "He found one way to keep her."

Padraig shook his head. "No, I don't think that's the way of it." He admitted. "There's more to it than that, even when she tried to be free of him, there was more to it than that. Besides, she's a woman. She knows what's best for her."

Seonaid stopped. Padraig looked over his shoulder and frowned. "Did you want to tend the animal yourself?"

Seonaid prayed for patience, though why she bothered was a mystery. "So you're saying because she's a woman marriage is best for her?"

He turned to face her squarely, her son following his example, standing by his side. "She needs a husband and the Bold is a good man."

"Aye, he is a good man, one of the best and he deserves a woman who knows that."

"Like you?" he challenged.

It always came to this, for everyone, and no amount of denying ever made a difference.

"Do you think I climbed into his bed? Is that what you think?"

He had the decency to flush then he bent down to Deian. "There's a lad in the last stall. His name is Jamie and his dog just had pups." He pointed to a young stable boy who stood toward the back of a row of stalls.

Seonaid blushed this time. Her own son and, with the rise of her ire, she forgot he was there, listening. Little bodies had big ears.

Padraig nudged him. "Why don't you go see if he wants to show you the animals?"

Deian struggled with shyness for a moment, looked to her for support. She smiled and nodded. "Go on then, mind stay within earshot."

"I will!" he garbled, as he shot down the length of the barn.

She felt the brush of Padraig's arm, as he came to stand beside her.

"Thank you for that." She offered, refusing to look at him.

"He's a good lad."

"He is that. Better than I could have dreamed."

"You don't usually bring him to the castle."

So he had dropped the question of her attraction to Bold for another question everyone wanted to ask.

"He's too young. I don't want him underfoot when there are so many people about."

"Is that why you rush home when the Bold charges out to fight."

Stunned, she whipped around to study him while he studied the path her son had taken. "Aye, but that's not what most think."

"When we ride off, Bold shuts these gates up, tight orders. Sometimes for days, if not weeks."

"I can't be away so long." She whispered.

"Doesn't Ingrid watch him?"

Seonaid snorted. "Oh, aye, and she was watching him when I went home two days ago. Only she left just after dawn, making him wait alone until I returned near dark." A shudder ran though her at the memory, as Padraig turned to stare.

"She left him alone?"

"Aye. I finally tracked her down this morning. She was with Deidre."

"They both left him?"

Seonaid shook her head. "No, I don't believe so. Deidre seemed as surprised as me." She hesitated before adding, "I'm happy to have Deidre in my home, but Ingrid worries me. She's not right these days."

"You and Deian should move to the castle."

"No," she moved further into the stable, stroked the neck of her horse, "no, there's more danger here than out where I live. Something's not right here at Glen Toric and I'd rather Deian not be close to that."

* *

Maggie.

"Ian." Maggie sat up in bed. The whisper of her name rode across dreams on the cusp of sleep.

Why would he do that? Why would he wait until she was at Glen Toric, before giving her a sense of himself? He had done that before.

She reached out to lay her hand lightly on Talorc's shoulder and waited, as the comfort of his presence stilled her heart. If she'd known how it would feel to have him close, she never would have fought the bond. Even the now familiar sound of Brutus's snuffle reassured her against the phantoms of the dark.

Only, Ian wasn't a phantom to be frightened of.

"Ian." She whispered, fearful of waking Talorc, who wasn't happy with her attachment to her twin. He treated it as a threat, as though Ian might try to take her away. Ian would never do her harm.

But they were a pair, bonded. Too hard to explain.

She waited in the still of the night, her gaze piercing the shadows of the room, her ears strained to hear what couldn't be heard. No figure separated from the gloom. No sound broke through the quiet. Despite his call to her, she didn't feel him near.

After a few minutes, she lay back upon her pillow and wondered if snuggling would wake her husband. If it did, he could take the blame. Hunger that lapped at the core of her came from his teachings. She smiled, placed a hand upon his broad chest, flexed her fingers,

and sighed. Better to let him sleep rather than
risk Ian witnessing the wanton she had
become.

If Ian were close.

She rolled to her side, shimmied her
back against the curve of Talorc's front. Deep
in sleep, his arms wrapped around her, one
hand covering the slight swell of her belly,
and pulled her more securely into the nest of
him.

The gentle sounds of night lulled her to
a doze, neither awake, nor fully asleep. Like a
warm breeze, the call caressed, woke her,
wide eyed and worried.

"Ian," she whispered, caught between
dream and a doze. More under illusion than
reality, she grumbled, "Stop waking me. Talk
to me in my sleep." And fell back to slumber.

This time, when Ian called, she did not
bolt into wakefulness, but stayed inside the
dream. She was in a small boat, on a quiet
stream, asleep, but not quite. She turned
toward the shore, where she knew she would
see them.

Ian grinned broadly, the boy by his
side, tugging to get free, to cross to Maggie.
A mere observer, she couldn't speak, could do
no more than look down at her lethargic self.
One hand dangled in the water, the other laid
protectively over her belly. Her mind smiled.
She felt good, content in her life. Young Ian
was safe in her brother's care, for now.

Then she frowned. Looked to the swell
of her tummy and wondered why, after six
months' time, the babe was still separate from
her.

A breeze rippled, seductive, teased her
neck. A warm, wet, enticing nudge of breath.
It had to be Talorc. She stretched, able to
move to him when she had been unable to

move to Ian. She turned her head to give him access and saw the goblet in her hand.

All thought of Talorc, of the babe or Ian vanished, as she focused on that goblet. She hadn't tasted it, but she knew it was a strange bitter brew.

Drink! Drink! The command hissed and she did. She drank as Ian's voice, distorted with the distance, called out, "Downed ringa. Down ringa".

She frowned.

Downed ringa? Donn it rinka. She gasped, as the dire warning rang clear.

"Don't drink! Don't drink!"

She looked at Ian, confused by what he said as rain drops fell. She opened her mouth to catch them and felt a vise upon her belly so powerful she jackknifed with the pain.

The idyllic moment vanished. The boat rocked, hard, the water a wild torment. It kept lapping at the boy, trying to suck him in to the depths of it. Frozen, she could not move to help him, to go to him, all she could do was cry and wail, "Nooooo!" which made the boat rock with greater ferocity. Then Ian grabbed the boy, held him to his chest.

"Not yet, Maggie, you can't have him yet."

Tears streamed down her face, as she was rocked to and fro and the cries of her name mutated from Ian's voice to Talorc's.

She opened her eyes. The rocking stopped, though Talorc didn't let go of her shoulders. Frantically, she grabbed him, pulled him in and hung on for the life she so dearly needed. "The babe, Bold, I don't have the babe." And then she scrambled, like a demented thing, to see, to look for witness of the loss, but there was no sign of blood, of water, of a small, unformed life between her legs.

Tenderly, she felt her belly. No pains.

"Tell me," Talorc asked, with the wariness of a man who didn't know how to step into women's business, but was desperate enough to try.

She turned to him. "Hold me, Bold, just hold me." And he did, he held her close, settled her trembling, waited for the fear to ease from her. He stroked her back, her head, the length of her hair. He wiped tears from her cheeks, and kissed the paths that he stroked. When, finally, the trembling stopped, he looked down at her.

"What was it, Maggie?" But she couldn't tell him, she couldn't say that the babe was not yet with them, and mayhap, would never be. She couldn't say that something was wrong.

"Just a dream. It frightened me."

"Frightened you?" He nuzzled her neck. "You, me, even Brutus, the mangy wimp." He chuckled and turned her cheek, so she could see the great beast of a dog quivering beside the bed.

Her smile was meager. The dream had shaken her, moreso for the two times Ian's voice had woken her to catch her attention.

"I don't want you fearful, Maggie. You're safe here, you can count on that."

She didn't want to worry him, chose instead to distract. "I know," she smiled as she raised her hand to cup his cheek. "Show me." She leaned up to tease his lips with hers, "Show me just how close you can get, to guarantee my safety."

"You're a dangerous minx."

"Am I?"

"Aye." He lowered his mouth to hers, willing to be distracted, to blind her to the terror of the darkness.

She felt his lips first, as they brushed against her own, teased until she leaned up, further into the kiss, demanding an order that Talorc was quick to obey. It was more than a kiss, he suckled and laved her mouth, her neck, the inside of her arm, all the places she thought quite ordinary, and none of the places that should have made her shy. And in his doing so, her hunger rose until she tormented him in turn, with her own lips and tongue and nips of teeth.

They rolled, taking turns in submission, sometimes meeting in the middle.

"Oh, Bold," her words caressed his swollen hunger, as she dared to be bold herself and lave and suckle that part of him that separated who they were.

He groaned, hard and loud. "Did I wound you?" she teased. He hitched her up his body.

"Aye, you wound me to the core and I want revenge!" He lifted her hips and plunged deep into her softness. As he sheathed himself, he pressed the heel of his hand against their joining. Maggie could no more hold back the moan that came from the depths of her, than she could stop the convulsive rhythm of their union, her desperate reaches to match his thrusts, until her cry mingled with his hoarse shout, his shudder of release toppling her pulse of the same. She landed hard upon him, the fierce beating of their hearts against each other's chest. Her hair fell like a silken wave around them both.

He caressed her derriere, eased them both to their sides, still tangled, still one.

When he spoke, his words were no more than a series of pants. "Tell me, wife. Tell me what you dreamed."

But, like so many dreams, it had dissolved with only a few reminders. She frowned. "The babe, Talorc, it's not young Ian. Not yet." And she let sleep claim her to a night of restless darkness.

Talorc left William and Padraig to stand by the door of the low sod building, while he waded into the stream, to fetch a bucket of water. The river was frigid, would have iced, if the current hadn't kept it moving too fast to form any covering. He welcomed the way it numbed to his knees, for it sent a shock of alertness to his senses.

He turned back to find both of his men had shed their clothes, ready for the steam. Talorc reached them, handed over the bucket so they could go in before him. He rid himself of his own garments, and ducked under the low lintel.

William ladled water onto fiery rocks mounded on top of coals nestled in a small depression in the middle of the dirt floor. Around it there were low benches, with slightly taller ones behind those. Talorc grabbed the sheet he had left there, and wrapped it around his middle, so he wouldn't burn his backside when he sat.

He breathed in deeply, of the steam, of the mint that had been added to the fire and felt every passage in his head clear. "Aye, this is what I needed." He adjusted the sheet so he could lie back upon the bench. "But where is Aed?"

William, happy with the amount of water he had put to hot rock, finally sat down himself. "He's with your lady wife. Seems she had a dream of sorts, wanted to ask him about it."

Talorc grunted. He didn't like her with the storyteller, their heads close together in discussion. Not that he didn't trust Maggie, despite her peculiar caring for puny men. He couldn't deny her dream last night, or the way it terrified her, had her grabbing at her belly.

He shook it off. A dream was merely a dream. There were other, real problems, to sort through.

Padraig doused himself with a ladle of the frigid water, until it dripped from his hair, to his nose, down his massive beard. Like a dog straight out of the loch, he shook it off. Talorc lifted his forearm over his eyes, to protect himself from the slash of water.

"You've watched all the boundaries?"

"Aye. Winter or no, there's been activity."

"Any sign of one of ours meeting them?"

William no longer smiled. "Ours and theirs cross each other. But no sign that they stop to chat."

"What did you learn from Old Micheil," Padraig asked, "when you were closed up with him all day yesterday?"

"Says the same as you, there are comings and goings out east." Talorc ran a hand down his face. "He's too close to the Gunn border for my comfort, but he's too stubborn to stay at the keep for longer than a report."

"There are others closer to the border."

"Aye, Seonaid is out there. She claims it's quiet like, but then she's a woman, and not trained to look for problems."

"Tracks skirt her, but don't go near."

"She's the one you have to move closer to the keep, Laird." Padraig argued, "A woman and child on their own . . . it's not good."

Talorc doused himself with the frigid water, felt his muscles bunch with the shock of it. He knew the truth of what Padraig said, but it was not that easy. "She doesn't want to come." And my relationship with Maggie is just that new, just that fragile, he thought. It was no secret that Talorc didn't want the other woman near enough to cause a problem. "I tried to get her to join up with Nail's people, but she doesn't want to move. Says it was her father's croft, and it's rightfully hers."

"As if we would take it from her." William grumbled.

"She needs to marry." Padraig kept to the woman like a dog to a bone. "That would keep her boy safe."

Talorc looked at William and they both laughed. It was not a humorous sound. Neither explained their reaction, but William did offer, "Her cousin Roger and his family live close."

"And what has he said?"

"Signs of too many intruders." The burly man looked at Talorc, "He thought we had gone that way, when we went to fight the Gunns. He was that shocked when he heard we hadn't. He's thinking of moving his family closer in to the keep. Maybe they can convince Seonaid to move with them."

"You think?" Padraig brightened.

"No." Talorc shook his head and frowned at Padraig. Seonaid was too independent, too eccentric to fit in with those at the keep. That's why she liked to stay by herself. As for the rest of it, Talorc was beyond thinking. He'd thought and thought, and all he did was bite the tail of an idea, only to find he was right back where he started.

"You have to move her to the keep, Laird."

So that was the way of it. "She's gotten to you, then? As if you don't know better."

Padraig kept his eyes on the fire. "Maybe she would marry me."

William barked with laughter. "She'll not marry any but the Bold, and well you know it."

"I visit with her, when I watch the land. She's no' so cold."

Both Talorc and William shot Padraig a look. It was William who asked, "Does she know when to expect you?"

"Great Gods!" Padraig bellowed, "I'm not green you know. What I do, how I do it, and when I do it is for my mind. Woman or no, sweet or no, I keep my actions to myself, without sign of order." He scowled at Talorc. "Do you see any one as the betrayer, Bold?"

He shook his head.

"Beathag?" William asked, but Talorc was quick to shake his head against that one.

"I thought it, it made sense. She still thinks I murdered her poor lass, but she's not the one."

Padraig argued. "Why? Why do you say she's not?"

Talorc drew in a deep breath of the minty air, as William poured more water on the rocks. "Remember when we rode out, to chase the Gunns off our borders?"

They both nodded.

"Well, I told Conegell to keep a watch on her, then I had Brock mention, in front of Una, that we missed the southeastern crag when there were problems there."

"So you think Una's the one?"

"No, but she can't keep a secret in her head, and as her Conegell was always near Beathag, Una tends to find reason to be around Beathag."

"Una told Beathag."

"Aye, and Conegell, good man that he was, faced me with the truth of it."

"Could you imagine having to be owning up for your wife's blabbing?"

"Well, if he has a fault, it's in his silence."

"So what happened?"

Talorc couldn't quite make heads of it. "Beathag went to my Maggie, and told her she knew we had a weakness by the southeastern cragg, and with Gunns about, it should be sorted out. Maggie sent men over there straight away."

"Do you think she knew she was being watched?"

"No, Una didn't know that much."

Both of the other men grunted in understanding.

Aed popped his head in the door. "Room for another," he smiled broadly. Talorc motioned him in.

"Your wife is a lovely woman, Bold." Aed had too much energy for someone thick in the heat of steam. Talorc frowned. Aed, oblivious of the animosity, settled himself on the bench and continued. "Very brave, what with the dreams she has and all."

Talorc grunted. It was enough that he thought Maggie lovely, better than lovely, beautiful and spirited and feisty as a Sidhe.

He didn't want other men to take such notice. He looked at Aed's bony protrusions. All skin and bone and no meat. What did Maggie see in such men?

"Did she tell you of her dream last night?"

"Aye, she did. I think it means the boy is not ready to come over yet."

"She said he couldn't." Talorc admitted. His worst fear, his worst nightmare, was that the boy child was meant to be someone else's. Which meant he couldn't come over, because his true father had yet to mate with his mother.

"Aye," Aed settled his skinny butt on the bench, his arms and legs like thin tree branches, making Talorc wonder if a man like that could father a son to Maggie.

He stood, abruptly, and wondered why he was standing.

Aed didn't stop his rambling. "The boy can't come yet, because you're to have a lass. That's what it all looks like to me, Bold. Can't have a lad when it's meant to be a lass."

"A lass?" Talorc sat down hard. "You're telling me the dream means she's to have a lassie? A wee little girl?"

"Sounds like that to me, but you can't be certain with these things. Not if you don't remember them clear from waking." Aed shook his head with frustration, "She said she got distracted by the night, and forgot much of her dream. What, do I ask you, can so distract that one forgets the importance of dreams?" The storyteller shook his head, as if the world did not make sense.

The shelter grew quiet, an uneasy silence. Aed looked up, confused. Padraig and William coughed. For Maggie's sake, Talorc kept his mouth shut. She was a mite shy about some things.

He changed the direction of his thoughts. "She spoke of water, her brother Ian."

Aed perked up and smiled. "Makes sense, doesn't it? Her brother is on the other side. She would have to go out in the water to get near enough to hear him."

"Aye," Talorc nodded slowly, but as the thoughts rushed in, his head bobbed with more earnestness. He slapped Aed on the shoulder, hard enough to pitch him toward the stones. "Sorry, man," Talorc righted him, brushed at the ash on his arm, "Sorry." Aed was puny, but smart.

A lass.

Talorc let out a bellow of laughter. A sweet lass, just like her mother . . . well, more tart then sweet.

She would enchant him.

He had been troubled about Maggie's dream, but with the ease he felt more open to listening.

"Aed," definitely more amicable, "I was thinking, mayhap in your stories, in our history, you know of any who might just hold bad feelings for his people."

Aed screwed up his face as he thought. He had a repertoire of stories that outlined the history of the clan. Legends of warriors who had fought under Talorc's own father and before. Accounts of lovers and loves crossed. He was even bold enough to tell the story of Seonaid and her boy, despite the frowns that Talorc threw his way.

Maggie said she would find out who the father of Seonaid's child was, but so far she had only drawn more questions. It was best that way. Seonaid, for the few moments she had been here, refused to talk to Maggie. Diedre, on the other hand, was not shy of speaking about the two. About how Seonaid and the Bold were such close friends. Of how he had saved her once, when a Gunn snuck up to her farm. Of how he always traveled to the woman's farm, even if it was out of his way. And how he talked to her about everything.

It had all been true. Talorc had done that and more for all his people. He checked on all those who lived in remote areas. It was part of who he was as laird. As for talking, well, Talorc knew what he could talk about and what it was best not to speak of.

"Come on, Laird, Aed's about talked out." Padraig and William led the way out of the sweating room, into the early gloom of the afternoon and down to the stream.

Talorc joined them in their roars, as the cold water washed over steam dampened skin.

"Oh, Aye." William shouted, as he sloughed water over his face, his head, "Firms a man up."

Padraig laughed. "And shrivels his privates."

"Speak for yourself." Talorc charged, as he sloshed from the water, his back to the others.

The sweat had eased his muscles, cleared his head but couldn't wipe away the worry that someone, out there in his clan, caused trouble. The stories hadn't helped. There wasn't much he could do about it now. Maybe it would be his turn to dream up answers in the night.

He threw his shirt over his head, and wrapped his plaid around his waist then up, over his shoulder.

"Come on men, I think we'll have a bit of fun before we go back. Let's have a tug of the rope with the keep guard."

William grinned. "How many to a side?"

"Six of them, to our three," Talorc looked at Aed, "Unless you want to join us."

"No," the storyteller backed off, "but I'll tell the tale of it after we sup."

They headed up the slope, shouted to the warder guard, on the wall that protected the keep.

"Any men for a game? Tug of war?" Padraig shouted. "Six warders on one side, Your Laird, William and myself on the other."

"Aye," one of the guards shouted down, "and if it took six of us to beat your three, then a sorry lot we would be. Fair odds, here. Kenneth, Liam and Colban to you three, and I'll bet my best harness!"

"Oye, what about me?" Adam shouted from above, "Why can't I put a hand in?"

"I could do better than Liam!" Cal argued.

Talorc punched Padraig, "Go get Naill and Sim, find Bruce, and anyone else you can find. If they want even odds . . ."

A wild screech tore through air.

Talorc froze.

They all froze, William, the warder guard. Before any could react, Talorc was off and running.

"Maggieeeeeeeeeee!" he roared, because no one, no living body in this world would scream for him with such pain and terror but his Maggie. Her voice rocked his world, pummeled his belly. And as he ran, he called, the sound of a wild, stricken mate determined to let its partner know help was coming.

He hit the hall to chaos, people running, others standing immobile and frightened. Again, that eerie wail.

"Up here, Laird!" Nora called from the balcony, "Up here!"

He charged for the stairs, took them three at a time, and barreled into his room to be confronted by a wall of women, their backs to him, busy as a hive of bees.

"Where is she?" he roared, because he could do no other.

Ealasaid turned. Faithful calm Ealasaid. "Out!" she ranted at him, "Be gone with you! We haven't time for you." But with her back turned, she had opened a gap, where he could see Maggie, her face scrunched with pain, her hair wet and plastered to her skin. She looked up, a wounded animal on the verge of hysteria, and reached out an arm. She mouthed it, though no sound came. She wanted him, needed him, more than any other.

Then she was gone, scrunched up around her belly. Her plaid, her dress, hiked up indecently, with all the women there, mopping and pressing and blood, so much blood. Puddles of it, pools, a near loch's worth of blood streaming from between her legs.

He didn't care what Ealasaid said, he didn't care if this was women's work. It was his wife, in the same pain as his last one had been, and look where that got her.

He reached Maggie's side, wrapped his arms around her, so she could lean over the one, the other a brace to her back. He kissed her head, his tears blending with the sweat that formed in large droplets on her forehead.

She moaned, a keening sound, and he heard her gag. Again, nothing came out. She wasn't there, really, she was caught inside her pain, a long way from where they all were. Her eyes were glazed with shock, her skin pasty from loss of blood.

"There's no more babe, Laird." Ealasaid huffed, and then he heard her voice hitch to a sob. "And if we don't stop the blood, there'll be no more Maggie."

CHAPTER 5 – GRUESOME CELEBRATIONS

In all the turmoil the store rooms, and in turn the caves, were empty. No guards at the front, anyway. She slipped in, as quick as a snake, and slithered through the rooms. She knew where she was going, hoped her man would be there waiting, though he probably wouldn't be. Too many guards these days, watching too close for a man to pass as a woman, for anyone, without taking note of who they were and when they passed.

Oh, aye, but she needed to see him, to celebrate, excitement running high in her veins, between her legs. She had killed the child, probably the mother too. There had been so much blood.

Och, and the Bold, poor thing, was in torment.

She bit back a laugh, afraid of the echo, and rounded a corner into the body of a man whose smell she knew, oh, so well. Her man.

"Did you bring food?" He whispered into her ear, causing her to heat even more.

"In the basket." She lifted her arm, showing the large woven basket she carried, holding up a candle in the other hand so he could see. "But I'm hungry, too." She offered.

He looked over his shoulder. The darkness shifted, revealing at least three more men. "Me first?" He asked, then turned away to pull a hunk of cheese from beneath the cloth that covered her wares.

"Not here," she hissed. They were too close to the store rooms, too close to where bored guards would hunt down any sound.

As he bit into the cheddar, his other hand cupped her breast. "I thought you were hungry?"

And she was, damn him, and ready for all he offered, even to the others. The thrill of danger spiked the heat in her. "You're not a silent lot when you get going." She charged.

"No, I suppose not." He smiled against her face, "but neither are you."

"Go on, the lot of you," she pushed at his shoulder, "lead me out of here to where I can tell you just how bad it is in the castle. To where we can laugh and make merry at the torment caused."

He slapped her backside. "I'll make you scream."

"Oh, aye, you always make me scream, just as I make you beg."

She saw his frown, but she didn't care. She had the power, stolen from the Bold, one loss too many for the man.

There had been a time when she thought the MacBede wench had broken him by leaving. But he brought her back and with her a brewing babe. The man was too full of himself with all that. He deserved to be brought down.

She accomplished that. The arrogant bastard would be no more. His heart would be broken, his spirit trampled and his reputation shredded.

Oh, aye, she had the power now.

CHAPTER 6 – DEVIL'S CLAN

"If you're staying, be useful. Lift the girl, get her to the bed," Ealasaid commanded, and suddenly Talorc pulled from his stupor.

He lifted Maggie in his arms, held her as Ealasaid bustled forward, her commands cutting through his stupor, as she pulled back sheets. "Gerta, get that hide on here, so she doesn't ruin the bed, and Caitrina, help your mother, move the pillows to where we'll lay her hips. They need to be higher."

Talorc tilted his burden, hips higher than head, as Deirdre held a sheet, once white, now scarlet, between Maggie's legs.

Too much blood. Too much bloody blood. "We need cold." He commanded. "There's ice at the pond but not down by the stream, don't waste time with that." He looked about the room, caught his cousin Seana standing in a shocked stupor, "Go tell the men, we need ice and now!"

He was glad to see Seana run, to do his bidding, to escape a smell sharp with scent of battle. It was the blood, Talorc told himself. Not a battle, not an attack. It was a matter of nature.

He felt useless, helpless as he stood there, pushing against the pressure of Deirdre, who pushed hard with the sheet, against the

apex of Maggie's thighs. The bed was readied,
a hide down, fur side up for comfort, a cool
sheet over the top. He laid her down
carefully, with pillows under her hips. As
soon as he did, Ealasaid pushed forward, to
lift Maggie up and over, as she placed a
twisted sheet under her.

"What are you doing, woman? Moving
her about so."

"You ever use a tourniquet on a man?"
Ealasaid barked at him. "Well, leave us to our
own devices."

"Don't let her die."

Ealasaid stopped, her beefy arm
swiping at the sweat on her forehead, her eyes
on her patient. "Your Maggie is stronger than
Anabal was, Bold. She's stronger, there's a
greater chance she'll make it." She bent to her
task again. Talorc lifted his wife, so the
woman could get everything where it needed
to be.

Maggie's head lolled from side to side.
He thought of her concussion, of the
temptation to go to her twin, and jostled her.
"Maggie, wake-up, don't die on me. Don't you
dare put me through this again."

"Stop it, Laird," Gerta tugged on his
arm. "Let us tend to her. She's better sleeping
against the pain."

Pain. For the second time, in the short
time they had been together, she lay upon
their bed, near death.

"Why, Gerta?" He asked, as though
there were an answer. "Why does this have to
happen?"

The old woman clammed up, her lips
pressed so tight they nearly turned blue.
There was an answer, when he expected none.
No one could explain nature. But wrong doing
was another thing, entirely.

Something was wrong.

Talorc whirled on Ealasaid, "What happened here?" his fury tinged with panic. "Why is she bleeding like this?"

"She lost the babe. She's a red head. Put the two together and you've got blood. Lots of it. So get out of the way." Ealasaid refused to look at him, though he heard the choke of a sob. "This is no time for talk!"

Gerta tugged at his arm, again, someone pushed gently at his back. A man collided with him, at the door, a slab of ice in his arms. Helpless, Talorc watched as the ice was passed to the women and the man scurried out of the room. Away from the tragedy. Talorc followed, crushed by his inability to be of help.

There was nothing he could do. When Anabal had been in this state, he had mourned, but at the same time he had the hope of a babe. But there would be no babe this time, no chance of one. That was already gone. Now, his only hope was that Maggie live.

Please, God, let her live.

He slid down the wall, elbows braced on his knees, head in his hands. The hallway filled with quiet murmurs, as clansmen joined his vigil. Old Micheil pressed a goblet of whisky into his hand.

Talorc could not swallow. "Give it to Maggie; see if it fires up her life."

"I did that first. They've poured it down her throat." Micheil urged him to drink, but the threat of tears lumped in his throat. He turned away.

His Maggie, his feisty spirited girl, now limp as a doll and as pasty as raw dough, lay on the other side of that door. She had not chosen to come here. He used her own family against her, fueled the MacBede clan to add pressure and added the hefty weight of a battle won to cap it. He thwarted her own wishes and connived to handfast her. He seduced her to child, allowed her to think it was her brazen nature and not his hunger to spill his seed in her womb. He trapped her, against her own ideals, against her sense of time. He'd rushed her, when he could have waited, should have waited.

And now, here she was, the child lost, her reason for staying with him gone.

I vow she shall never be harmed by me or mine, in any manner.

Twice she lay near death under his roof, amid his people. He had promised differently.

"Laird," Conegell hunkered down before him, "Something's wrong."

Talorc's head snapped up. "Aye, my wife is losing blood. That's wrong."

"Like your first wife."

He turned away. "You don't have to be telling me what I know." He was cursed, there was no doubt now.

"It was a drink she took and it was no different for your Anabal. She fell ill with a drink."

Drink? The same as Anabal? He hadn't known that, but now, two wives, years apart, at different stages of carrying a bairn, lost babes by the same means.

An enemy could not survive for years inside Glen Toric. They would have exposed themselves.

"Anabal's birthing came on too soon. That's not uncommon. Nor is losing a babe before time."

"Too fast, Laird. A woman's first child does not come on so quick; one moment standing and laughing, the next folded up and screaming." Conegell insisted. "The women are talking, trying to remember the shock of your first wife's dying. They weren't easy in it then, even less so now."

Talorc fought despair that would only muddle his mind. He had to think, had to listen, with a clear head. "If what you're saying is true, then someone among the clan would have to be the cause of it."

William leaned in, "Old Micheil was betrayed."

Thoughts forced Talorc to stand. His words put before the others for consideration. "We don't know the man was betrayed. And I can think of no one who would do this. No one who could live among the clan and remain an enemy."

Conegell took a deep breath. "Beathag gave her a drink."

William snorted, "Maggie knows better than to drink Beathag's concoctions."

Talorc waved him away, weighed the accusation. "Maggie might drink one of Beathag's brews, but not Anabal. And Anabal loved the old woman as much as Beathag loved Anabal. I don't see it, but yes, the old woman might hurt my Maggie. The hitch is, she would never harm the child she nursed from birth." Talorc frowned.

Beathag was an easy solution, but such things were usually the fault of shallow thinking. He needed more information. "Conegell, you've followed the woman. What do you think?"

"You asked me to watch, but when she goes to your Maggie's room, I can't follow. Una does."

Buoyed by purpose and duty, Talorc waited, impatient for information. When none came, he looked up, gestured. "Well? What did Una say?"

Conegell shifted. "Beathag put a goblet down, but Lady MacKay dinna' drink, not then. She talked to the old nurse, sweet like, and thanked the woman. Una said Beathag left, and then Lady MacKay took a sip. There were two flasks there; the one from Beathag and one with fresh water."

"You're saying she drank from the wrong one." Talorc closed his eyes. This made sense, a stupid error. She knew which to drink from and took the wrong one. Life was that fickle.

But when he opened his eyes, Conegell was shaking his head. "The women don't know. Some say yes, some say no. They're all fretting about it, about the way Lady MacKay made a face with the taste of her water, but swallowed anyway."

"She knew it wasn't water?"

"No," Conegell shook his head. "It's more like, she wasn't certain. She looked at the goblet, as if something was wrong with the goblet, not the brew."

"Did Una understand why she would do this?"

"You know how Una talks round and round till it makes you dizzy. But she said she was certain Maggie drank of the water." They all stared at Conegell, he continued. "But she says it like it's a question, like she can't figure it out. She says Ealasaid keeps saying Lady MacKay never drinks Beathag's drinks. They use different goblets. Maggie knows Ealasaid's goblet and Ealasaid fetched the water herself."

Talorc swallowed air, rubbed the base of his head where a knot twisted.

"From Una's description, Lady MacKay
looked at the goblet again, smelled it, then
her face turned ashen. She dropped the goblet,
clutched at her inners and started to scream as
she fell. Both goblets toppled when she went
down. No one knows for certain which one
was which. I'm thinking, Lady MacKay will
be the only one who knows if she drank from
Beathag's or the water's flask."

"Where's Beathag?" Rage, a powerful
menace, threatened Talorc's control. With
effort, he breathed deep, forced his tightening
muscles to ease. There was no loosening the
knot in his stomach, or at the top of his spine.
The hollow calm of his words obscured the
tempers edge he rode. "Where is she? Where's
the old hag?"

It made perfect sense, after all Beathag
was a Gunn. A Gunn spy, planted within the
MacKay clan. He smiled with thoughts of
vengeance.

But his smile waned. It made no sense.
Beathag was free to return to the Gunns, but
had cringed from such freedom. She never left
the hall. Never went for a visit. Had no way
of meeting the enemy.

And Beathag would not, could not,
murder Anabal. She had been the girl's nurse,
had raised her from a wee babe. She adored
her charge.

If she had poisoned Maggie, that would
mean two culprits with the same outcome. Not
likely. It didn't ring true.

"We locked Beathag in her room,"
Conegell put his hands on his Laird's
shoulders, as if to temper his temper. But the
rage had twisted into frustration. "The old
woman was as startled by the scream. I saw
her, saw the look on her face. She ran, fast for
old legs, tears running down her cheeks, she

near twisted her hands off, and she kept
saying 'not again. Oh, no, my lass, not again."

His instincts were true. Beathag, guilty
or not, did not set out to murder anyone. "Did
you watch her make the drink?" Talorc asked.

"Aye. Her worry made me think. All
these times I follow her, I see her take the
goblet up to your wife's chamber, but I never
see her gather herbs or go down in the rooms
where they make the potions. She fills the
goblet with a small chunk of sugar, a spoon of
malt, an inch of molasses and a pinch of
yeast. The rest is ale, straight from the cask in
the kitchen. Today was no different."

"Does she pull anything from a pouch
on her way to the room?"

Conegell shook his head. "She adds an
egg some days, but not today. The cook
wouldn't have it."

"Are you certain that is all she puts in
there? Could there be anything up her
sleeve?"

"I've run it round and round my head
and I'm certain, Laird. I've watched real
close. But I watch her, not the brew, and
that's the worry. She leaves it on a shelf,
gives the yeast time to come alive and stir the
flavors."

The chamber door opened and Deirdre
popped her head out. "The bleeding's
stopped."

Talorc groaned, felt tears of relief
surge. He fought them. "Is she awake?"

"No," Deidre looked back in the room,
"Well, not really. Her eyelids flutter, which is
a good sign. But I have to get back." She
darted out as quick as she had popped in.

Talorc stood, alone, surrounded by his
men. He had tasks to do, for Maggie. Just
what, refused to surface. He had to get a grip

on his thoughts. "William, Conegell, go to
Beathag and talk to her. See if there's
anything she wants to say, or thinks about all
this." He turned to Padraig, "Take Niall here
and go to the kitchens. Watch who comes and
goes. Listen to their thoughts, suspicions.
Don't let them know why you're there, just
snitch at the food and flirt, like you would
otherwise.

"Liam, you stay here in the hallway, to
do any bidding that's necessary. I want you to
note who comes to see how Maggie fairs.
Bruce," Talorc didn't turn when he addressed
him, "send Malcolm up, he can help with
running messages. And between the two of
them, one should be here at all times."

It was then that Talorc eyed Sim, who
stood to the back of the other men, just
behind Liam, "I'm going to ask a great task of
you Sim, and you're the only true choice."
The young man stood taller. "I need you to
get to the MacBede Keep, as fast as you can .
. . but first, check to see if there are any
unusual tracks around this keep. Do you
understand? If there are tracks, forget the
MacBedes and come straight to me. If not, if I
don't see you in the verrrry near future, I'll
know you are on your way to her people.
They'll want to know the hope of a child is no
more."

"Should you wait, Laird?" Bruce had
the gall to ask.

"Wait? To see if she lives or dies, do
you mean?" Bruce looked at his feet. If she
lived, how different would they react. If she
died . . . her eyelids had fluttered. Talorc
would hang on to that.

"Go now Sim, and promise we will send
another, on the morn, to say if she lives or
dies. And Sim," Talorc looked him straight

on, "tell them I broke my promise. We think she was poisoned by one of our own."

CHAPTER 7 – LETTING GO

Maggie lay on the bed, white as chalk. Covers pulled up to her waist, where a twisted sheet and a piece of wood for a tourniquet handle, rested on her belly, the twist now loosened. Ealasaid leaned against the wall, spent from her efforts.

"What needs doing?" Talorc asked. She shook her head, words more energy than she had.

Gerta pushed forward, "Y' need to sit." And pushed Ealasaid into a chair. "You," she pointed toward Una, "and you," Deidre this time, "help me strip the bed down, and take that God awful thing from around her."

Ealasaid shoved away from the chair, "She'll be needing water."

They all looked to the spilled pitcher on the floor, and the drying puddle of blood beside it.

"Liam's outside," Talorc told them, as he eased the knot at the top of the tourniquet sheet, "tell him to fetch fresh water from the stream and warn him he's to taste it before she has any."

"You can trust my Liam!" Caitrina snapped, and walked to the door to inform her husband of his task.

"Caitrina," Talorc stopped her, "have Liam tell the rat catchers," the young boys who made certain the keep wasn't over-run with vermin, "to find me some live ones." The girl shuddered, but didn't ask questions as she did his bidding.

Talorc lifted Maggie into his arms, as Gerta removed the twisted sheet from around her waist.

"Hold her a bit, while we get this bed freshened." Ealasaid stepped in front of him, "Sit over there. We'll get her into a fresh gown as well."

Caitrina came back into the room with a bucket full of water and a scrub brush.

"What are you doing?" Talorc asked.

Caitrina scowled as Gerta answered. "She's going to clean the floor."

"Don't."

"Laird, we can't leave it as a memorial, now."

"Don't clean it. Not until I say. And don't step over there either." There were answers on that floor. He needed to find them.

Maggie's gown was lifted, to be changed, and revealed a deep purple circlet of bruises. Great racking shivers coursed through her.

"Shock," Talorc mumbled. He held her close to his chest, as he reached over, lifted the lid of the trunk at the foot of the bed, and pulled out fresh blankets to wrap her in. He had experience enough with injuries during battle. He knew what he was dealing with. What he didn't like was the limpness. She was no more than an empty shell of flesh.

"She needs water, Laird. She's lost too much of the liquid inside of her. She needs water."

"It's coming." He had to stay calm, for Maggie. If he let his fears, his temper, surface he would be no help. He had to stay focused.

"Bring the bucket here, Caitrina," He felt it, ice cold. "Over there, by the fire, there's a kettle. Bring some hot water so we can wash her before we dress her again."

Talorc helped to get her clean, dressed, back on the bed and under heavy piles of covers. Liam came in with another bucket of water, and took a sip without being asked, ended it with a respectful nod to Talorc.

At least he did not take offense to his Laird's request.

"You're a good man, Liam MacGhei." Talorc nodded him off, then turned to Ealasaid. "How many people do you need now?"

"Gerta will do, the rest can go, though you'll be hard pressed to get them to leave."

"I want as few people in this room as possible."

Ealasaid nodded. Talorc looked at the others, then tilted his head to the door. As they left, they skirted around the blood soaked floor, and toppled pitcher.

Ealasaid was set on getting Maggie to drink the water, but Maggie refused it. Every try, the liquid spilled over and down her neck. Talorc stood beside Ealasaid. "Use a cloth," A slanted look let him know she wasn't stupid.

She dipped a clean cloth in the cup and dribbled it over Maggie's lips. Loss of blood, weak as she was, Maggie managed to tighten her lips against refreshment and moaned.

"She doesn't trust the water," It also told him which goblet she had drunk from.

"Maggie," He held her head upright, his face straight on hers, even though her eyes were closed. "It's fresh water. Liam tried it; I'm tasting it right now." He grabbed the mug and took a taste. "It's sweet and clear and refreshing. Ah, I think I'll drink more." He took her face in his hands again. "Want a wee drop, of the same cup I drank from?" he didn't expect an answer in words. He knew it would come as he tipped the cup to her lips. It went past her lips, into her mouth. She swallowed.

Talorc closed his own eyes and said a quick prayer.

"Give her more, Laird," Ealasaid bade him. He did so, murmuring to her as he gave her small sips, watching as her weakness ebbed. Not by much, she'd been through a hefty ordeal, but it ebbed enough that her eyes opened a mite and her tongue had the strength to lick her lips, though not strong enough to offer words.

"Good, Laird. You've done good." Ealasaid leaned wearily against the wall.

He sat on the edge of the bed, cupped Maggie's face in his hand, as his thumb rubbed over the rise of her cheek. She turned into the caress. He kissed her forehead and rose.

"She's sleeping." Ealasaid leaned over to lift Maggie's wrist. It was not as limp as it had been earlier, with the lack of so much blood. The older woman sighed, deep.

"I truly thought we had lost her, Bold. I don't know what I would have done."

"Don't you worry about our lass, here," Gerta told Ealasaid, "You've nursed her before, when no one thought she would make it. She's got spirit, she does, spirit through and through." Gerta sat back, tears in her eyes.

Tough as hide, old Gerta might be, but she had a soft spot for his Maggie. As did Ealasaid. Maggie was safe with the two of them.

"I have to go, ask questions, but you need to make me a promise. Any slight

change, better or worse, you send for me.
Liam is right outside with Malcolm."

He strode from the room, did not stop
when others tried to stop him. He ignored it
all, for the stables. Without blanket, saddle,
stirrups or even halter, he mounted his horse,
broke free of the keep at full gallop. Hard,
fast, he rode up over the folds of the hills,
down one, up another, until he came to a spot
hidden in the roll of the land. Soaked with
sweat, his mount heaved in breath, as Talorc
dismounted, careless that the animal might
take off and leave him with no way home but
by his feet.

He didn't care.

Didn't care about anything.

Numbness had grown in proportion to
Maggie's lifelessness. He had functioned
because he had to, for her. Now there was no
need to cope, to be of use, to see that all was
done with logic, precision.

He stood, alone, empty. There was no
comfort. Fear pummeled his belly.

He would lose her. He would truly lose
her. And not just to death.

He had broken his promise.

He had not protected her.

She was lost to him. Life or no.

Emotion shattered his nothingness,
filled the hollow with shrieks of a thousand
banshees. One moment, stillness, the next, a
warrior's roar erupted from the depths of him,
bounced off the hillsides and came back, an
eerie echo, creating a wild, tormented chorus.
It grew from the pit of the earth, up through
his toes, his legs, his belly, and out his throat.
He shouted his fears, his anger, acknowledged
the tears that streamed down his cheeks, and
sank to his knees, where he begged, pleaded

for the Lord to save her, to keep her well, to allow her life.

As if in answer, every moment of their time together flashed through his mind. Guilt swamped his meager soul. He had cajoled, tricked, seduced and inveigled Maggie into his world, his life, his heart-- against her own wishes. He had forced her into being his wife and then he had failed to keep her safe.

He didn't deserve her.

The truth of it rocked through him, filled him with a self-hatred that he had never before tasted. No room for self-doubt for the Bold.

But he wasn't the Bold right now. Maggie had shown more guts, more determination, more giving in one afternoon, than he had offered in the whole of their time together.

He did not deserve her.

Fury forced him to this moment of self-discovery. He pulled his sword from its sheath, and stabbed the ground, over and over until the blade snapped. He gripped the handle of his wounded weapon, pierced through earth until that too gave way, but he did not give up. He punched and pounded and howled until finally, exhausted, he fell onto his back, eyes closed as salty tears streamed down the sides of his face.

He loved her, to the bottom of his black soul. He loved her with such passion that he would give her the one gift she would treasure.

He would set her free.

CHAPTER 8 – TORN APART

Determined to be strong, Maggie grasped the bedpost to steady herself and shut her eyes against a wave of nausea. The room spun, Maggie tilted.

"Stop moving." Fiona snipped, too focused on Maggie's pleats to look up.

Eyes opened wide, Maggie swallowed against the illness. She did not want to be fussed over. The whole of the MacKays, as well as her own kin, had fretted enough. All of them, from the oldest to the youngest had bustled about her, seeing to her needs, putting their hands on her forehead, bringing food to fatten her up.

All of them but Talorc.

"Where is he?" She pulled away from Fiona's tucking and pleating. On edge from days of attention, ready to be up and about, sick or not.

Fiona grabbed her daughter's skirts and tugged her back into place. "Where is who?"

Maggie snorted and spun around, which managed to unravel half of Fiona's hard work. "You know who I mean, Ma."

Fiona ignored the accusation. "Come here," she waved Maggie to her. "Let me fix it." Mother waited, daughter stood firm. Fiona flicked her wrist again.

"Alright," Maggie gave up with a sigh and stepped forward. She managed to hold still, all but an impatient tap of foot and drum of fingers. "I'm about to walk into the hall, to see and be seen by the whole of the MacKays, but my husband has yet to come for me."

He hadn't just failed to fetch her; he was never there, ever, any more. The last time she'd fallen ill, he sat with her hour after hour. Now, he claimed he was too busy trying to find out how the poison came to be in her cup.

A memory shifted. She frowned, fingers and feet stilled.

There was something elusive about that cup. She remembered lifting it to her mouth and then . . . nothing. No thought, no recollection, nothing. Perhaps that was best.

"Where is he, Ma?"

Head bent to a task she didn't work at, Fiona pressed the edges of her own pleats. It was a familiar gesture, a thoughtful pose, as she fought for comfortable words in an uncomfortable situation.

"There's something you're not telling me." Maggie accused.

"Me?" Fiona looked up, looked down, rose to her feet and smoothed her plaid. Delay tactics.

"Aye, you." Maggie snapped, then watched as her mother drew in a deep breath. Oh no, she thought, no and shut her eyes again, as if to block the words she knew would come.

"He wants you to return with us."

The world spun, Maggie's stomach plummeted. "Why?"

"He . . ." Fiona hesitated, as though leafing through thoughts the way one leafs through a book for information, "You must

know your father and I agree, as do your
brothers . . ." Fiona's lips thinned. "Maggie,
it's not safe for you here. Not until he knows .
. ."

"I'm safe enough."

"You've been hit in the head, poisoned.
God knows what else might happen."

"Mother, I was warned. I may not have
heeded it, but I was warned. Ian told me, in a
dream, not to drink the water."

"So you claim, and you've always been
a canny dreamer, but tell you or no, you still
drank, and swallowed."

"I know better now."

Fiona dropped into a chair, motioned
for Maggie to take the opposite one.

"Your Talorc is feeling regret. Not only
did he push you, when you weren't ready to be
pushed, but he sent you to danger. He nearly
lost you twice for it. All the signs say he was
wrong to take you. You were right to fight the
match."

Such a twisted mess, she had to battle
her own arguments. "Ma, it's too late to go
backwards. I've accepted the risks in being
married to the Bold. He must accept the risks
in being married to me."

Fiona shook her head. "You don't
understand, Maggie. He's the reason you are
in peril. And besides, love," She leaned over,
brushed hair away from Maggie's forehead.
"Men may have more brawn, but women are
stronger and braver in affairs of the heart."

"That's just too bad. He's going to have
to live with that."

"Maggie." Fiona stood, not to be
thwarted. "We're leaving on the morrow and
you're coming with us."

"I have no say?"

"He'll not make it easy for you, and neither will I."

"You act like I'm a guilty, thoughtless child. You put me in this place and now that I want to be here, you mean to take me away?" Unfairness swamped her.

Maggie met Fiona's steady glance, but her steadiness did not stop Fiona's arguments. "At least come home until he finds out who is guilty of wishing you harm."

Fury edged Maggie forward. "Am I never to make my own decisions?" She jumped up, paced, voice rising with each step. "He regrets making my decisions earlier, but refuses to stop doing so. I have a mind to . . ."

Fiona grabbed Maggie by the shoulders, tears pooling in her eyes. "It broke my heart to lose you to another keep, but daughter mine, to lose you to foul play, och, I couldna' stand that."

Like a fish on dry land, Maggie's heart flipped and flopped between tender emotion and frustration. She could have used her mother's argument a hundred times as a child, raised in a household with men who insisted on facing death square on. Everyone knew that each battle fought, diminished the odds of their surviving.

This time, Maggie was on the other side of the fear. It was her safety that tormented now.

"Ma, life comes and it goes. We can't determine what it is for God to fate."

"Easy for you to say."

Maggie threw her hands up. "You face such dangers with my brothers without argument."

"Don't try that." Fiona snapped. "You were the one who cursed them for making me face their risks."

"Aye, and you never said a word. You never made their decisions for them."

"They were sons. Why do you think I craved a daughter so?"

Maggie huffed. "I'm a woman now, Ma. Grown, married, carried a babe in my belly. I don't even live with you, it's time I act on my own mind and that says I won't go."

"Even for a visit?"

"I've done that." Now all she wanted was to be held by her husband. They had lost their child, their babe. She wanted to be held, to be told of his love for her. Instead, he stayed away, avoided her presence, from the day she drank the poison.

He chose to send her away.

"It was not my fault." She argued aloud. Fiona moaned, deep in her throat, and reached to hold Maggie, but it wasn't a mother's hold Maggie wanted.

Perhaps Talorc never loved her. Perhaps she was no more than a goal that had lost its value.

"I've done nothing wrong."

"Maggie."

She spun to see Talorc in the doorway.

"No one thinks you did anything wrong,"

She yearned to run to him but held back, by battered emotions. He chose to send her away. It was there, in the way he stood, remote, just a few feet away. He could be all the way to England and be closer.

She sighed. "It's your chamber, as well as mine. You can step into it."

He didn't move. "Are you ready to go below stairs?"

He didn't want her, could barely be near her. The reality of it yanked at her security. There was no energy to fight him. Emotions cloaked, she refused his offered arm when she reached him. She'd not force herself to his care.

"Are you coming, Ma?" She looked over her shoulder. Talorc took her elbow, urged her forward.

"Fiona will follow us."

How different this time, to the first, when he'd taken her along this same hallway to meet his clan. He had wanted her then, confessed or not. She had known, had sensed it. Now the affection was gone, the caring an act of manners, not heart. She had become a stranger he couldn't be rid of fast enough.

They reached the stairs to solemn silence. No shouts of joy, no cheers of welcome. Not this time. She had lost a child, an heir to the Laird. The clan's respectful stillness, in a time when Talorc refused to share the sorrow, nearly broke her.

Needing support, she reached, gripped his arm, surprised by his gentleness, when he laid his hand upon hers. She glanced up. His gentle touch contrasted with the harsh mask of his expression, focused far from her.

Face taut, he studied the people in the hall, reminding Maggie that one of them had murdered their child. It seemed impossible. The only one at odds with Maggie was Seonaid, who kept her distance. Seonaid understood men, not herbs. She had little time or tolerance for Maggie, but that was her general tone toward all women.

She was a loner. Not a murderer. Possessive, not crazed.

As Talorc guided Maggie down the staircase, she tried to see what he would have seen, but failed. No one prompted her to fury. Not even Beathag, who stood on the outskirts of the gathering alone, fearful. Some suspected her, but Maggie did not.

She glanced up at Talorc again. He refused to look at her. She stopped, mid-step. The surprise forced him to glance her way, a frowning slant of a look, gone as quick as it had come. It was the first time he had looked directly at her since the poisoning.

He was probably as reluctant to touch her.

Fine.

She pulled her hand from his arm, lifted her skirts ankle high. He whispered her name. Head high, she ignored him, made her own way down the stairs, with a smile for everyone gathered below. As she moved, she noticed Beathag again. The older woman sat huddled in the back of the great hall, her shivers visible from across the smoky chamber.

"Excuse me," Maggie nodded, as she wove through the crowd, toward the pitiable old nursemaid. She was halfway there when someone walked straight into her.

"Seonaid?"

"I'm sorry, I didn't see you there before I moved." The brunette swiped at her plaid, as if soiled from their encounter. Maggie stepped away.

"So, you're better." Seonaid's cold concern chilled Maggie's spine. "What a shame that someone was fool enough to gather water and wild venomous plants in the same place."

"Is that what happened?"

"That's what's said."

"Interesting." Maggie murmured, and looked back at Beathag, only Beathag wasn't there anymore. Maggie swiveled, tried to spot the older woman.

368

Seonaid interrupted the search. "I knew you would not stay."

"Oh," Maggie's fury rose. "It is not I who chooses my leaving."

"No?" Seonaid frowned, leaned closer. "Perhaps I have not seen you in a true light." Maggie raised an eyebrow. Seonaid continued. "Perhaps you and I should speak."

"Now?" Stunned, Maggie looked up, half wondered if she was looking into the eyes of a murderess. "It's a bit late for us to be talking."

"About your going?" Seonaid gripped her hard, "You could come back."

"Aye. I've a mind to" Maggie yanked free, confidence building. Talorc hadn't been with her, but neither had he been confiding in the other woman. "If you don't mind, I'm looking for someone."

"Beathag?"

Maggie tilted her head, surprised by Seonaid's unusual persistence. "You don't want to be talking to Beathag. She's so overwrought with what happened to you that she can't even speak."

"So I've heard, she just shivers and shakes. But it's not talking I mean to do, not that it's any matter to you."

"The woman's crazy. It's my thought she did poison you. She is a Gunn, after all."

"Is she? And why isn't she with them now? Her charge, bless her soul, isn't here anymore."

Seonaid lowered her eyes, the frown grown deeper, marring the perfection of her brow. As though to convince herself, she murmured. "Beathag's nothing but a hag. I doubt the Gunns want her any more than we do."

"Who says the MacKays don't want her?"

Rather than answer her, Seonaid looked over her shoulder and Maggie knew Talorc was there, before he took her arm.

"Go away." She didn't bother to look at him.

"Maggie?" He tugged.

She shrugged him off. "Go away."

"Whatever you have to say to each other, you can say to me."

"I'm thinking she doesn't look well, Bold," Seonaid lied. "She needs to be going back to bed."

Talorc had the grace to ignore her, but he did study Maggie. His gaze a sensation, it rippled through her. She had missed it. But he was sending her away. "I'm fine, Bold, better than when I was above stairs."

"I don't want you upset, or bothered."

Maggie looked anywhere but at him. "You're the only one who bothers me now." Which was true. Her eyes shifted back to his face, filling up on memories.

He frowned at his feet. Except for him, and her parents, who verged so close to charging to her rescue they looked like racers waiting for the cloth to drop, she and Seonaid had been given a wide berth.

She pushed Bold toward her kin. "Go. Calm them."

He hesitated, for a moment, then did as she asked. Surprised, she blinked. His compliance meant one of two things, either he really didn't care what happened to her, or he trusted her to take care of herself.

That didn't matter right now. She needed to see Beathag. Questions about the cup skirted her memory. So much rode on explaining what happened and how to keep it from happening again.

Beathag was not to blame, but the old woman might be able to help her grasp the evasive answers. Besides, Maggie hated to see the old woman in such a fretful way, when she had done nothing wrong. She wanted to help her find some peace.

There were two doorways near where she'd been sitting, one to the hallway and all the rooms beyond. The other door, an outer door, led to the kitchens. If the woman had gone to the hallway, she could be anywhere in the keep. It would take less time to search the smaller area of the kitchens, less time wasted if it was the wrong choice.

Beathag was there, rooted in the midst of preparations for a feast. Deep in thought, she no longer shivered, ignored the busy women who muttered about her being in the way. Maggie moved toward her, when suddenly, without warning, Beathag came to life. She moved toward the sugar bin, stopped short, then acted as if she were there, lifting the lid, chipping off a chunk, raising a piece to be dropped in some invisible container.

The old woman enacted the same parody for a spoonful of malt. From there, Beathag crossed to the molasses cask, again she stopped short and mimed turning an imaginary spigot, only to shut it off with the quick precise motion needed to stop it in mid-flow. When she made to move to the yeast, Maggie cut her off.

"Beathag," Had this disaster set her beyond recovery? Was she now as lost within her mind as she was within this community?

Eyes bright, Beathag squeezed Maggie's hands then pulled away.

"What is it, Beathag?" The older woman shook her head and went back to her routine, until she put an imaginary object on a shelf. As she went to leave the kitchens, she reacted as if something brushed against her. She stopped, cringed into herself, and then looked over her shoulder. Her eyes followed the empty space as though tracing the movements of the person who had bumped her. Her expression changed from fear, to irritation, to a frown, and finally confusion.

She swiveled, her hands on hips, tilting her head with a scowl.

"Beathag, tell me." Maggie tried, but it was Talorc who answered.

"She's trying to remember what happened the day you fell ill." He stepped further into the kitchen. "I keep telling her it wasn't in the brew she made, but she won't stop retracing her steps of that day. It's the only thing that stops her shivering." Beathag continued to re-enact her movements. "What did Seonaid want with you?"

"Seonaid?" Maggie didn't care about Seonaid.

"She didn't bump into you by accident. It was deliberate. She had something to say, and I'd like to know what it was."

Maggie frowned and looked away, as she fought to capture an elusive thought. Something Talorc said jogged an idea loose, but not loose enough to tumble into her senses. It tickled at other ideas as if they were all hinged together.

He had her by the arms. "What did she want?"

Maggie pulled free. "Did you say bumped?"

"It was done on purpose."

"No," she waved that away. "Someone brushed past Beathag when she went to leave the room. Someone who did not belong there, and did something to anger Beathag."

"Beathag is too meek to get truly angry."

"No, she's not." Maggie's head snapped up, "She's not so much timid, as she's aware this is not her place, her home, her position meager. She knew she couldn't challenge, that didn't mean she fell in line with all that was done and said."

Talorc was not pleased. "We never sent her away, though we told her she could go if she wanted. She chose to stay, and was accepted."

Maggie snorted. "Accepted or tolerated?"

"We were never unkind."

There was no point in arguing the matter. Maggie resolved, right at that moment, that she would give Beathag a home that appreciated her. "You would be amazed at what she sees." Which brought Seonaid to mind.

His eyes narrowed. "Would I?" Then he looked at the older woman, as if to witness what had been hidden from him. "Do you think she would harm you?"

"Never. But Seonaid is wary of what the old woman sees."

He stilled. "Why would you say that, lass?

"I'm not a lass any longer," she studied him, wanting to see a flicker of reaction. "I'm a wife now, a full grown woman." He glanced away.

Beathag scuttled up to Maggie, tugged at her arm. "Up there, on the shelf." With a tenacious grip, she pulled Maggie further into the kitchen. "She changed the cups."

"Who, Beathag? Who?" Talorc joined them.

Exulted, Beathag put her lips together, to name the culprit. There was a twang, a snuffle of air and a thud. Beathag's words bubbled out on a gurgle, as an arrow came through the front of her throat.

Stunned, no one heard the second twang, the whir of an arrow. Shoved by shock, Maggie stumbled backward. Talorc caught Beathag before she could fall, and shouted for the nearest man to take her. Unloaded of his burden, he started to run toward the back entrance.

Time warped, moments slowed, actions dragged.

Mid- stride, Talorc turned, spotted Maggie, his mouth opened to shout, but no sound came. The determined gleam in his eye dulled to horror, his face churned with fleeting emotions, as his body twisted in mid-air, as though it had lagged behind thought, to follow the path of his gaze.

Maggie shook her head. Talorc's spin took minutes, rather than seconds, as his emotions bombarded her, huge waves of horror, anguish, torment, fury.

What had she done?

His silent bellow of fury erupted and time dropped back to reality in a swirl of screams and shouts and chaos.

She felt, rather than saw, her mother reach her and collapse in a faint. She felt her father's arms on hers, the blast of his breath against her skin, as he lifted her, shouting at the same time for Talorc to get the bastard.

She was dazed. Numb to all but the sight of Beathag's empty stare, as she was led away.

Did she live?

Maggie tried to ask, tried to turn to point but could not, which forced her to look down, to see why she couldn't move. There was an arrow pinning her arm to her side. She blinked, saw the end of it barely out of the entrance wound. Which meant the arrow must be coming out her back. Clean through.

She could not breathe, felt panic rise to swallow her, as darkness overtook.

* * * * * * * * *

Talorc raced from the keep out to the back gardens and stopped. He stood still, men on either side of him. His heart beat so hard he thought it might fly from his chest. With one gesture, the men fanned out and moved forward. Swift, but observant, their eyes scanned for signs of fleeing feet, hidden figures.

The drum of his heart, the race of his blood, urged to charge into a fray. Still, with tremendous effort, Talorc held his ground and waited. His neck prickled, a moment of confusion before he distinguished between reaction and instinct.

He pushed down the sight of his wife, the memory of an arrow lodged in her body. Time will come for recriminations. He had not kept her safe.

He could not think of it. Not now. Now he had to act. He breathed deep, centered himself on the pursuit and was rewarded. Musty air.

The ground was fresh, with summer in the wind, yet a scent of damp earthiness lingered. He turned toward the root cellar. It had been opened, recently.

More men rushed out from the main building. He stayed them with a hand, motioned toward a stick, which young Colban grabbed and tossed to him. Talorc used it to reach for the metal handle of the door, to give distance should the enemy be ready and aimed for battle, but before Talorc could lift the handle, it inched upward, opened from the other side.

He stood back, as did his men, out of view from the entrance as it was pushed open. The weight of it slapped almost back in position, before caught by a woman's backside, as she pushed through the opening, back bowed with the weight of a heavy load. Once free from the low lintel, her head lifted and she turned, wielding a basket of onions, her hair mussed, sweat dotting her brow.

"Deidre?"

Startled, she looked at him. "Talorc?" Then at the men who formed a crescent around where she stood, a mere woman on a domestic errand.

"Fetching onions?"

She lifted the basket and raised an eyebrow, as she turned to go back into the kitchens.

"Did you see or hear anyone, anything, while you were out here?"

"No. Should I have?" She brushed past him, but he stopped her.

"Talorc," Deidre tried to pull away, her jerk loosened the pile of onions. The top ones fell. "Look what you made me do." She scolded, "Big Birtha is waiting for these."

He bent to help her.

"Bold!" Padraig was anxious to get on with the search. Talorc nodded for him to go, but not before he signaled, with his eyes, for someone to go into the caves.

"Leave Nail and Sim with me." He added.

Deidre's head shot up. She glanced at the men leaving, the ones staying. She settled the basket on her hip. "May I go as well?" It was a sarcastic question, she was already aimed toward the kitchens.

"By all means." Talorc murmured. An infinitesimal nod had Nail following her.

Talorc looked at Sim, who was already down on his haunches, checking the tracks that traversed the courtyard outside of the kitchen.

"You know what I'm thinking?" Talorc asked.

CHAPTER 9 – A WOMAN'S GAME

"Maggie!" She heard the thunder of her brothers' approach, lifted her lids and saw them, as stormy as they sounded, bearing down on her.

But her vantage point disoriented her. Where was she? In her father's arms? Just inside the keep? Why?

She blinked at all the faces that stared at her. Shock, terror . . . a bare breath of sound escaped with awareness. She had fainted. Stout hearted, strapping Scottish lass that she was, had fainted like some fragile Sassenach woman.

And it all came back . . . the boy, too young to be left alone, yet not with Seonaid at the keep . . . poisoned water. . . Seonaid's distraction. . . Beathag lost and confused . . . switched mugs . . . arrows . . .

"Bold!" She screamed at the top of her voice and, as she did the flash of another memory flipped through her mind.

Talorc spinning around, seeing the arrow, horror, fury, guilt. A moan of worry rippled through her.

"Let me down!" She cried, as a chorus of voices shouted.

"Maggie, you've been wounded."

"Who was the bastard?" Crisdean was yelling.

"Let's go!" Feargus the younger led the charge. Voices rang around her, as her father fought to keep her steady.

"Let me down." She screamed, and fought so hard her father was challenged to keep her in his arms.

"Do as she says, Da, before she does herself an injury." It was Douglas.

"She's been . . . Maggie."

She had jumped out of his hold, spun her back to her siblings and grabbed her father's arm for support. "Break it off!" She commanded over her shoulder. "Break the bloody arrow head off."

Her head spun, her heart pumped hard but it was the energy, the wild need to move, that overtook everything. "Break the damned thing." She was frantic, refused to be calmed. All she could think of was Talorc's face, the horror, the guilt. If she didn't show him she was fine . . .

Alec snapped the arrows shaft, just short of where it left her back. "I think it only caught the flesh." He smiled as he looked up at the others. "Good thing she's a ripe one and not too scrawny. It merely took the extra flesh!"

There was no time to argue with his teasing. Pinch of flesh or no, the shock of it shuttered through her. She refused to buckle, it was crucial that she not be put in another sick bed.

Maggie clutched the feathered shaft at her arm and yanked it free. "Let's go," she bit out, as she ran to the kitchens, through them and toward the door that led to the courtyard beyond.

"Don't, Maggie." Douglas grabbed at her good arm, but she yanked it away to push through to the outside. She didn't look, only ran straight into Deidre.

She was coming to understand the intensity of battle, how the world slowed, as it had when the arrows shivered through the air and as it did now. She could trace every movement, each offering its own thought. She felt the force of the impact, heard her own scream of rage and pain as though a slow, eerie cry. It wove around Deidre's shout of fury.

A basket flew up, as a shower of onions rained around them. There was a glint of silver, an undulation of metal in the air as Deidre's arm reach out, to catch . . .

A dagger, shaped in the old way, with a wavy blade.

In Maggie's mind, even as she screamed, even as she shuddered from the collision, she thought, the dagger, lighter than the onions, flies higher, spirals . . . mustn't let her have it. And as she thought, she lunged for Deidre, who lunged for the weapon.

They crashed as time converged on itself. Once again, moments flashed. They were a tangle of skirts and arms and sharp burning scent of wounded onions.

Maggie had twisted, to land atop Deidre, and learned the advantage to her extra size. As much as Deidre squirmed and flayed, she could not pull free. Her fight changed, she pulled at Maggie's hair, her teeth bit into Maggie's good arm, as her fist swiped at the injured one.

Maggie had pure mass on her side. Ignorant of her own pain, she hefted a mighty blow to Deidre's side and felt the other woman deflate. She punched again, in the same place, in case Deidre faked her weakness. She raised herself, her arm across the woman's neck, pressed hard with all the angers inside her.

Anger for her babe, gone before it barely made a mound of her belly, and poor Beathag, and Anabal and Anabal's bairn, who lived for only two days. And for all the others Deidre must have hurt. Maggie pressed with all she had, only to weaken, as the blast of energy that propelled her out to the courtyard, and into the fray, suddenly drained.

She collapsed atop her prey.

Someone grabbed her around the middle and tugged. She swung on them, a meager assault, a last touch of aggression from a flow that had all but petered out. And then she felt herself pulled in tight, with such care that her aches didn't ache so terrible.

It was Talorc's arms that comforted her, held her. Finally. She was safe, secure, could let her tears fall. In her husband's arms she mourned for a cherished dream of a babe that was no more, for the pain that now threatened to swallow her, and for the sorrow that he may never hold her this close again.

"It was her, Talorc." She whispered, "It wasna' my fault."

"Shhhh, my love, shhhhhh."

"She poisoned your Anabal. She shot Beathag and me, and poisoned the water . . ."

As someone wound a cloth around her wounded arm to soak the blood, his great body rocked her. Maggie didn't look to see who intruded on this moment, but cherished Talorc's tender embrace. Weariness engulfed her, dried up her tears.

She leaned back, looked at her husband, to find grief staring back at her.

"Talorc?"

He looked away, up to where her father was and rose. He did not carry her inside, to

381

their chamber. He passed her to her older brother. She fought the exchange, at least had the will to do that.

"I'll walk myself." She kept her head up. If there was nothing left of her, no hope, no dreams, no warmth, at least she had her pride.

Her family surrounded her. The people she had never wanted to leave, and now wished gone. She loved them, but if they meant separation from Talorc, she would do without.

With shaking hands, her mother adjusted Maggie's bandage, to better staunch the seepage, but what did it matter when her heart was bled dry. The pain was a welcome distraction.

When they reached the door, she turned to Talorc, who faced Deidre, now awake and held by two huge men. "You know she was the one?" Maggie asked.

"Aye. She's always been a good shot with the arrow, but no one has ever seen her fetch for the cooks in the kitchen before. We found the bow in the root cellar."

"She switched the chalice. So when it spilled, people would think it was the cup that Beathag always used. They would think it was Beathag's brew that poisoned me."

He nodded, his eyes focused on the slush of the courtyard. "I don't understand." He looked to Deidre. "Why? What harm has the clan ever done to you?"

"You stupid, foolish man." Deidre railed, "You refused to see. Straight in front of your face, it was!" Deidre stopped struggling once she had Talorc's attention. "I did it for Seonaid. So her son could claim the Laird's place."

"For Seonaid?"

"No!" The woman in question stepped out of the shadow of the kitchen, rushed to Deidre, only to be held back by Padraig. "Not for me." She sobbed. "I didn't want this."

"Deidre!" Ingrid ran from the castle, tried to reach her sister. "What have you done?"

For a moment, Deidre faltered, the sight of her sister halting her. "You almost caught me, Ingrid. But I'm glad you didn't. You don't belong in my world."

"Deidre?" Tears streamed down Ingrid's cheeks.

Deidre smiled at her, a small, sad shaping of her lips before she turned her anger on Seonaid. "You were so blind! But I saw." She nodded toward the Bold. "There he was, all so good, all so grand, yet he never claimed his own son. He never watched over or took care of his son's mother!"

"No!" Seonaid wailed and pulled free, fought her way to take Deidre's face in her hands.

"No, my sweet love, the Bold is not the father of my child. Never."

Deidre looked from one to the other, as though trying to assess. "Of course he is." But Seonaid only shook her head, tears in her eyes.

"He is," Ingrid hissed, "but who can blame him for not wanting Seonaid. She's more man than woman."

"Don't." Deidre ordered.

"It's true." Ingrid cried. "Why would you fight for what she's not willing to fight for?"

"He's the father of her son!" Deidre shouted.

"He's not," Seonaid wilted, tears flowing.

"Then who?" Deidre demanded.

Seonaid kept crying. Big Birtha knelt beside her, wrapping the woman in her arms. "Och, Deidre, it's not pleasant things you talk of." She cooed to Seonaid, stroking her hair. "But it's time they're spoken of."

With trembling hands, Seonaid swiped at her tears, nodded, as she pushed away from the cook. "It was no' the Bold, Deidre, it was my brother. Lochlan. That's why he was sent away. He raped me, Deidre, beat me and took me more often than I can count.

"But one time," she shuddered with her tears. "One time he was careless, out in the field. I was trying to run away and he caught me. That's how Talorc found us.

"He nearly killed Lochlan, but I stopped him. He was my kin. Shamed as I was, shamed as I am, he was my kin."

"No," Deidre's eyes filled with confusion. "Not Lochlan, not him."

"You've yet to see the bad in him, but it's there."

"Oh, aye, you call it bad, you call it evil or wicked, but he makes the blood rise. He challenges a woman. He's my husband, Seonaid. We've pledged our troth. No doubt you wanted him for yourself but he's not that kind.

"He claims it was Talorc who was caught with you, that was why he was banished." Deidre snarled. "He's planned it all so your son could be Laird."

"His son, Deidre, my boy is my brother's son!" Seonaid snapped, before turning to flee. Padraig stopped her with the bulk of his body. Just stepped in her path, pulled her against him. She head bowed, she leaned against him, her body shaking.

"Deidre," Maggie confronted, "you defiled your clan. Betrayed your family, your people."

"You know nothing." Deidre argued.

Talorc stepped forward. Maggie shook her head at him. This was women's business. That's why he had been unable to protect her. He thought it was man's business, strategy of his own kind.

"You wanted Seonaid to wed Talorc, to put her son in line to be Laird." Maggie said, "Only Talorc didn't wed her."

"He was the traitor to his clan. Marrying a Gunn, turning our clan into measly traders. He was to be destroyed and we nearly did it. His strength waned with the loss of battles. One more and he would be cast aside, weakened, but then you came!" She screeched, pointing her finger at Maggie. "You, from some tyke of a family, fired his blood. You needed to be killed, sacrificed. Your power for my power.

"A second wife murdered, and no one would trust him. Not only would he have lost the aide of the MacBedes, he would have gained them as an enemy. Other clans would shift allegiance.

"And the Bold, ah yes, he was pitiful in his need for you. Losing you, when you were under his protection, would have broken him," She pointed at Maggie and sneered. "already has and you're not even dead yet."

"Enough!" Talorc shouted, over the chaos of words flung in fury. "You will lead us to the renegades and we will fight one on one, like true men. None of this using women to play games."

"Never." She sneered.

"Oh, aye, you and your Eba, banned to live in the wilderness."

385

"Banned?" she snorted, "Not banned, left to be with my own."

"The renegades? Word will be sent to the Gunns. Together we will run you all to earth for the vermin you are. United we will hunt you, track you, until you all pay the price for what you did to our clan and those we protect."

With Talorc's pronouncement the ground shook as feet stomped, hands clapped, a beat of exile. Shouts wove a tune through the drumming, but Diedre's crazed laugh silenced them.

"You are too late," she shouted, eyes blazing. "All those lasses, stupid girls, lost to their clans? Missing?" Her eyes scanned the crowd. "They were ours, we took them! We destroyed them. Whatever remains of their bodies, at the least their heads, have been left at the borders of all those who lost them."

Rigid with stunned disbelief, all listened to the mad woman. "They were dumped with empty bottles of MacKay whiskey and pieces of plaid that could only be dyed from plants on our land."

"What have you done?" Talorc whispered, beyond fury.

"Ruined you," Diedre spit. "Destroyed you."

As the words fell, like wounding shards of glass Seonaid raised her head alert as a deer sensing danger. Swift as that deer she broke free of Padraig's hold, leapt for the dagger Diedre herself used against Maggie and plunged it deep into her friend, shoving deep and hard and up, into her friends heart, with a brutal twist of the wavy blade.

Blood gurgled from Diedre's mouth, gushed from the wound to spray the truest of war's paint. Eyes wide from the moment she saw death's approach, Deidre crumbled to the unforgiving courtyard. Panting, Seonaid loomed over her, the knife gripped in her hand, dripping with her friend's blood.

Chaos erupted, shouts, cries. Seonaid spun around, knife raised, challenging any to come near before she threw the weapon aside and strode from the swarm of confusion.

"Come, lass," Feargus pulled Maggie toward the keep.

Maggie fought to turn back, pleaded. "I should be by his side." He needed her, the clan needed her at his side.

"Later, love," Fiona crooned, as she had when Maggie was a child. But Maggie was no longer a child. She was a woman. She had been wed.

"Bold." Maggie called, her voice a meager thing, next to the noise of the crowd.

"Maggie," Feargus took her by the shoulder. "You'll be coming home with us."

"We can't leave." She argued.

"After the battle." Her mother urged her out of the turmoil.

"I'm a married woman." Maggie argued.

Her mother pushed her own. "He's allowed it's not so."

"We said our vows. We've promised." Maggie continued, as they moved against the flow of people."

Her mother stopped, then, took Maggie's face in her hands, ignoring the jostling of the horde. "No man nor woman is held to vows made under force, and not from the heart."

She had known this, she had known they were going to play this game. She could not fight it with her family.

"We will wait until he returns from fighting." She said, and watched as her father caught her mother's eye. They wouldn't wait. They would take her before she could confront him.

And suddenly she understood just how Deidre felt to be wed with no husband to claim her.

"There is one more thing I can do for my husband." She announced to no one, to everyone.

"The only thing you can do is rest and mend."

"No, mother." She stood firm. "There is one more thing and I will see it done."

****

Burrowed deep in discussion with his top chiefs, with the MacBede men, Talorc felt the approaching silence even before it hit him. Feargus MacBede looked up first and cursed.

"What now, woman?"

Fiona bore down on them, her face set.

By everything Holy, this could only mean one thing and would be all about Maggie.

He needed her gone, free of him, without the chance to do something selfish and foolish. Especially now. Time was the enemy. He could not afford to be torn between her and what needed doing.

Seonaid slew the only voice that could lead them to the renegades. Oh, aye, the clan wanted Diedre to pay for her crimes. But their hunger was for greater vengeance than a quick, clean kill and, most certainly, not before she had told them everything she knew about the renegades.

They needed information.

They needed to know how many clans would be charging for vengeance. How to circumvent too many dying before they could be aimed at the true enemy.

If Talorc could convince them, in the heat of battle, that they fought the wrong people.

Lies have a tendency to stick, no matter the evidence.

He didn't need this, but still he rose from his place at the table and moved to intercept his wife's mother, drawn by need. There was no time and yet, for Maggie, there would always be time.

****

Aulay Gunn halted his men, told them to wait as he rode ahead to scout the lay of the land. Plan their strategy. Escape a palpable rage that blinded.

Revenge vibrated, a tight rope strangling reason. Aulay needed reason.

"It makes no sense, I tell ya.'" He argued with the two men who rode beside him.

"What makes no sense? Butchered lasses? Scraps of plaid? Bottles drained while our poor wee ones were tortured?" Gil snarled, proving he wasn't so much deaf as beyond reason.

"They're mean bastards, tight as a horse ass, you know this. They'd not waste using bottles made for trade. They'd fill their own jugs before they'd do that and then, they'd not leave them behind and have to find another to use.

"So why waste what could bring them money? Why leave traces of who they are?" He looked back at the band of men who had

ridden out, warriors, craftsmen, farmers.
Restless, edgy, beyond control if he didn't
find answers fast.

He turned back to his captains. "Easy
enough to provoke us to fight without this.
And why would they hurt those who could not
fight back? Only a sniffling coward does
that."

"Heathens!" Erik cursed. "Not just our
lasses but others. Did you not speak to the
runners?"

"Aye, I spoke to them." Messengers
from other clans still reeling from the
gruesome remains left on their own borders.
"And what they're saying is that the MacKays
have lowered themselves to butchering women
and goading every ally they've ever had, as
well as inciting enemies. Now why would they
do that?"

"Because they're fools," Gil offered.

Again, Aulay shook his head. "The
MacKay does everything in his power to
protect his clan, not destroy them. Doesna'
make sense." And he knew it, just as he knew
the destruction of the boats had not been
MacKays doing, which left him with a bigger
problem.

Still clinging to his view, Erik voiced
Aulay's dilemma. "Then who is responsible?
Every other clan around has been brought into
this fight. Who's left?"

Aulay shot Erik a keen glance. "That's
what I've been trying to say. We're being
used."

"No!" Gil fought the mere idea.

"Oh, aye, the Gunns and every other
clan in the highlands is being used to destroy
the MacKay." They rode in silence before
Aulay added, "and use your noggin', whoever
it is expects the rest of us to be weakened by

the fight, for the MacKays won't go down
easy.

"So who hates the MacKays more than
us and thinks they can take the whole of the
highlands?"

"It's not so hard to hate the MacKays."
Gil said.

"And it's not so hard to use us against
them." Erik added.

This time it was Gil who nodded.

"We've some angry men with us." Each
looked over their shoulders. On horseback
they were furlongs ahead of their clansmen,
most who followed by foot. Even with the
distance, Aulay sensed fury burgeoning
beyond control.

"I'll go spread the word that we may be
fighting someone other than the MacKay." Gil
offered but Erik stopped him with a curse,
pointing to the hilltop ahead of them.

"We're too late."

Aulay's curse rode on a wave of
disbelief. "A woman and a boy, riding from
the MacKay's? He sent a woman?" He spat.
"You, Gil, go stop our men. Erik, come with
me. We'll meet the riders and see what is
going on here."

Blood curdling warriors cries stopped
Gill a second time as the Gunn's, a mass of
roiling fury, surged forward.

Aulay motioned Gil to turn, ride with
him and Erik, fast as their mounts would lead,
to reach the MacKay riders. The two
approached swiftly, down the slope. Above
and behind them, on the edge of land the two
riders left, a long line of MacKay warriors
appeared.

Had he got it wrong, Aulay wondered?
Were these two riders a tease?

Never, it still made no sense.

The woman, with a wild mane of hair, rose on her galloping horse, feet braced in some sort of stirrup. She waved one arm madly, the other held at her chest with a swath of cloth. She halted her ride down in the gully, an awful position, as Aulay's men could not see him if he met her there.

Her cry filled the gully. "Stop them! The MacKays are not at fault for this! Stop your men!"

Obviously the boy had some training for he urged her to ride up the hill.

Erik reached them first, his mount rearing as he pulled on the reins. He circled the two, pointing to the high point, where the Gunns could see their Laird. Aulay and Gil arrived, blocking any other exit as they, too, corralled the two.

Women, they were both women though one was dressed as a man.

Eyes sparking with determination, the one with the wild red hair sat stiff, her head high, nostrils flared. Proud and strong, much like the beast she rode. An attractive woman. Maggie MacBede, now MacKay, he guessed.

He turned to look at the other one. At this range rider's breeches, sheathed dagger, a bow and quiver of arrows over the shoulder failed to disguise a woman's figure.

Seonaid MacKay. Well known to the Gunns. Her cottage, near enough to their border, teased his men with her presence, a woman as beautiful as she was contrary.

He would deal with her later.

"Maggie MacKay." He fought to hide his gripping tension. "Bold as your husband claims to be."

"Aye," She nodded, allowing them to edge her still higher on the slope. "And your ransom to ensure my husband will not fight you or yours."

"Why should we bother with ransom? You seem to know what has provoked us. The murder of young women."

"It was not our men. But we know who it was, and need you to join forces with us."

Caustic and hard he laughed at her naivette. "Give me more than that. I need more to stop them." He gestured to the approaching army as they had reached the rise. He didn't trust this any more than he trusted the battle they headed toward.

"Lochlan," Seonaid broke-in. "It was my brother and renegades from all the clans who did this. Lochlan." She, too, held her head high.

"Lochlan?" Oh, aye, finally something made sense. Lochlan MacKay, a conniving, evil man.

"Laird Gunn, tell your clansmen to stop their charge!" A command weakened by the tremor in her voice. He didn't blame her. The ground shook, the air burned with the approach.

"And," he shouted, "who's to stop your men?"

For the first time, Maggie MacKay looked to the land she had crossed not moments before.

"Oh shite!" She sniped. "Who told him?" She grasped Aulay's arm. "He doesn't know what we are about, but he doesn't want this battle."

"No doubt you were not his first choice for ransom."

She shook her head, proud and defiant. Aulay felt a twinge of sympathy for the man.

"We've no time for him to listen." She pleaded over the growing rumble of the ground as both sides stormed closer. "You're going to have to trust me." And without any sign of fear she maneuvered her horse, signaled for Seonaid to follow suit "We'll take your back, you take ours."

And so their mounts' rumps faced the threat from the Gunns.

She turned her back on the enemy.

Without time to consider alternatives, Aulay nodded for Erik and Gil to follow his lead as he turned his back on The Bold, their backs to a charging army charging.

Five against two armies, stood firm. Propelled by a black well of hatred, there was no guarantee his men would stop despite their own laird.

And what of the MacKays, with no notion their Laird's bride meant to form a truce? Aulay knew, if he wasn't trampled by his own men he may just end up with a knife in his back.

He heard The Bold's shout to halt but still, the Gunns surged forward.

He rose in his seat, held his hands high, fury pumping through him, that his own men could, quite possibly, betray his lead.

Slowly, Gil and Erik moved toward the advancing army. Shouts lessened, speed slowed until, finally, they held still, close enough Aulay could see the rise and fall of their chests, as they heaved in their own restraint.

Then he turned to the MacKay.

"It seems we have a common enemy." He called across the divide.

"Aye!" The MacKay returned. "A wily fox who would be best cornered from all sides. Are you with us?"

Aulay paused as horses side stepped and snorted. "We are with you." He confirmed.

Maggie, Seonaid by her side, led the Laird Gunn to his adversary, the Laird MacKay, before leaving them to form, if only for this day, a bond.

Two troops, from opposite sides, joined. They would meet the other clans and amass a power far greater than any renegade troop.

CHAPTER 10 – CONFRONTATION

Seonaid stood on the battlements, looking out over the land she'd called home the whole of her life. Her son's home.

Her brother's son.

The whole of the clan knew of her humiliation, her family's shame. The evil that ran in Lochlan's blood. The same blood that ran in her viens.

Every day she feared that evil,that it would rise to consume her. She watched young Deian, for some sign, but all she saw was a playful lad with a huge heart. Had Lochlan ever been like that? Something other than a clever bully?

Early on, she sought ways to focus anger, fear, so it would not turn on those she loved. She donned men's clothes, she learned to fight as a man learned to fight and struggled against the softness in herself, the vulnerable.

No more. She was tired. Deep inside tired and somehow the revelations allowed her to sink into that depth, to stop fighting, to stop bracing herself with secrets.

She had to think of Deian.

"You're wearing a bliaut." Padraig's deep voice flowed over her as soft as a breeze, making it worth it to have on the garb of a woman.

"Aye." Men's clothes had been a shield, given her a sense of power. A futile gesture. She had no power.

"It becomes you."

She turned to him then, grateful as she always was to this man. "Thank you."

He flushed, shrugged, concentrated on the view she had been looking at. "It's land worth fighting for."

"Aye," she didn't know what else to say to him, knew better than to speak the truths she felt. That she hungered for him, cared for him. "Impossible." She admitted, and put a hand to her lips, as though she could stop the words already slipped.

"What's impossible?" He asked.

She shook her head, then thought to confide in him. "I will be leaving on the morrow, with Deian. We are going to a place in the west, where a society of women healers live."

"You're what?" Quiet, harsh, he faced her.

"If they'll have me," She continued. "and Deian. I'm no healer, but I can help protect them. And though he's a male, Deian is young, they should not mind."

He took her shoulders. "There's no reason for you to leave."

Stunned, she stared at him. "Have you lost your senses, man? I bore my brother's child! I'll never live past that. Worse yet, Deian will never be able to live past that."

"You could marry me."

You could marry me. She would never forget his offer, the harsh hope in his voice.

But she could not marry him. She could never marry anyone. Oh, but that he asked, a mere four words she would cling to for the rest of her life.

Sadly, she shook her head. "No," she huffed out a weary sigh, "I canna' marry you." She touched his cheek. "But I'm that grateful that you asked." And she walked away.

* *

Talorc held his face to the wind, as the day threatened with a hint of pink against the deep gray of night.

He willed the day to hurry on its way. He willed it never to come.

She would be leaving with first light.

He tried to stay away, but the renegades had no strength in direct combat. Their power had been in malicious whispers, building hidden fears. Their games had been lost when the Gunns joined the MacKays to oust the trouble makers.

It hadn't taken long. They'd cornered them in their own hole, scattered them like cockroaches to light. Talorc found Lochlan drunk and reeling, laughing at the accusations, taunting with his misdeeds up to the moment Talorc speared him to the ground.

Pinned, like an insect, not killed he'd whined and blubbered.

They'd not kill them, any of the renegades, but leave them wounded and bleeding in cages, to starve and thirst as they fought off the vultures, hanging from arches in the same places they left the bodies of their victims.

Talorc's work done, he now stood on the battlement, determined to see Maggie once more.

Maggie.

Feelings, crammed deep, so they wouldn't interfere with his thoughts, now rushed to the surface.

It was true. Maggie had doubled his strength, his power. Even in the end, she was the one, not him, who sorted out and found the answers to the evil played against them.

They had vowed forever. He would live true to that vow, but never would he ask the same of her. She deserved a man who could protect her.

The deep gray softened with light. Talorc looked toward the windows of his chamber, where he knew his Maggie would be preparing to leave his bed.

He doubted he could ever sleep there again.

Perverse hunger had him willing someone, anyone, to pull open the shutters, so he could get a glimpse of her, from here, on the far side of the battlements. Where no one would expect to find him.

The shutters flew open with a crash he could hear from across the courtyard, and he got his glimpse. It was her, wild mane caught in a wind that howled as fiercely as he wanted to howl himself.

"Bold!" her voice rang through the air, to waken the worst slug-a-bed.

His heart thrilled at the sight of her hefting air into her lungs. She was riled, just the way he loved her to be. It warmed his blood, had it pumping hard in response. "Bold! I know you're here, somewhere. I feel it in my bones."

Fiona came up behind Maggie, to urge her back in the room, but Maggie shrugged her off.

And she was right. Her instincts spot on target. He was here, playing the coward to her courageous heart.

"I'm here, Maggie." He shouted, refusing to portray himself, as he saw it. Better she remember his strength.

"You're set on sending me away?"

How could she ask that? He had robbed her from her home, her family, and failed his most basic responsibility to her. He had failed to protect her.

"Now that the babe is gone, you have no use for me?"

"Don't be foolish, Maggie." he shouted back, but without force, for suddenly he realized this was not a private conversation. They were shouting across a courtyard that was filling with each word.

"Do you think I can't carry another? Or is it that you don't want to try for one?"

"Maggie." He warned, but she would not be stopped.

"Tell me Bold, just how many times have you been injured?"

He snorted and headed for the stairs to the courtyard.

She leaned further out the window, "How many?"

"I'm a man, Maggie, a warrior. It's my job to be wounded, to defend you." Which he had failed to do three times.

"And I'm a warrior's wife, but I'm beginning to wonder if you're a man or not."

Talorc's head shot up, his jaw dropped. Even the birds stopped singing to the dawn with that one.

Maggie leaned so far out the window, Talorc was certain the only thing that kept her from falling straight out was the hold her mother had on her skirts. Try as Fiona did, to pull Maggie back, to hush her, his wife could not be stopped.

"They call you the Bold, but I think you're nothing but a coward." She turned, to shove her mother away and leaned back. "And don't you dare move until I get down there to give you a piece of my mind."

He couldn't have moved if he had wanted to. He just kept staring, dumbfounded, at the empty window, where Maggie shouted like some goddess fishwife.

Only she wasn't a fishwife. She was a woman with strength and determination. She was a woman pushed to an edge she didn't want to fall over.

It felt like the whole of the clan was standing in the courtyard, fidgeting with embarrassment, for they had come out to watch an explosion that blew up beyond their expectations. Talorc knew they could no more move than he could. He also knew they wanted to ease away, discreetly, as if they hadn't heard the slander against their Laird.

She had called him a coward. She had questioned his manhood.

There was only one thing left for him to do. Stand-up and take her fury head-on. But that was not what would prove him courageous. Nor would it prove him a man. Those would be seen in his soul, when he still had the courage to set her free and to do so without ever letting her know the anguish it cost him.

****

Maggie tore down the stairs, her skirts hefted above her knees, so she could run all the way out to the side courtyard. Her heart pounded. Not from exertion, but with fear that he would have disappeared.

She never should have shouted out such rubbish, for all his people to hear. She should have run down the stairs straight away and confronted him close up. She may have overplayed her hand, lost him completely.

That would not happen without a fight.

Jamie and Crisdean tried to stop her, but she sidestepped them, managed to barrel through the doorway to stand, heaving for breath.

He was there. Standing right where she told him to stand. When he raised his hand and crooked his finger, she went to him. She owed him that much. She could have sunk into the ground for being so brazen in front of . . . her head shifted to see the huge crowd of people watching.

Did they always have to have an audience?

She looked back at Talorc.

"I'm not going." It was all there was to say.

"Fine."

That was not the response she had expected. "I thought you were sending me away."

She watched as he took air into his lungs. Did it take so much patience to deal with her?

"Maggie, you can come or go. It doesna' matter. Sim is taking a missive to the Campbell's where they say the priest has settled for the winter. It says I forced you to wed me, against your will. Your father wrote that he forced you as well."

"That's a lie." She watched him shake his head.

"The church won't recognize a marriage of arms."

"Aye, you made up my mind for me. You took me to Handfast against my better judgment. You took me away from my family, my home. You promised me a husband who took risks with his life every time he left me." She began to pace. "You expected me to be strong enough to face all of that, when you are too weak to face the loss of one babe."

He grabbed for her shoulders, stopped at the sight of the bandage that covered a wound still fresh. "I almost lost you, three times."

"And I almost lose you every time you leave this keep."

"It's not the same."

"It is. Don't you see, you know how to defend with the sword, you know how to match wits with another warrior, but you're a fool to think you could fight a woman's game."

"Why do you think a laird needs a wife if not to fight the battles from his blind side?"

She stepped back, her eyes narrowed, her jaw clenched. She wasn't done yet. She knew the rest would come, she could feel it spoiling within her. And then it did, the words flew from her lips, as she shoved so hard at his chest, he had to take a step back or fall on his bottom.

"If you're the man your clan thinks you are, if you're the Bold, then prove it. Have the courage to take me as your wife. Have the courage to risk the planting of a babe. Prove it to me by the morn, or I swear I will leave knowing you're nothing but a . . . a . . . trembling. . ."

"Don't say it Maggie." He warned.

"Are you going to prove me wrong?"
She sassed.

His jaw twitched. "Do not say that word again."

"Stop me."

"Maggie," his threat rumbled through her, goaded her.

"Coward." She brazened, then spun on her toes, hefted her skirts and took off, three steps.

Suddenly she was airborne, flipped and hanging over his shoulder.

Her head popped up, to see a crowd of faces, as stunned as she felt. And then they started to grin. It was contagious. Old Gerta winked at her. Maggie had to duck her head, from embarrassment.

She meant to confront him, push him to take her back, but in doing so she'd made a public spectacle out of their bedding.

He didn't go to the keep, but headed straight to the stables, where they'd first come together, as man and wife.

"Out," she heard him roar at the men tending the livestock.

There were no empty stalls, but there was a soft mound of hay, where it was stored. He set her down, on her back, as the last man left the barn with a slam of the latch.

"Coward?" He stood above her, hands on his hips.

She swallowed, half exulted, half afraid. She wasn't at all certain he was above throttling her. And deserve it she did. She had pushed harder than she meant to, but couldn't back down now. "You could prove me wrong."

"You want to be married to a coward?"

Even her voice shook with nerves. "I want to be married to the Bold."

"We never exchanged the gifts."

Excitement surged. "We could now."

"Aye." He nodded slowly, reached up, removed the pin that held his plaid at his shoulder. The fabric fell to the floor, to lie like a train behind him.

"Here." He handed the broach to Maggie. "If you look, you will see wheat in the design."

She took it in her hand as tears came to her eyes. He cradled her face in his hands, his thumbs brushing at the moisture as he spoke.

"May this wheat be a symbol that I vow to provide for my home."

It was her turn. She too, took the broach she had hastily clipped to a plaid she wrapped around her. There'd been no time to dress before confronting the Bold. It was the MacBede plaid. Her mother had removed MacKay plaids, despite Maggie's argument. Now it held good purpose. She unwrapped it, leaving herself in naught but a kirtle.

It took her a moment, for her hands trembled, but she managed to fold it while Talorc waited. When she handed it to him, a symbol of weaving and sewing, she said, "As I will provide for our home."

He removed his dagger, placed it in her hands, held silent, as the intensity of the moment gathered around them. He looked to the beams of the old barn, as if garnering the courage to go forward. With tender tears his gaze finally met hers.

"I vow to protect our home." His hands cupped hers, "And I do, Maggie. With all my strength, and with your insight and . . . " She stopped him, by resting her head against his mouth, against his words.

If they had been prepared, if they had known this moment was coming, she would have had a Bible ready, to give to him with her own pledge of protection. But there was no Bible, only their hearts.

She trusted that God would be with her as she whispered. "You vow the protection that comes from the blade. I vow the protection that comes from the hilt of the dagger." She traced the line of it as she spoke, "A cross for the strength of faith. But together," understanding where she was going, he placed his hands on hers, again, so they could hold the hilt as one. "Together we will face the crosses that life bears. We will be united in each other, in our home, in our love."

"Together," Talorc promised, "We will fight our battles as one, and never let them tear us apart."

Symbol or no, the dagger was thrown aside, as he pulled Maggie into his arms. "I don't deserve you."

She tilted her head so she could look up at him. He truly believed what he had just said, as if she were someone precious and special. But she had been raised with a team of brothers, who had wailed that they didn't deserve her, either. Only they didn't mean it in a good way. She couldn't help but tease. "Oh, trust me. You deserve everything I have to give."

His eyes sparkled, "Do I?" and she knew he thought of something else entirely.

She stepped back, "Like the sharp edge of my tongue."

He advanced. "Twined with mine."

"I'll go toe to toe with you."

"It would be easier if you just wrapped your legs around my waist."

"We'll butt heads."

He laughed. "I've a head that would love to have you take it on."

"Talorc!" She shouted, hands on hips. "I mean it. I'm not nearly as good and precious as you make me sound."

"And delicious. Don't be forgetting that, now."

She looked to the barn door, aware that the clan was out there waiting for results.

Just as they had once before.

"Maggie, we're married, because you insist. Are you now going to pretend we aren't doing what's necessary to bear an heir?"

She was stuck on 'insist.' "Are you going to write the church and tell them you were forced?"

His smile was huge.

"Oh, no you won't." she stormed for the door. His hand slammed against it, trapping her with his body.

"I love it when you get riled."

She couldn't look at him. "Good thing."

"Come here, Lass."

She didn't have an option, not that she wanted one, for he had pulled her flush to him.

"Do you feel that, Lass?" Aye, she could feel the heat of him, as well as the hard hunger of him. He shifted his hips as if she could miss it otherwise. Maggie rolled her eyes.

He prodded. "Do you believe the church would let me claim that you forced me to feel like this?"

"I could have seduced you."

His chuckle rustled her hair. "Maggie, every time your name floats through my thoughts, I'm seduced."

She moaned against her own desire.

"Do you want me, too, Maggie?" The arrogance was gone from his voice.

"Aye." She wanted him.

"Why?"

"Don't," she grabbed at his head, pulled him down to kiss her.

"I have to know, Maggie. I have to know why you want to be married, why you want to stay."

The arrogance had been traded for anguish. She pulled back, to search his eyes. "I could ask you the same."

He groaned. "Don't you know? Don't you know how I've felt from the moment you landed in my arms?"

"Your hands."

It was a sorry sort of chuckle. "My hands. From that moment I knew I had to have you for myself. Selfishly. No care for you. I had to have you.

"And then you came into my life, all soft yet strong. Vulnerable yet ready to jump into the fray. You caught my heart, Maggie. I love you, desperately. I'm famished for you." He buried his face in her neck, kissing, suckling, shifting to her ear, the rise of her cheek, her eyes.

He cupped her face in his hands, and stopped kissing her, though she sensed it wasn't easy.

"Tell me. Can you handle the depth of my love for you? Does it make me weak in your eyes? Because if that's true, you might as well run now."

"No." she shook her head. "No. Love takes courage. A man has to be Bold to admit to it." She traced the line of his cheek, "And I love you, Bold, with the same hunger, the same need, the same blush with the thought of your name."

She stood on her toes, to whisper to his lips, "In this we are equal."

He lifted her into his arms. "Do you know what that means?"

"No," she shook her head.

"It means we're both too desperate to make it any further than this barn."

And they were.

THE END

Excerpt

THE PROTECTOR

DUE FOR RELEASE WINTER OF 2013

This is a work of fiction. Any resemblance to actual events or persons is coincidental.

In the Year of Our Lord 1226 . . .

Roland looked about his bed chamber. Ten years ago, when he'd left for crusades, this had been his father's room. That shouldn't have changed.

He crossed to the bench by the fire, stretched his legs so Ulric could remove his boots.

"There were representatives of the king here, to welcome you home." Still naïve enough to be impressed by royalty, even watered down versions of the King's aide, Ulric reflected on the night.

Roland didn't respond. Having spent the entire evening with emotions clamped tight, he was not about to say what he thought now.

As Ulric pulled Roland's tunic over his head, the young page murmured. "Your sister Margaret was here."

Cowed goose! The curse was silent, the only thing Ulric would have heard was a grunt of agreement.

Yes, Margaret was here, with her husband and family and their retinue of servants. And yes, the King's men were here, as well, ready with invitations from court for Sir Roland. Neighbors, friends, fellow knights all here for Roland's homecoming after ten years absence.

But his wife wasn't here, nor his father. Not even his best friend.

Two of those three were dead and one was responsible for those death.

"Leave!"

Ulric's head shot up.

"Just go," Roland muttered wearily, embarrassed by his outburst, as if he cared, truly believed, deep inside, that his wife would be the same sweet child he left behind.

"I can certainly undress myself. Go."

Ulric bowed and stepped back. "I'll be on the other side of the door, my lord. In the ante-chamber, if you need me."

Roland shooed him away with a flip of his hand. When the door closed, he stood and paced against a volcano of emotion roiling to erupt and condemned his foolishness. He learned, early on in his travels, never trust. Comrade in arms or the Pope's man, goodness was a commodity, only as thick as the benefit it offered. Kindness was measured by a mercenary's scale. The reminder calmed to a bitter smile.

Ulric, so impressed with all who arrived at Oakland, to witness his the homecoming he failed to notice that no one, other than town's people, greeted him at the port, not ten miles from his sister, Margaret's home, though they all knew he was due to arrive. He had been welcomed to her home by servants. Banners and waves and the wild shouts of welcome, that Ulric enjoyed, were supplied by strangers, not his family or his peers.

Margaret had already left for Oakland.

The King had sent a guard of honor for Roland and his knights, but the King's men were at Oakland.

It seemed that the whole of the English country side knew of his exploits, knew of his victories but word had only moved one way. No one deemed fit to forewarn him of affairs at his demesne. Not even Margaret had the courage to face him alone.

So he returned to a horde of supposed well-wishers. A horde of greedy gossips full of whispered stories and curious glances. All waiting hungrily to see him react.

He refused to give them that pleasure. Let them stew in their lost tittle-tattle. They'd fed off his flesh for the past five years, he wasn't about to give them more.

Caskets full of precious herbs were stacked against the wall. With one sweep he sent them crashing to the floor.

His wife, Veri, the winsome lovely child who had tended to his wounds, pulled his father away from the threshold of death; the wise young bride he had left untouched and innocent, to ensure her protection while he sought the crusades, had taken his best friend as lover and murdered his father.

The roar that filled his lungs, threatened to escape. He swallowed against it, punched at the solid wood poster of his bed. The wood cracked, Roland's hand throbbed, but the shout was squelched. He drew in deep draughts of air, released each one to slow measured counts. A trick he had learned on his travels.

The herbs crunched under his feet. He thought about his step-mother Hannah. She would have used them, but not properly. Only Veri truly understood the use of such things.

Veri.

Did she know of the damage she had wreaked? Dori would never be the same. His sister Dori, so jolly and loveable, now sullen and angry. Excusable. It was her husband Derek Veri seduced to her bed. Once in her bed, Veri lured Derek to murder.

Derek died for his sins.

Veri had not.

Locked in this room with its thirty foot drop to the rocks below, a twenty-four hour guard outside the door, she escaped.

Stories were flung at him, asides and whispers, throughout the celebrations of his return. Did he know of her powers? Shape-shifting into a bird and flying away. She bewitched the household guard, had them under her spell. She could make men do anything . . . escape . . . murder . . . anything.

Roland doubted both. His eyes shifted, glanced at the wall where the tapestry of a boar's hunt, hung. He knew of the door hidden there. No one else knew of it, not even his family. Only the lord and his heir would know of that route out of the castle, to ensure against a family turned traitorous.

The pacing stopped. He stood amid the jumble of herbs, his anger contained.

"Ulric!" He shouted for his page. Immediately, the boy popped his head around the door. "Clean-up this mess. Then you can go to sleep."

"Yes, milord." Ulric hurried with his task, as Roland prepared for bed.

He would need his sleep before he set out on his quest. To hunt down his wife, see she meet a fitting death, as gruesome as Derek's had been.

The mess removed, Ulric gone, Roland slid under the sheets of his father's bed, and slept as he slept the past ten years while on crusade, a dagger beneath his pillow, a sword along his side.

How long he slept, he was not certain but, he was awake, abruptly. To the silver light of a near full moon and a fire burned down to coals and ash. He offered no sign of wakefulness, one slight hitch of breath the only clue.

He knew better.

Eyes closed, he waited, to see if the creak of a door proved dream or reality. The well oiled hinges of the chamber door would not make a noise.

A soft swoosh of stale air brushed his face.

Reality.

Rage rode on his blood, hot and viscious.

No living soul, no person he cared to see, knew of the hidden entrance to this chamber. Yet, it had just been breached from the far side of the moat, through a tunnel both steep and slick.

Ten years he'd been gone, not even back long enough to witness a sunrise, and the treachery against his family reignited. This time it would be different. This time his skills had been honed by years of the unholy, holy wars called crusades.

He almost smiled. Almost. But that would have alerted his intruders, told them he was awake. Instead he mimicked the deep, easy rhythm of sleep, his lashes lowered to hide the gleam of his eyes, as he studied the deep shadows of the chamber.

There was no shift in darkness, just a heavy, ominous silence. If not for the damp, musty smell he could have argued the earlier noise imagined. But he knew better, knew to wait and quell his thirst for immediate action. He counted breaths, focused on them, aware that time had expanded to a place where moments became hours.

When it finally came, the carelessness of the move surprised him. The door pushed open in one rash movement, rather than slight, silent increments. Footsteps brushed the gravely dirt of the threshold, distinct enough that he counted nine pairs of soft boots cross into his room.

Did they truly believe he had survived a decade of perilous travel to fall prey now? Did they imagine that upon his return, he would fall back into the naïve and gullible soul he had once been? And he had been, to believe he could leave his child bride behind and return to find an innocent virgin untouched by an insatiably greedy and cunning world. He had allowed that small spark of hope to linger in his heart until this evening.

When the truth was put before him, he must have seemed a fool to think it could have been different.

He snorted, a sleepy sound, shifted, stretched, eased back as though in slumber. The dagger and sword he had gone to bed with, now in hand.

The merest hint of light allowed assessment of the room without notice. They had filed in, one at a time, so the door would not have to be opened more than the width of a body. As though the first rasp of hinges would not have woken him.

The nine of them huddled within the entrance, shrouded from head to toe in black capes. Their whispers reached him, low indistinct murmurs, as they divided with the soft shuffle of feet. Three crossed to the door, four toward the raised alcove on the far side of the room. Two stood near the tunnel entrance, until one of them separated, moved, without cloak or weapon, to the bed where Roland lay.

An innocent approach. Roland knew too well the deception of innocence.

Still, he waited.

One step, two steps, the intruder drew near, almost aligned with Roland when he stilled, looked over his shoulder. One misguided movement and the dupe handed over any chance of control.

Roland leapt naked from bed, his attack so swift all was accomplished before the echo of his mighty war cry could fade. With one arm he pinned his victim against his chest, a dagger to his throat. His other arm stretched out, sword at the ready, to defend against approach.

Short of leg, the captive stumbled as Roland forced him to step backward until they stood with the stone wall at their back. A well-orchestrated move, it gave the knight both hostage and freedom to attack. From this vantage he could judge the room and the people within it.

A battle waged at the door to his chamber. Ulric outside, alerted by Talorc's shout, fought to force his way in. Three caped figures struggled against Ulric's strength as they wrestled to bar the door with a wooden beam. If they managed to slide it into the iron slot, they would effectively lock Ulric out and Roland within. With great effort, they gained the advantage.

Roland watched it all, and assessed the danger that confronted him.

The three by the door were too weak and fumbling to be a concern. Their capes quivered with their fear. The figure before the fire stood tense and erect, perhaps on the brink of escape. Certainly close enough to the tunnel to get out unnoticed, if Roland allowed it.

He would not.

There was a second three-some, much like those who had battled Ulric for the door, huddled fearfully within the windowed alcove. Separate from them, yet within the same alcove, stood another, deep within the night's shadow. This one stood observant, with no quivering sign of any emotion beyond curiosity. This one drew his caution. The greatest adversaries were those whose sense over-road emotion.

The strangled croak of his name from the man in his hold, pulled Roland back to his captive. His knife had cut far enough into a fleshy neck to bring a fine line of blood to the surface. Easing the pressure, Roland looked to the man's face.

God's teeth!

Galvanized by horror, Roland thrust the man away. As he did so, a collective wail filled the room. The other intruders spun away, their capes billowing like kites full of wind. One moment he had been surrounded by assailants, the next they turn their backs? He stood armed for attack and they offer him their most vulnerable side?

What fools! What bloody useless fools!

Nothing made sense, nor did it offer the release Roland so desperately craved. He needed the revenge, to exorcise the demons within him.

He wanted to avenge his father's death. Retaliate against the turn of a winsome, eerily intelligent child to the snares of the devil. He wanted to thrust his sword, slice with his knife, draw blood and prove that he was not a weak gullible fool.

"Friar Kenneth!" He roared at the one familiar element in this bizarre scene. "What the devil is happening here?"

Trembling badly, the friar dabbed his throat. Roland's scowl deepened.

He wanted to tear apart any and everyone who had brought him to this pit of hatred. He wanted it now, though he hadn't known how brutal his fury was, until he faced the one man who would not allow such vengeance; the one man who could force Roland to face the anger, to soften the hatred.

It was the ugliest irony of fate.

"Your timing is pitiful," he accused.

"Yours is much better, had I been your enemy."

"Perhaps you are," Roland suggested. The portly friar eyed him sharply, before shaking his head with a weary sigh.

"It is true then. You have been much hardened by your ordeal."

For a mere moment, Roland's eyes widened in disbelief. It was a flash of reaction before he shuttered his expression and leaned against the stone wall behind him.

"I am no harder than the experiences your God has thrown to me."

"My God?" The friar questioned, but didn't expound. Instead, he looked toward the other intruders, noticed their backs. Even in the meager light Roland could see the man flush.

"Perhaps," Kenneth suggested, as he now dabbed at beads of sweat upon his forehead leaving little smears of blood from the cloth that had staunched the bleeding of his throat, "if you would dress, we could discuss our reasons for descending upon you in this manner."

Roland looked down at his naked state and frowned. Were the clergy so modest? Those he met on crusade had not been, but it mattered not to him. He reached for a robe, shrugged into it as he looked toward the others, then back at Father Kenneth.

There was something in the friar's discomfort, the decided embarrassment, that sent Roland's mind scrambling back to moments before; collective gasps, turning of backs, the struggle with the door beam, the small stature of his captives.

As awareness dawned his mind slung it back as absurd, until he could no longer deny the evidence.

"You've come to my room with an army of women?" He asked in disbelief.

Father Kenneth reached for the heavy cross that hung from his neck. "Aye, the sisters of Our Lady's Convent."

"You bring nuns to my room?" Still Roland could make no sense of the matter as his gaze raked over the scene before him, "and in secret? Using a passage that

my family knows nothing of? As though women such
as this could not be met within the hall, and with
respect?"

With an explosive shudder, the wooden door to
Roland's room was rammed from without. Barred from
the room, Ulric tried to break through. "Hold free!"
Roland barked. "Hold free Ulric, I am in no danger!"

The hall would have filled with the first of his
warriors cry. The whole of the castle would be on the
other side of that portal.

"They have locked you in, m'lord." His page
argued.

"Aye," Roland rolled his eyes, "it took three of
them against one of you, and you are no more than a
tyke. I am safe, so desist. It is naught but the friar and
nuns."

Silence hung ominously in the air. Roland glared at
Kenneth. The friar hesitated patting softly at his cross,
before he offered, "we've come to speak of your lady
wife."

Like a storm, the stillness shattered into roiling
shards of life, arrows of ice propelled by Roland's
voice. "Lady wife?" He tilted his head in question, "I
have no lady wife. No," he leaned back against the
poster of the bed. "The only woman in my life is a
murdering whore who hides behind a worthless
marriage document. Though she is no virgin, our bodies
never 'joined.' The union was not secured."

"Roland!" Kenneth warned but the knight refused
to listen.

"What is it you have to say about this woman? Has
she stolen from the convent? Has she murdered any
children? Turned to sorcery?" Fueled fury carried him
away from the friar, three great strides before he spun
back. "What could she have to do with you?"

He stopped, stood, sucked in deep draughts of air.
He tried, unsuccessfully, to calm himself.

"Speak!" His bristled command burned with the
sting of anger. But Father Kenneth said nothing, as if
waiting for the fury to burn itself out.

A man of small stature, round at the center, Kenneth's brown hair encircled his bald crown much like a halo, in keeping with his benign countenance. With no fear for his own safety, he reached up to rest a hand on Roland's shoulder. A touch to calm, to ease tensions, much as he had done when Roland was a boy.

Roland flinched, but did not pull away.

"Come by the fire, son, so we can talk of these stories you have heard."

"Stories?" Roland wrenched his shoulder from the friar's touch, and stalked back to the fireplace. "Was it a mere accident that my wife gave my father a goblet of poison? Did she not run away with my sister's husband? Was he not found? Tortured? And all for a pack of stories?"

Arrogantly, he lifted the chin of the woman who stood there, to see her face more clearly. It was lined with years and experience. Though the tension was clear, it was neither based in fear nor anger. Nor did she look ready to flee.

She was not afraid for herself, but concerned by the hardness of Roland's heart. He knew it, sensed it, but cared not. Hardness had saved him from far more pain than soft feeling ever had.

"Good sister, have you come to tell me the wonder of a wife who brings such end to men's lives?"

"Roland," Father Kenneth interrupted, "This is the Mother Superior from Our Lady's Convent. Mother Rose."

He released her chin to offer a mocking bow, "My apologies, Mother Superior, for my insolent behavior."

The stately woman nodded, acknowledged the apology, if not the sarcasm behind it. Resignation over-rode her concern, for she eased as she gestured toward the high-backed chairs and bench beside the fire. "Shall we be seated?"

Roland nodded, appalled at his own lack of behavior. He knew better, knew that he should not condemn without hearing them out. To give himself time to calm, he threw wood on the fire, stoked the

flames to burn hotter, brighter. He'd be damned if he
would light lamps. Better they not see into his eyes, to
see what he really thought. Better to know their minds
first.

Mother Rose settled on one of the chairs, Father
Kenneth behind her, a hand on the back of her seat as
though, together, they had more strength than alone.
Roland took the bench, one leg crossed over the other,
formal, patient. Not so the other nuns, the rustle of
habits, the barely voiced whispers proved their
agitation. Roland refused to reveal his own.

Kenneth pulled him back to the reason for their
visit. "Tell us what you have heard of Veri?"

Roland recoiled. He couldn't help it. He had yet to
translate his Veri, the sweet young child, to Lady Veri
the murderess. Two entirely different beings. It was a
cruel blow to be reminded of the former, to be
reminded of the change.

Still, he had no desire to offer any insight; he didn't
want to help her case, even indirectly. "Why don't you
tell me? What do you think I would have heard?"

The sister glanced at the friar who patted his cross
again, a sure sign of agitation.

"I will tell you," Mother Rose offered, "as we have
probably heard the same tales." She took a breath.
"You have been told that your Lady Wife" at his raised
eyebrows she corrected herself, "Lady Veri, is a witch.
That she was . . . wanton. That she shape-shifted and
flew from this room to escape retribution."

"How clearly word spreads." He trusted his voice to
disguise the disquiet he felt

"You have also been told that she poisoned your
father, gave him a full goblet of wine with a spell on it,
so that he was the only one to drink of it and die."

"What sort of spell could do that?"

Rose ignored his sarcasm. "Do you believe all the
lies?"

Roland snorted, "Do you think me a superstitious
fool? Surely it is as obvious to you, as to me, that she
had no need to shape-shift and fly from this room to

escape. Nor do I believe that she 'spelled' the wine. She had an uncanny knack with herbs. If anyone knew how to measure a potion just so, it would be her."

Friar Kenneth leaned forward. "Roland, do you truly believe she was of a nature to take a life? After she spent so much time saving it?"

The question stuck, like a fishbone to the throat. Roland rose against it, though he fought the desire to pace out the agitation. Instead he stood before the fire, fixed by the dance of flame.

With a yearning hunger, he wanted to believe the friar's insinuation that Veri was still good and sweet and honest. He wanted to believe that the stories flung at him, upon his arrival home, had no basis in truth.

He hated the fact that he knew better.

The crusades had driven deep the reality of mankind's cruelty against man. It taught him to trust the world's ability to twist innocent souls toward evil. He'd seen precious little evidence of goodness' reign. It just didn't happen.

That Kenneth still believed in such fairytales was a measure of the man not the society that reared him.

The Veri Roland remembered would never have taken a life. On the contrary, she had found him alone and dieing in a meadow, the victim of an ambush, and saved his life by tending to his wounds.

Before Roland left for crusades his father had been reduced to a wasted shadow of his former self. Veri healed him with her uncanny ability with herbs. Child or not, she saved them both. That was why Roland had given her the protection of his name, a secured future at Oakland, in gratitude, and with his father's blessing.

His father who was no more.

Time changed all things, all people.

"Roland?" Kenneth prompted.

He turned back, sadness tamped, if not distanced. "Who knows what manner of woman she became. All females transform when they come of age, especially when they are steeped in the affairs of a castle as great and powerful as Oakland. Ambition has taken the least likely and made devils of them."

"She was not like other women, Roland," Mother Rose tried, "she was not raised . . . "

"Raised?" This did lift his interest.

When the child had found him in that bloody meadow, she had been alone, had nursed him alone. It had always been a sticky point to him. Orphaned, absolutely, but why would a child of no more than eight, possibly ten, years be abandoned? And where would she have acquired such skills? She claimed her father was a coal maker, her mother knowledgeable with herbs but still . . ."

"We knew of her at the convent. Actually, I knew of her before you found her."

"And you left her abandoned in the wilderness?"

The mother superior concentrated on the lint of her habit. She stroked, plucked, but did not look up, as she formed her reply.

Rather than give confidence to Veri's plight, this new information made her even more suspect. She was something other than an abandoned child of the wilderness. She had allies. She had adults who would guide her.

The church was always hungry for land. His step-mother and her sainted Father Ignacious where testament to that.

"She was not so much alone, as you might think." Rose finally met his eye, challenged him with the directness of her stare.

"And a convent, such as Our Lady's, is well versed in healing and herbs." Roland nodded, as a picture grew within his mind. That it was not equal to the picture the Mother Superior would wish him to see, mattered not to him.

"Yes," she nodded, smiled, "we are known for our healing. As a child, Lady Veri spent many hours among our gardens, though she did not live with us."

"There must have been someone."

"There was," distressed, Mother Rose looked to the alcove, studied the women there. She seemed to reach some conclusion for she continued. "There was a grandmother, an old woman, terribly feeble. Veri had only just lost her when she found you."

"I see," he lied. He did not see at all. Answers to questions that plagued him for years, that Veri's simple answers had never quenched, were now being answered. But why not before? Why had she never mentioned the old woman? Why had Veri lied back then? When Ignacious had flung accusations of the devil at her, why had she not said she was associated with Our Lady's?

Obviously, her falsehoods started well before he left Oakland. Hell, they started before he had even brought her here.

The sister's words had not paused with Roland's thoughts. He barely registered what she was saying until he heard, ". . . she had enemies."

His head shot up.

"Enemies? An odd thing to say of an innocent, hapless child. How would she gain enemies?"

Rose looked over her shoulder to Kenneth who stretched his neck as if to ease a tight collar. When he cleared his throat, Roland realized he had never seen the friar in such a state of discomfort. Never. Kenneth was the calmest of men, with a soul known for soothing others. Roland frowned.

"She gained enemies here, Roland. As you know, Father Ignacious never approved of her, your step-mother, well . . ."

"Threw her in the dungeon once, nearly had her hung."

"Precisely." Kenneth nodded, smiled that he was making his point.

"That was why I took her to wife, to ensure her place, her acceptance." Roland argued.

Kenneth shook his head. "It was not so easy as that, Roland, as well you know. There was no heir . . ."

"No heir?" Roland roared, striding from the fire to stand solidly before the sister, as close to Kenneth as he could get. "Just what the hell was I then?"

"Settle down," Kenneth moved to stand between Mother Rose and Roland. Roland stepped back. "You were heir, and now. . . you rule Oakland. But she, Lady Veri, did not carry your seed."

"I should say not. She was a child when we wed, when I left. There was time enough."

"If you survived."

A bitter smile crossed Roland's lips. "Oh, I survived, in my own manner. The question is, how did she survive? What skills did she utilize to keep her in my absence? It has been ten years, since I left. From what they tell me, five years since my father's death, God rest his soul.

"What has become of her in the meantime?" Roland sat back down, his legs crossed nonchalantly, as if he cared little for the importance of the conversation. "It seems you may be the only ones," his arm swept out to encompass all of those present, "who do know where she has been all these years."

"Your wife has been with the sisters since she left this place." Father Kenneth blurted baldly, his wry half smile evidence enough that he knew this came as a surprise. Roland had to restrain himself from bolting forward with the shock of it.

Searches for Veri had been extensive, yet no one had thought of a nunnery. Evil people did not seek sanctuary within Holy walls.

That was the belief of the masses, but Roland was not of the masses. On campaign to the Holy Lands, he met many spiritual men, and many men of greed and lust who'd claimed vows of poverty and chastity. Holy walls held evil as well as good.

"What is it she wants?" He stretched his legs out before him as he lounged in his place. "Does she wish to come back, to claim the riches she so hastily abandoned? Does she wish to administer to me as she did to my father? Will she play the loving wife?"

"On the contrary, Roland, she wishes the marriage to be annulled."

Roland sat up, no longer hiding his interest. "Annulled?" It was the second time Kenneth had surprised him with his words. First, that Veri had been hiding in a convent no more than half a day's ride away. Second that she wished the marriage annulled. This was a contingent he never envisaged; though now, perhaps, he realized he should have.

Of course he should have.

She would hold him to an offer she did not deserve.

She would imagine herself safe within the walls of a convent. To retrieve her would be to challenge the church. Not just the one convent, but the whole of the church. For an act against the part would be seen as an act against the whole. She would be free of him and his vengeance. Or so she would think. She wouldn't know that nothing, not even the church, could withstand Roland's anger.

But, in her mind, she had sanctuary. So being, what would it cost Roland to buy his freedom? What price would she put on the annulment? They must think him desperate for without it he would never be free to marry, to produce an heir. To her mind, she had him cornered.

Hiding his thoughts he asked, "What does she want? What price, for the dissolution of the marriage?"

The friar looked to Sister Rose. She nodded and turned to Roland. "Her only wish is that you listen to her side of the story. That you not judge her on the word of others."

Roland shot off the bench as swiftly as his calm shattered. "Not judge her?"

Again, he was taken by surprise. She asked a high price indeed, but not to be paid, as he would have thought.

He stalked to the fireplace, his back to all within the room as, once again, he fought against emotion. The fire beckoned his gaze, mesmerized him as he remembered Veri, the child she had been.

Such a fey thing, no surprise many thought her a witch. In truth, even as a child, her ability to heal was unsettling. But he had been grateful for that ability, as his father had been after him.

Why don't they like me? The question had haunted him. She had asked that when still new to Oakland, and with good reason. She was no more than a peasant child, who spoke the language of old, the Celtic tongue. That, in itself, made her suspect. That she should be given absolute care of his father, when he was so near death, did not gain her allies. Yes, she had, had enemies back then, until his father had strengthened. Until she had proved herself worthy of being a part of Oakland.

He had to shut such thoughts out. That was the past. It mattered not that he yearned to believe in Veri. That she alone, could re-instill his faith in mankind. Should she prove not guilty of the crimes, should she prove to be the same innocent soul who found him wounded and dying within a meadow, then the world would tip once more. It would become a place of light rather than darkness.

He hungered for that.

He knew the impossibility of it. She had lied to him even before he had left. The world was not a place of goodness.

She was his one weakness.

He must not weaken.

Pivoting, he faced Kenneth and the sisters of Our Lady's. "She wants me to hear her story?"

Slowly, thoughtfully, he walked around the room, toward the three huddled together in the alcove. He glanced at the shadowed features beneath the cowls of their cape hoods, before he gestured toward the others. "And are these her witnesses? Are each of these women," he studied the three closest to him, "here to claim Veri's goodness?"

"You have heard many lies," Mother Rose told him, "It is time you heard many truths."

"Truths? Such as the wolf spoke when he wore lamb's clothing?"

He fought for calm, but something in the air, some elemental charge of energy, filled him, tested his senses. Not danger, such as Roland had come to know, but something else entirely. Anticipation, exhilaration, it swirled through him, as though he was on the verge of victory.

He had her. He had her within his grasp. He knew where she was and how to bait her from her den.

"She relies on others? Afraid to speak for herself?"

Father Kenneth beckoned Roland back by the fire, "You need to hear the whole of it, Roland, and you need to let your mind open before she can show herself to you."

Mother Rose crossed to Roland, took his arm to guide him to return to his former place.

He shook her off as the friar continued, "You are not the man you were, but that does not mean the fellow of balanced judgment is not within you." The friar acknowledged the bench again, "Come back, be seated, we will discuss this."

They were too insistent.

"What are you afraid of, Friar Kenneth? Mother Superior?"

"That you will not listen to reason"

Roland didn't believe him. There was more to it than that. Rose's gaze flickered between Kenneth and one of the sisters, as though seeking guidance. Roland suspected the Mother Superior was a woman who wore calm as easily as another donned a hat. A woman who confidently made her own decisions. Yet worry shadowed her eyes.

She was troubled. Why?

Roland looked about him again. The gaggle of nuns by the door, more within the alcove and the Friar with the Mother Superior. Once again, he noted the woman in the alcove. Not the women, but the one woman; the one who stood off to the side, deep in shadow, looking through the window at nothing but blackness as if the discussion held no significance.

The one who Rose looked to for answers.

Slowly Roland pivoted, to view the woman straight on.

Oh, they truly were fools, totally inept at strategy.

They had brought their queen to the king's lair.

Check mate!

"She is here!" In two strides, he cut off the protective move of others, made toward the figure, and was upon her. With one tug he pulled back the hood, to stare into the face of his treacherous wife. "You fool!" Elation spilled over, as he beamed his victory.